Taking Apart the Poco Poco

A NOVEL

Richard Francis

Simon & Schuster
•New York •London •Toronto•
•Sydney •Tokyo •Singapore•

SIMON & SCHUSTER
Rockefeller Center
1230 Avenue of the Americas
New York, N.Y. 10020

Previously published in Great Britain by Fourth Estate Ltd.

Manufactured in the United States of America

1 3 5 7 9 10 8 6 4 2

Library of Congress Cataloging-in-Publication Data

Francis, Richard, date.
Taking Apart the Poco Poco / Richard Francis.
p. cm
I. Title.
PR6056.R277T35 1995
823'.914--dc20   95-9744
                                  CIP

ISBN 0-684-80337-2

1

Raymond opened one eye, and then woke up. He could see when he was asleep, but saw more when he woke, as if you could open your eyes twice: the kitchen jumped several inches nearer. He knew without looking how it was outside. Dark, but with the palest breeze stirring. Long before the sun rose, a smidgeon of light was borne in on the wind, not enough to dilute the generality of night, but sufficient to produce a faint silveriness as the breeze curved and twisted its way across the lawn.

He sniffed.

There was a chicken on the washing-machine, its smell icy and remote, as if a real chicken was managing to keep itself at a distance within a shell of polythene and stone. It made a howl rise to his throat but he tamped it down so that only a whimper came out. There were other smells too, a tedious assortment of vegetables, the gassy boiler, plastic tangy lino, bright metallic instalments of water (with an overlay of chlorine) from the drops that blipped out of the sink taps. From above, the prone sleepy odours of the humans, all in place, Stephen and Ann smelling separate, John and Margaret together, not so much tangled as striped, where they'd been lying close but still. The breeze slid under the back door like a sheet, hectic with outdoors, lawns, dirt, plants, trees, a distant but still heady bloom of crap. Raymond's nose followed far-off possibilities and his heart thumped at what the day might offer. Then he brought his nostrils back home. Everything was in order except . . . there was a faint smell, previously unnoticed, by the flat cool odour of the window. It was black, malign. Raymond took a step towards it and then halted.

★

Upstairs in bed, John was half dreaming, the wrong half. His mind was testily awake but it couldn't control what it was thinking. It was thinking that he and Margaret were two lumps of fat in a big square pan, slowly melting. He tried to cry out but could only hiss and sputter. He thrashed his limbs (slightly) but this was only the movement of melting lard. It was tiring too, so tiring, holding your actual body together.

He imagined looking at his own beseeching face in a mirror and watching his nose ploop downwards until it pinkly ran, his eyes dissolve into tears, his insignificant double chin swell out like the first bulge of tide-turn heading shorewards, like the glowing edge of newly erupted lava. He tried to remember what he looked like, as if memory itself could provide the necessary blueprint for his features, a sort of backbone to his face, but he couldn't achieve anything but the most minimal roster, two eyes, a nose, a mouth, getting plump, growing old. It was like one of those crude police composite pictures. I recognised him, constable, running away from the bank. His face looked as if it was drawn in charcoal, and his head was paper-thin.

And then, almost to his relief, the damn dog knocked over something in the kitchen, and he had a definiteness to clutch hold of. You have to know who you are. He was a dog-owner.

'Fuck that dog,' he said.

As if that was a cue, Margaret spoke immediately, in clipped, cold, long-awake tones: 'First, your *actual* body. Then eff that dog. It's a real education, listening to you in the middle of the night.'

John was agreeably surprised. He had no memory of saying anything about his 'actual body', and the thought that he had done so struck him. Perhaps he hadn't been as far gone as he'd felt. Moreover, he liked it when a woman, in other words Margaret, used clipped, cold tones. It made them, women, sound inviolate. Why shouldn't he generalise? Just because you were married to the one didn't mean that you had no knowledge of the rest. Just because you'd been married all those days, weeks, months, years, decades, above all, all those nights, married so long you felt sometimes like a blood-relative, that didn't prevent you from knowing a certain amount about women as a whole. For a Don Juan to go to bed with women as often as he, John, had gone to bed with Margaret, he'd have to have had thousands, tens of thousands, of them. No,

2

thousands. Surely you could multiply up from the one? (Or, from a certain point of view, the two.)

What a way to be promiscuous: generalising. To say women do this and women do that, and try to convince yourself you were an expert.

But Margaret did sound inviolate when she spoke in those clipped, cold tones, as if she would like to carve her words on glass. Not virginal exactly, that would be overstating it, but at least not like a blood-relative either.

'I hope he hasn't broken it,' he said.

'What?'

'Whatever-it-is.'

There was a silence. There was simply a woman beside him, a female lump in the bed, surrounded by a sort of no man's land of sullenness.

'Are you going to look?' she asked.

'No.'

'*If* you're so worried.'

'I'll leave it till the morning. It'll be a surprise.'

'Happ-*y* anniversar-*y*.' Her sarcasm made it rhyme.

'Damnation.'

'How nice. Eff the dog. Damnation the anniversary.'

'I didn't mean it like that.'

'Raymond broke a vase. Happy anniversary. My life is full of treats.'

'Oh, *Margaret*.'

But of course the anniversary must have been at the back of his mind. That's why he'd half dreamed of the two of them as side-by-side knobs of lard in a pan, presumably. Marriage was like cooking, on a very slow heat.

He wondered whether to try for an erection. This is neither the time nor the place, he heard a voice say in his head, his mother's voice, or rather a cruel parody of it, slightly speeded up and raw at the edges, as if a male comedian were imitating her. Why, who knew? Obviously she'd never had cause to speak to him on that subject, and in any case she was dead. Perhaps a certain part of his brain was still asleep, not a half now but a small patch, enough to provide a stage. But surely what the voice was saying could hardly be further from the truth? The time was night. The place was bed.

3

The date was their umpteenth wedding anniversary. But from another point of view the voice might be right after all.

He wondered whether to send a hand across to find out. It would be difficult to tell. Hostility could be a good sign, neutrality a bad. And in any case he didn't have an erection yet. There was a time when one would just arrive, like a pint of milk on the doorstep. But nowadays he had to unfurl, stage by stage. The process reminded him of one of those nature films, when they show a flower opening, speeded up, though in this case it was slowed down of course. And it could stop, he knew from bitter experience, at any moment, hanging at half-mast like a nondescript purple flag in a sad wind, commemorating the death of someone hardly anybody had ever heard of. Margaret would be so kind at these moments. 'You,' she'd say, '*you*'ve got nothing to worry about. You don't have to prove anything to me.'

One generalisation he was sure about: women were sweet and sympathetic on that score. Lord, Lord, he thought, I feel as if I've been impotent with hundreds of them.

He could tell without touching that it was still at the not-quite stage, slightly rubbery, like something you bought in a pet shop to throw for your dog.

'Damn thing,' he said.

'What?'

'The dog.'

'If you're so bothered, I told you.'

'Goodnight, love.'

'What there's left of it.'

He turned away from her and scrunched himself deeper in bed. He liked to sleep face down, as babies did before the link with cot deaths was established. It did seem a defiance of the laws of nature: he sometimes wondered if he were the only adult to do so. He'd been right about his erection. He felt as if he were lying on a soft bone. As it softened further, it reminded him of going to sleep, and he slept.

She had been awake for hours. She had woken up suddenly, with a terrible Monday morning feeling. Since she'd stopped going to work so that she could 'be there' for the children, Monday morning feelings didn't necessarily happen on Monday mornings. When

4

Stephen was still at infants' and she had to meet him at the end of school, she'd be quite capable of having a Monday morning feeling at five to three in the afternoon. She'd doze off in front of the fire after watching some lunch-time television, and then find herself wriggling and jerking her way out of sleep in panic, as you might if you found yourself in a burning building, shoving at the exit. Stephen, Stephen, she'd say, the magic word, the spell. And it would summon up in her mind a pale wedge of a face, marooned at the school gate. With those spectacles on, which always made her want to cry when she thought about them.

Stephen had been so piercingly pleased when they were first fitted. She and John had stood side by side in the optician's office, feeling that they were participating in the proceedings of a terrible court which brought innocents to judgement and meted out cruel sentences. 'I don't know where he's got it from,' they both kept explaining. 'We've always had very good eyesight.' The optician simply nodded impatiently, as though to say, yes, yes, I've heard it all before, they always say that. But it was true. She couldn't think how it had happened. Her good eyesight gene had met John's good eyesight gene, and something about the way they clicked together had given Stephen poor eyesight. Perhaps a part had been omitted, like a missing piece of jigsaw puzzle. Or some short-sighted ancestor had surfaced, at exactly the wrong instant, while she and John were making love.

The optician held a mirror for Stephen to see himself. His little face lit up.

'Looks like my head's got wheels!' he said. They were round spectacles, not as bad as the old National Health ones, but round enough. She saw what he saw, his head like a roller-skate, a tea-trolley. What a convenience, a head with casters. You could turn him upside down and manoeuvre him about like a supermarket cart. A sob flew out of her mouth before she could stop it. She added some titters and sent them quickly in pursuit, to turn her sob retrospectively into a laugh.

She had opened her eyes to blackness, and lapsed back in relief at the realisation that this wasn't a five to three in the afternoon Monday morning feeling. Stephen went to school and back by himself now, anyway; he was a sensible boy and didn't have to cross any roads. It wasn't even a Monday morning Monday

5

morning feeling, it was the small hours of Thursday. There was no point in pressing the little light-button on the clock to see what time it actually was, because infuriatingly it had been designed to give you exactly not quite enough light to make out the numbers by. Perhaps her eyes weren't as gung-ho as she'd thought, after all. The experience would be like policemen getting younger every year. Possibly she was missing things all the time, notices, instructions, clues. She seemed to be able to read all right, but it took her for ever to arrive at the end of a book. Had it always?   •

But anyway she could always tell what time it was when she woke up at night. She would have a specific conviction that it was one fifteen, or nearly three. She was always right. At least, she always assumed she was right. She didn't of course have the means to check.

This time it was around two. Hours yet, and nothing to do but sleep. She relaxed back luxuriously into the fug of the bed. And then, suddenly, she chilled. The Monday morning feeling came back. Tomorrow, today, was going to be the day. *The* day.

How could she have forgotten? She hadn't thought about anything else yesterday, or the day before, after the hospital had rung to make the appointment. The woman at the other end of the phone had asked, cosily, 'Are you busy on the eighteenth, luv?' as if she was setting up a Tupperware party.

'The eighteenth of which?' Margaret had replied.

'This eighteenth. Thursday.'

'*This* one?' She was appalled. She'd only gone to the doctor yesterday. Who ever heard of an appointment coming through this quickly on the National Health Service?

'That was quick,' she said in a trembly voice.

'We had a cancellation, duck,' the woman lied.

'I see.'

She had looked down at herself. Even in her dress, which made her bosom one thing, you could tell, when you looked, that there were two of them. After Thursday, though, there might really be one. If they pulled her in so fast, they surely wouldn't hesitate to cut it off straight away. She'd put the phone down and walked into the kitchen almost sideways, like a crab, practising being an unbalanced woman, protecting her soon-to-go breast in the lee of the one remaining. I'll be nearly a man, she thought. She wanted to faint. How could you *want* to faint? Fainting was something that happened to you. But no, she felt she had a choice. Do I faint, or don't I? Better not. She needed to keep going, for the time being at least. There would be time to faint later. And to tell John. She could faint and tell John later. When they took away her breast she would have so *much* time. She would have all the time she devoted to being her usual self now. Another life would stretch ahead for her, with nothing to do except be a woman with one breast.

John would be devastated. She guessed he would cry. Not just meanly. Naturally, like any man, he would want a woman with two breasts, side by side like a pair of plump twins, and no doubt some of his tears would be for that. But some would be for her too. He had his faults, but he would cry for her, she knew that. And she didn't want him to. She didn't want him to cry for himself, and she didn't want him to cry for her.

But the main reason she didn't tell him was that until she did, it wouldn't be quite real.

She was fairly confident he wouldn't find out for himself. There was a lump to the left of her left nipple, but it didn't show. You had to feel it to know it was there. A patch of the flesh had stiffened. It wasn't hard but it wasn't as soft as the rest, it was like a biggish lump in that school custard of years ago. She wasn't quite sure exactly when she'd first noticed it, a few weeks previously it must have been, and they'd made love once or twice since then, but John hadn't shown any awareness of it. He touched her breasts, of course, but didn't feel them all over as he used to in the old days, when they were a novelty. That was only natural. Nowadays he mainly squeezed her nipples as if they were a couple of buttons you had to press to achieve the desired effect, like turning on a sexual television. And why not, it worked. He only had to do it, and she would feel a wanting sensation, and would loosen up down below. She *was* a sexual television. And on Thursday, she'd suddenly thought, I'll only have one button, just like a proper set. In the privacy of their lounge, with *Neighbours* blaring away on the unsexual television in front of her, she'd wept at the prospect.

She wanted to cry again, when it all came back to her while she lay in bed in the early hours of Thursday morning. But she didn't. Instead, she thought for hours, in the darkness, the same thoughts. Beside her, John breathed on, complacently. Sometimes he gave a soft snore. It sounded like a small electric saw engaging with wood. She had a vision of it engaging with her breast and, though her eyes were already shut, she squeezed them tighter, as if you could shut them twice. Hour after hour passed; certainly at least one. The thoughts would come round in sequence, like couples in *Come Dancing*: meeting Stephen from school; the optician's; Looks like my head's got wheels (each time she got to this a lump dutifully rose in her throat); the eighteenth, luv luv luv; faint and tell John later; school custard; sexual television.

On the umpteenth go round, a new thought struck her. It was when the woman on the phone said: 'The eighteenth, luv luv luv.' 'The eighteenth of which?' *This* eighteenth, the eighteenth of April.

Their wedding anniversary.

How could she forget?

No, that wasn't it, she hadn't forgotten. She'd remembered it all along. Yesterday, while she was passing the local newsagent's, she'd thought of it and gone in to choose John a card. *To my dear husband*. They mostly had fishing rods, pipes and cars on the front, and as it happened John didn't fish, didn't smoke, and wasn't the least bit interested in cars, even posh ones. Thank goodness. If they had a Sunday afternoon walk they would both pity the men who washed and polished their cars at regular intervals along the local streets, lost souls who thought they could wash and polish their way to heaven. A car is a useful device for getting from a to b, John would say. Of course he had to keep theirs moderately clean for work. They would take it through the car wash at the Elf garage every couple of weeks or so. She had to go with him as he always claimed to be afraid to go through the car wash by himself. Anything could happen to you in there, he would tell her.

So in the end she bought him a card with a dartboard and a bottle of beer on it. He didn't play darts much, but he did like to drink beer, so it was as close to the truth as she could get.

Even while she was choosing John's card she was worrying about her breast appointment. She actually thought, with premature bitterness, as if she was trying bitterness out, I wonder if you can go to a big shop, a shop in the middle of London perhaps, where they have a selection of cards to fit everybody, and find anniversary cards for women with one breast to give their husbands, perhaps with a picture of half a bottle of champagne and just a few bubbles flying up from it. Or maybe women who've had one cut off aren't expected to send anniversary cards at all, since they're no longer the women their husbands married.

Although she thought about their anniversary in the same mental breath, so to speak, as her hospital appointment, she never once thought about the two things taking place on the same day. She was seeing the breast specialist on the eighteenth of April; her wedding anniversary was on the eighteenth of April. But those two dates stayed unrelated in her mind, as if they were different eighteenths of April, or eighteenth of Aprils. And after all, they *were* different. One eighteenth of April held a consultant with a knife in his hand, as a cage would hold a wild animal; and the other eighteenth of April contained, as a smartened-up living-room might contain, the subdued celebrations of their nineteenth wedding anniversary, with a bottle of sherry on the sideboard. It suddenly occurred to her how women could be unfaithful to their husbands, could lead a double life. Imagine you wake up on the morning of the day in which you are going to see your lover, a Thursday, let's call it, like today. You don't think of it as a particular Thursday on which you are going to tell lies, and not just tell them, but *do* lies as well. What you have are two separate Thursdays side by side, like a two-car family. You could be a two-Thursday woman, with a man in each day. Heavens, she thought. She almost giggled, silently, but then she remembered. It's funny how you can forget for a moment. She would make a fine two-man woman, she would, with one breast between the two of them.

If you could see ahead, she thought. If I could have known how I'd be spending my nineteenth anniversary. She spent a long time wrestling with those ifs, wondering what difference they made. Was there some corner she could have turned, some path down which breast cancer would not have been lying in wait? Would it have made a difference if she'd not got married? It seemed ridiculous. And yet two dates which were the same date: you couldn't help feeling that was trying to tell you something.

'Your actual body,' John said suddenly, quite clearly. She froze. She peered over at him, but however hard she stared he was just a mound. He was breathing regularly, still asleep.

Your actual body. Perhaps his dream was trying to tell her something as well. She said it to herself in her mind, said it in different

9

ways. *Your* actual body. Your *act*ual body. Your actual *body*. It began to seem to her like a foreign language. If only she could translate it. Was it a diagnosis? Or advice? How could John, asleep, know that something was the matter with her actual body, since he certainly didn't know when he was awake? She wished she could take the phrase in her hands and wring it dry of its meaning, as you could squeeze a dishcloth. Your act*u*al body.

There was a crash from downstairs. The dog had obviously knocked over something in the kitchen.

Something woke Ann up, she didn't know what. Her first thought was of a horror film, where you see the dead girl, and then a shadow moving off from a lit doorway. They don't show how it happened or who did it, just the shadow.

There wasn't a shadow of course because the room was in darkness. Her doorway wasn't lit because her door was closed. There *was* a crack of light all round it, because they left a night-light on on the landing, for Stephen's sake. He said he didn't mind being in his bedroom in the dark, but he was worried about going to the toilet. Ann didn't believe him. How often did he go to the toilet in the night? Hardly ever. He went the second night that they put the light on for him, but that was just for show. You could tell by the noisiness of his pee. Even the flush seemed to flush louder than usual. And in any case he always made jolly sure his bedroom door was open. She would find it more frightening to have her door open than closed, just in case a shadow walked past the doorway. Even if it was the shadow of mum or dad, or Stephen, it would make no difference: she'd be dead of a heart attack before she found out.

This hadn't been a shadow, of course.

Had it?

She peered fearfully at the lit cracks round the door. Oh dear, supposing one of them dimmed, and you could tell that something was moving on the landing beyond! Even lit cracks were too much for her. She couldn't bear to look at the door any more, in case it happened.

But it couldn't have been a shadow that woke her. It must have been a noise. Probably Raymond knocking over something in the kitchen. The shadow of a noise. Perhaps it had scuttled past some doorway in the world of sound. Oh God.

She put her fist to her mouth as if it was an apple, and bit it slightly. Don't be a moron, she said to herself. She was lying here, imagining a masked invader, when it was just Raymond. Raymond had paws that were too big for his legs, so he knocked things over, it was as simple as that. Raymond was a moron, even by dog standards.

She felt much better, getting that sorted out. Now, what had she been dreaming about? Most dreams didn't like the light of day, even when there wasn't any light of day. All you had to do was open your eyes and they jumped back where they came from.

What was it?

What was it?

Oh, yes, she was just in time, it came back. She'd been dreaming about God, she might have guessed. She was always dreaming about God. No, not exactly God, Jesus. She was never quite sure of the difference. Jesus was a sort of Prince Charles, waiting to become God when God died. But God wouldn't die, that was the problem. The Queen probably wouldn't die, for that matter. Jesus would be a heavenly Prince of Wales for ever and ever amen, handsomer of course, and wearing His sheet thing instead of naff suits, and with long hippyish hair in place of the desperate haircuts the real prince always had. His haircuts made him look as if some part of him, you couldn't quite think what, not his hair exactly, had been amputated.

Jesus had been walking, with that lovely graceful stride He always had, as if His feet didn't quite reach the ground, across a field of cabbages.

Cabbages?

Yes, cabbages. Why not? They were much nicer than sheep. You killed sheep and ate them. You ate cabbages too but it wasn't the same. Cabbages wouldn't baa pathetically on the way to the slaughterhouse. She remembered how the neat heads had stretched away like a vast class of well-behaved schoolchildren with their hair brushed flat, brushed green, sitting in rows in their field.

What did it mean? As she thought about it, she almost remembered Jesus turning round to look at her, say something. His eyes were deep, twin pools. They were brown and deep. They sucked you in. When humans looked at you their looks just bounced off. Perhaps not with True Lurve, if there *was* such a thing, but when the average person looked at you it was take-it-or-leave-it. Their eyes could just as well be buttons. If they wanted to give the old come-on, they might jerk their looks to one side a few times, like a fisherman trying to make his hook stick in the mouth of a fish. Jesus's eyes were like a pair of high-powered magnets, only soulful. That's why the disciples had dropped what they were doing and run off after Him, leaving their wives and children, their dead fathers, their fishing, all the rest of it. The eyes were like body magnets, clung, wherever He went you had to follow. Or soul magnets, to be accurate. Your soul went clung, and your body followed as fast as its legs could carry it.

His eyes sucked at her across the cabbage field. My child, they seemed to say, follow me. He put His arm out towards her. His sheet thing hung down like a white wing. The eyes, the eyes. She felt surrounded by them. They turned her knees to water.

This bit she'd made up, she was sure of it. Her dream hadn't got that far. She was just imagining she'd dreamt it. But it didn't matter. If you dreamt of Christ going across a cabbage field, in that sleepy drifting stride of His, with His white wings fluttering like a huge bird about to very very slowly take off, it amounted to Follow Me whether He turned to look at you or not. But follow Him where? What were the *cabbages* trying to tell her?

And then she had it. She was so pleased she nearly said it out loud. The evangelists, that's what they meant, that's who. Philip, Jessica, and Jessica's brother, Kevin. In Kevin's little van, buzzing off to that hoe-down, scooting through the countryside with their skin erupting all over the place. The evangelists, of course. They were *human* cabbages when all was said and done.

Stephen woke up just before the noise. Perhaps he heard the fall, without knowing he was hearing it, like hearing a dog-whistle. Perhaps things shrieked in very high-pitched voices as they went through the air. Then: scrunch. Something big becoming something little, all in a moment.

Stephen had broken a teapot a long while ago. It was lovely to witness the tiny occasion in which it stopped being a teapot and became a pile of broken pieces, all loose on the floor. For a second, before his mother caught her breath and gave him a shouting, he'd felt a strange sensation of relief, as if it had been a strain all along having a teapot in the kitchen. A broken one was more peaceful. The bits didn't have to teapot any more, they were free.

But this scrunch was not nice because he didn't know what was scrunching. Something had broken in the dark. It could be anything. It could be anyone who had broken it.

Stephen broke things because he didn't fit. Also he wore glasses. Things always jumped when they came in front of your glasses, and sometimes they jumped out of your hand. He imagined someone big, too *big* to fit, with black spectacles. People in the daytime had white spectacles, to see the day. The big man wore black spectacles for the dark, or perhaps a bag over his head.

Those men on the television had bags over their heads. Woolly ones, like head jumpers. You couldn't buy them in the shops. You couldn't go into a shop and say, Can I have a head jumper please, I want to rob a bank. Their mothers could have knitted them. But you couldn't ask your mother, either. Stephen saw the television men in his mind's eye, sitting in their den, peering through black spectacles as they knitted their own head jumpers, their tongues curled out.

The television had said:

Reconstruct the bank robbery which took place last month in Blackburn, in which a bank manager and his family were held hostage for the whole of the night before the raid by a gang of armed men. Their ordeal began as the manager approached his car after leaving work on Wednesday, March the twenty-second. A man sprang out of –

And there he was, with his gun, and his head jumper. He shouted in a rough voice. Robbers and murderers always talk to you as if you are deaf. The bank manager seemed to shrink, like a slug when you put salt on it. The robber wagged his gun. He borrowed the bank manager's keys, and then he put a gag over his mouth and tied up his hands. He made him get into the boot. Stephen was surprised at how nicely the bank manager fitted, he had never thought of people folding in the middle before, especially grown-ups. Then the boot lid was slammed down and locked, and the robber drove the car off.

He drove into the countryside. There were trees and fields. There was another car parked there, with more robbers in it. The bank manager's car drew up and stopped. The cars just stood there, one in front of the other. The television said: *They waited until it grew dark.*

Then you were in the bank manager's house. His two children were sitting at a table, doing their homework. They were bent over, writing things and looking pleased.

'You children could take a leaf out of their book,' mother said.

'Moth-er,' Ann said, 'they're just smarming up to the television.'

Of course. Stephen hadn't thought about that before. *You* couldn't see the camera, but they could. That's probably why the robbers seemed so rough. Perhaps they wouldn't even have bothered to put bags on their heads if they weren't doing it on television. The mother was in the kitchen. She was cooking things in the same way as the children were doing their homework, as though they were all in church.

Then you saw a hand putting a key in the front door, which burst open and the bank manager nearly dived in, his spectacles wild and staring, the robbers just behind, their guns poking up, their heads in bags, shouting and shouting. The bank manager's wife put her hand up towards her mouth very slowly, as if she couldn't quite remember where her mouth was.

Mother turned the TV off.

'It's all right,' she said. 'You mustn't worry about it.'

Stephen stared at the black screen. He imagined the robbers still inside it, like people in a room when the lights have been switched off. It wouldn't matter to the robbers, because they had bags over their heads anyway. They carried their own darkness around with them, so it made no difference what it was like outside. They reminded him of the way Percy and Bubbles, the class goldfish, sat, or lay, or stood, in their bowls, whichever it was, and watched the dry world going past outside. The robbers were safely in the dark however bright it got, even if people shone torches and searchlights on them. And it didn't matter if somebody turned the television off either, because they were as dark as could be already. In the night, when everyone was in bed, a house was like a switched-off television. That's why Stephen was glad the hall light was on. But if the robbers were in the kitchen it wouldn't make any difference, they'd be dark men in a black room, like fish in water. Raymond was there too but he wouldn't do anything. He wasn't interested in strangers. The only people he ever barked at were members of the family; the only person he'd ever bitten was Stephen.

14

Stephen didn't want to call out. He'd called out a few nights ago. Not because of a noise that time, but what amounted to the same thing, a silence. He'd woken up to a silence so deep it seemed to have a sound of its own, a sighing sound like a lonely forest in a slight wind. It was like the sound someone leaning over your bed might make when he is trying to breathe faintly so he won't wake you. Stephen had been so frightened that he didn't dare to shout, and yet at the same time he didn't dare not to. Like the breather's his noise was quiet, a whispered scream, the sound Raymond made when he woke up and stretched all four legs at once. Nobody heard it at first but he couldn't make it any louder, there was only room for that exact sound between himself and the silence, so he just kept on and on making the same noise until at last it wore away his mother's dreams, and she came into the room.

'Stephen,' she said, 'whatever is the matter?'

His heart was thumping so hard it was moving him up and down, a small boat on a big sea. He couldn't speak at first because when he tried the thumps seemed to become sobs.

'Stephen,' she said again, 'wake up!'

'I am awake,' he told her.

'You've had a bad dream.'

'No. I woke. Up and. I thought he. Was in here.'

'Who? He who?'

His father came into the room now. He switched on the light. Stephen groped over to his bedside table, found his spectacles and put them on. His mother and father became detailed.

'The robber.'

'There's no robber here, Stephen,' mother said quietly.

'The bank-robber.'

'That's the Blackburn bank raid,' she told his father, 'the one with the hostages. He saw a bit about it on television. Before I switched it off.'

Stephen wanted to say, *after* you switched it off as well, but he didn't dare.

'That was a bank manager whose family they took hostage,' his father explained. 'I'm an *assistant* manager. It won't happen to us.'

They might be assistant robbers, Stephen thought, but he didn't say it.

'Do you want the hall light on?' his mother asked.

15

'I don't want Ann to know.'

'Ann's asleep. I looked in. She's snoring like a pig,' father said.

'She'll find out. She always finds out.'

'We'll tell her you need it on in case you want to go to the toilet,' mother said. 'Especially with your spectacles and everything.'

And since then the landing light had been left on all night. Ann moaned of course, she said she couldn't sleep. If he made a fuss now, with the light already on, it would be too much, he knew it would. You get so that you know when something would be too much. But in the meantime a man could be leaving the kitchen, creeping into the downstairs hall, beginning to climb the stairs . . .

Stephen shut his eyes.

They didn't feel shut enough, so he opened them again. The oblong of light in his doorway was like a block of butter with blurred edges. He found his spectacles and put them on. The light sharpened. He shut his eyes, with his spectacles still on, and this time they felt properly shut. But still the man was coming, further and further up the stairs.

One thing he knew how to do, he knew how to dead-eye his teacher, Mr Sherlock. Mr Sherlock would look around the classroom for somebody to answer a question and Stephen would know it would be him: all the children always knew when it would be them. It did no good turning your head away because Mr Sherlock would see the sort of swirl your head made, which would be just as bad as catching his eye with yours. But you could make your eyes go dead. If you made them go dead enough Mr Sherlock could look right at you and still not think of asking you a question. Stephen had tried to dead-eye a bird once as it flew past his bedroom window. He wanted it to stop halfway across the glass, stuck in the blue like a wasp stuck in jam. It did seem to stop for a little while.

Stephen, his spectacles on, his eyes shut, lay in bed and deadeyed the robber as he climbed the endless stairs. It took all his energy to keep him where he was, he had to force his eyes to stay dead. Quite suddenly he fell asleep.

Raymond stared at the spider. His legs trembled with the stillness of his stare, but his head was a rock. His head's unmovingness made him want to howl, to pee; the lack of biting made his teeth almost unbearable in his jaws. The spider rested calmly on the cool window, the most opposite thing in the world to a dog: incuriosity personified.

But it was necessary to wait, in case suddenly it should choose to twitter arbitrarily across the glass, to a quick nowhere a few inches away, a journey only a spider could make, one which had no starting-point nor end, and which failed to pass through anywhere in particular en route. The journey would be as detestable as the stillness, since it would lack the justification of dog journeys: to find out, sucked along by your nostrils, or to celebrate, driven forward by your wagging tail. But it would at least let him off his leash, enable him to pounce.

Around him, as he waited, the ghosts of the family assembled. Beyond the window, a previous day dawned, nooned, moved towards evening. Sudden long drops appeared, like cracks in the glass. Guttering ticked somewhere, tick-tocked out of time with the kitchen tap. One member of the family had just come in, John, and he smelled of newly landed rain, the bright cold scent of the upper air, a sudden rich flowering of his damp coat, redolent of buildings, streets, polish, the car, cigarette smoke, women's perfume, a tangled garden of odours, among which was an ancient smell of dog, perhaps Raymond himself, distanced by time and the coat's journeyings. Something seemed ready to happen. They were standing about looking at Raymond expectantly. He longed to justify their gazing.

He would do anything.

He wagged his tail, cautiously, hoping to suggest he'd done it already, that the abrupt party had taken place. No one noticed, no one pulled his ears. The conversation seemed to turn away from him. He wondered if he should fetch his towel, but he didn't know where he'd left it, and as soon as he moved people would disperse, their concentration had so short a span. Then he would be back, tossing, tugging, proclaiming it, and their attention would be elsewhere, leaving him to the chill embarrassment of cavorting unappreciated.

And then, by chance, a fleck in his eye as it swept despondently across the floor, past those human feet that were itching to go: a spider!

It was green, fat-legged, nasty. It was waiting, in interminable spider fashion.

17

Raymond had leapt, without even a precautionary sniff to verify his eye. His teeth clacked as the side of his head hit the exact section of the floor on which the spider was performing its wait. His tongue nudged it, cornered it against a tooth, flipped it in. He raised his head towards his alerted family in triumph.

And then he realised.

He'd smelled tomato from the beginning, thinking dimly that there must be a tomato in the room somewhere. Now he could taste it also, a retchy flavour like decaying undergrowth in deep unsunny woods. What he had in his mouth was the floret from a tomato top.

He shook his head, biting, growling tiny individual growls, one unit at a time, as if confronted by a spider's minute resistance, but they knew, they all knew. These people, who normally saw nothing, smelled less, they knew. He had seen, on many occasions, the blind feet of each of them plonking into heads of crap, while a dog, any dog, would never miss one, would run his nose over each piled configuration, never more than an iota away, never touching, participating in its complicated richness, leaving the totality precisely intact. But when it came to a tomato floret that even *he* had only chanced upon by accident, the humans all knew it was there, they didn't miss a trick. They gibble-gabbled loudly, excitedly, Raymond Raymond buried in the middle of their talk, laughter round the edges. There had been a detestable unwanted affection in their tone. Stephen stroked his head, giving out sudden childish sniggers like hiccups. He, Raymond, tried to smile, always a dangerous undertaking for a dog, his face long and forward where it should be back and flat, the smile in three dimensions, thrusting outwards like a snarl. He'd wanted to stake a claim to a little of their laughter, to bite some of it off, so that he would find himself on their side rather than his own. But to no avail. Stephen poked a fist at his mouth, challenging his teeth, Ann picked up his front paws, made him totter like an unsuccessful man, they all poked, patted, harassed him while the floret snuggled into a gap between his teeth with the persistence of a spider after all, until at last he managed to shake it loose, and it plipped sadly to the floor.

The ghost of the previous spider dissolved, along with those of the family, and Raymond was alone once more in the kitchen, with a new spider on the window-pane. Or a new candidate for spider.

There was no one to see him but he could not attack because of the chance that the beast would metamorphose on the instant to a tomato floret, as it had before. Embarrassment, the worst of all the emotions in a dog's gamut, would be intolerable even with no one else to see. *He* would see. The ghosts of the sleeping family would see. The spider which wasn't there would see. So he waited in trembling rigor, in canine imitation of the spider's vegetable stillness.

As he waited the window began, faintly, to pale, at the exact speed of time. But still the spider didn't move; it was obstinately static even in comparison with the momentum of oncoming day. A bird sang somewhere and at last Raymond's immobility became more than he could bear. He settled on his haunches and tensed his back legs in preparation for the spring. His tail stiffened and rose like a phallus till it pointed straight back. He leaned backward to get purchase for his leap, his tail prodded a tea-towel that overhung the rim of the washing-machine like a table-cloth, there was the wobbling clatter of a plate, the sploosh of water, the skidding noises of a floundering object. Raymond stopped on the exact edge of his leap, stopped so suddenly that an invisible Raymond leapt out of him, hurtled through the air and crunched against the window. The stopped Raymond gasped in sympathy; the spider yet again did not move.

Behind him something flew through the air, wingless and leaden, hit the floor with a thump that eradicated memories, embarrassment, second thoughts at once, and allowed Raymond to leap, throw his front paws up on to the window-sill, plunge his head upwards, flick his tongue out, flirt the spider in. It landed cooperatively between two teeth, an up and a down.

Raymond closed his jaws and the body burst like a spare pimple, a portable spot, a loose blister, providing in a section of his mouth a sudden tangy, dry, old taste of spider. He wagged his tail in triumph and turned back to examine the kitchen.

In the middle of the floor was the thawing chicken in its misty bag. Above, the half-moon of its plate peered down over the edge of the washing-machine. Raymond backed up to his blanket and settled down on it, but he continued to stare at the bag, ears strained forward in hopes that a feathered hen in the deeps of that bald chicken would at last emit a faint Antarctic cluck.

2

'**D**amn that dog,' John said.

'John, I'm getting really tired of hearing you say that. You've no idea how tired I can get, hearing you say damn that dog all the time.' Margaret raised a saucepan of the porridge that Stephen always asked for, as if it were a club. It maddened John to see her. She always made Stephen a whole panful, even though she knew he would only eat one bowl. Then, shuddering, she would glug the remainder in great slews on to kitchen paper and chuck it in the bin. He actually asked her once why she didn't make the right amount. She clutched her cardigan closed, as she had that time he'd been to bed with Linda, that one and only time in his whole life when he'd gone off the rails, but said nothing. With a sudden quick perception he realised she *did* know. She made Stephen so much porridge because he had to wear spectacles. He was condemned to go through life with not enough eyesight, so she gave him extra porridge instead. Then of course the more Margaret thought about the measliness of his consolation prize, the more guilty she felt about the spectacles, until she zigzagged her way almost to tears.

It had frightened John to realise all this. Normally he went through life with the sense that everything he looked at had just shut its door on him. Not just people but everything: trees, paving stones, the dog. If he'd come by a moment earlier or a moment later he'd have seen what they were *really* like. This one time, in the case of Margaret, he had. He'd felt a sudden hatred of her, as you do when you have a glimpse of what makes someone tick.

'He only said damn that dog once,' Stephen, ever a stickler for justice, pointed out.

'He said it in bed as well,' Margaret snapped. She spooned some porridge into Stephen's bowl.

Stephen took off his spectacles and tried to shake the steam from them. He put them on again and looked at his father in astonishment. At least, his spectacles showed astonishment.

'Did you say it in bed, dad?' he asked.

'Yes. Hours ago. Hardly *all the time*.'

'It still counts,' said Stephen. 'Why did you say it in bed? Raymond was down here.'

'Because he knocked that blasted chicken over.'

'At least he didn't eat any of it,' Stephen said. 'He may have given it a lick, though.'

'I wish I'd known what I was thinking of,' said Margaret, 'getting it out of the deep freeze in the first place. I knew all along that we were going to have steak today, for our anniversary. I keep remembering our anniversary and forgetting it at the same time.'

'Do you hear the crunch of bones when somebody's run over?' Ann asked. 'The actual *crunch*.'

'I've never seen anyone run over,' John said testily. 'Or heard them either. And I don't see why you can't put that chicken back.'

'You're not supposed to refreeze poultry,' Margaret explained in a prim voice.

'It still seems fairly hard to me,' he told her. 'I expect it was a cold night.'

'I'd better cook it up, all the same.'

'Bang goes the steak.'

'It was the chicken that banged,' Stephen reminded them.

'What would you do if I ran away from ho–ome?' Ann asked. She had an infuriating tendency to talk with a catch in her voice, as if about to weep, when she wanted to make an effect.

'That's what toddlers do,' Margaret said, sitting down at last. 'Not girls your age.'

'Lots of girls my age do it. They become drug addicts and sell their bodies.'

'Ann!' John almost shouted, furious. 'We've got Stephen here, if you haven't noticed.'

'It was on the *tele*vision,' said Ann, as if that made it all quite innocuous. 'They become addicts and sell their bodies to pay for their drugs.'

'If they'd sold their bodies, they wouldn't have anything to put their drugs into,' Stephen said.

'You don't know everything, big brain,' Ann told him.

'He knows enough, without your help,' Margaret said.

'How much do you think I'd get for mine?' Stephen wondered. 'It might be better to buy a small one. You could put it in your boot. You wouldn't have to fold it in the middle.'

'Stephen', Margaret said quietly, 'and Ann. If you carry on like this, I'm going to cry.'

John had another perception of what she was thinking – no, not another, merely the second instalment of his previous one. She had a vision of a tatty card, pinned to the noticeboard in the forlorn post-office round the corner: *Small boy's body for sale. Hardly used. Short-sighted, but otherwise perfect cond.*

'You could think of something nicer to talk about on our wedding anniversary,' John told the children.

'That's why I'm depressed,' Ann replied. 'That's why I keep thinking ho–orrible thoughts. I forgot your anniversary.'

'I didn't,' Stephen said self-righteously.

'Yes, you did. *I* told you about it. Then I forgot all about the bleeding thing myself.'

'I made a card,' Stephen said. 'I'll go and get it.' He stood up. 'I've finished me porridge, mum.'

'My porridge.'

'Your porridge.' He left the room.

'I could strangle him,' said Ann. 'Mr Goody-Two-Shoes.'

'It doesn't matter about a card,' John said. 'Your mum and I didn't get cards either, did we, dear?'

'I did,' Margaret said. 'I may as well go and get mine.'

'Yes, you do that,' John said wearily. 'Rub it in.'

'We're two of a kind, eh, dad?' Ann said, suddenly good-humoured again.

Margaret came back with her card first. They could hear rooting noises from upstairs as Stephen searched for his, and low cries of frustration as he kept on not discovering it in the chaos of his bedroom.

'Here you are, dear,' Margaret said. She gave him a quick peck on the cheek and put the card in his hand. He opened it. There was an idiotic picture of a dartboard and a pint of beer. He almost blushed to see it, but gritted his teeth and kept the blush at bay. Suddenly, perhaps because he'd been thinking forlorn thoughts on Margaret's behalf, he felt despair in his own right. This was what he amounted to, a dartboard and a pint of beer.

'Oh well,' Margaret went on. 'It's the thought that counts.'

'I didn't even have the thought.'

'Oh well,' she said again.

'But I'll do something tonight. You know, bring you something.'

'You don't need to. When we've been married as long as we have been.'

'Oh yes I will. You wait and see.'

'We'll have steak in any case. I'll cook the chicken and *then* refreeze it.'

'That'll be nice.'

Stephen reappeared, with his card.

Stephen had drawn a picture of a pig on his parents' anniversary card. He liked drawing them, even though he'd never actually seen one close up. He'd seen lots of them in the distance. Whenever they passed a pig-farm when they were driving anywhere in the car, daddy would call out Piggies! and everyone would look. Pigs, at least seen in a distant field, always reminded him of bottoms, they were so pink, bottoms on four fat legs, scrobbling about in muck. He had called Mr Sherlock a pig yesterday, when it was his turn to start a Chinese whisper in class. Mr Sherlock is a pig, he whispered to William, and William whispered it to Helen, and on it went. He liked Mr Sherlock as a matter of fact, but you always had to say something rude. Strangely this whisper wouldn't Chinese, so when Mr Sherlock heard Angela Connelly whispering it to Susan Yates, it still said the same thing.

'Thank you very much, Angela,' Mr Sherlock said. As usual Angela burst into tears.

'That's a very nice pig,' daddy said. 'Is it me or your mother?'

'It's just a pig.'

'It's lovely, darling,' mummy said. 'I'll probably put it on the wall, when we've finished with it.'

She said It's lovely as if somebody had just said it wasn't, and suddenly Stephen realised he shouldn't have done a pig in the first place. What had he been thinking of? He should have done a bunch of flowers, a cake, a house with a tree beside it, and the sun shining down from above. He should have done a picture of mum and dad holding hands. But he hated doing pictures of people. They always looked like children's pictures of people, and whatever he did he couldn't make them any different, so he'd chosen a pig instead. It was easy to make a pig look really like a pig. But of course it ended up being childish in a different way. When he was young he'd believed your mother was just your mother. It didn't have anything to do with her being a her; she could be a man or a child or even an animal. So drawing a pig on her anniversary card made it look as if that time in his life had come back again. If your mother was a pig you wouldn't know she was a pig. Piglets would just think their mother was their mother. Of course it was his father's anniversary too, but *he*'d never been anything but a man, even when Stephen was very little, so the card really belonged to mummy anyway, which was only fair, since daddy had one already.

'I'm sorry it's a pig,' he said. 'I'll cross it out if you like.'

'Oh no you won't!' His mother held the card right up, in front of her face. 'Your pig, Stevie, is exactly what I wanted.'

Stephen's pig was like an anchor, holding her steady, an anchor in the deeps of family, of family-after-all. This morning was proving as horribly Monday morning-ish as she'd anticipated while piloting her half of the bed through the long night. Normality wasn't a comfort, it filled her with despair. As she laid the breakfast table and put Stephen's porridge on, she'd felt her heart was about to break. Perhaps she would only be going through this routine a few more times.

Since her National Health phone call she'd been torturing herself with the thought of losing a breast. While she had scuttled about getting the breakfast, though, it occurred to her that this might be only the beginning. First one breast, then the other, then her whole body. Why on earth did it take so long for the penny to drop? She suddenly envisaged lying on a sweaty bed, desperate with pain, terrified of dying. There was no comfort anywhere, no hope of comfort. And then somebody came into the room and stood by her bedside. He was a dark, shadowy presence, and she imagined him

24

looking a bit like Nelson Mandela. Mr Mandela bent forward, through her haze of pain and fear, and offered her a golden possibility. She could go back to her normal life, her normal one-breast life, that was, and live it as before, on condition she didn't complain about her lot. Tears fizzed in her eyes at the privilege of this offer. Having a breast missing was the merest detail. And then more tears, a second generation of tears, fizzed at the notion of a position so dire that a breast would appear as a mere detail. They fizzed so violently that they pushed the earlier tears to the surface and out, so she hurriedly had to wipe them from her cheeks with her cuff, hoping no one would notice. She felt a swift hatred of Mr Mandela for the heartless pressures which lurked in the depths of his offer, the ruthlessness with which he forced her to accept a personal catastrophe as the best of all possible worlds. And here she was, in her kitchen, exactly as if this was normality, when really she was at her wits' end.

While she bustled about making Stephen's porridge she was on her knees, with horrors on either side of her, death by cancer the devil, mutilation the deep blue sea. The normality all around seemed like a mockery. When John damned the dog yet again she wanted to murder him, to beat his brains out with her heavy porridge pan. It was so unfair, it was so hideously complacent of him, to have as his greatest annoyance the nocturnal clatter their dog had made in knocking a frozen chicken to the floor. The triviality of his preoccupations made her want to scream with fury. And dear little Stephen trying to adjudicate, with those middle-aged moons perched on his nose. Her sense of an imminent parting somehow reversed itself, and she had a picture of Stephen being advertised for sale in that tiny, despairing post-office round the corner. *Wears specs. Otherwise near perfect.* They wouldn't need to advertise *Ann*, by the sound of it. She was ready for off already. Her ugly talk about drugs and prostitution was the final straw. Margaret thought to herself: breast, spectacles, and now Ann wants to be a drug-taking *whore* when she grows up. And John forgot to buy me a card. And my marriage is out the window. I'm as much use to him as an old piece of furniture.

When she went upstairs to fetch the card she had remembered to buy, albeit in the midst of her woe, she had a sudden, private cry in the bedroom. She surrendered to it whole-heartedly, almost

25

boo-hooing, though she did her best to keep the sound down. It was actually enjoyable, she cried so completely, even though only for a short time. Afterwards, when she was downstairs again, numb, wan, cried-out, Stephen came trotting along with his pig-card and made her want to laugh. She remembered that life could be jolly, people could be thoughtful, that families were families. Normality hadn't been amputated in anticipation of her breast, it was still here, she still had a stake in it. There could be nothing more normal, more friendly, than Stephen's pig. It gave her something to cling on to. I'll be normal in the gates of hell, she thought triumphantly. In her heart of hearts she knew she wouldn't, but Stephen's pig would at least help her to get through breakfast.

Ann had done herself a slice of toast. She nibbled it slowly. I shouldn't be doing this, she thought, it's bad for my anorexia. Her dream of Christ among the cabbages was still vivid in her head. Sometimes dreams faded or became silly, even *more* silly, by the time you woke up in the morning, but this one seemed the same. Also, her interpretation of it was unchanged. The cabbages signi-fied going to the hoe-down with Philip, Jessica and Kevin, in Kevin's little van, along with a few hundred assorted blackheads, whiteheads, greenheads, pimples and pustules, the outward signs, for reasons known only to God, of passionate, sincere religion. She should be fairly immune, she wasn't either sincere or passionate. There was nothing like a touch of hypocrisy for keeping the zits at bay.

It was a funny kind of hoe-down: it was going to last all day. At least, it was going to last Philip, Jessica and Kevin all day, plus her-self now she'd decided to go along. They had volunteered to help get things ready. Christians were always volunteering to help get things ready. The idea was they should pop and fart their way across the countryside in Kevin's clapped-out van to some mansion in north Cheshire that had gone evangelical, and then set out trestle tables and paste sandwiches and do whatever else was necessary to get a hoe-down on the go. Quite likely the other hoe-downers would also be there early to prepare for the evening: Christians would far rather have the anticipation than the event. After all, it was the only way of making sense of life on earth as opposed to the hereafter. They would prefer to pootle about making everything just so than come along, get their legs under the table, and take a whack at life with a knife and fork. A hoe-down must mean the end of the day when all the workers could put their hoes down and take it easy; but the evangelical version, if the mob she knew was anything to go by, was all about picking up your hoe and working your way through the whole shebang. Typical, in other words, Christianity.

Philip and Jessica had cleared it at school, of course. And no doubt Kevin had cleared it at Reddish Windscreens, where he worked his way through the here while waiting to go to Bible College, the hereafter. Days off all round. Ann had done no such thing, equally needless to say. For one thing, she hadn't decided until her dream that she was definitely going to attend. For another, it would take some of the cloyingness out of the hoe-down if she went there by skiving off. The arrangement was that if she decided to go after all, she would call round at Jessica and Kevin's house first thing, instead of catching the bus to school. Philip was doing the same. Ann had no intention of asking, or even telling, her parents either. They would grumble about her missing school and probably, deep down, they would feel a bit sniffy about her tagging along with a gang of God-botherers. She felt sniffy about it herself. And the last thing she could do would be to tell them about the dream. It would frighten them stiff. Who wanted a daughter who saw visions? They would see it as the first stage on the road to becoming a Moony. She, Ann, didn't believe in dreams either. At least, not as such. She was sure she'd given her dream the right interpretation, but so what? You could dream that God wanted you to transform yourself into a biscuit, but you'd obviously be loopy if you chose to dress up as a fig roll.

Another problem was her parents were quite likely to suddenly take it into their heads to go off and celebrate their hundred and fiftieth wedding anniversary, leaving her in charge of glum old bug-a-lugs. If she wasn't at home they couldn't spring anything on her. What she'd do would be to ring up from the hoe-down and just tell them she was spending the evening with Jessica. It wouldn't even be a lie.

But still, she couldn't help feeling she was doing the dirty on them to a moderate extent. They would be expecting her to catch a bus to school and instead she would be travelling to the wide blue yonder in Kevin's beat-up van. It was a bit like being dead, on a limited scale. For a day she'd have vanished from their lives. Certainly it was running away, on a sort of cheap-day-return basis. Christ's eyes came back to her: they were two brown bulbs in the heart of the kitchen, moist and poignant as sea anemones in a rock pool, folded in upon themselves, drawing and sucking. But it was one thing being sucked all the way to north Cheshire on a school-day; it was another leaving your parents, and even Stephen, stone cold. She didn't really believe in the Christ business about leaving everybody in the lurch, and letting the dead bury their dead. There was a nasty side to Christ, which you could see very plainly in the evangelical bunch. As a prodigal daughter she didn't believe in the parable of the prodigal son, either, where the creepy one who cleared off is given the works, and the nice one who stayed at home is just told: tough.

She had a sudden mental picture of Kevin's van careering towards the hoe-down, and her mother and father and Stephen jumping in front of it in a bid to stop them; and being run over. She could hear their bones crunch. She asked them about whether bones crunched because she wanted to give them a clue; also to stop them going on and on about their crummy anniversary: any moment it might occur to them to go out tonight, and if it did they would ask her point-blank to babysit Stephen, and she'd be in a fix.

After that she gave them some more hints. It felt less dishonest, and also it was a form of inoculation. If she made them think about girls going on to the street, then her going to an evangelical hoe-down wouldn't be so bad. She wasn't exactly inoculating *them*, when she thought about it, since they would never know she was going to the hoe-down in the first place, she was inoculating her-self. I'm only going to a hoe-down, she reminded herself: it isn't the end of the world.

Raymond lay curled in his basket, his head on his haunch, letting the breakfast drift over him. His only concession to its remote possibility was one open eye, brimful of reproach. His body remembered a time when the smell of toast would make him leap and howl, and he twitched a little as the memory tried to bound free. Toast took the scent of grain to the edge of meatiness. But this toast was not for him, it was *other*.

He had grown accustomed to other by now; it was like an invisible fence around all the things in this household he wasn't allowed to have. Sometimes an arm – usually Stephen's – poked over or through the fence and gave him a piece of whatever it might be, but not when the family were all sitting together. At such times other was like steel. Being in a group reminded them they were humans, and they lost interest in the alternative of being a dog. There was no point in even trying. All the energy Raymond was prepared to invest was that required to hold the lids of one eye open against the imminence of toasty sleep, and to fill that solitary eye with sad emotion. He was very tired. Something had perhaps happened in the night.

'Oh well,' said John. 'What sort of day have we all got in front of us?' He felt a sudden need to jolly things along after a bad start.

You swine, thought Ann. There must be something about me, I must send out lie signals. Even my father can pick them up. Every time she stepped off the straight and narrow she fought for her life. The tiniest fib had to be defended as if it was the hugest whopper.

'Today starts *off* with double French –'

'I'll take Raymond to dad's to see –'

She and mother, speaking at the same time, *both* sounded like liars. Today *did* start off with double French, for all those too feeble to play truant and go to the hoe-down.

John thought: Margaret seems eager to tell me all. Why?

Margaret thought: I'll do this, I'll do that, just as if life was going to go on for ever. And all along I'll be carrying my breast around with me as if it's a time-bomb.

Raymond heard Raymond and cocked his ear, in case he needed to catch it. But it didn't come towards him across the room as it sometimes did, towing something lovely in its wake, a scratch on the head, a dog biscuit, perhaps even, given dog-optimism, a piece of toast. This Raymond went from one side to the other. But it was worth his second eye. He opened it and his two eyes followed the Raymond, glowing bright in its sequence of dark words, as it travelled from left to right, to the back door, out. He was going to be taken for a walk. That word, walk, hadn't been said, but it didn't matter, the Raymond was going in its direction, palpably. He sniffed Raymond delicately, marginally enlarging one nostril.

29

Yes, it smelt of outdoors, in the faintest, most abstract way, of trees and pee, paving stones, crap. The other nostril rapidly followed before the word was out of range. There was more, yes, the old man's garden, kitchen, the old man's fat hand, bliss. Food. It could be anything, crisps, chocolate, toast, meat, there were no limits to what the old man could give, there was no *other* in the old man's house, the old man was leader of the pack, top dog. Utterly top. Top dog of the *humans*.

Raymond got up and shook himself, preparing to go.

'Raymond heard that. He's getting ready,' said Stephen. 'I told you he understands all we're talking about.'

'You never said any such thing, you little *li*ar,' Ann said.

'Ann,' John remonstrated, almost on auto-pilot, thinking: why does Margaret sound flurried?

'I'm always saying it,' said Stephen. 'I might not have said it this actual morning.'

'To dad's to see how he's getting on,' Margaret continued obstinately. 'Then I'll go for my jog. After that I'll see.' She pinked. She'd known the lie was there, but she still fell into it, like a comedian falling into a hole. 'What about you?' she asked John, to take the attention off herself.

John watched her pinkness, wonderingly. She looked suddenly lovely, flowerlike. He felt himself blushing in reply, as it were. One's middle-aged wife doesn't resemble flowers. And anyway, something was the matter, he was sure of it. A terrible thought struck him: perhaps she looked like a flower *because* something was the matter.

'You're blushing!' she announced. Her voice still sounded remote. 'Children, your dad's blushing! I think he must be seeing another woman, and on our wedding anniversary too!' With the comic possibility, her voice began to warm up, as she'd known it would.

And why is she dredging *that* up? John thought. Linda yet again. Considering she never mentioned her, as per her promise, it was amazing how often she mentioned her. Why this time?

He didn't want to pursue the why. He did want to unblush. He had to switch his train of thought. He suddenly remembered how, in the early days of their marriage, when he was frightened of premature ejaculation, he would also have to switch his train of thought. He used to make himself think about leprosy, the non-existence of God, a sharp object being poked in his eye, rotting food, anything nasty or depressing.

Now all he had to do was think of the answer to Margaret's question, or rather his own. What was he going to do today? Oh shit. Today was the day he *had* to beard Gardiner, his manager. It was his last chance. Gardiner would be sending in his report tomorrow.

That did the trick.

'I've got a stinker of a day at work today,' he said. 'That's what I've got.'

'It's the same for all of us,' Ann chipped in. 'We've all got the stinker of a day. Except for mum of course.'

'I'd better just go up, and,' Margaret said vaguely, and left the room. John watched her go. He felt his mind was split exactly half and half between thinking about her and the prospect of bearding Gardiner.

'My day's all right,' Stephen said stoutly. 'It's just the same as usual.'

Disappointed at Margaret's sudden exit, Raymond subsided into his basket. Noticing, Stephen said, 'Here, Raymond, have a piece of toast.' He picked up Ann's half-nibbled toast from her plate. Raymond howled in joy, leapt in the air, and snapped it from his grasp in a single twisting movement.

'You shouldn't have done that,' Ann said.

'You always say that. Why shouldn't I?'

'Because it teaches him bad habits. Anyway, it was my toast. If you give him *my* toast, he'll be grateful to you instead of me.'

'You'd never give him any anyway.'

'That's not the point.'

'Don't let's argue about a piece of toast, kids,' John said. 'We've all got enough on our plates today without that.'

'Anyway,' Ann continued, never able to let things lie, 'how did you know I wasn't going to eat that piece of toast myself?'

3

John kissed Margaret goodbye, just a daily kiss, a sort of hand-shake between his lips and a patch of her cheek. Ann was up in the lavatory, where she usually seemed to be. Not that he kissed *her* these days. He'd kissed her for some reason or other a few months ago, and she'd actually shuddered. He'd asked Margaret if it was all right that Ann didn't like kissing.

'Of course it's all right,' Margaret had replied. 'Before you know it she'll be kissing her lips off. And all the rest of it,' she added grimly.

Women were peculiarly practical about sex, as John had long ago decided. Sometimes Margaret could have the almost savage practicality of a surgeon; at others her practicality was cheerfully obscene. His attempts at bringing about the second attitude were not usually successful, however – the chemistry had to happen by accident. For the most part she was at neither extreme, just functional. It was men, he'd decided, (because if you could generalise about women, you inevitably generalised about men as well) it was men who were romantic and idealistic.

Stephen didn't mind being kissed, though. John squeezed one under his nose-and-spectacles, and went on his way.

As he backed out of the driveway he realised his windscreen wipers were going. He switched them off but they remained on, as though trying to swish the April sunshine from the windscreen. Because there was no water to lubricate their passage, they squeaked and groaned like put-upon children. John thought to himself that this wasn't the sort of thing that should happen to an assistant bank manager, it would make you feel such a fool, driving up with them going backwards and forwards for the staff to see; then felt a fool for having such a pompous thought in the first place. Perhaps somebody would flash him. He always felt disproportionately unnerved, even humiliated, when that happened, a car equivalent of being told you hadn't done up your zip. If his car was running normally he wasn't the least bit interested in it, but the wump-wump of the blades and their cries and creaks of pain forced him to pay attention. He decided to be bad-tempered for the first part of the day.

He drove past the Poco Poco on the corner of Denby Lane and Manchester Road. They were demolishing it, as one might pull out an elephant, or extract a dinosaur. It had been a monstrously ugly building, a huge box for people to have romances in. He'd met Margaret in it. He'd felt quite sickened, over the last week or so, to see them knocking it flat with a great metal ball swung from a crane, particularly with their anniversary coming up. Yes, he *had* remembered their anniversary, he suddenly realised. He ought to have told Margaret: I remembered when I saw them knocking our dance hall down.

The sun was shining on the new houses beyond for the first time since they were built, but it didn't make him feel any better, not with the wumping of his wipers and the thought of his memories going down the drain. Thousands must have been put on the value of those houses, with that eyesore being removed, so somebody would be pleased. The ball was lying idle on the ground now, like an enormous conker, because most of the building was down – only the lower part of the walls and the entrance steps remained.

As he drove on, peering through his wipers at the dry day, John realised that he was prepared to think about *any*thing, good or bad, as long as he could keep the thought of Gardiner at bay. And yet, if he didn't beard him today, he would be – it sounded melodramatic, even as a thought, but it was true – he would be done for, as far as his prospects were concerned.

When they knocked down the dance hall where you'd met someone, you couldn't help having a horrible suspicion that it meant that you'd never truly met them in the first place. It had all been a dream. Just as if it turned out that the vicar who married you wasn't really a vicar but somebody who had dressed up as one, an escaped prisoner on the run perhaps, wearing a bald wig, a dog-collar, those sticking-out teeth you can buy, then you wouldn't really be *married* after all. The licence wouldn't be worth the paper it was written on, you could tear it up.

He visualised the pieces drifting down like confetti on the non-couple as they stood, not exactly side by side, unbride, ungroom, middle-aged now, at the wrong end of their marriage. Your vows – something twitched with interest, deep down in his anatomy – your vows would be void. Margaret Margaret, he thought, forcing himself to be nostalgic, where we met will soon be nothing more than a hole in the ground. Toot toot, he added gleefully as a confused old lady stepped towards the path of his car, but he slowed down and avoided her all the same.

The destruction of the Poco Poco, and all it stood for, induced a further moment of wildness in him as he drove along Broadstone Road towards Reddish. He had a sudden mental picture of his loans officer, Mrs Clarke, rushing through the debris on all fours for some reason, her private parts puckered and busy as she ran away from him, her white rump nodding before it disappeared behind a pile of rubble.

Turning the corner of the road was like boom turning a corner in Life. Home and family left behind; but school not in front. From now on nobody in authority knew what she was up to. She was free. She could do whatever she liked. Go shopping, take a walk in the hills, start a new life. What she was going to do was travel to a hoe-down with the spotty ones. What a treat!

She walked down Wellington Road towards where Jessica and Kevin lived. The old ghouls at the bus-stop glared at her across the road, but there was nothing they could do about it. They were the sort of people who became enraged when they saw somebody not go to their bus-stop. If you asked them, they wouldn't have the faintest clue why.

Ann looked across again, to make sure she wasn't exaggerating. No, they were still looking at her. On impulse, she gave a sudden wave. Bye bye, darlings. Needless to say they just carried on looking. Ann made out loud the noise people make when they look at things uncomprehendingly: der. They wouldn't know what a wave was if one came up and bit them. What must they think? That her arm was flapping about in the wind?

Suddenly Ann felt embarrassed, in that foul way you do when you are walking along the street minding your own business, and somebody suddenly calls out 'Hello!' in a welcoming happy voice, and it sounds so like the sort of hellos people call out when they're talking to *you* that you answer automatically, and only then do you realise they're greeting someone else. Doing that makes you feel such self-hatred that if you had a gun handy you'd shoot yourself on the spot. Instead you have to stagger along as best you can, suppressing your moans and trying to look as if it's the most normal thing in the world for your mouth to open from time to time and let out a big hello even though you don't know anyone in sight.

Luckily this time there was nobody around, except people in cars who wouldn't know whether her waves hit the target in any case, and the two ghouls themselves, who were still staring and saying der. For two pins she'd do a V sign at them, except that they weren't worth it, and in any case she didn't want to be a fascist doing V signs at people. That would be almost as boring as just staring at people with your brain gone dead. She could feel their gaze on her even when she had turned back on her way, as if two pairs of eyes had been fired like squashy cannonballs, and had hit her in the small of her back.

She could still feel them as she walked past Stephen's school and then into Springdale Gardens just beyond, where Jessica and Kevin lived. Even the tulips in their front garden had a Christian look about them, standing in such neat rows you could easily forget they were supposed to be pretty. Ann knocked on the front door and it was opened by Jessica.

'You've come,' she said in that special voice she used, which was normal volume but had a whisper round the edge of it, as if she was confiding in you ALONE, a fat lot of good if all she could tell you was the obvious.

'I wouldn't miss it for the world.'

'But you've got your school things on.'

Jessica was all got up for the hoe-down, in jeans and a shirt she'd probably borrowed from her brother Kevin. They were both beanpoles. The get-up suited Jessica, as it happened. She was far too pure to have anything as sordid as breasts, but it didn't show in a shirt, and in any case she'd made up for it by having a little bunch of ears of corn pinned to the front to emphasise the bumpkin look.

Her long brown hair, the prettiest part of her, was loose, hanging down halfway to her middle.

'I hadn't made up my mind till I was on my way. I've got my other things in my school bag. I wanted to keep my options open.'

'I thought you wouldn't miss it for the *world*,' Jessica said obstinately. She was very literal. Anybody else would realise straight away that Ann had sneaked out of the house without telling her parents, but not Jessica. Jessica was that great rarity, a *good* Christian.

Ann had come to the conclusion that Christians had a tendency to be worse than ordinary people, anything from slightly less nice in the details of life to really terrible in every way, but this sliding scale didn't seem to apply to Jessica, or if it did, only very marginally. If you had extremely sensitive evil-detectors, and they were switched up to maximum, you might just be able to detect that Jessica's goodness was of a rather bad kind. She would always be willing to lend money to Fiona Buchan, for example. Fiona perpetually didn't have quite enough money to buy herself a Kit-Kat in morning break, or pay for her bus fare going home. Instead of doing without the Kit-Kat or the bus she would winge and moan and cadge. After forking out a few times, people would tell her to get lost. Jessica wouldn't, though, she'd always lend it.

Jessica didn't start off with more money than anybody else, not even than Fiona probably, but there was a Christian quality to her supply which meant she always had some spare to give to the poor, a sort of cash version of the loaves and fishes. Jessica didn't complain, she didn't frown, she didn't moralise, she seemed perfectly happy shelling out. And yet, and yet. Just as you knew that however cold the surface of the earth was, rocks hubbled and bubbled down below, so Ann sensed that there was something hot in the very centre of Jessica.

She paid up so *perfectly*. The smile was perfect. The friendliness was perfect. The not remembering that this had happened yesterday and the day before that and the day before that was perfect. It was like watching an actor who convinced you that who he was, was real. At the end of the day he was still only an actor. What Ann's evil-detectors thought they detected was *virtue*. I'm virtuous. Being virtuous means I give my money to creeps like you. That's your job, Fiona, being a creep that I can be virtuous to.

'I didn't know I wouldn't miss it for the world until I decided I wouldn't miss it for the world when I was on my way,' Ann lied. 'I saw the light.'

Jessica's mouth opened. It had a tendency to do that. More than anybody else's, Jessica's mouth reminded you that your jaw was on a hinge. It was a pity because she was actually not bad-looking. She had some zits, of course, on the lower part of her cheeks and on her chin, but her eyes had a wide-apart, slightly elfin look, with high cheek-bones beneath. But then she'd open her mouth wide suddenly, like an animal, and your impression would change. Her teeth looked like stalactites and stalagmites, in a dark pink cave. Her tongue looked very tonguey. Her mouth when it was wide open was so much bigger than anything else on her face that you automatically looked into it, instead of looking at her eyes, as you did when it was closed. Perhaps she did it to cool herself, like a crocodile. This time it was more likely because she wasn't following the logic, if there was any, of Ann's explanation.

'For goodness' sake, Jessica, can't you let me in? Are you waiting for me to say the password or something?'

'The password', said Jessica, her face lightening, 'is breakfast.'

'Oh no,' said Ann. 'I've had mine already.' Now she thought about it she could smell bacon and eggs wafting about on the breeze. Kevin was a tremendous eater, being so tall. So was Philip, and he wasn't. Ann had once explained to Stephen that your body was hollow, so your food plopped first down one leg, all the way down, squidging into each toe in turn, and then building up and up until it reached the top, and then down the other, and then slowly up your trunk, till it finally reached your head. Stephen hadn't believed her, naturally. 'Why does blood come out when you cut yourself?' he'd asked. 'Why not bits of chewed-up meat and vegetables and cups of tea?' 'That's what blood *is*,' she'd replied. Obviously it was a vast over-simplification, but all explanations were vast over-simplifications. Kevin's food had a long way to fall. Philip's didn't. He just ate a lot because he was greedy.

'I'm sure you could fit a bit more in. Now that you've seen the light,' Jessica told her.

First dad jumped off the ship. Stephen imagined him sailing through the air, plump as a bird but without wings. Sploosh. Then

37

Ann, raggedy in the wind, blowing over the wave tops until one finally gobbled her up. Next would go Stephen himself. His spectacles would fly away and the sea would change from sea to a solid block of green on which he would terribly splat. He would cry as he fell but no one would hear, just as the falling chicken had cried in the night. When it landed it sounded as if it broke, but, when they came down in the morning and inspected it, it was whole. Perhaps you could break into such small bits nobody could tell you were broken at all. Perhaps when you were dead and frozen you were broken already. And after Stephen, mum and Raymond. They would drop together like those people without parachutes who hold hands, though in mum and Raymond's case it would be a dog lead. Of course Stephen wouldn't see them because he would have gone already.

Stephen paused in the hall as a horrible thought came into his mind. Perhaps when you died you might not even know *you* were dead. You might just think everything had stopped.

'Have you got your swimming things?' his mother asked.

For a moment Stephen was too choked to speak. 'You don't put on your swimming trunks when the ship is sinking,' he said. 'You haven't got time.'

'No, dear, of course not. But you do put them on when you go swimming with the school. Think of what all the girls in your class would say if you didn't.'

'Of course I've got them.'

'Well, swim carefully, darling.'

She kissed him. She used to kiss him on the garden path but now she did it before she opened the front door, so that nobody would see. Now she opened the front door. The garden path glittered in the sunshine. For a moment he thought it *was* the side of a ship, stretching downwards. He stepped on to it, opening his arms for balance. He couldn't fall down it, because it was in fact flat, but he could run.

'Don't run, Stephen,' his mother called. 'You're not late. I don't want you running into the road.'

He ran hard towards the road, and pulled up at the last moment. He was always hoping to skid but it never quite came out.

'Stephen! I'll have to take you to school if you're going to behave like that. I thought you had more sense.'

38

He looked back at her. She always looked sad when she was angry. She ran a hand through her hair.

'I'm sorry about the pig, mum,' he called.

'The pig was perfect,' she called back.

He looked at her a bit longer, wondering what she meant by that. The pig could only have been perfect if it wasn't a pig at all but something else, something you *should* have on your anniversary card. Still if his mother wanted a pig, let her have it. It was a bit of luck he'd drawn the pig in the first place, seeing that for some reason she wanted one. If it was his anniversary he'd much rather have something different, even a dartboard and a pint of beer, like daddy. At least they were some use. Pigs weren't any use unless you killed them and ate them, and who wanted something you had to kill and eat on their card? You couldn't even ride a pig. At least, he'd never heard of anybody riding one.

He tried riding one down the street. It was so fat he had to keep his legs apart and round, like the round parts on nutcrackers, where you put the nut. It made it very hard to walk. The old woman with the poop scoop came along, and looked at his legs as she went past. Her dog looked at them as well. Stephen had bought a poop scoop for his mother but she never took it with her when she went out with Raymond. Before she took him for a walk she would always say, Raymond, behave! which meant, Raymond, don't go to the toilet. There was a patch of garden, at the bottom behind the place where they had bonfires, where Raymond was supposed to do his business. But if he felt the need to do it on a walk he just did it anyway. When this happened mum would put her hand up by her eyes so she wouldn't see it, like the blinkers they put on racehorses to make them go straight ahead. She would say Raymond Raymond in a quiet voice without moving her lips and each time she said it Raymond's ears would twitch a little although he pretended they didn't, and he would go to the toilet even more to show he was taking no notice.

Riding the pig was very wobbly and made Stephen's legs ache, so he stopped, and walked instead. He had a feeling that the old lady and her dog were creeping up on him from behind so he turned to look, but they were going away from him down the road. He walked on till he got to the cold corner. The cold corner was where their road met the big road. He had to go round the corner, and walk along the pavement by the big road for a while until he got to school. You had to stiffen yourself when you went round the cold corner, because a wind lived in the big road. When you turned the corner you always walked right into it. Sometimes, if it was even windy in *their* road, the wind in the big road would be so strong that it would flatten your eyelashes and squeeze so hard into your nostrils that they would hurt. It might even make your eyes cry. Today it wasn't as bad as that but it was still cool.

He began to walk towards school, which he could see in the distance, beyond the wind, bright green grass which always looked nicer from here than it did when you got to it, when you could see all the brown showing through as if it was getting bald, and the red buildings like pieces of meat in a butcher's shop. He walked looking straight ahead, just like his mother when she wasn't looking at Raymond going to the toilet, but in this case what he wasn't looking at was Ann standing by her bus-stop on the other side of the big road. She was always the only schoolgirl standing at that particular bus-stop, but there were usually two grown-ups standing there as well, and he didn't want to call hello to her in front of them. He knew she didn't want to call hello to him either. He'd never asked her but he knew she wouldn't, not with the other people there. And, in any case, what did they have to call hello about when they'd seen each other already that morning? So he kept his eyes fixed on the school, and watched it bounce slowly larger and larger as he walked.

After a little while he got to the bus-stop on *this* side of the road, which was empty, as usual. He didn't know why they'd bothered to put a bus-stop here since nobody ever seemed to want to stand by it. The only person who liked this particular bus-stop was Raymond. But it was an important landmark because when Stephen got to it he would begin to count his steps, and after ten of them he would look sideways, without moving his head. He was always exactly opposite Ann when he got to this point, and he liked to take a quick look to check whether she was there or had already gone.

This morning she'd gone.

But something strange had happened, which made him look again, this time with his whole head. The other two people were still there!

Yes, it was the same two as always. How could Ann have got the bus and left them behind? He stopped in his tracks and concentrated on looking. He took his spectacles off just in case they were missing her in some way, but now nobody was there, not even the bus-stop. The big road went halfway across and then went soft and swimmy. He put his spectacles on again, but she still wasn't there.

He looked left and then right. As luck would have it, gaps were approaching from both sides. When they were level he rushed across them, like Moses and the Israelites crossing the Red Sea. The pavement on the other side, when he got to it, felt dry and safe, like the river bank of a slow grey river that was full of large, dangerous fish.

The two people at the bus-stop were a man and woman. The man was a man who often walked past their house. He was tall and sad, with a blue anorak and grey hair. He always had a cigarette in his mouth as if it had been nailed there. The lady was quite fat, even her eyes were fat, and she was carrying a shopping bag. She tried to smile at Stephen, but missed, and her smile faded away. Ann still wasn't here. Perhaps, Stephen thought, the bus had come early, and she'd caught it while the other two hadn't. He felt very relieved at this thought. He stood waiting with the other two for a little while. He wanted to cross the road again, and carry on on his way to school, but he didn't like to. He wondered if he should explain to the man and the lady that he'd come over to look for his sister, but he didn't like to do that either. He looked at them again, just in case. The man's white cigarette and the lady's fat eyes made them look as if you couldn't tell them anything, at least as if Stephen couldn't. Of course he could just run, and leave them untold. They would never be able to catch him up. It gave you a cold feeling, though, even colder than the wind, when you thought about running off without telling the grown-ups you were standing with. Still, that's what he would have to do. Even if they had head jumpers to put on they'd never catch him. He imagined that the lady had one in her shopping bag and the man one in his briefcase. When his back was turned and he was running, they might put them on and follow, but if he ran fast, through a gap, he would leave them behind. He could run very fast. He looked down the road, to see if a gap was coming, and froze in horror.

The *bus* was coming, Ann's bus!

41

It was near, it filled up all the road, he could smell its bus smell. Ann *must* be here. He wanted to look again, but he didn't dare. The thought crossed his mind that she might have become invisible. The man got on. He put his ticket in the clicker and went straight upstairs. The lady got on. She stood by the driver, paying him. The bus was still here, waiting. It was too big not to get on when it was waiting for you. Anyway, Ann should be getting on herself. He was her brother. She had become invisible.

He got on the bus in place of Ann. The bus driver was still doing the lady's fare. He walked past them, and down the aisle, looking for a seat. He expected the driver to call out and ask him for his money, which would be very embarrassing. All he could say was Ann has it. But the driver was busy being busy with the lady, and took no notice of him.

Margaret had a little secret, which she shared with Raymond. She didn't go in for secrets on the whole, and didn't like women who did. There was a distinct sort of woman who was always whispering things to you and telling you not to tell them to anyone else. Her 'friend', Lynne York, was one of them. Come to think of it, she was the only one she knew, at least of the really hard-boiled secretive sort, but Margaret still felt sure that there was a whole section of the population like that, all basically the same. She imagined them even looking the same. Lynne was an oblong woman who wore flouncy clothes. They knew each other at the Guild. Margaret didn't really think of Lynne as a friend, so that when she pictured the word in her head she put it in quotation marks. As a matter of fact she was probably in quotation marks herself, from Lynne's point of view. She was simply somebody for Lynne to confide her secrets to, an ear on legs. There were no doubt many other people to whom Lynne confided them. Perhaps she saw everybody as ears on legs. The most important point, though, was not how Lynne saw other people but how Lynne saw herself: she was like Santa's sack, chock-full of wrapped-up goodies. But there was an underlying sadness about her, irrespective of the flouncy clothes and the little voice scrabbling inside your head and making your ear go hot. Surely if you wanted to be full of secrets it was because you really wanted to be a *femme fatale*, and couldn't be; in Lynne's case, because you were too oblong. You didn't have any adventures of your own, and you couldn't *offer* adventure to whoever one would offer adventure to, men presumably; so you offered other people's adventures to women instead.

Such secrets as Margaret had weren't to be offered to anybody, if she could help it. She could only think of three, in any case. The first had been a secret so long it was almost a secret from herself. The second was the secret of her left breast. If, if only, the lump proved to be benign, she could tell John about it, and there wouldn't be a secret any more. If the other thing happened, John would be told about it anyway and there still wouldn't be a secret any more. Either way the secret would only be a secret till the end of the morning, and then it would harden into fact or melt away altogether.

The only person to know her third secret was Raymond, and he wouldn't tell. In fact, it was his secret as much as hers. Stockport had enacted a by-law a year or so ago, forcing people to clear up their dogs' messes after them, on penalty of a one-hundred-pound fine. Stephen had been much struck by the severity of the punishment involved, and had promptly bought her a poop scoop for her next birthday. He seemed to have a picture in his head of people being dragged kicking and screaming from streets and parks by the authorities, as if it was the French Revolution all over again. As it happened the public took very little notice. The old lady at the end of their road observed the by-law religiously, but she observed everything religiously, and she might even be the only one. She would go to heaven all by herself, which would probably suit her, along with her dog, of course.

Margaret had tried to be good when she'd first had her poop scoop, but confronting dog muck coiled on the pavement like brown demonic toothpaste was almost more than she could bear, and she'd very quickly begun to backslide. Now she only did her duty when Stephen was in the offing, and at other times she'd got into the habit of not even taking her poop scoop in the polythene bag she carried for it, almost as though to ensure that she would resist any temptation to do the right thing.

Instead, before going on a walk, she'd take Raymond to what John called the crap-patch at the bottom of the garden, and try to hypnotise him into going to the toilet. In fact Raymond was relatively easy to hypnotise. She would stare at him, and he would

43

stare back, his eyes moist, and intense, and yearning. At this stage his eyes seemed to say, we're on the same side you and I. I know you're a woman and I'm a dog, but in the end that distinction doesn't count. We understand each other. Then she would stare at him a little more, and his eyes would slowly fade until they were completely blank and gormless: he simply didn't have the concentration to keep up his soulful expression. It was at this point that he could be hypnotised, but unfortunately he was so dim-witted he had no idea what instruction she was trying to give him. He had no vocabulary at all. He didn't even understand words like 'Fetch' and 'Sit' as other dogs did.

To get round this problem she endeavoured to think not in words but in sensations. She would try to summon up the experience of wanting to relieve yourself, and somehow transfer it to her eyes so that it could then be transmitted towards Raymond's blank, receptive face. On a couple of occasions she'd evoked the sensation so vividly that she'd had to rush off to the lavatory herself. But it had no effect on Raymond whatever, despite his protestations of a few moments before that the two of them were allies on the elemental plane of life. The tension of not understanding what his mistress's hypnosis was referring to would become too much for him, and he would eventually let out a despondent whine, or occasionally even growl with frustration. Sometimes, it was true, he would in fact squat and do his business, but when she worked it out the frequency was no more than the law of averages would demand. On these occasions she would congratulate him effusively, practically kissing his black unkissable lips, and of course he would respond with gusto, as he always did, being a friendly, open-hearted dog, but she could tell by a kind of polite expression on his face that he had no idea what he was being congratulated for. Obviously if you've just been to the lavatory because you felt the need you don't expect a reward. The long and the short of it was that he never learned from his experiences. All she could do before going for a walk was tell him to behave and hope for the best.

'Behave, Raymond,' she said, as soon as they'd come in from the back garden and she'd put his lead on him. She said it quite roughly, like a bad-tempered schoolmistress. He blinked, and swallowed nervously. Then she opened the front door and he switched on his tail as abruptly as one might switch on a propeller. He tugged on the lead so hard that he whined a little with self-induced pain. She followed him out, barely able to swing the front door shut behind her before he was pulling her down the path.

She looked up Glenwood Road towards Wellington Road at the top, as she always did, for no particular reason. Stephen and Ann would be safely at school by now. She looked just for good luck. By letting her eye scour the blank road and pavement she relegated any possibility of two prone crumpled forms lying there to the abstract world of statistics. The odds that anything could have gone tragically wrong, that a hit-and-run driver could have flattened her children, that a murderer could have murdered them, that a bolt of lightning could have emerged inexplicably from the bouncy blue sky and struck them down, were trillions to one. Or billions. Anyway, millions. But somewhere, today, such a thing would happen to *some*body's children, you could read about it in the paper. There were enough people in total to let even the longest odds gobble up the occasional child or two.

It occurred to Margaret that all her thoughts seemed to be growing teeth. First, the Monday morning feeling, creeping up on her in bed, and biting her left breast. Now these long odds attacking Ann and Stephen. She was in a morbid frame of mind, which was hardly surprising. In her own case the odds didn't even have to *be* very long. They could be small fat ones, appropriately since their target was her breast. The odds needed to be only, who knows, three to one, four to one. But if I have to confront such short odds, let no long ones attack my children, she thought. Enough is enough, fair is fair. The self-sacrificing nobility of that idea suddenly made her lips tremble, and it was all she could do to stop herself crying in the street, particularly as she realised immediately that it wasn't true, there were no guarantees, whole families could get cancer more or less simultaneously, or be run over, or some horrific combination of the two. You could be transformed overnight, in the blink of an eye, from a perfectly ordinary family to a well-known local tragedy. All your years of normality would count for nothing, like a bad investment, and when people said your name they would always say Poor Margaret, and shake their heads, or even brush away a tear. She didn't deserve *that*, they'd say. I don't deserve it, Margaret said, and then realised she'd spoken, or at least muttered, out loud. Raymond cocked his ears, and then shook his head, as if to shake the stupid incomprehensible words on to the pavement, where they belonged. 'Come on, Raymond,' Margaret added, as if that was what she'd intended to say all along, and, turning her back upon the possibility of her children lying dead in the road, she set off in the other direction, round the corner into Gower Road, to go past the Poco Poco, over Manchester Road, and into Ash Grove, where her father-in-law lived.

The Poco Poco was nearly gone. She'd gone past there a few days ago, at an earlier stage of the demolition, with Stephen.

'I should think there's only about one Poco left,' he'd said. That had obviously triggered off a whole train of thought, because a few moments later he'd added, 'Whoever invented the human language must have been a very bad speller.'

As Raymond towed her past, Margaret wondered how much of the Poco Poco was left now. Just a final o, perhaps, a good letter to end on. The place was a dump, anyhow. She found it impossible to remember how it had seemed to her when she was young, when, for example, John was just a lad she was going out with, and not her husband. When she tried to picture it, she saw herself as she was now, but crammed into a silly mini-skirt, and John, stocky and bank-managerish, in a matchstick-man suit, both of them doing a stupid dance to loud horrible music, like actors who have been embarrassingly miscast. No, it had gone, let the building follow it, then her breast, then herself, one by one, on to the scrap heap. That's where everything ended up; in the end.

As if, thoughtfully, to change the subject and snap her out of her mood, Raymond chose this moment to do his business on the grass verge in front of what was left of the Poco Poco, so that the demolition men, just now clocking on, could get a perfect view of him. It was probably not the sort of thing that would worry demolition men, of course, but still she felt the paralysis of shame overcoming her. She could never help feeling implicated, as though Raymond were her representative, going to the lavatory in public on her behalf. She looked fixedly in another direction, muttering Raymond, Raymond, under her breath, but of course he took no notice.

'Hello, love,' said one of the demolition men cheerily as he trudged past. He was wearing a filthy shirt and jeans, and was fat and hard-looking at the same time, like an uncooked potato.

I don't know what he's got to say hello love about, Margaret thought bitterly. I'm holding a lead that has a dog relieving himself on the end of it, my left breast could be whipped off at a moment's notice, and I got married years and years ago today. I used to dance in the Poco Poco once upon a time but now you're knocking it down and all that's left is the o.

'Good morning,' she said. As with any cheeky man she made sure she didn't sound too friendly; but she didn't let herself sound hostile either.

As Raymond crapped, a man came up, possibly drawn by the smell, though he didn't sniff. They never sniffed. All he did was make a noise at Margaret. Raymond sniffed *him*, however, as he passed. He smelled like a walking building. Raymond half rose to follow, but then remembered what he was doing and sent his rear suddenly back to its mid-air poise. The man trudged on, to an area of broken-off walls and dense, unsorted rubble. As Raymond's nostrils followed, they stumbled upon the sharp bitter pong of rat. His ears shot forward, and his tail sprang further up as if blown by a strong wind, a rat wind. Raymond had only ever smelled rats before in the distance, their remote blurred odour sometimes discernible round intricate corners in the great tangle of smells you could sniff by the iron grids of drains. He had never seen one, but his nose found within that smell an implication of short grey fur, bony body, long pink tail, wedge head, sneering teeth. He whined with joy, shut his bum abruptly, and flung himself forward in pursuit. His lead became an iron bar, and his whole body, except his tongue, stopped dead.

He twisted his head to see Margaret and she returned his stare, giving him her look, the same look that she'd given him in the crap bed at the bottom of the garden earlier this morning, place of deep rich smells where day after day she took him and then, with her look, said don't, when his whole being, particularly the latter half, strained with desire to *do*. It happened so regularly that he remembered it, Margaret's earnest look saying no, not harshly but with that firm perversity of humankind, opposed to crapping, fucking, and eating breakfast, even though they crapped, fucked, and ate breakfast themselves. Meanwhile, of course, the crap bed in the garden said yes, and he, Raymond, was straddled disconsolately between the two imperatives, negative at the head end, affirmative at the rear. Occasionally the rear end won, and he would not be able to stop himself. At these times Margaret behaved strangely, stroking and caressing him, as if to comfort him in his remissness, and her pity would paralyse him with shame. On their walks it was a different story. The need became overpowering, he was not in Margaret's territory and, however much she looked her look, he felt no shame.

Raymond turned back to look at the retreating figure of the man who smelt like a building. He couldn't follow him, so there was no point in remembering him any more. The man disappeared from Raymond's horizons, and he turned away again, letting the lead slacken, and noticed his pile of crap. He sniffed it. Yes, it was properly done. It was his and it smelt of him. The smell was in sharp focus, and would be recognised by other dogs, even by dogs who didn't know him in the first place. Margaret tugged on his lead and they were off again.

They crossed the big road, turned down a smaller one, and then things began to change. The smells of road, pavement, windows, trees, pee, were more joyful, the breeze danced, tugging his fur, the air lit up, brighter than before, as if, though he had not even been asleep, he had opened his eyes for the second time: something was about to happen. Each paw-step became magical, he was entering a new part of the day. Now he could catch it on the breeze. He was entering the territory of the top dog, of the top man. It was a place where all experiences, even ordinary ones like sitting under a table, became privileges.

Oh dear, thought Margaret, I don't know why I do this. He's *John*'s dad, after all.

Stephen found a seat with nobody sitting in it, so he could be by the window. It was on the road side, which meant that he could see the road itself, and the other side of the road. The bus shook and started off. The window of the bus made everything look strange, and when they went past the top of Stephen's road it looked like somebody else's road. That gave him the horrible feeling that if he went down it he wouldn't find his house there any more, and he suddenly wanted to cry. A sob came up in his throat and was just about to escape when he managed to swallow it again. It had sharp edges as it went down, like a giant cornflake. But he was being Ann and Ann wouldn't cry. She did this journey every day. Every day she must get on this bus and look out of the window and discover that they'd taken her road away and put a different one that just looked the same there instead. And every afternoon when she got off the bus she would find that their old road had been put back again, and their house had returned to its place, and their mum and dad had come alive once more. Stephen wondered if Ann ever felt frightened that some day a mistake would be made – somebody would forget – and she'd come back and not be able ever more to find her way home.

As long as it's not today, Stephen thought. It's bad enough having to be Ann in the first place.

The problem was he didn't know where she got off. He'd been to Ann's school, but only in the car. He didn't know whether he'd even be able to see it from the bus. And if he missed the stop what would happen to him? He wouldn't be Ann any more, he'd just be Stephen, and the bus would be going Anywhere. The sob came back into his throat. This time it felt like a giant cornflake on the way *up*. At any moment it would shoot out.

Then he remembered: Ann went to school with her friend, Jessica. She was always talking about what they said to each other on the bus. Possibly Jessica was on already. Stephen stared at all the people in front of him, but none of them were her. He twisted his head round to look back, but none of *them* were Jessica either. Perhaps she was upstairs. He tensed his legs, ready to get off the moment he saw Jessica arriving at the bottom of the stairs.

They stopped once, then again. Jessica didn't appear. The second time they stopped, a man got on. He looked at the seat beside Stephen, but Stephen dead-eyed him, and he went towards the back of the bus. At the third stop there was still no Jessica. This time another man got on. He paid his fare, and came straight down to the spare seat beside Stephen. Stephen looked up to dead-eye him too but saw immediately that it would do no good. The man was small and ugly, and he had a very red face which almost seemed to *shine* red, as if there was a light bulb inside his head somewhere. Stephen's dead-eye just bounced off.

The man sat down. He turned to look at Stephen. He half shut his eyes so that they could look twice as hard. Then he spoke. He had a deep rough voice which sounded strangely like a talking belch.

He said: 'I dunno, I dunno, where de blotherin thing.'

Stephen wasn't quite sure whether he was speaking a foreign language or not. Each word smelt as it came out, a bit like sweets, a bit like strong medicine and a bit like pongy breath. 'Where de blotherin thing?' the man added.

'I don't know,' Stephen replied.

The man seemed to decide whether to be surprised. He looked at Stephen for a moment, screwing up his eyes so that there was only a tiny crack of look left. Then, after a while, he suddenly jumped, as if Stephen had just that *second* said his 'I don't know', and had completely caught him off guard.

'What you don't know?' the man asked in return. 'What you don't blotherin know?'

'Where the thing is.'

'What thing?'

'The blotherin thing.'

50

'Where de blotherin thing,' the man said, that obviously having reminded him. He turned away from Stephen and inspected the aisle, as though it might be there. Then he bent down and picked something off the floor. It was a crisp bag. He opened its mouth and stared down it, looking just like a doctor when he stares down your throat. Stephen almost expected him to ask the crisp bag to say ah. Perhaps he thought the blotherin thing was inside.

Stephen remembered the other day, when he'd seen a Polo mint on the floor, and had suddenly had the feeling somebody was inside *it*. Somebody who needed to be rescued, like the people who drowned in the swimming-pool where his class at school went every Thursday. There was always a terrible noise in the pool, much more than was being made by him and his class, and there were cries and screams in it, from drowning people he could never see. He couldn't hear anybody in the Polo mint, but perhaps this was somebody you couldn't see *or* hear.

Luckily Raymond was in his basket in the corner, so Stephen went up to him and got breathed on. That got him to the size of a dog. Then he went out into the garden to find Cyril. Cyril was the cat from next door, who always lay on the roof of their garden shed when it was a sunny day. It wasn't sunny, but luckily Cyril had fallen asleep when it had been sunny before, and hadn't woken up yet. He woke up though when Stephen approached, and yawned a wide and trembly yawn. He didn't open his eyes at first, as if he was trying to say Stephen wasn't important enough to be looked at. Unfortunately Stephen wasn't quite close enough to get the breath from his yawn and when he got closer Cyril woke up properly and began backing away up the shed roof, probably thinking Stephen was a dog now he'd been breathed on by Raymond. Stephen hoped he would catch a bit of cat breath on the wind but no luck. You could always tell when you'd been breathed on by a cat because you'd smell a cat-food smell. Stephen wondered whether cat breath smelt of cat-food because they ate so much of it, or whether their insides smelt like that anyway, which might be why they liked cat-food in the first place. Stephen didn't like it, it was too strong. Cat breath didn't travel very far because cats had such tiny nostrils. It was just like only having a very tiny gun, you couldn't fire things a great distance.

Cyril got to the top of the roof, began to back down the slope on the other side, lost his footing, or rather his pawing, cried aaagh, and disappeared from view. Cyril was sometimes very neat and agile, nipping about with his paws hardly touching the ground, and sitting with them so neatly side by side that they reminded Stephen of when his mum folded up the washing; and at other times he just looked like a ball with legs poking out at random. He was like that now. Stephen could hear the ball aspect of him thudding down the roof, and the random paws scrabbling against that funny tarry stuff that looks like a very thin road, which they put on shed roofs. Cyril wouldn't breathe on him now, so Stephen went back into the house.

He found a piece of paper and drew a picture of a cat, complete with two tiny nostrils. Then he did a cloud coming out of his head, like those clouds of words that they do in comics, but this one was empty, because it contained only breath. Then he put his nose right down to the paper until it was actually touching the cloud, and breathed in. That took him down to the size of a cat.

The next step was easy because he already had a toy mouse. His aunty Chloe had given it to him for Christmas many years ago, when he was young. It was called Patrick. It was an odd mouse because it didn't have any particular legs. It had a long curved head and body, like a grey banana, and a long tail on the end of it. Patrick wasn't a very nice mouse, and didn't get on with the other animals that lived in the toy-box beside Stephen's bed. He was a particular enemy of Rabbitty, a small furious one-eyed rabbit that Stephen and his mother had once found sitting on a garden wall in the pouring rain, and had dried out. Stephen picked Patrick out, hid him behind his back so that Rabbitty wouldn't see, and went off to the toilet so he could sniff his breath in private. That took him down to the size of a mouse.

Then he went into the garden. Some ants lived in the patio, in the cracks between the paving stones. Luckily several of them were running about now. He put one of his fingers into the crack and waited for an ant to run on to it. First of all they all ran away. Then they began to get used to his finger (which was like a pink tree to them) and came nearer and nearer. This was what made it exciting, seeing them gradually approach. Stephen had tried fish-fishing, but it was boring because you couldn't see what was going on underwater: ant-fishing was much better.

At last a very tiny ant, presumably a young one, scuttled over the end of Stephen's finger, but he stepped back off into the crack before Stephen could do anything about it. Then another one, slightly bigger, did the same, and this time Stephen lifted him in time. The ant ran about in panic, on top of his finger, then down the side, then underneath. Stephen poked his nose down, missed, poked his nose down again, and hit, but a bit too well. He breathed in the ant's dying breath. When he took his nose away, the back part of the ant was squashed, and the front part was waving its legs feebly in the air, as if waving goodbye. Stephen scraped it carefully off his finger against the edge of the paving stone, so it dropped into its home crack, and could be buried by its friends. At least he hadn't died in vain. Stephen was now the size of an ant.

He went back to the Polo mint and began to climb up its white side. It was like climbing a cliff of solid ice in Antarctica, but his feet must have picked up the stickiness that the feet of ants and other insects have, because he was able to scramble up it quite easily. He slipped between an o and an l when he went across the top. The o looked like a bright white dry bath-tub. When he'd got past it, the mint sloped downwards as it went into its hole so he sat down and began to toboggan on his bum. He had never been anywhere so white as on this mint. The air was so fresh and minty it made the inside of his nose seem to ring. The surface was smooth as glass and he slid faster and faster until he got to the steepest part, when he slid as fast as you could go, but he still didn't hurt himself when he got to the bottom because the drop was only about a quarter of an inch altogether.

In the circular place at the bottom there was no one to be seen, only a shoe, like Cinderella's. He picked it up. Perhaps it was a valuable one. He looked at it closely. It seemed pretty ordinary to him. He sniffed it. It smells of the human foot, he thought.

'Stephen, what are you doing, messing about with Ann's shoe?' his mother asked.

He tried to answer but realised he'd folded his tongue into a sausage and poked it through the hole in the centre of the Polo. His tongue bonged about in his mouth like the clapper of a bell.

'Stephen, what have you got in your mouth?'

He rested the mint against the front of his front teeth, pulled his tongue out and said, 'A Polo.'

'Where did you get that from? I told you –'

'I found it on the floor.'

'I would have thought you were too old to –'

'I found Ann's shoe on the floor too.'

'I wish Ann would take her shoes off like normal people. When she comes in from school she just seems to explode.'

The blotherin man gave up on his crisp bag and threw it back on to the floor. He turned back to Stephen.

'I've not had no breakfast,' he explained. Then added: 'I had egg, bacon, tomato and fried bread.'

'How did you have all that if you didn't have any?' Stephen asked him cautiously.

'Et it in my fucking dreams,' the man said. He turned and looked across the aisle to a man who was sitting in the next seat, a man who had an enormous coiled ear, as though ear-stuff had just been piled up on the side of his head. 'Where de blotherin thing?' the blotherin man asked him loudly.

Despite his big ear the other man took no notice.

The blotherin man was possibly looking for his dream breakfast. Stephen pictured the fried egg on thin little insect legs, much like the legs he, Stephen, must have had when he climbed into the Polo, with a smiling yellow egg face, and the splat of white all round its head like a bonnet. The blotherin man was in hot pursuit with his knife and fork.

'I had porridge,' Stephen said. 'Porridge can't run away. It's the wrong shape. It would just sort of spludge.'

The man turned back towards him. His face wasn't as red, and he spoke in a different voice, not such a furry one, as if another man inside him had finally got to the mouth-hole. You could tell he wasn't worrying where the blotherin thing was.

'What you talking about?' the second man asked.

'Porridge,' Stephen said.

The second man looked politely blank.

'Breakfast,' Stephen explained. 'When you said you had your breakfast in your, you know, dreams.'

'I just have some of the old bottle,' said the second man. 'Just to get me on the go, like. On me working days. If I want to go mad I wait till the end uv the week.'

The bus stopped again, but only ordinary people got on and off.

54

'The other one doesn't,' Stephen said.

'What other one?'

'The dream one. He has egg and bacon.'

'Good for hum,' the second man said. His face reddened up, as if the dream man was showing through. 'Yum fucking yum,' he added tiredly.

'And tomatoes,' Stephen said. There was a pause, then he asked timidly, 'Does he wear a jumper?' He didn't like to say the next bit, so he said it so softly the man wouldn't hear. 'On his head?'

But the dream man had come back in any case. He opened both his eyes as far as they would go, which wasn't very far. They were small and shiny, like sweets you take out of your mouth to check, when you've been sucking them. His face became as red as red. 'De blotherin thing,' he muttered, as if to remind himself who he was.

The bus began to slow again. Stephen's stomach felt nervous. Yum, he kept thinking, just because the man had said it, yum yum. He was sure this was the stop where Jessica would appear from upstairs, and then everything would be all right. He could get off, and it would just be where Ann went every day, so it wouldn't be difficult and unknown. He could even ask Jessica how to get back.

Some other teenagers got off, but Jessica still didn't appear. The bus set off again. When it was too late Stephen thought to himself, I could have got off with the other teenagers. They were probably going to Ann's school as well.

Stephen's dad often said ten to one. For a long time Stephen had thought he was telling him the time, except that he said it when it was obviously not ten to one at all, but seven o'clock, or a quarter to nine. Then Stephen realised that they were words you said to make what you said into something that was true. Ten to one those teenagers were going to Ann's school, Stephen told himself. Ten to one Jessica wasn't even on the bus at all, even upstairs. Ten to one the same thing had happened to her as had happened to Ann. Perhaps they'd *both* exploded.

And now he was just Stephen, on a bus that was going any old where, probably somewhere he'd never even heard of, with the blotherin man sitting on his outside as a jailer sits outside the door of a jail. The sob came back up, soft and easy, not like a cornflake at all, so it was there before he even knew it was coming, and this time he had to let it out. He was allowed to now he was Stephen again and didn't have to be Ann any more, but even so he kept the bloop as small and quiet as he could because he didn't know what the blotherin man would say.

Kevin and Philip were at the table in the Downtons' little dining-room, gobbling fried eggs, tomatoes, bacon, fried bread. Philip stood up when Ann came in, so Kevin had to do the same. What knights in shining armour these evangelicals were, except they weren't. Kevin did shine a little bit, though. His hands especially were extremely pink, where he'd nearly been successful in scrub-bing oil or windscreen rubber from his fingerprints and nail-rims. Even his zits looked clean and flat, and almost translucent too, like small pieces of stained glass, blue, mauve, purple, set flush into his skin. He crinkled up his eyes when he looked at you, as if he was looking through cigarette smoke, even though he was far too Christian to smoke. He had quite long hair which was well brushed so he seemed to be wearing a hair cap. His clothes, like him, were long and lanky and lacking in style. In fact he wasn't wearing anything in particular, but for the sake of argument you could call it a pair of jeans, a tartan shirt and a beige-ish jumper.
Philip's clothes, by contrast, were always too small. Ann couldn't quite understand it – they must start off being too small. He was like a fatness equivalent of those men who always have one day's growth of beard. This morning he was wearing a green car-digan with leather buttons, their heads straining to one side with the tug of the buttonholes, like the heads of hanged men. He wore dark grey flannel trousers, as plump as liquorice Allsorts, with the teeth of the zip just showing at the top of his flies. His hair was cut short like a scrubbing brush on top. His zits looked younger and more active than Kevin's, congregating on his neck just below his ears, and swarming over his jaw-line on to his cheeks, with a few of the advance guard having reached his nose. There were a couple of white-capped ones in the groove between his left nostril and his cheek, like two tiny explorers in pith helmets encamped in a ravine.
'Good morrow, sister,' Philip said.
'I'm no sister of yours,' Ann told him baldly.

56

'Sister in God.'

When Philip said something like 'Good morrow, sister,' he was pretending to joke, but underneath he was really sincere. He would go to the stake on the grounds that she was his sister in God. Well, not go to the stake, he wasn't the going-to-the-stake type, but he would probably let somebody throw a rotten tomato at him. Perhaps under the sincerity there was a joke after all, like getting one layer of rock under another in geology. Ann couldn't tell about that. She kept assuming that none of the evangelicals could be really sincere in their heart of hearts because she couldn't imagine being really sincere herself. No, that wasn't completely true. Poor old Kevin was sincere, too much of a drip to be anything else.

'Have some breakfast,' Kevin suggested. He sat down again behind his. Presumably Jessica would have to provide Ann's if she wanted any, which she didn't.

'We've got a big day ahead,' said Philip, sitting porkily behind his pile.

'Just because we're Christians there's no need to eat till we pop,' Ann said. She was going to say *you* are Christians, but chickened out at the last minute and changed it to we. She was being aggressive enough already. She felt a bit like a spy in danger of blowing her cover. 'Me no want fried egg,' she added, by way of making the peace. She would have said it with a German accent, just for luck, but couldn't remember how one went.

'Have this one,' said Jessica, coming in with a plate of food.

'I've 'ad mine already, duck,' Ann replied in moronic northern, less embarrassing than Red Indian because it was more or less how she spoke anyway.

'I'll have it then,' Jessica said, and sat down. It was obviously hers anyway, exactly the amount not to be greedy, and arranged so neatly on her plate that if there was an equals sign you could have given the answer. She cut dear little pieces of every item in turn, and stacked them on her fork so that each mouthful, even though it was small and tidy, hardly more than a nibble, included a democratic representative of everything.

'You'll make a lovely mother,' Ann told her.

Jessica blushed. 'Why do you say that?' she asked.

'Because you eat so nicely.'

That wasn't of course quite true – nothing is ever quite true.

Jessica's husband would probably leave her before she ever got the chance. Watching that tidy eating every morning could reduce a strong man to tears.

'Don't be silly,' said Jessica.

'Anyway,' Philip said, his last gobble waiting for him on his fork, 'when we've finished this lot we'd better be off.'

'What time are we supposed to get there?' Ann asked.

'About half eleven they're expecting us,' Kevin said.

'In your little van thing you never know,' Ann told him. 'The only thing that's sure to work is the windscreen.'

The house smelt of crotch, sour, dark, delicious, authoritative, a young smell for an old man, and one which provided an essential component of his aura of top dog, cock of the walk. At second sniff the crotch changed, however. It was not young, imperious, pungent, after all. What Raymond's nose had encountered was the long shadow of crotch, crotch perceived through time, crotch that included its yesterdays. It was a subdued old man's crotch that hadn't been washed frequently. This gave the old man, for round-about reasons, a patina of virility all the same. Partly it was that the first sniff's impact lingered; added to which, dirtiness was more a young dog's characteristic, at least at home where it was Stephen who was most likely to smell of wee. So the old man seemed spry enough, even if he didn't, when you sniffed deeply, smell of fuck nowadays. But what made him *magic* were the treats buried in his pink hand, as bones might be buried in the garden, but never were when you came to dig them up, even though, misty as in a dream, you had an image of burying them there once upon a time.

A boiled sweet, a chocolate, a torn-off piece of toast: the hand grasped Raymond's muzzle and slipped each goody in, sharing with him, in its silent manoeuvring, the knowledge that Margaret would disapprove. The only drawback was that Raymond couldn't emulate the humans by eating silently, with his mouth closed. He had to scuttle off to a corner and stand there, his eyes peeping back round his ears while his lower jaw went nakedly, fla-grantly up, down, up and down, until finally he could gulp away the evidence with almost a sense of relief. Margaret was watching, he knew, but she didn't prevent him from slinking back for the next treat. And how could she interfere, in any case? Her smells were not as strong as the old man's when all was said and done. She could tell Raymond off about it later, but that didn't matter because he would have forgotten about it by then, and would therefore be justified in taking no notice whatsoever of her complaints.

Why do I bother? Margaret asked herself. Since Nancy died he'd really become a rather horrid old man. For one thing, he didn't seem to keep himself one hundred per cent clean, although it might be he gave that impression because he'd not shaved all that well. There was nothing worse than seeing little white stalks poking out of an elderly man's cheeks, like so many would-be dandelion clocks. Then there were his bottles of sauce, lots of them, clustered together on his table like a clump of fungi. They all seemed to be different from each other, specialised. She had a mental picture of him testing them out when alone as a wine connoisseur does, spitting clots of different-coloured sauces into a bucket; and a shudder rode up her body like a great wave. Beastly thing. As she watched him sitting at his breakfast table, he poked one of his great swollen-looking fingers into his eye and wiggled it rapidly about, as if his eye were really a hole, like one's ear. The rhyme about little Jack Horner putting in his thumb and out came a plum came into her head. With his other hand he was feeding something that would rot Raymond's teeth into Raymond.

'You're managing all right,' she repeated. It would have seemed rude to make it into a question.

'I'll get you a cup of tea,' he said, pulling his finger out of his eye at last, picking up his teapot and giving it a shake. Raymond meanwhile was munching something in the corner, peering round at her like a naughty boy, fearful that she might come and put a stop to it.

'You stay where you are,' she said. 'I'll fill the kettle.'

'I love that teapot,' the old man said unexpectedly. 'It's home.'

'Good heavens,' Margaret said, and as the water splashed noisily into the kettle added quietly, 'silly fool.'

'Since Nance died, I've felt, I have to cling on to what I've got.'

Her back was to him as she lit the gas, and she screwed up her face as if she was in terrible agony, her mouth open in a silent scream. It was oddly satisfying, and reminded her of being young again, but of course as soon as she thought *that* she remembered she might be screaming in earnest soon enough. As she had earlier this morning she made an involuntary noise, this time more of a whimper than a sob.

'My tea caddy as well,' dad added, as if frightened that his caddy would be mortally offended. 'Are you all right?'

'Yes, "dad", I was just clearing my throat.' It occurred to her that she said 'dad' in quotation marks, just as she said 'friend' when she was thinking of Lynne York. She even paused a little before and after the word, where the quotation marks should be. It wasn't that she wanted to be unfriendly but every time she said the word dad she felt she was knocking a nail into her own father's coffin, and putting in the quotation marks seemed to soften the blow.

'Things that you've had all these years,' dad said. 'Sometimes I think to myself, if they could talk.'

'If what could talk, "dad"?' Margaret asked, coming up to the table to collect the pot.

The old man blinked. 'You know,' he replied lamely.

He means his teapot and his tea caddy, Margaret realised. She burst out laughing, horrified at doing so. I just can't control my emotions today, she thought. Perhaps it sounded like a sneeze. Anyway, dad pretended to take no notice.

'They've seen such things,' he said gloomily. 'A whole lifetime. Two whole lifetimes. It's funny to think a teapot goes on and on but a human being just dies. You know what I mean. A person is so much bigger. There's so much more *to* them.'

'Teapots don't go on and on in our house,' Margaret told him, hoping to break his mood before he reduced her to complete hysterics. 'Stephen broke one only the other day.'

'Of course with a teapot there's not a lot *to* go wrong. Only if you drop it.'

'That's what Stephen did do.'

'When you've got something complicated, like a washing-machine, that's a different story.'

'Oh yes.' She poured boiling water into the teapot.

He turned back to look at her. His face seemed hot and personal. She removed her eyes from his gaze, as you might withdraw your hand from someone's clasp which you didn't want, and let them drift across the room. It was true, what the old man had been driving at: this room was the long shadow of some remote date, late 1940s perhaps, or early 50s. The cooker on which she had boiled the kettle was enamelled New World, with the stubby far-apart legs of some redoubtable old lady (not that Nance had been redoubtable in the least, she'd been like a nervous bird); there was the stoneware sink with its wooden draining-board, slimy when wet, fuzzy when dry, and its limp plastic curtaining in front, on rings, failing to conceal buckets and floorcloths and a dustpan and brush, as if, inexplicably, it had shrunk; there was the utility dresser, with the funny black tin vents in the middle of the cupboards, like toy aircraft propellers, through which tins and packets of food peeped sadly out. Stale, dry, ancient smells emanated from the dresser: tea, nutmeg, Bisto. They smelt like smells from before the world began. Margaret carried the teapot over to the table. Dad's gaze trotted alongside as she went, as Raymond used to before he got old enough not to be well behaved.

'That washing-machine,' he said, as if she needed prompting. She either had to pick up his stare again, or turn to look at the washing-machine, so she turned to look at the washing-machine. The washing-machine had no connection with the 1940s. It seemed spanking new, like a false tooth, though they'd had it a couple of years.

'Do you remember the row it made when we first bought it?' dad asked. 'Got on our nerves. Then one day, in I came into the kitchen, the machine is screaming like a pig in an abattoir as per usual, and there's our Nance saying, "Dear Lord, stoppest this horrible screaming noise."' His hot eyes studied Margaret mercilessly as he waited for her to comment. 'That's what she was saying,' he insisted, '" Dear Lord, stoppest this horrible screaming noise."'

'It must have been getting on her nerves,' Margaret said. 'I'll pour the tea.'

'I just stood there watching. She didn't know I'd come in. She said, "Stop Thou its shaking-about everywhere." I'll swear, those were the actual words she used.'

'We all say that sort of thing from time to time. You shouldn't have been spying on her. It's like watching somebody do something private.'

'She wasn't just saying it like you say God or bother. She was really praying. I went straight to the telephone and rang up the manufacturers. I said, "There's something badly wrong with this washing-machine." You see, we'd thought it was because it was doing everything so fast that it made such a racket, being a modern one, but it turned out it needed a new engine. It was a dud.'

'So Nance's prayer was answered.'

'Her prayer wasn't answered. My telephone call was answered.'

'I suppose it depends how you look at it.'

'You don't think it was God who sent a repairman out to honour the guarantee, do you?'

'But it was Nance's prayer that made you phone up.'

'Only because I couldn't stand it. It made me ashamed. You don't want to tell me you believe in that nonsense, Margaret.'

Margaret thought: don't I just? I was praying to Mr Mandela earlier on. But of course she didn't believe in God, at least not in a God who listened to prayers. Too many Jews had been killed in the Second World War for anyone to believe in that kind of a God. However it was beastly to have to think of yourself just as a bit of machinery that had gone wrong, like dad and Nance's washing-machine.

'Lord this, Lord that, she never stopped mithering. It got me down. She talked to Lord Jesus more than she did to me. I said to her one day, perhaps we could have a bit less of your blessed Lord Jesus.' He took a sip of his tea, and as if the tea had done something to his vocal cords carried on in a trembly little voice: 'A couple of months later she keeled over and died. Right in here, while she was filling the kettle.'

Oh dear, thought Margaret, he's telling me I should have been more tactful. I knew that story about Nance ending her days filling the kettle, I could hardly not know it, he must have told me two hundred times. Nance lying on the floor with the kettle still clutched in her hand, and water everywhere. An honourable way to go, death in combat. He's telling me it was tactless of me, a fellow-woman, to have filled the perishing kettle for him. Brought back tragic memories. Meanwhile *he* can't even take the trouble to remember it's our wedding anniversary. And if I remind him he'll probably hold that against me too, rubbing salt into the wound. Well, I'll tell you this, Margaret said inside her head, you silly old devil, I'll never fill your kettle for you again as long as I live. I note you are not too overwhelmed by grief to have accepted another cup of tea. And, while we're on the subject, in another couple of months I could be dead myself of breast cancer, and here you are talking about death all the time. Well, I hope I *do* die in a couple of months, it'll serve you damn well right.

He was looking at her again, beseechingly. 'I want to tell you something, Margaret, that I've never told anybody before.' He tore off a piece of his toast and marmalade and passed it to Raymond quite openly, as if she would now have more important things on her mind to worry about than that. Raymond gave her an insufferable look that said, 'You dare,' but there was nothing she could do about it without treading on dad's exposed nerves. It struck her that he was just an old rogue, having his way now as he always had done in the past.

'Oh yes,' Margaret said as coolly as she dared. 'The only thing is I've got to go off on my jog shortly, then I've got –' she was going to admit to an appointment, but thought better of it '– to see a friend of mine. Lynne York.'

'You know I inherited a bit of money from Nance. From life insurance.' He lowered his voice as if somebody undesirable was likely to hear: 'A couple of thousand.'

'Yes, that was –'

'Well, Nance did all that herself, you know. A few bob a week from the housekeeping. I didn't approve of it. Now I've copped the lot. She did it for me, Margaret. I never thought about that aspect at the time, I never thought, it's to my advantage. I suppose I took it for granted I'd go first, like men do.'

'I'm sure it gave her some happiness to think –'

'I made a point of never seeing this man, the Pearl man, when he called. He used to come in the afternoon for his money, when I was at work, but even when I'd retired, I never went to the door. I used to say, it'll be the Pearl man, it's you he wants to see, you're the one who's daft enough to give him your money. It was what you might call an obsession with me, never seeing his face. I used to imagine that he was actually pearly himself, like one of them cockney people in their blazers, pearly kings. I knew he wasn't, of course, but it suited me to imagine he was.' He drank some of his tea and for a moment Margaret had hopes he'd finished, but his face returned to her, transmitting its lostness full blast, without any let-off. 'And, of course, one thing leads to another in your head, and in the back of my mind I started to think of him as if *he* was her blasted Lord that she was forever going on about. I knew he *was*n't, the butter hadn't slipped off my spuds altogether, but like I say, I imagined what it suited me to imagine. I expect it was to do with the pearly gates. So every time she did her Lord Jesus this, Lord Jesus that business, I pictured her talking to this Pearl man. Between you and me, I suppose I was jealous. And then of course I go and tell her where to put her blessed Lord Jesus, in other words, her blessed Pearl man, and then she goes and dies on me, and the self-same Pearl man puts more money in my hand than I've ever had in my life before. He was a nice fellow, too. He obviously thought the world of Nance. You see where it leaves me, don't you, Margaret?'

'I wouldn't let myself think about it –'

'But on the other hand, what kind of God is it who goes around repairing washing-machines?'

The bank was the corner unit of a pre-war row of shops in Houldsworth Square, Reddish, except that there was a gap beside it which always reminded John of a gap in somebody's mouth where a tooth has been removed. Indeed a shop had gone from there, one of those unhappy ones that keep changing hands but which throughout it all are compelled to sell unlikely things like carpets, which were its final speciality, or bathroom sinks and taps, which were the one before. The bank had acquired it and turned it into a car-park, put it out of its misery. It was gone, as the Poco Poco was now going, though John had no excuse to feel sentimental about it because he'd never bought a carpet or a bathroom fitment there in his life, and nor had anybody else.

The council had decided that it was too dangerous to allow access to the car-park directly from the main road, so you had to go past it, down an alleyway and round to get in, disappear up your own arsehole, as Gardiner put it. Gardiner wasn't a man to mince his words, and hadn't been far off coming to blows with the highways official who'd explained the restriction. He was the bovver-boy sort of bank manager, newly promoted into a branch where he could keep rickety local businesses in order, rather than one where he might be required to grease plumper companies on their way.

'It's your job to be nice to people,' he'd told John first thing after arriving there from Heaton Moor. 'I can't stand being nice to people, me. Unless they've got lots and lots of money.' Then, as a gloomy afterthought: 'I can't stand being nice to them even then.' It was true: sometimes clients came out of Gardiner's office weeping. The branch's record on defaulters was improving by the week.

John drove round and into the car-park. There was an old gaffer on duty, Henry or some such name, fat and wrinkled simultaneously, like a pink prune. The car-park was tiny, of course, and could accommodate exactly the dozen cars that were used by the staff, but shoppers and local businessmen tended to pinch the places if they got half the chance, so the answer was to employ an old-age pensioner on a miserable pittance for three-quarters of an hour a day until everyone was installed. If you wanted to go out at lunch-time you used a cone, probably nicked from some road-works, to guard your place.

Henry had an amazing ability to forget his clientele. You always had to stop your car, wind down your window and say 'It's only me,' before he'd let you in. On the other hand, he seemed to be able to keep tabs on everybody who *wasn't* you.

'It's only me,' John said.

'All right, sir.' His voice sounded like a prune too, dry and sludgy at the same time.

'Is Mr Gardiner in?'

'Oh no, sir.' Henry shook his head and tutted slightly as he spoke, as if John had made a ridiculous suggestion.

'Blast,' John said. He'd been hoping to do the bearding straight away, before embarking on 'morning prayers', which would inevitably take hours if he had a particular need to get them over with quickly. 'And damn,' he added.

'Your windscreen wipers are going,' Henry told him.

'I know my windscreen wipers are going. They've stuck on. I'm going to get them seen to.'

Henry looked at him balefully. 'Mr Gardiner won't be coming in today,' he said. His tone suggested that he'd decided to withdraw Mr Gardiner because John had spoken too sharply about his wipers.

'Why the hell not?'

65

'You'll have to ask somebody else, sir.' This time the suggestion was that he had not been informed whether John had been cleared to receive information of a confidential sort.

'Thank you very much.' Everybody always seemed to know something he didn't. It was this phenomenon which caused his suspicion that whenever he looked at anything, even a pebble on the beach, it had just stopped doing whatever it *really* did, and was acting dumb for his benefit. And related to this suspicion was his feeling that there was a lot more sexual intercourse going on in the world than he knew about. He acted for the most part on the assumption that he was a 'normal' married man, but often had the unpleasant sensation that normality was in fact a grotesque exception to the usual run of human behaviour. 'Look at him,' people, especially tellers, said to each other behind his back, 'he's *normal*.' And collapsed in mirth. 'What about Mrs Clarke?' he asked, almost as a sop to his pride. He had no particular need to know if she'd arrived, but he wanted to be suggestive, to balance his mental picture of Mrs Clarke in the remains of the Poco Poco against Henry's information as to Gardiner's comings and goings. If only the Bible had been right about the possibility of committing adultery in your head, what endless, innocent pleasure one could achieve, how non-disruptive and non-traumatic could be a life of sexual experiment and promiscuity.

'What *about* Mrs Clarke?' Henry asked.

'Is she in?'

'She will be, when you shift yourself,' Henry told him, with a leer. John actually imagined, for a second, that Henry had been able to see a bestial image of Mrs Clarke shimmering somehow beside his head. Then he realised what the old man was driving at, glanced in his mirror, and saw Mrs Clarke sitting patiently in her car, waiting for him to stop blocking the entrance to the car-park.

'I'm sorry,' he said feebly, and drove forward with a jerk.

When he'd parked his car he stood waiting in some trepidation for Mrs Clarke to get out of hers. As she turned to lock her door he forced himself to inspect her closely. She was of course dressed, in a thick winter skirt despite the sunshine, a wool top, a short jacket. She was dressed as completely as a well-wrapped parcel. How extraordinary, the thought of having seen her bottom. The image, in this workaday car-park, was as exotic as that of a flying-saucer.

His scrutiny now was so close as to be cruel. She was middle-aged, getting towards plump. That distant glimpse of her rear among the ruins was suddenly replaced by a detailed, close-up, intuitive picture of dimpled baldness, podgy backside cleavage, and he was filled with such overwhelming desire that his head swam. He removed his burning X-ray eyes so that he was looking at her off-centre, conscious of turning red as he did so. His voice cracked as he said. 'Good morning, Mrs Clarke.'

'Is anything the matter, Mr Edwards?' she asked, turning towards him.

Something in her tone made him look at her square-on again. Friendliness, that was it. To an extent. Friendly concern was part of the story, but not all. There was eagerness as well, surely he wasn't imagining it. He had a sense that their relationship was all ready to get on to a new footing entirely, that the two glimpses he'd had of her in his mind's eye had changed things between them for ever.

'What should be the matter?' he replied, as roguishly as he dared. It was a cowardly response, but he felt the need to trawl up more information before going any further.

'I noticed your windscreen wipers were on, while you were coming in.'

For God's sake, he thought impatiently. 'They're just stuck,' he said. 'I'll have to get them seen to.'

'Oh, I see,' she replied, smiling a little.

No he couldn't be imagining it, there was something a slight bit suggestive, just a hint of the wicked, in the way she said that. Now was the moment. The chance to make a pass. To say, if I was looking a little overheated, it was at the sight of you, Mrs Clarke. To say it in that slightly jokey tone he'd heard other men use, so that it sounded like nothing more than silly banter, but you could leave your eyes switched up to hot so that the message was communicated anyway. A man can't always stop his windscreen wipers being on, he could add, if things went well.

He actually began.

'If I was looking a little overheated,' he said. But it didn't come out jocularly, it sounded like something huge, slipping and sliding its way through a bog. If he carried on there'd be nowhere else for either of them to go. 'It's because I'm a bit put out. Henry's just told me Mr Gardiner won't be in.'

'Didn't you know?' she asked, the intimate possibilities that had been jiggling in and around her features dispersing as she spoke. Then: 'Who's Henry?'

'Henry,' said John. 'You know. The car-park attendant.'

'Oh,' she replied. 'You mean Ken.'

'I thought he was called Henry.'

'I don't know where you got that from. His name is definitely Ken.' She didn't even sound amused any more, just cold and superior, part of that same universal conspiracy of which even Henry was a member, under the pseudonym of Ken.

'I could have sworn he was called Henry,' John said despairingly, as he and Mrs Clarke walked round to the front of the bank.

5

The blotherin man got redder and redder as the bus went along till Stephen expected him to burst into flames. He also grew more blotherin. And his voice became belchier.

Now Stephen wasn't Ann but only Stephen, he wondered whether he ought to ask somebody what he should do. The trouble was, the blotherin man didn't seem to be the right person. But if he asked anyone else, he would have to ask them *over* the blotherin man, which would make him even angrier than he was now. Also the only person nearby was the man with the big ear, and he didn't want to ask *him*. He wished that the man who ate breakfasts at weekends would come back to the blotherin man's mouth-hole.

'Cherwant?' the blotherin man suddenly asked, and pushed across the gangway of the bus at the man-with-the-big-ear's shoulder. The man-with-the-big-ear's eye came round and looked at him. Stephen couldn't see his other eye because it was on the far side of his nose, which was almost as big as his ear. The blotherin man's eye that was nearest Stephen was nearly shut, which meant that he was giving him a hard look back, as he had done to Stephen a little while ago. The man-with-the-big-ear's eye didn't move at all, or even blink. Finally the blotherin man gave up, and turned back towards Stephen.

'Blothr,' he said sadly. The man-with-the-big-ear's eye carried on looking at him, just to make sure, then went to the front, then hopped back again just to make sure sure, and then, having definitely stared the blotherin man out, went back to the front and switched itself off.

'Cherwant?' the blotherin man suddenly asked Stephen as if the word had just come back to him. 'Cherwant? Cherwant?' He said it so fast and often, and in such a belchy voice, he sounded as if he was sneezing.

'I want to go home,' Stephen said in reply.

'Cherwant?' the blotherin man continued, taking no notice.

Stephen didn't say it again. The word home had nearly made him cry. He remembered what Ann had said this morning about running away, and wondered if he would have to sell *his* body, too. Who in all the wide world would want to buy it? And what would he do without it if somebody did?

The bus slowed down again. This time the blotherin man got up. He looked back down at Stephen with his fiery face, but didn't say anything. Then suddenly he twisted round, gave a spiteful poke at the man with the big ear, and scuttled along the aisle to get off. The man-with-the-big-ear's eye glared for a moment, then looked up at the ceiling in surprise, and then began to look at ordinary things again. What did it care? The blotherin man was gone.

Gone.

First Ann. Then Jessica. Now the blotherin man. As he went on further and further he was leaving everybody he'd ever known behind. He remembered the terrible time when grandma died, and grandad was crying. It was dreadful to see an old man cry, it made him want to cry himself, or shout, but he did nothing, he stayed perfectly still, so his mother and father probably forgot he was even in the room. He listened to what grandad said.

Grandad said, 'I don't mind her dying. Well, I do, a course I do. But I don't mind her dying as such. It's her *staying* dead that makes me feel so depressed. I'm getting older and Nance'll just be stuck where she was. That's the bit I don't like about it. She'll stay still, and I'll go on, though where I'll be going to at my age, Lord alone knows.'

Stephen's mother suddenly noticed him. 'Your grandad's feeling a bit upset, dear,' she said in a whisper as if she didn't want the old man to hear, though he was nearer to her than Stephen was.

Upset? Stephen thought. He's not upset, he's crying. He didn't think of grandad's tears as tears but as a terrible leak, such as you might get in a house when the roof has blown off.

Stephen thought of grandad's words now. The bus was taking

70

him further and further into the unknown. The blotherin man was the last person in the world that he felt he knew. Where I'll be going to at my age, Stephen thought, Lord alone knows. The bus began to shake, as a preliminary to moving off again. Stephen caught sight of the blotherin man through the window beyond the man with the big ear. He seemed to be swinging his arms in the air. He was always *doing* something, not just sitting or standing like other people. The bus began to move off. Stephen suddenly got up from his seat and rushed down the aisle.

'I've got to get off here,' he cried out.

'Make up your mind,' the driver said grumpily, stopping the bus again. He pressed the hissing thing that made the door open. 'And by the way, I'm not deaf,' he added in his sour voice. Stephen didn't care. He was down the step and off, in the outside. For a second he felt free.

Mr Hawthorne, the manager's assistant, was keyholder, and had the responsibility for opening the safe and doling out floats to the tellers. He passed them over with meaningful looks and nods of his head, as if he were buying the services of the tellers for later. Mr Hawthorne would have had no trouble with delivering an innuendo to Mrs Clarke. John could just hear him saying, 'It's you who's making me overheated, Mrs Clarke. Perhaps you could think of some way to cool me down.' He said that kind of thing all the time. And Mrs Clarke would reply, 'Now, now, Mr Hawthorne,' and there would be no harm done. Of course if you looked at it from a severely practical point of view, not much of *anything* would have been done. But John had reached a level of dissatisfaction where even a safely delivered come-on would have given him a feeling of release. Just to be told off in that caressing voice women used for interlopers who haven't interloped too far would be enough. Has any woman ever told me off? he suddenly wondered. Have I ever nearly gone too far (apart from the one time, when I went even further, which didn't count, since it was *only* the one time, a fluke, a sport, an aberration)? And what did women really intend when they did? The tone was so forgiving when directed at a professional nuisance like Hawthorne, but if he, John, tried it, he felt sure the voice would harden up, express outrage or shock, and he would be left with an experience of burning embarrassment. Even as he thought that thought he had a sense of embarrassment anyway, at the meagreness of his ambition in wanting no more than to be suggestive without being crushed.

'Yes, Mr Hawthorne, no, Mr Hawthorne,' the tellers said in pert chirpy voices as they received their little money-bags from Hawthorne's lingering fingers.

'Good morning, Mr Hawthorne,' John said as he went past.

'Good morning, Mr Hawthorne,' Mrs Clarke said.

'Good morning, Mr Edwards. Hello, Mrs Clarke, lovely day for it.'

'Lovely day for what, Mr Hawthorne?'

'Working in a bank. It's a lovely day for working in a bank, isn't it, Mr Edwards?'

'So what's become of Mr Gardiner, Mrs Clarke?' John asked.

'He's not coming in today.'

'I wish he'd let me know.'

'I think he left you a note on your desk. You were dealing with a customer at the time. He's got an appointment at the hospital. And he's got his quarterly report to finish off, so he said he might as well do that at home, to save too much coming and going.'

'Is he ill?'

'I don't know. I shouldn't think so. It's probably just a check-up.'

'Let's hope so,' John replied, thinking, but I would prefer heart. Heart attack would do, kill him off. Or if that's too much to expect, a stroke would be acceptable. He imagined Mr Gardiner drooling, lost for words. Opening and shutting his mouth in that lost way people have, as if they can't remember what their mouth is for.

'Talking to yourself, first sign of madness,' Mrs Clarke said with a girlish giggle, meant to excuse the impertinence. Perhaps, perhaps, she wants to be familiar with me, John wondered. Possibly she's somehow intuited that I had a vision of her on all fours in the Poco Poco. That memory might be hanging in the very atmosphere around us, like a storm hanging in the air on a thundery day.

'I hope you weren't able to hear,' he replied, to his own surprise capitalising on his previous failure, and achieving something close to a leer in his tone.

72

'Of course I wasn't,' Mrs Clarke said in a comforting voice, missing his bait by a mile. 'And I wouldn't have dreamt of listening if I was.'

'I'd better open the mail,' John said, feeling snubbed. 'Tell all concerned I'll take morning prayers in half an hour.'

He went into his office. Yes, sure enough, there was a memo from Gardiner on his desk. He, John, had been seeing a customer in the interview room late yesterday afternoon, but had returned to his office before going home. He'd presumably looked at the note on his desk without seeing it. He hated it when he discovered blanks in his life, like missing pieces in a jigsaw puzzle. It confirmed his sense that there were things of fundamental importance going on of which he had no knowledge.

John, the note said, *I won't be in blah blah.*

John deliberately let his eyes go out of focus, so that he couldn't read the rest of it. That must be how Stephen saw things without his glasses. Or rather, didn't see them. And it was Ann who liked saying blah blah. He was not-reading the note, in a method borrowed from his children. But not even children could have such childish motives as he did. He didn't want to read it because at the moment the very thought of Gardiner filled him with despair. That was probably why he hadn't seen the note last night. Whatever the note said, no doubt nothing more than brusque do this, do that, it would mock him like a hyena. He screwed it up and threw it in the bin.

He had never understood why all the mail had to be opened by the senior manager on duty, whoever it was addressed to, but that was the rule. In any other industry some secretary would have this job, and leave him to make better use of his time, but not the bank. He sorted the letters in straggly piles for himself, Gardiner, and the various heads of departments, writing down the name of the sender and that of the chosen recipient in the mail-book as he did so. It all seemed to be routine stuff, except for the Amos Baking Company who wanted a further loan, mainly, as far as he could see, in order to enable them to repay their previous ones. They were working towards a cash-flow system independent of the baking of bread. He put a note in his phone log to remind him to ring them later. As he was doing so the heads of department trooped in, and he settled down to morning prayers, going through the day's business with each in turn.

73

When they were trooping out again, he suddenly called: 'Mrs Clarke,' and stopped her in her tracks.

'Watch it, Mrs Clarke,' Hawthorne said, with a wink.

'What did you want, Mr Hawthorne?' John asked him.

'*I* don't want anything, Mr Edwards,' Hawthorne said, and went out grinning. John could only see the back of his head, with its coarse-looking, carefully cut, pale brown hair, but the grin was visible right through it.

'Yes, sir?' asked Mrs Clarke, and John realised with a shock that now was the moment he had to say something. It was because he now felt in charge that he had asked her to stay behind, but by the same token being authoritative made him feel too formal, too dry, to bring the conversation round to the direction he wanted it to go.

'Mrs Clarke, can I ask your advice?'

'Oh dear, I'm always terrified of giving advice.' Suddenly girlish: 'Just in case someone takes it.'

He had meant to say, Mrs Clarke, can I ask you a question? And then, according to mood, according to his exact state of mind when he reached the end of the word question, he would plunge on towards something risky, or play safe. He hit a state of mind, however, halfway through, a sudden bump of terror, and skidded the rest of the sentence round a corner, bringing it to a safe stop. The suddenness of the manoeuvre made him feel sweaty about the eyes. And then, of course, when it was too late, Mrs Clarke looked just as if she would have been ready and willing to go along with him.

What bloody advice could he ask her? Shut your eyes, shut the eyes of your mind, and just grab something.

'Could you suggest anything, buy my wife, little anniversary present, forgot, nip out at lunch-time.'

He stood there, shaking inside himself as if he had inner arms and legs and body encased in the outer ones. He felt like giving out a terrible, despairing moan, like a dinosaur dying in a swamp, and for the same reason: he had failed the only test that mattered, the survival of the fittest.

The only consolation was that Mrs Clarke seemed calm and unsurprised, as if this idiotic question was just the sort of thing she'd expected.

'Naughty you, Mr Edwards. Chocolates or flowers never do any harm. Or both.'

'She's always talking about going on a diet.'

'Everybody always is. You could tell her she doesn't need to, that would be nice. And she probably won't eat the flowers.'

'No.'

'I *love* flowers.'

'Do you?'

'All women do. You can't go wrong. Just like all men liking football.'

'*I* don't like football.'

'Oh well,' she said, lowering her voice to what was almost a tease, with that ability to achieve almostness that other people, especially women, seemed to have, so that he never felt completely sure of his bearings, 'all men except you.'

'Yes, well,' he went on, lowering his voice also, and trying to catch the precision of her approximateness: 'I've got to this age without it.'

But it didn't work. In a harder, workaday voice, Mrs Clarke replied, 'I hope your wife didn't get to *her* age without flowers.'

She sounded like his mother. Mother, he thought, remembering her visitation. Mrs Clarke didn't sound *like* her, in point of fact, merely like someone doing the same job. And so she should. He wanted, as so often, so much to be a true bastard, and so far the nearest he could get was being slightly greasy.

'Or if you want to get her something a little more expensive,' Mrs Clarke went on, 'there's always a Liberty scarf.'

'A Liberty scarf?'

'I think she *has* been neglected. Silk, with a nice pattern.'

'But I want to do it at lunch-time. Where could I get a Liberty scarf in Reddish?'

'Oh, there's a shop. Along Hyde Road. I could show you if you like.'

'Thank you, Mrs Clarke,' he said. He didn't trust himself to say any more.

'All right then.' Brightly: 'Twelve thirty do?'

He needed to drink. 'Twelve thirty will do nicely,' he said. His lips felt ridiculously cracked as if he'd been crawling across a desert, and his tongue was huge, like a toad's.

'I'll give you a knock,' she said smokily, smiled, and trotted out of the office.

After a few minutes, he followed her and went into the Gents toilet. There wasn't a drinking fountain there so he had to put his head in the sink and pour water from the tap gently into the lower of his cheeks, which could hold a tiny puddle. Then he righted his head, the water sluiced down into the middle of his mouth, and he could swallow. The amount was always much less than you wanted, and you had to do it over and over. It was a miserably functional way of assuaging thirst, very much in the spirit of the bank. But when he had finished he was able to relax and feel triumphant. He had managed it. He was going to spend his lunch-break with Mrs Clarke. It was fast moving by most standards: only an hour and half had elapsed from the time he'd seen his mirage of her cantering through the wreckage of the Poco Poco to the time when they'd arranged a meeting.

Who was he trying to fool? They'd arranged a meeting to choose his wife an anniversary present. As a come-on that took incompetence to the point of insanity.

When he came back into the house Raymond's head was still full of the smells and tastes of the old man, and his legs still contained his walk through the streets. He lay on his blanket and tried to feel tired, so that he would be content with being back at home, but stillness made his restlessness worse. He stood up again and then went to every room in turn, hoping that one of them would be different in some way from how it was before, but none of them were.

There was the scrunch of tyres, and a toot. His heart leapt for a moment at the possibility of something new, but then Margaret was down, shooing him backwards, speaking in the kind worried voice that meant don't, the voice she used when forbidding him to use the crap-patch at the bottom of the garden. With equal rapidity she was gone, and by the time Raymond got his head over the window-sill in the front room, the car was already moving off.

Her going changed the house. Raymond had the sudden sense that its walls surrounded the whole world, leaving only a tiny patch in which he was stranded. He trotted to his bowl in the kitchen to check if it had become full since he last inspected it, but it was still obstinately empty. Then he went into the front room and tried half-heartedly to fuck the settee, but it didn't convince, so he climbed up on to it instead. By now, at least, the walk had nearly faded from his legs; and so, for want of anything better to do, he chose to fall asleep.

Jogging was not the sort of thing Margaret did, except that she did do it. For two pins she wouldn't have gone this morning, and in fact had rung Judy before she took Raymond for his walk to dad's. She'd said she had a lot on her mind, but Judy had immediately become sad and alone and argumentative.

'I don't want to go on my tod,' she'd said. 'I do too much on my tod as it is. And jogging's good for the mind, in any case. It brings things to the surface. It lets you have a clear-out.'

'I suppose it's better than brooding,' Margaret, always a soft touch, had replied. She had been going for two or three weeks, at Judy's instigation. Judy drove them through Reddish, past the Amos Baking Company, and they turned off by the school on to the narrow road that curved down towards the Vale. There was a farm on one side, as if to inaugurate the countrification, complete with cows.

They pulled into the little car-park that served the Vale, and walked past the pond where the same fishermen as always sat on the bank, sunk in gloom, like so many fishing gnomes. Beyond the pond a long viaduct looked as if it were taking a bite out of the scenery.

Judy and Margaret walked through a copse and up a slope to the ridge where they began their jog. At the top of the ridge was the Brinnington housing estate, the roughest in the area. Down below was Reddish golf course, and as she jogged along Margaret spotted a tiny golfer teeing off. Even at this distance she could sense the severity with which he eyed the seat of the little invisible ball on its slender invisible tee. Then his arms and club whirled like a demented clock. He obviously missed his target, because he looked furtively about him and then his arms and club whirled again. This time he was more successful, because he began to pack his things away.

'But not him,' Margaret said out loud.

'Not him what?'

'Chopping people's heads off.'

Judy ignored the remark. 'I'm glad you were able to come with me after all.'

Margaret was beginning to pant. She noticed that her heart was thumping.

'Is it all right, me being able to hear my heart?'

'That's the whole idea.'

'Oh. Good.'

'But like I was saying, you need it for the mind as well as the body. When I'm running I don't know whether I'm running after Terry, or away from him, but it makes me feel better either way.'

They thudded on in silence for a while. Then Judy added: 'It's nice to imagine he's the footpath and I'm squelching him as I go along. I can talk when I jog,' she added unnecessarily. 'I would feel so trapped, mentioning it indoors.'

'Mentioning what?' Margaret gasped.

'The whole trauma of how he left me. I've never told anyone.'

'I think I've got a rough idea.'

'No, I don't mean just running off, I mean *how* the sodding bastard ran off. As you can tell I feel quite calm and neutral about it now, ha ha. I think some things happen that are bloody things in the first place, and however much you think about them afterwards, bloody things they remain.' She repeated her last words with relish: 'Bloody things they remain."

'He ran off with your best friend, I knew that,' Margaret said, trying to forestall the agony.

'She wasn't my best friend. She was *a* friend. She and her husband. We knew them as a couple. We were having dinner with them, at their house. The four of us. Then Terry gets to his feet and says, cool as a cucumber, Sheila and I love each other, and we're going off now so we can live together for always. Oh clear off!'

A dog, out for a walk with an old man, had run up in greeting, and was dancing around Judy's ankles. His owner called him back, glaring at the two of them.

'They always go for me,' Judy said. 'It must be the way I sweat. Mosquitoes go for me too. Anyway, there we were, this Graham and me, just staring at each other across the table, totally pole-axed. Then of all the incredibly stupid things I could do, I just stuck my fork in my meal, and carried on eating. Graham did likewise. What a pair of clucks. While Terry and Sheila were making hay somewhere. I can remember thinking to myself as Terry was making his announcement, I ought to empty my plate over him. And her, for

78

that matter. But then I thought, don't be hasty, you're probably getting the wrong end of the stick. You'll regret it later. In my life, every time I've thought I'd better not throw my dinner over someone because I might regret it later, the only thing I've regretted later was not doing it. So I ate the damned dinner instead. I probably thought I was being dignified. We sat there saying, pass the pepper, pass the salt. No, we didn't, but we might as well of, have.' Although she was sharp and verbal, Judy was the sort of person who sometimes took two shies at being grammatical. 'We didn't say a dickey-bird,' she concluded sadly.

Bloody things they remain. Judy's words seemed to thud into Margaret's brain with each step. She thought of bloody not as a swear-word but as if it were describing something covered in blood. This was probably because every time she saw Judy she thought to herself, Judy will be a pretty woman when she comes off her period, but Judy never did, remaining drawn and pasty-faced and slightly metallic-smelling. So when she said bloody things they remain, Margaret had received a blurred picture in the back of her mind of a used Tampax hanging on and hanging on, impossible to get rid of. The thought of Judy obstinately clearing her plate, along with the other bereft partner, was revolting.

They reached the end of the level part of the ridge, and ran down a steep slope on to a meadow at the bottom. In the distance the office-blocks of Stockport gleamed in speckled April sunshine. Judy and Margaret always followed a large triangle round the meadow, so that they finished by going up the slope on to the ridge again, and retracing their steps. At this mid-section Margaret liked to fade out Judy's prattle and become lost in her own thoughts. If she didn't she would become more and more conscious of her body complaining. This time however what happened was that the picture of the bloody Tampax was replaced by a picture of her own bloody breast. Cut off it resembled a ghastly dissolving summer pudding. She pictured a huge bucket of amputated breasts in some hospital disposal room. It was as obscene as those buckets of heads that used to accumulate under the guillotine in the French Revolution. The breast-bucket looked like a container of sea-creatures, red and pink jellyfish. Margaret's knees went weak as she pictured it.

'Are you all right?' Judy asked.

79

'My knees feel weak.'

'That's a good sign.'

'According to you, everything's a good sign. Having a heart attack is a good sign. Legs giving up the ghost is a good sign.'

'Don't get nowty. What I mean is, you're stretching yourself.'

'I feel as if I'm shrinking,' Margaret said, thinking damn, damn, I've engaged her in conversation, which is the last thing I want to do at this stage. 'Before I know it I'll be running round here on little stumps,' she added, trying to scotch their conversation light-heartedly, but of course the word stumps brought her morbid thoughts to the forefront of her mind. 'Guess what, it's our ani-versary today,' she said quickly, to get rid of them.

'Thank you very much,' Judy replied.

'Oh, sorry,' Margaret said, but she thought to herself, for heaven's sake, you can't expect everybody else to get divorced just to please you. But at least Judy had lapsed into silence, and Marga-ret was free to think again.

What is there about me this morning, she thought, that makes people want to tell me their woes? First dad, with his parting from Nancy. Then Judy, and her parting from Terry. And all along, my own possible parting from my left breast. Her breast was like something that bleeped or flashed in a science-fiction film and attracted catastrophes towards itself. Funnily enough the oddest sensation she'd had since taking up jogging was that of her bosom bouncing up and down out of time with her paces, as if it were just tacked on and the normal state was to be flat-chested like a man. As she ran now she kept wondering if one of her breasts was bouncing slower than the other, the cancer perhaps weighing it down ever so slightly. Whatever the normal state is, she thought, suddenly chok-ing up, it can't be half and half.

'*Are* you all right?' Judy asked.

'I couldn't breathe for a second,' Margaret replied. 'I suppose that's a good sign too.'

'Why are we going to the middle of Manchester if the hoe-down's in south Cheshire?' Ann asked. She was sitting on the horrible old back seat which Kevin had installed in his van himself. It had wounds, out of which fuzzy stuffing bulged. 'You could be blind-folded,' she went on, 'and be given a smell to smell, and not be given any clues what it is, and you'd say without any hesitation it's the smell of a car seat that's gone mouldy. There's only one thing it *could* be.'

'You can swap with me if you like,' said Jessica sweetly. 'It was rude of me to sit in the front in the first place. I wasn't thinking.'

'We like it in the back, don't we, Annie?' Philip said.

'We love it, Philip,' Ann replied. 'Or should I say, Philippy?' When he spoke you could actually smell eggs and bacon on his breath, in the way you could smell booze on the breath of a drinker. Mr Humphries at school had been telling them that when you smell you in fact sniff up molecules of whatever it is you are smelling, which meant that Philip's words were literally coated with scrapings of breakfast, like an unwashed plate. It also meant that she was having to eat his breakfast second-hand.

What a bugger Jessica is, Ann thought. She makes jolly sure she's safely ensconced at the front with her brother. *She* doesn't want to have to sit back here with Philip squinching down his half of the twangy old seat, so that your bum keeps trying to edge towards his lap as if it's got a mind of its own, and can think of nowhere better to go. No, Jessica keeps her bum to herself, on its own individual seat. Then she offers to swap, which she knows is impossible without opening the van with a tin-opener, or stopping it, in which case it'd probably never start again. Then she admits she was rude to sit in the front in the first place, so she gets forgiven. She could work things round until she was practically made a saint on the spot.

'Because we've got to pick up some supplies the Brindleys have ordered,' Kevin said. 'From a bakery off Deansgate.'

'Who?' Ann said. 'What?'

'Us,' Kevin replied, in his taciturn fashion. 'Things to eat.'

'Life is full of things to eat,' Ann said.

'It's bound to be,' Philip put in.

'I don't see why.' Ann felt argumentative. 'Why should it be full of things to eat?'

'That's the difference between life and death. *Things to eat*,' Philip said triumphantly.

She looked at him fishily. 'What a philosophy of life,' she said. She ran her eyes over his bulges so that he would be able to detect every horrible lump and hillock of himself in the movements of her head.

'It's not a philosophy of life,' he complained. 'It's just a fact. You don't eat when you're dead.'

'I'm sure you'll manage it somehow. You'll be like the ancient Egyptians and take a packed lunch along with you.'

Even in the dimness of the back of the van she could tell his face had gone red.

'Life after death is not – '

'Only joking,' she told him.

'I don't think it's a thing to joke about.'

'Probably not. But you know me. I'm only a heathen.'

'Heathens always make the best believers.'

'Not my sort of heathen. My sort stays a heathen till they rot.'

'If you thought that, you wouldn't be coming to the hoc-down with us.'

'Day off school, why not, oh bloody hell!' She swung her head back into the recesses of the van so hard she banged it on the metal side. 'Ah,' she cried.

Kevin began to brake.

'Keep on, for God's sake,' she called out. Even while she said it, she thought to herself: do no harm to fling a bit of blasphemy around, tone up their little systems. But at the same time she felt frightened out of her wits as one stupidity led to another, like an Australian soap opera. First of all, just because she glimpses him through Jessica's window, she immediately assumes he's likely to notice *her* at the back of the van. As a result she whacks her head, so he hears the interesting sound of a van emitting a dull bong as it putters past, followed by wailing and moaning from inside. To crown it all, Kevin suddenly starts to brake, which given the general state of the vehicle is liable to make it fall apart altogether, and leave the four of them sitting on their seats in the middle of the road, in full view of everybody.

Luckily it started off again, and they accelerated with that wobbly slowness rockets have when they're setting off for outer space.

'What on earth is the matter?' Jessica asked, turning back towards her.

'I bumped my blasted head,' she replied.

'I know you bumped your *head*.'

'I got the shock of my life. I looked out of your window and I saw Stephen standing outside the university. My little brother.'

'Are you sure?'

'Of course I'm sure. I saw somebody, and I thought, that's a funny sawn-off-looking person, he looks just like Stephen, and then quick as a flash I realised it *was* Stephen.'

'Why do you think he looks sawn-off?' Philip asked.

'How should *I* know? He just does. Perhaps it's because he wears glasses.'

'But why is he at the university?' Jessica asked. 'He should be at school.'

'So should I. That's why I nearly had a heart attack.'

Jessica's eyes widened. The penny had finally dropped that she, Ann, was skiving off.

'At his age,' Philip said, laughing eggs and bacon at her again.

'They're probably being taken to the university museum,' Ann said as the explanation occurred to her. 'I was taken there once. There was a guinea-worm on display, that burrows into people. It was the best thing in the whole place.'

'Da. Dididididi,' Kevin suddenly said, very emotionally. Ann realised it was a sort of Morse code for swearing. 'I nearly ran right into that woman,' he explained.

'You can't hit the target every time,' Ann told him, sympathetically.

6

The blotherin man's arm had grown very long, like somebody's arm in a cartoon. He didn't touch people with it but put it in front of them as they walked along. He shut his arm in their face, like shutting a door. But the door wasn't stuck to anything, that was the trouble with it. At least on one side. It was stuck to the blotherin man on the other side, of course. Stephen remembered going up into the Peaks with his family, though even when it was just inside his head the word family had a sort of sad echo, family family family. In the Peaks there were lots of walls that hadn't been stuck together. They were just loose, as if they'd been built by giant children, and one of them had fallen down, leaving its gate behind, fastened to nowhere.

Nearly all the people going up and down the pavement were young. Not young like Stephen himself, but grown-up young. Many of them wore horrible clothes, torn jeans or skirts that were saggy and long. One girl was all in black with a white face like a witch. He had come here once with the school, to go to the museum. Inside the museum they had a worm on show, that lived inside people. When they wanted to get it out of somebody they used a little crane as if they were pretending that the worm was very very heavy, though in fact it didn't seem much bigger than a normal one. But it was terrible to think of it burrowing through someone's body instead of ground.

The blotherin man's door was quick. Students came trotting along the road and then bam it was shut in front of them. Most would stop dead for a moment, unsure what to do. One student, though, took no notice of it at all but pushed straight through, spinning the blotherin man like a top. The blotherin man cried out, more than he needed to, and staggered more than he needed to as well, flapping his arms about as if he'd suddenly been hit by a hurricane. Then he stood very still, glaring at the walking-away student who had done it to him. But the student was thinking about something else already, you could tell, so the glare had no effect. The blotherin man gave up and shut his door in front of somebody else. 'Erma forkin wino,' he said in his horrible cheesy voice. Some students walked round the door; others stood there, eyes bugged, just as if they were laying an egg. One even puffed out her cheeks with shock, so that she looked as if she was going to make the laying-an-egg noise. The ones who waited were spoken to by the blotherin man. First he said again who he was, a forkin wino. Then he said:

'Spare coppa far cuppa.'

When he said this he pointed at coppa and cuppa with the hand that wasn't a door, as the two words hung in the air between him and the student. Stephen could see by the look on his face that he couldn't understand how coppa and cuppa could sound so similar and still mean different things. Once he looked just as if he was going to say something about it, but then he remembered that he couldn't talk about what he was talking about, not unless he had two mouths, so all he did was say it again, more fiercely this time, so that watching him Stephen himself made a small egg-laying noise, carpupupup, though the student just looked fed up, stepped round, and went off.

Some of the students gave the blotherin man money. They put their hands in their pockets or their bags, got some out, and gave it to him. They went red when they did it, and looked the other way, more as if they were taking money away from him instead of giving it. As soon as he'd got the money the blotherin man took no notice of them any more. He reminded Stephen of a troll, making people pay to cross his bridge. When they didn't pay him anything he would look at them as they hurried away, and instead of eating them say 'Gar' in an angry voice, or 'Gar on.'

Stephen watched the blotherin man for a long time. The bits of sunshine felt warm when they landed on him, too warm not to be in school. It made him feel as he did when it was too dark for him to be up in the night. His place was in the classroom now, being taught by Mr Sherlock. The outside morning belonged to other people, except the little patch that was his at playtime. Someone else ought to be standing here at this moment looking at the blotherin old troll, not him, not even Ann.

Ann would be at school herself, unless she was dead. But if she was dead she'd not left any sign behind, no body in the road or on the pavement. Nothing. Except she might have been cleared up by somebody before Stephen ever turned the cold corner. He didn't know how fast they did it. He'd never seen a dead body lying about in the whole of his life, even though crowds of people must have died in that time. Everybody died, but he'd never seen a single one lying on the street. The only dead body he even knew about was grandma's. They must clear them up very fast. Or perhaps – his stomach went cold as ice as the thought struck him – perhaps you didn't always leave your body behind. Something might happen to make you die *completely*. You might be hit by a car so hard there was nothing left at all.

He tried to think what Ann looked like. No, she was gone, not even a memory. He tried again but this time the face of Katie Lucas, a girl in his class, popped into his mind instead. Perhaps you could be whacked with such force that you were knocked out of the world altogether, and left no memories behind.

He tried to remember his mother, but she had gone too. For a moment this was a relief: *she* hadn't been hit by a car, she'd been waving to him as he went down the road. Next, his father. No, no father either. The only person in his whole family whom he could picture in his mind was Raymond. His shivers came back. If he went home after this – if he *could* get home – and found them still gone, what would he be able to tell the police? He wouldn't even be able to describe them. Nobody would believe a word he said.

Ghosts are blank, Stephen suddenly thought, ghosts are blank because they are people no one remembers any more.

He had been so busy thinking that he hadn't been watching what was going on around him, like being asleep with his eyes open, which his mother said he did sometimes. He hated the idea of it, because it meant that his dreams were prowling about on the outside of his eyes instead of boxed safely inside his head. But now, like an Indian looking through the branches of a tree, Stephen looked through his thoughts to what was going on beyond. The students were still parading past and the blotherin man was shutting his door in front of some of them. Something made Stephen look across the wide pavement towards the road.

The something was Ann's face. There it was, through the window of an old van, staring back at him from the dimness.

Stephen thought: I'm thinking with my eyes wide open, so my thoughts are on the outside like my dreams were. He thought Ann's face was the memory of Ann's face, and his heart thumped bouncily with relief that his memory had come back. Perhaps in the next car his mother, the one after that his father, his memories driving past one at a time, his grandad in the next, his dead grandmother after *him*, and then all the things from a long time ago, when he was young, until memories of when he was a baby would parp parp gently along in tiny woollen cars.

Ann's face shot away into the complete blackness at the back of the van, there was a clonk, a muffled cry, the van began to stop, then got up speed again and carried on. It *was* Ann then. A memory wouldn't zoom away like that. She was being kidnapped. She had seen him but before she could call for help they'd pulled her back and driven off. It must be the people who'd come in the night, the bank-robbers. They'd wanted him, too. There were probably too many students about for them to kidnap him at the moment.

Stephen watched the van disappear up Oxford Road. He wondered if there was room in the back for mum and dad to be in there as well, folded up like that bank manager had been in the boot of his car. He had to tell someone.

He went up to the blotherin man.

'I saw my sister in that van,' he told him.

'Yr suster isna in that van.' As the blotherin man spoke he let his door swing open and a student inside hurried out quickly, without paying.

'Yes, she is. I saw her.'

'What van? There isna a van isna here. Isna a van, no soster inna, isna. Blotherin suster.'

'It went away again.'

'Forkin saster. A fork di sister.'

'It went. She was inside it. And my mum and dad.'

But the blotherin man was taking no more notice. He said mern and da a few times to himself, but Stephen could see he didn't know what the words meant, he thought they were just words to play with. Then he went back to stopping the students.

★

87

Miss Fielding was as pure and perfect as an egg. She was so pure that there was no need to feel any sexual desire for her, which, all things said and done – or rather, very little said and nothing done – was a relief. Her skin glowed, as an egg's shell might glow, in certain lights. She looked downwards, not out of timidity exactly, but by way of completing the oval effect. She had lovely legs, however, which was not very eggish of her, though they weren't especially long.

'Just long enough to reach the ground,' John said.

'I beg your pardon?'

He was growing senile, at terrible velocity. He would be like a poor old man in a newsagent's, trying to summon the courage to reach up and take one of those magazines that they keep on the top shelf, switching at the last minute to *Wireless World* or *Caravanning Monthly* if he feels somebody has noticed him. What made it pathetic was not feeling lust, because on the whole you respected people who felt lust. It was the thought of what those beautiful nasty-looking women must think as they looked up at some doddering old chap from their flat page, with flat eyes. It was no use saying it's only a picture and can't feel things, because the old man had invested two pounds fifty of his measly pension to imagine it *was* feeling things. I should know, thought John bitterly, because I've done it myself. And now here I am saying things out loud that I shouldn't be saying out loud. I'd better watch myself, my God. Perhaps sex-criminals could be much the same as other people, only more absent-minded.

He had spoken out loud because of left-over feelings that he'd had concerning his arrangement with Mrs Clarke, that opportunity lost. Why hadn't he the guts at the time just to ask her to lunch? She would have accepted, and no mention would have been needed of the cursed anniversary. He suffered from slow-motion courage, all ready to come out fighting when the battle was over.

'Never mind. How can I help you, Miss Fielding?'

'Your windscreen wipers. They're still going.'

He suddenly remembered his resolution to be bad-tempered this morning.

'Are they? How interesting. And how did you happen to discover *that*? I don't imagine you can see my windscreen wipers from the counter.'

'It was my turn to go across and buy a bottle of milk. For the coffee. I was going across the car-park and I heard this funny sort of crawly noise, coming from your car. It turned out to be your wipers.'

'Thank you for telling me, Miss Fielding.'

'Yes, sir.'

She turned and left the room. As soon as she was gone he realised he should have asked if the engine was still going. No, surely she would have said. In any case, he was bound to have turned it off. Why he hadn't noticed his wipers hadn't shut off with it, Lord alone knew. He must have got used to them being on by then. Not to mention of course Mrs Clarke coming into the car-park right behind him, and his desire to leap out of his car and grasp *her* by the leg.

The trouble was he always took his car for servicing in the other direction from his house, to a garage in Heaton Moor. But that would be too much of a palaver to do at the moment.

Inspiration. That brother of Ann's pal, what was his name, lugubrious sod, Kevin, he worked in a windscreen place in Reddish. They'd have their contacts, surely.

He looked up Reddish Windscreens in the *Yellow Pages*, and dialled. 'Yep,' came a voice at the other end.

'Is Kevin there?'

'No.'

'Oh. Is he out?'

'He's not in.'

'You know what I mean. Has he just nipped out, or is he not coming in at all?'

'He's had to go to church. He took the day off.'

'How can you *have* to go to church? It's not a Sunday.'

'There's a lot of sin in the Reddish area, so they say. It's probably like the hospitals, you get a bit of a backlog. I wouldn't know myself, I'm too busy fitting fucking windscreens.'

'The reason I was ringing Kevin, I've got some trouble with my windscreen wipers.'

'What did you expect him to do about it? We only handle the glass side of things here.'

'I thought he might know someone. I'm at the bank, in the high street. Someone nearby. They're going non-stop, I'm worried about my battery.'

'All right,' the voice said, in that resigned way voices have when

89

they've seen their way to making some money, 'I think I know a lad who'll come over.'

When he put the phone down John was sweating with relief. He hated negotiating with people in garages, the way they tut-tutted and shook their heads when you told them your make and model, as though everybody in the world knew that that was a car only a mental defective would buy. Worst of all was trading in, the mournful friendliness, the lame reasoning: I don't know why it is but you can't get rid of green cars for love nor money, no offence – the most offensive words in the English language – no offence, but that year is regarded as nothing but trouble, I'm sorry but a cash transaction isn't such good news in my line as people seem to think, I'd sooner give credit.

Even though he knew exactly what the dealer would say, and how he would say it, John always gave in. Deep down he felt that he didn't want to make the transaction sordid, for the dealer's sake as well as his own. He convinced himself, while the negotiation was under way, that there was a residual virtue in losing out, a tiny grace implicit in getting less than you ought to for a used car.

That was what was intoxicating about the prospect of having an affair. The boot was on the other foot. You had to manipulate, to persuade, to work on the other person in her capacity as a body owner just as in other circumstances you were worked on in your capacity as a car owner. It gave you the chance, for once in your life, to be, when all was said and done, horrible, and your only regret would be that you didn't get the chance to be horrible more often.

Suddenly he remembered his mother's voice in the night, that strangled version of it, saying this isn't the time or the place. Why had it sounded like that, as if some man were squawking it out in imitation of her? She hadn't squawked in life, at least not in that way. He thought of her as he'd seen her in that filing cabinet for dead bodies at the undertaker's. When he'd come back to the bank and pulled open a drawer in his own cabinet he'd suddenly expected to see a cool dead head looking up at him, instead of all those neatly ranked letters from people wanting him to loan them money.

The undertaker had said, 'Would you wish to view the deceased?' exactly as if he'd been saying, would you like to take a test drive? Inside his head John had said, no, no, I don't want to see somebody dead, especially my mother. I want to remember her how she was.

90

But then he wondered if he was just being cowardly, too terrified to have a last moment with his own mother, willing to let her go into the fire unlooked-at. His dad wouldn't look. The first thing his dad had talked about after her death was the fact that their washing-machine had broken down a few months previously, not long after they'd bought it. In his confusion he associated the two events. Perhaps it was his try at dodging the whole issue, thinking about a machine conking out, something you could repair.

The for and against had been so balanced in John's mind that when he opened his mouth he didn't know which he would say, and was surprised and frightened to hear yes, because he thought that if you simply left the alternatives to get on with it, the easiest one would come out on top. The drawer opened with the exact squeaky rumble of a real filing cabinet. There she was, rather pale, her eyes a little sunken, but otherwise hardly changed. The end of a joke came into his mind, about somebody being dead and not doing a lot. Her body was like a full-size puppet in a ventriloquist's case, waiting to be used again.

Perhaps the only way his mother's soul could speak to him now was in that squawky voice, the nearest approximation she could get, carving words out of the air without any voice-box to do it for her. Neither the time nor the place, true enough. However it hadn't been true last night, when he was in bed with his own wife. But perhaps it hadn't been referring to then but anticipating now, this wedding anniversary morning full of crude, ugly thoughts. Living in eternity you would become vague about time.

Oh mother, he said, suddenly wanting to weep. His inner voice sounded as rasping as his mother's. I'll concentrate on Margaret, I won't fantasise about Mrs Clarke again. He spoke knowing he was being insincere, as he always was on the rare occasions when he said a prayer.

'At least we were spared the sound of his little bones crunching,' Ann said reflectively from her dark pit, which now smelt not merely of rotting car seat but of dead animals from the boxes of pies heaped up behind her, and also of that public-convenience pong which egg sandwiches in quantity always give off. Large detached houses clumped past Jessica's window as the van staggered through sub-urbia; BMWs zipped past Kevin's right shoulder.

Jessica turned back. 'What little bones?' she asked, looking concerned. That was another reason her future husband would leave her, besides the neat eating habits: her ability to feel concern. Married to her you'd never be able to squash a wasp or say something fascist about sections of the population who got on your nerves without Jessica training her concern on you as somebody else might train a machine-gun. 'Crunching?' she added in a plaintive little voice.

'Stephen's,' Ann told her.

'Stephen's? Stephen's little bones?'

Ann hollowed her voice: 'I had a premonition this morning,' she announced. 'I suddenly saw it in my mind's eye, while I was eating breakfast. I was in this van going to the hoe-down, just like we are now, and Stephen flung himself in front trying to stop me. And over him we went.' She left out the fact that her mother and father had flung themselves as well, it would be too much. 'He must have been trying to prevent me committing a si-in.' Her voice nearly broke under the strain of describing little Stephen in this unlikely role.

'What sin?' Philip asked promptly from the dimness beside her.

'Going to the hoe-down.'

'There's no sin about that. It's a church hoe-down.'

'I should be at school.'

'Why should you be? Doing God's work is more important than learning French. If you put it like that, *I* should be at school.'

'We got permission,' Jessica said, hot-faced at the thought of being accused.

'I didn't,' Ann said.

Philip paused for thought. 'That was because it was a last-minute decision,' he said. 'You might have got permission if you'd had time to ask.'

'I can't be excused that easily. I lied to my parents.'

'Ann,' Jessica said in that out-loud whisper of hers. 'What did you tell them?'

'Nothing.'

'Telling them nothing isn't lying,' Philip said.

'It is when you should be telling them *some*thing,' Ann told him. It was nice winning a religious argument when she didn't have a religion. 'Anyway I had this vision. Little Stephen puts his hand up. "Stop!" Then scrunch scrunch. Leaving only a pair of slightly cracked spectacles lying in the road. Yuk, I wish we didn't have these heaps of pies back here. I got a whiff then and I could smell poor Stephen, how you'd smell if you were squashed, like dissecting rabbits in biology.'

'They're just pork,' Kevin said, the first time he'd spoken, but the back of his head had been giving out the tiny vibrations of someone listening to every word. After all, in Ann's vision, he would have been the driver who crunched Stephen's bones.

'There's no *just* about it,' Ann said. 'When they mash up pigs they put in everything, snouts, bums, the lot. What the Christians will be eating at this hoe-down is animal murder, in pie form. Not to mention the unborn children of a load of chickens.'

'The eggs aren't fertilised,' Philip said.

'Which?'

'The eggs in egg sandwiches.'

'And whose fault is that?'

'And you didn't need to shout out bloody hell like you did.'

'The point is', Ann said, 'that when I saw Stephen in real life, outside the university, I couldn't believe my eyes. I thought he was bound to be squashed flat the next second, and it would have been me who'd wished it on him.'

'I doubt if this van *would* squash anybody flat,' Kevin said. 'It's quite light-weight.'

'Well, it certainly wouldn't have done him any good. You don't see someone about to be run over and say to yourself, it's all right, this van's light-weight.'

'He wasn't *going* to be run over.'

'But I didn't know that. I thought my vision was coming true.'

'I don't think you ought to have visions,' Jessica said. 'Unless you're a saint.'

'Which means a *Cath*olic,' said Philip with contempt.

'You can't choose,' Ann replied. 'If you have visions you have visions.'

'I think we can control what happens in our heads,' Jessica said with revolting self-righteousness. 'If we can't control that, what *can* we control?'

'All I can say is, your head must be very different from mine.'

'Do you often commit sins? What you *think* are sins,' Philip asked.

93

'Only when I'm in the mood.'

'You shouldn't joke about it,' said Jessica.

'You shouldn't be so boring.'

'We're talking about a soul here,' Philip said.

'I tell you what, you save yours, and I'll save mine.'

'But that's the whole trouble,' Philip said, 'you don't seem to want to save yours.' He lowered his voice so Jessica and Kevin wouldn't be able to hear above the van's roar. 'I'd like to save it for you.'

'You know what you sound like? You sound like Jamie Davies that time he shoved his great big lips on me. At Linsey's party.'

'Which Jamie was that?' Jessica asked.

'The one that looks like a prawn.'

That shut them up, but only temporarily. A few moments later, Philip began again. 'It is possible to live a life that is completely perfect, in every way,' he said. 'God being good, and asking us to try for perfection, He wouldn't ask us to try for something we wouldn't ever be able to reach.'

'You what?' Ann said.

'I'm talking about perfection.'

'Oh, that.'

'That. What else *is* there?'

She turned her head to what would have been a window, if this hadn't been a van. She imagined she was somebody in Charlotte Brontë, in a long dress and petticoats, sitting on a window-seat and looking out of a casement at a handsome man in tight trousers stalking away across the landscape. 'So much. So much,' she said wistfully.

'Nothing that really matters.'

'I like things that don't really matter. Things that do really matter make me sick.'

This time Philip stayed shut up. Ann continued to look through the non-existent window. Just ahead Jessica's actual window fizzed and bubbled like a TV screen at the wrong angle to see properly. But then Ann *did* glimpse something through it, a doleful strip of hedge, a field full of cabbages in neat rows, something white, surely, in the distance. It was gone as soon as she'd seen it, swinging past the blank side of the van, but she had a strong sensation of being pulled, as if those deep eyes, dark as the darkness through which their beams now travelled, were at full power again, as they had been last night in her dream.

She found herself pressed intimately to the side of the van, another joggle and she'd find her way out, passing through some doorway secretly positioned between the atoms. Perhaps Jesus wanted to lead her *away* from the spotty ones, who knew where? He might even agree with her that Christians were nastier than everybody else. She imagined flying through the side of the van which burst outwards to let her go like a great tatty flower coming into bloom, and then bounding across the field of cabbages with long lilting slow-motion strides to the man who stood there waiting with His white winged arms and His huge brown eyes, while Philip and Jessica and Kevin sat among their heaps of pies and sandwiches and watched her, open-mouthed.

And at that moment, in a hushed sort of voice that sounded as if it was coming from that exact imaginary Kevin who was witnessing Ann's miracle, Kevin said: 'Look at that.'

Ann turned to the front of the van and there, through the windscreen, an enormous webby eye was rising over the horizon, an eye that was swollen, intricate, revolting, like the eye of an insect, an eye that looked at her with such mechanical menace that its very beam seemed to clatter and clank.

Ann realised that in her shock she had cried out. The van lurched to a stop.

'Whatever's the matter?' Jessica asked.

Philip shoved himself along the seat towards her, by way of comfort.

Kevin muttered, almost to himself, 'It's only the radio telescope at Jodrell Bank, for heaven's sake.' He was probably nervous about his fellow-evangelicals hearing him say anything as risky as for heaven's sake.

Judy let Margaret out at her gate, and sat looking up at her wistfully from her big car. Margaret felt she ought to say something more – she always did at these moments. It was to do with looking down at somebody.

'I'd ask you in,' she said suddenly, so suddenly she didn't know she was going to say it herself. Usually she just boringly repeated their next arrangement: so I'll see you again tomorrow, same time, lovely, thank you very much. Perhaps she'd mentioned asking Judy in this time because she knew she couldn't. It was a safe cul-de-sac of politeness. In hopes it would stay safe, she made sure her *but* came out as forcefully as possible: 'but.'

Judy had a tendency to go without warning into a public performance in the middle of a conversation. She did so now: 'What, like I am, all of a lather? Have a shower? No way, all your neighbours would say we're a couple of lesbians.'

Margaret almost clapped her hand over Judy's mouth, hard, to smack the word lesbians back. As it was she couldn't stop herself from glancing up and down Glenwood Road. Nobody was about, as usual. Judy seemed to take a delight in bringing everything down to rock-bottom. Perhaps that was what had made her husband leave her, the desire for a little more romance. What a hypocrite I am, Margaret thought as soon as she'd thought that, John and I hardly set an example, what romance do *we* have? It was so easy to be superior when your own marriage was still intact. Then her left breast seemed to glow, like a warning-light. Though in other respects, Margaret thought dutifully, heeding its warning, Judy might soon be ahead of me in the superior stakes. And in the intact stakes.

Then she nearly sobbed with fright. It was amazing how you could worry your way through an argument in your head and miss the whole point about what was happening to you, her left breast was actually *glowing*. Thinking about it made her want to shriek in despair and terror. But she didn't. If she had, she'd have ended up telling Judy everything. Judy was the last person in the world to confide such information to. She'd probably laugh. She'd talk about it very loudly. She'd en*joy* it. And worse still, bringing it out in the open would make it real.

'But, I was going to say, I've got an appointment shortly,' she said. She felt she ought to say a little bit of the truth, as a sort of fee for withholding the rest.

'So have I,' Judy said. 'I've got a living to earn. In fact,' she went on, lowering her voice confidentially, at least confidentially for her, so that it only carried a hundred yards or so, 'I've got a do on later that'll make you laugh. Naughty but Nice.'

'What's naughty but nice?'

'The do is. That's what it's called.'

Something about the elephantine intimacy of Judy's tone must have struck a chord in Raymond, because he suddenly started howling from the house. Heavens, thought Margaret, how often does he do this while I'm out? Perhaps he howls for hours at a time and infuriates the whole neighbourhood, but people are too polite to complain. People round here *were* very polite, except perhaps the old lady with the poop scoop.

She tried to concentrate. Naughty but nice. Judy had a job to do with organising people who sold products at home, like Tupperware, only it wasn't Tupperware, it was all sorts of things. As Margaret understood it, it was a bit like running a mail order catalogue, but in the flesh.

'Not the one in Wigan, that I'm going to now,' Judy explained to her. 'That's Frills 'n' Fashion. It's the one I've got tonight. It's strictly wives, all the men have to go to the pub. Then we have, you know, those nighties that are hardly worth putting on in the first place. And bras with holes in for your nipples to poke out of, peek-a-boo bras they're called.'

Margaret burst out laughing. Inside, she wasn't laughing at all. Imagine, one of those peek-a-boo holes with the nipple poking out, and the other one empty and gaping, like an empty eyesocket! Her laughter felt horrid and bruising, like being struck by a laugh equivalent of that conker thing they used for knocking down the Poco Poco.

'I'm glad you see the funny side,' Judy said somewhat tartly. She seemed smaller still in her big car. Even while being shaken by laughs that seemed as arbitrary as hiccups, Margaret realised that jokemakers didn't like people laughing at their jokes *too* much. It must be a bit like having a pet dog which showed too much affection for other people, though come to think of it Raymond, who was still howling, was welcome to show as much affection for other people as he liked. Judy gave an irritated smile. 'That's not the funniest bit, as a matter of fact,' she went on, 'but perhaps I'd better not say any more, in case you do yourself an injury.'

Margaret's laughter had died away. She didn't in fact *want* Judy to say any more, in case it started up again. But she didn't dare tell her so for fear of making her more upset still. 'Oh, go on,' she finally asked.

'Well,' Judy said, her enthusiasm coming back, 'they look at all these basques and knickers and things, and then they come to order. With the Naughty but Nice stuff you only have to put the code number on the order form, you don't have to put a product description. They talk about what they're going to put down but there's one thing they never mention. Somewhere in amongst it all they squeeze in one secret little code number they don't tell *any*one about. V,82,61,1. I know it off by heart. Each one thinks she's being so daring. Do you know what it is?'

'Of course I don't.'

Judy opened and shut her mouth. For a moment Margaret seemed to have become inexplicably deaf. Then she realised Judy was miming.

'I'm sorry,' she said.

'For heaven's sake,' Judy said, 'I'm miming as loud as I can.' She mimed again. Her eyes bulged and she looked exactly as if she was shouting. How *thick* she is, Margaret thought.

'I *still* can't,' she told Judy.

'A vibrator!' Judy suddenly shouted. She'd switched from silent to out-loud without lowering the volume level at all. Margaret looked up and down the street again, appalled. Still nobody. The silence was intense. She sensed ears straining behind windows. Suddenly it occurred to her that Raymond had even stopped howling.

'For goodness' sake, Judy,' she said.

'Oh well,' Judy said philosophically. 'Why worry? One thing I can tell you about vibrators, from my experience. Everybody wants one.'

'My old woman with her poop scoop wouldn't want one.'

'Everybody who goes to Naughty but Nice parties wants one, I can guarantee.'

'That's the difference,' Margaret said, but Judy showed no signs of taking the point.

'I've got to whizz,' Judy concluded. 'I won't get any brownie points for turning up smelly. See you.' And with that she drove off, tooting as she went.

Margaret stood on the pavement watching her disappear and thinking: lesbians, vibrators. If you could call it thinking. Perhaps I think too much, she thought, I'm not enough of an animal. Judy seemed pure animal, she belonged in a zoo. I ought to have more dirty thoughts, Margaret told herself, that's my New Year's resolution. On the other hand, Judy hasn't got a man, and I have, so dirty thoughts aren't everything. Maybe she doesn't match dirty thought to dirty deed. But, come to think of it, nor do I. I don't do dirty deeds and I don't have dirty thoughts either. When we make love I don't do much more than lie on my back and think of England, except that I don't think of England. No, that's not quite fair, I get worked up, but how long does that last? Exactly long enough. Probably about a minute. And how often? Sometimes a couple of nights in succession. Sometimes weekly or worse. Let's say on average every five days. One minute, every five days. It was hardly worth toting your body about in the first place.

She opened the front door. Raymond reared up at her, tail wagging, black lips curling in a grin, whining with joy. 'I know, I know,' she said, pushing him down. She wanted to carry on with her train of thought. He rushed off and brought back his sodden towel as an offering. He always brought her that. Just like a male, the same routine every time. Because it takes two to tango. John was to blame as well. He never did anything startling, like taking her in the middle of the night. He never seemed to show any initiative. But then, nor did she. It was amazing anything got done at all.

I am now going to think a dirty thought, Margaret told herself, so bugger off, Raymond. He'd begun to climb her again. 'Get *down*.' His eyes clouded over as he realised she meant it, and he trotted off to the kitchen to inspect his bowl. She watched him with a kind of sympathetic contempt. His bowl was a refuge against life's disappointments, but he never seemed to learn that when he went to it in such circumstances it was always empty. It was bound to be empty, because he ate what was given him when it was given to him, in one or at the most two horrendous gobbles. A poor memory didn't seem the answer since he wasn't so much forgetting that the bowl was empty as remembering it as full, and it had never in his life been full at such times. She wondered if he actually needed a second disappointment to confirm his dim view of existence. The bowl clattered sadly, just out of sight behind the kitchen door. His tongue, ever wet, sloshed around its bare earthenware. He gave a deliberately audible sigh. Honestly, thought Margaret, I've got no staying power, I can even be diverted from thinking dirty thoughts by the sadness of my dog.

She went upstairs. The landing was bright and cheerful. She loved her landing. By some sort of accident it had turned out to be a place with a delightful atmosphere.

'This is a delightful landing,' she said out loud, in an effort to feel reckless. She revolved her eyes in a way that would have been siren-ish if there'd been any man to see. She wondered if she ought to think her dirty thoughts here. It wasn't really private enough, though: its jolliness, its quality of tumbling light, was mainly brought about by a large window looking out on the houses on the other side of the road. If she pulled the venetian blind shut the nice-ness of the landing would go at the same time, and be replaced by a guilty atmosphere. People going past might wonder what was going on. She didn't want to think her dirty thoughts in a guilty atmosphere, she wanted to think them with bravado. She went on into the bedroom.

Their bedroom was just as nice as the landing, when all was said and done. The yellow curtains at the window, and the yellow duvet cover, emphasised the brightness of the day outside, though the sun didn't shine directly in till later in the afternoon. Their back garden was sealed in by trees – mainly in adjoining gardens – which gave it a cosy, intimate quality, as though it were a secret garden. She'd started reading *The Secret Garden* to Ann when she was little but had stopped in disgust when she realised it was all about reforming your ways and becoming good.

I'm back on course now, Margaret thought, the dog's dis-gruntlement is behind me. There was a trembly feeling near her abdomen which seemed to herald enjoyable nastiness to come. She looked at her watch. Ten to eleven. Devote twenty minutes to dirty thoughts, have a quick shower, she should be able to leave the house by a quarter to twelve and her appointment, don't think about it, don't even mention it except from a strictly timetable point of view, wasn't till half-past for some mysterious reason, just when you'd imagine all the breast specialists would be knocking off for lunch but don't think about them. Back to the trembling in her tummy which was just about still there, and the lovely secret of the secret garden, green and cosy below the window, as long as you let your eye run quickly over the crap-patch where Raymond was so obstinate about crapping. You had to run your eye quickly over certain things like crap-patches and breast specialists on the way to a dirty thought.

She sat on the bed, then lay on it. From here she couldn't see the garden of course, she could only see the sky, but the great advantage was that absolutely nobody could see *her*. Unless the window cleaner came oh God. She tried to remember when he'd come last. The trouble with him was that he was irregular. He was a blond almost invisible young man who blamed everything on the weather. Still, that was all part of having dirty thoughts, not knowing if the window cleaner would suddenly peek through the window. The correct thing to do in the circumstances would be to tell him to come in. On her wedding anniversary? All the dirtier.

She could feel her cheeks reddening. It was time now to think a thought or two. Empty your mind of everything except filth.

She relaxed and let her ordinary thoughts slip away. Perhaps she let the filthy ones go with them, because her mind began to feel very blank indeed. She suddenly realised she could drop asleep just like that. It was the result of waking up in the night, and then going for her run this morning. Concentrate, concentrate.

A pair of anonymous female breasts came into her mind, big ones, much bigger than her own. Then another pair, then another. It wasn't anything to do with her appointment, whenever she tried to think dirty she started off by thinking of breasts. Once she'd come across a glossy pornographic magazine in John's briefcase, alongside a copy of *Caravanning Monthly* (odd since they'd never been interested in owning a caravan) and had found it exciting to look at the nude women pictured inside it. She wouldn't be the slightest bit interested in buying *Playgirl* and seeing pictures of nude men. Perhaps that was unnatural. On the other hand reading John's pornographic magazine had made her feel terribly eager to have sex with John. It was a pity that he'd been out at the time. But it was hard to feel erotic about a nude man *as such*. A handsome face, nice chest and shoulders, flat stomach, good legs, were fine, but the really nude parts didn't in themselves make her go hot under the collar. Men's bottoms seemed so weasly. And as for the rest of them, she suddenly thought of something Nance had told her years ago. Before John was born his dad had gone through a nudist phase, at the weekends at least. He would eat his breakfast with no clothes on. 'It used to put me off my food,' Nance had said bluntly, 'seeing his thing drooping over the edge of his chair.' It might have been that picture in her subconscious that had made Margaret recoil from the old man this morning. The point was that when she thought of love-making she thought of her body in the arms of a man rather than of the man's body in its own right. She had no idea whether that was normal or not. Too bad. When you were having a dirty thought you could think whatever you liked.

More breasts came through her mind. It was almost like counting sheep. She felt herself becoming sleepy again. Snap out of it, think of the breasts as swaying about in some depraved room, heaven only knows where you find rooms like that, in London mansions costing millions of pounds, or squalid council estates probably, but surely nowhere in Heaton Chapel, surely not in the streets she walked down day by day. She pictured furry pudenda bobbing about also, like partly submerged coconuts. If there was a door she could knock on, say just round the corner, just knock and be let in, and inside find such a room, would she knock? Of course, of course, she thought to herself, knowing that never in a million years would she do so. She would knock, and in she'd go, into the roomful of bodies, *now* she could imagine men's erections without spoiling it all, erections in the dimness like so many traffic lights on red, well, only spoiling it a bit, they couldn't help but remind you how daft sex was. Men's hands, thinking of their hands was better, a hand sliding up over the belly of a woman, suddenly groping and distorting her breast, her left breast.

She heard herself whimper, just as Raymond might. It was a whimper of annoyance at first, finding herself suddenly out of the game, like landing on a hotel in Monopoly. But then she whimpered with fear. She could feel her left breast glowing again, as it had when she was talking with Judy. Of course she was hot all over, what with the run and thinking in that dirty way, it was hardly surprising. Still, her left breast felt more hot than the rest of her, as if heat could come to a point. Perhaps she was creating the effect simply by thinking about it. She tried to put that explanation to the test by thinking of another part of her, her right foot, and seeing if she could make it heat up. Yes, it did feel warmer, thought not as warm as her breast. Of course that could be because although she was trying not to, subconsciously she was actually thinking more intensely about her breast than about her foot. A clinching argument suddenly came into her mind. She hadn't noticed the hotness of her breast from the time when Raymond sprang up on her until just a moment ago, and the reason was of course that she'd been thinking of something else. That proved it was all in the mind.

No it didn't. People who suffered from real pain, from real cancer, could forget it for a while, she was sure. Pain was all in the mind too, when all was said and done. Where else could it be?

Perhaps I'll die, she thought now. Pain was a road, leading to the destination of death. She almost blushed, it sounded exactly like the blurbs you read on the covers of pulpy books, but being embarrassed at her own corniness did nothing to reduce her fear of death. Thinking about a road made her suddenly visualise little Stephen standing forlornly on a pavement somewhere, just somewhere, nowhere in particular. He was motherless yet he was looking straight at her, his little round spectacles expressing such lostness that Margaret suddenly howled out loud. Oh God, oh God, she thought, I shall suffer all the agony and the horror of that way of dying, and yet instead of feeling sad or bitter I shall feel guilty, like some mother who's gone out to work instead of taking care of her children, only I will have gone for ever and ever amen. Dying in misery will count just as if it's something extremely self-indulgent. I will lose everything and will feel as much of a swine as if I'd *taken* everything. Poor Stephen, poor Ann, poor all of them, what will they do without me? Poor me.

Her howl triggered Raymond off again. Downstairs in the kitchen he began to howl too.

Raymond woke up. The settee on which he lay teemed with the ghosts of human genitals and backsides, John's and Ann's quite recent, John's so much so that the sharp scent of his semen was still packaged in his going-to-work-suit's odour of flat, processed sheep, but those of the other members of the family also, interwoven intricately with each other, the smell coloration getting fainter and fainter as you sniffed your way back into the past, until the bottoms were wavering, abstract things, barely discernible. Raymond, still groggy from his sudden nap, snuffled them all up, half hoping that by sheer accumulation he could precipitate a composite backside on the cushion beside him. But no, he was alone still, locked out from the big wide world. A square of sunshine lay on the carpet nearby, second-hand weather.

A fly shot past overhead, its wings clattering, and ponged into the window-pane. The impact stunned it for a moment, and it dropped almost all the way down the glass until it collected its wits again, bounced into the window a further couple of times, more tentatively now, and then flew back over the room, searching frantically for a way out. Raymond, eyebrows humped, watched it bleakly. After a moment it turned back, saw the window afresh, and hurtled disastrously into it yet again. Raymond settled his head on his paws, and sighed.

There was the sound of a car coming down the road. Raymond raised one ear flap slightly to take in the roar of the engine and the crunching of the tyres as they bit into the surface of the road. The roar lessened and became a deep throbbing, the tyres crunched more noisily than before. Raymond sent both ears up and forward. The car was coming to a halt. The brakes squawked, the tyres made a crumpling sound like massive paper, the engine puttered on for a little, then died away.

Raymond stayed put. A car door slammed. If he rushed to look it might not be Margaret but somebody else, taking her exact place in the world. With the window screening out scents he felt blind. He raised himself up slowly and deliberately and got down from the settee with such care, placing each paw in turn, that the strain made him grunt. Instead of walking towards the window he walked towards the corner of its wall, where the television was. He often lay under there, amidst the tangle of wires. At all costs he must not bark with welcome only to discover a strange cold face outside. The picture of a spider came into his mind, he couldn't think why.

As he walked he found himself being skewed towards the window anyway, as though blown by a strong sideways wind. He locked his eyes on to the television and strained towards it with all his will, but still his paws lost purchase and began to slide over the surface of the carpet. He lowered his head and body into the hunting posture to give himself better balance, but it was no good, he began to lean to the right, and to avoid keeling over altogether he quickly twisted in that direction and rushed joyously to the window regardless. Possibly sheer happiness might ensure it was Margaret there.

He leapt towards the sill in a flurry of smiling teeth, tail-wag, hectic paws, straining nose, and then rearranged all his exuberant bits and pieces into a delicate balance as he reconciled his sudden self to the narrow ledge. The shock made him pant, and he lolloped his tongue out to cool himself inside, but he was still smiling and by cautious counterweighting with his bum managed to get his tail wagging again. He looked out of the window, heart thumping.

It *was* Margaret!

She was standing talking with somebody who was still sitting in a car. Raymond strained his eyes to make out who it was, and as he recognised her, the memory of her smell entered his nostrils: the blood woman!

Her exciting tang was so vivid he wondered if somehow it had crept through the glass, and he pressed his muzzle to the window, whimpering in his desire to get through the barrier. Margaret, Margaret, the loyal part of his brain insisted, but the nose aspects of his consciousness were overwhelmed by the blood woman, and it was to her that he had to give his attention. He wanted her so much that the fur bristled on his neck and flanks. The smell said female but since it wasn't that of a female *dog* it also said meat; the fact that she could neither be fucked nor eaten only made her the more enchanting. A tickle began in his throat as if he was bristling within, and the only way it could be smoothed down was to howl.

He began a little one but then he looked at Margaret again and managed to squash it. Her scents were so much quieter that the thought of them had a momentarily calming effect, her sweat, urine, faeces, blood, coated with soapiness, and blandly human overall. But the blood woman's smells were urgent, and the memory of them replaced Margaret's almost at once. Another howl rose in his throat, and this one couldn't be stopped but came out high and true and modulated, bringing with it fleeting images of woods and underbrush, the jostling of a pack, a moon so pure and dominating that you could smell its sharp light upon the snow, an overall sense of being in the midst of a largeness that Raymond had never in his life experienced. His howl went on and on. His being, always prone to complications, always striving for simplicity, seemed at last to have folded in upon itself and become a thin line of sound. At the end of the garden Margaret was shaking, bending over, under the influence of the blood woman's savagery.

Then, at the height of his intensity, Raymond lost interest. His mind and emotions felt tired. He wondered suddenly if there was anything in his bowl. It struck him that he was very hungry. He jumped off the window-sill so clumsily that he staggered into the coffee table, and then trotted through to the kitchen.

His bowl was empty. All it contained was the smell of a previous meal. After a few sniffs he trotted back to the front room. When he arrived he felt refreshed. He tried to remember whether he had actually eaten anything from his bowl or simply sniffed it. The distinction was a fine one: remembered food was as insubstantial as the smelled kind. Either way the scent of food lingered in his nostrils, so he had a sense of well-being.

He walked back to the window slowly, licking his chops in hopes of finding the odd crumb or two in his fur, but he had no luck. In case he was feeling full he didn't leap up on to the window-sill this time, but put his front paws up and peered over them. As he did so the blood woman made a loud noise. She and Margaret had been there a long time. Perhaps they would stay there a long time yet. He yawned, moving his head back to give the yawn clearance. Perhaps it was time to sleep and let the possible food digest.

He lowered his paws consideringly to the ground, yawning again, and padded over to the settee. He clambered on to it and sniffed. There was the strong smell of dog, and he froze in his tracks for a moment. He sniffed again. Only himself. He lowered his hind-quarters.

At that moment the car engine started up again, there was louder talking by the women, and the car drove away. He flicked his ears forward. Yes, there was the sound of Margaret's shoes coming up the path. Just when he'd given up hope.

His sheer excitement made him forget for a moment that it was Margaret who was approaching, and he growled in case it was an intruder. Then he remembered, and yapped instead, leaping off the settee and bounding to the front door.

He pressed his nails against it and scratched sideways, trying to help it open. Her key went into the lock and then she was there, lovely Margaret back from wherever she had gone running, smelling of sweat and soap and of *her* in general, with a faint after-echo of the blood woman's blood, irrelevant though that was now she was gone and Margaret was here.

He leapt up and put his paws on her front; she spoke back gently, caressingly, making a repeated sound that was almost like an animal noise. He sniffed her again, and this time noticed fresh warm sweat mingling with the cooler sweat from her run. He tuned his nostrils more finely and smelled her again. She reeked, he suddenly realised, of lust. It was not an odour he'd often found on her before, at least not in this strength. As he flexed his nostrils appreciatively he discovered something else beneath the lust, an intermediate luke-warm layer between the sex-sweat and the cold sweat of her run. It was fear.

He whimpered slightly in surprise. Blind hunched fear, recently felt, just moments ago. Not directed outwards, not fear of man or dog.

She spoke again, harshly this time. He got down. It was time to give her his towel. He rushed off to find it, pounding and swerving round the dining-room so that the room itself seemed to be swinging at him from all angles. There it was, a patch of off-white glimpsed through the legs of chairs like a small crumpled animal or bird in a clearing.

He bounded over and grabbed it between his teeth. Though it smelled of domesticity and himself, the cloth seemed for a second to have another whiff to it also, that of a hunted creature, recently killed, of men somewhere across forest, across fields, awaiting it, of blue rainclouds tumbling, of the cold winds of winter, of hard pellets of rain beating down on him.

He whimpered with pleasure at the instant experience, and then with pleasure again at the thought that he was not really having it, but was safely at home with his beloved mistress at the front door. He rushed to her and dropped the cloth at her feet. She ignored it, and began to walk towards the stairs. His heart pounded in a kind of panic at the impossibility of pleasing her. If not the cloth, what *could* he give? Her smells had intensified, filling the hallway. She smelled unmistakably of bitch, human bitch, on heat. He whimpered again, in bitter frustration, woollen game on the floor, unfuckable bitch on the stairs.

He went into the kitchen and rattled his bowl, to give Margaret the chance of being nice to him for a change, but she carried on upstairs instead. He slouched back to the front-room settee and pretended to settle down to sleep, for want of anything better to do. He imagined Margaret inspecting his calmness. After a few moments he felt sleepy anyway, and was just beginning to doze off when he heard a howling from upstairs. Joyfully he began to howl in unison.

C H A P T E R

7

'**W**hen you said it wouldn't take a minute, you were right,'
Philip said grumpily. 'It's taken you half an hour already.'
Kevin pulled his head out of the engine to reply, and clonked it
on the bonnet. He didn't say shit but simply rubbed his head
gravely. 'Not far off,' he replied, and went back into the engine.

Another saint, Ann thought, the way he lets Philip ride rough-
shod over him. What was *Philip* doing to help, after all? Strutting
around the van puffing and blowing was about the extent of it.

A car came along the road and went past at insulting speed, leaving an afterwash of music behind. The notes seemed to pop into
silence on the hedgerow and the ditch as bubbles did when Stephen
blew them in the garden.

Jessica was no better than Philip. She was sitting obstinately in
the front passenger seat as if for all the world they were still hur-
tling along at twenty miles an hour to the hoe-down instead of
being stuck here by Jodrell Bank. It occurred to Ann that she hated
the way people's heads poked up in cars and vans, and you couldn't
see the rest of them. The heads looked so smug, with Jessica's being
smugger than most. When Ann's family went out for a drive, they
always inspected the heads in any car in front with great care. If one
of them had sticking-out ears they groaned, because it meant that
the car would be being driven very slowly, and if there was one
with sticking-out ears and a hat it was even worse, because the car
would be going very slowly and in the middle of the road.
Needless to say, Jessica didn't have sticking-out ears *or* a hat. In
fact, she had the tiniest sweetest ears you could imagine.

Not that Ann herself was doing anything to assist, come to

think. For the first few minutes after she'd got out of the van she'd felt almost as if she ought to hang on to something to avoid being dragged off over the fields after Jesus. The field here wasn't of cabbages as it happened, but of green, spiky stuff, young wheat or barley perhaps, but she felt the pull all the same, which was ridiculous considering she didn't believe in Jesus in the first place. She'd sat down spanning the ditch, her bum by the hedge and her feet by the roadside, so that her back was to the suction and she had a low centre of gravity. Even so, she felt giddy. It was like that feeling you have when you are sitting in the shallows at the seaside, and a wave is going out to sea again inside out, after having broken, and seems to want to pull you with it.

The trouble with sitting in that position was that the dish of the radio telescope at Jodrell Bank was silhouetted against the horizon more or less straight ahead, like a vast eye. Even though she knew what it was she couldn't get used to it, and every time she glanced in its direction she had a little shock. It was ridiculous since she'd seen it dozens of times before and never worried about it in the past. But now, because of her stupid dream, it gave her the shivers. There was no logic about it, not even dream logic, since even in her first glimpse she hadn't thought it was *Jesus's* eye. What had happened was that she'd been expecting Jesus's eye, and then seen Jodrell Bank instead. It was even on the opposite side of the van, it was opposite in every way. It was the oppositeness which had given her a fright in the first place. That's the typical result you'd expect from hobnobbing with this lot, she thought. You don't just start believing in God, you start believing in the devil.

'I still think I should go off and borrow somebody's phone and ring the Brindleys,' Philip said. He didn't actually say it to anyone, he said it to the landscape in general, as though only the landscape was likely to be intelligent enough to understand his point.

As before, Kevin raised his head and clonked it on the car bonnet. He's a simple soul, thought Ann, he's become used to doing that now. He just thinks it's something that happens before you open your mouth to speak, like having a migraine every time you eat a strawberry.

'What will you tell them if you *do* ring them?' Kevin asked.

'I'll tell them that we're stuck here, of course, what do you think?'

'They might come out to pick us up. And I'll have the van fixed in a couple of minutes, so it will be a waste of time all round. I expect they've got enough to do.' And with that Kevin returned to the engine once more.

'You wouldn't think we lived in the age of the telephone,' Philip told the breeze, 'the way we stand here like so many bananas.'

'Speak for yourself,' Ann told him. '*I'm* not standing here like a banana.'

Philip trotted over, as if grateful to be reminded that there was a human being in the vicinity, and not just Kevin. 'He's obstinate,' he said, lowering his voice but keeping it raised enough for Kevin to hear. 'He would never admit it might be beyond him.'

'Enjoy the sunshine, Philip,' Ann suggested. 'From the banana point of view that's what counts. Ripen, my son. Though you're probably ripe enough already.'

She regretted that as soon as she'd said it. If you weren't actually nasty to Philip he assumed it was a come-on.

'I've not gone yellow with black spots,' he said seductively.

'You've not gone yellow, anyway,' Ann told him.

Not having a sense of humour of his own Philip found it difficult to reply, so he cautiously fingered his septic spots instead, as if trying to check through his fingertips whether they were black or not.

'And don't press too hard on them,' Ann added. 'They'll burst.'

He cleared his throat but didn't say anything. Instead he wandered off, trying to look as if he were preoccupied with other thoughts, of a more noble kind.

There was silence, except for the small noises Kevin was making deep in the engine, and a high-pitched peeping from somewhere in the hedge. The sky was blue, with a few scrappy silver clouds. Ann closed her eyes for a moment. She could feel the cool breeze on her arms and legs, but the warmth of the sun came through it, like the warmth of a hot water bottle between fresh sheets. The pull of Jesus's eyes seemed to have diminished, and she felt calm. She opened her eyes again. Philip was standing in front of her, obviously hoping to cash in on any sleepiness that might be available.

'Sleepy?' he asked.

'My mind's like a razor,' she answered.

'Yes,' he agreed, as if that was just the answer he'd expected.

'I think that may have done it,' Kevin said. He clonked his head again, and shut the bonnet. 'I'll give it a try.' He stepped round the van and began to get in.

'Hang on a minute,' Ann said, pushing herself to her feet. 'Let us get in too, in case you zoom off. I wouldn't want to have to stop you once you'd started.'

'There is such a thing as neutral,' Kevin said, in a pained voice for him.

'There's such a thing as a flying pig, too,' she told him. Suddenly an image of Stephen came into her mind again, standing outside Manchester University as he had been this morning, his spectacles looking blankly at the van, and Ann felt so homesick she wanted to weep. She felt as if she were hundreds and hundreds of miles, years and years away from where she belonged. This stretch of road after all was one she'd never stood on before and in all likelihood never would again. It might just as well be a stretch of road on the Russian steppes. With Jodrell Bank stuck there it might just as well be a stretch of road on Mars. She remembered once, when she was quite small, going to stay with her cousin Emma, and having to share a bed with her. In the depths of the night Emma gave out a sweaty sleepy smell, familiar yet not quite right, and Ann realised that without knowing it she had always known the smell of her own immediate family, just as a dog does, and she'd cried quietly under the bedclothes so as not to wake Emma up.

She climbed over to her seat at the back of the van. Philip climbed over to join her, giving out little intimate puffings and pantings as he did so. Kevin turned on the ignition. The starter gave a mournful wail and faded. He tried again, and this time it caught.

'You see,' Philip said, turning round triumphantly, 'God does want us to get there, after all.'

'If He was so keen,' Ann asked, 'why did He let us break down in the first place?'

'Because nothing worth achieving can be done without a struggle.'

'It was Kevin who struggled. You just trotted round in the road talking about telephoning all the time.' She paused. 'Ye of little faith.'

'It was not little faith. I knew we were only being tested. But for all I could tell, the test might have been to see if we had the initiative to get alternative transport. As it turned out Kevin was being tested to see if he could start the engine again.'

'It's a funny kind of test for God to think up. Does He own a large garage somewhere?'

'He owns everything,' Philip said.

The van pottered on. Jodrell Bank swept by them. You could see so far across the fields that the countryside looked like Toytown. There were tiny farms, and cows looking spick and span. You couldn't tell at this distance that cows always needed their bottoms wiping.

And then, as they drove through the outskirts of a small village, the engine died away again.

She went to the Poco Poco with her friend Jen. It was November, and they had to wear coats. Maggie had an awful one with raglan shoulders which seemed to dominate its whole top half, as if you could have shoulders down to your waist. Her mother had bought it from a catalogue. What was terrible about it was not that it was unfashionable, Maggie wouldn't have minded that at all, wearing a coat that was just a coat, a coat designed to keep the weather out, and your body in. What was hideous about this coat was that it looked as if it was designed to be fashionable but followed a fashion no one else had ever heard of. It wasn't out-of-date or highly advanced, it was just separate. This is what the well-dressed Martian is wearing, it seemed to say. Needless to say Jen had a neat, slim-cut coat that curved out just the slightest bit at the hem, to give it bounce.

But what did it matter? Nobody at the Poco Poco would see it, she would check it in at the cloakroom when she arrived. And nobody would realise how horrible it was on their way there, in the sad bus light which made everything and everyone look horrible. People on the bus at night-time were always fat old ladies and tottering old men, whatever they were like before they got on and after they got off. For all anyone could tell she and Jen were fat old ladies and tottering old men as well. Only Jen knew that Maggie's coat was revolting in its own right, on the bus or off it, indoors or out, fair weather or foul. And to make sure there was no misunderstanding, Maggie told her about every five minutes that her mother had bought it for her, sight unseen, from the catalogue. She knew that Jen would keep this information in her brain, but she was still worried that the image of her in her coat could seep in through her eyes and find its way into her head anyway, so that Jen would start to believe that *this* was *her*. She had to keep pulling the word catalogue to the front of Jen's mind so that there was no room for anything else.

'The lead singer's trousers always split,' Jen said. 'Some time or other, they always do.' She laughed her sweet high-pitched laugh, which Maggie liked so much she'd practised it herself, but couldn't quite do it right. She could get the pitch but it put such a strain on her voice that she couldn't chop the ha-s, or rather, hee-s, off short enough, and if you left them long you just sounded like a mad person.

'I don't think seeing that will turn me on,' Maggie said. She liked to be hard-bitten about pop-stars. 'If he could make my coat split that's a different story. Being that my mother bought it from a catalogue.'

'I do know that your mother bought it from a blimmin catalogue.'

'If you could flap it fast enough I'm sure it would fly.'

'If you could flap *anything* fast enough I'm sure it would fly,' Jen said, and burst out laughing yet again.

The Poco Poco was half-empty, as it always was when you arrived. There were several more girls from school there, though. Luckily Maggie was uncoated by the time she got together with them, and wearing her moderately sexy mauve dress which was low-cut at the front, with nylon stuff you could more or less see through over her cleavage. There were records on at this stage because the band wasn't yet installed. The girls all began dancing, each one looking on the floor as they always did when dancing with other girls, so as not to be reminded.

Then the evening went vague. The next thing that seemed to happen was that the band was thundering away, Maggie and Jen were still dancing together with downcast eyes, and suddenly there he was, tall, thin, dark-suited, with fluttering black hair, dancing right between them.

He didn't dance like a boy, either shy or showing-off, but seriously, as you might dance by yourself in your bedroom. As he danced he swivelled slowly from Maggie to Jen, sizing them up in turn with calm eyes, as if he were deciding which apple to pick from the tree. He'll pick Jen, Maggie thought despairingly. Jen was neat and cool in a simple pink dress, very feminine. She wore her blonde hair in a beehive which made her look serene and dignified, like one of those ancient Egyptians on an old pot. Maggie felt dumpy in her flouncy dress. I've got better tits, she thought bitterly – Jen was staying at her house so she'd seen hers while they got dressed together, and to her surprise and glee they were minute – but there's no way of proving it. The more curvily she danced, the more her dress would seem fussy.

And then she realised he was dancing with *her*.

He came and went, that was the strange thing about him, almost as if he were a ghost. Later that evening he disappeared. Maggie could have wept. They'd been dancing together for hours and had hardly spoken in all that time, again not out of shyness, on his part at least, but because he was concentrating so hard. He danced each step as though it was a word he wished to say, not anything to do with the cacophony of the band, but a word about himself, clear and precise, so that there was no need to use the other kind. Maggie told him her name early on, and he simply smiled to himself, as though it was just what he'd expected. She faltered, miserably, in her dancing, thinking for the first time what a horrible name Maggie was, a name made out of twiddly mauve nylon like her dress. At the beginning of the evening she'd quite liked her dress, it was her coat she hated. Her coat, oh help. Imagine a being who owned a coat like that having the nerve to dance with possibly the most attractive man in the history of the world. He didn't seem like a boy, he did seem a man, though she could no more fix an age on him than she could a name.

'What's yours?' she asked timidly.

He raised an eyebrow.

'Name?' she replied.

He smiled and nodded, as if she'd told *him* something.

And not long before eleven o'clock he disappeared.

Jen and Maggie were leaving at eleven. Maggie had promised her parents they'd be home by then, but she interpreted this later, as she'd known she would, as meaning leave the Poco Poco by then. One of the girls said she'd seen him go upstairs to the bar where they sold proper drinks. She said it sneeringly, somehow managing to suggest both that he was therefore too sophisticated for the likes of her, and that she'd let herself down by dancing with someone who drank real booze. But her opinion, or opinions, didn't count: she was one of those fat girls who hate the thin world. The important thing was that he'd gone. Maggie felt like Cinderella at midnight. But at least I've danced with him, she thought to herself, my life hasn't been entirely wasted.

The last bus had gone, as they'd known it would have, so Jen and Maggie walked home. It was only about twenty-five minutes if they kept up a good speed. Maggie hated the way her legs clop-clopped under her balloon of a coat, so she was determined to walk fast. Suddenly she realised her man was back again, walking beside her.

But what about Jen? was Maggie's first thought, and then, immediately guessing, she glanced over her shoulder. Yes, there was someone for Jen, an ordinary-looking male, just someone her own man had got hold of for the occasion, hurrying along to join them because he had to catch up on legs, the way human beings did, *he* couldn't just appear. Jen looked round and saw him too. She looked resigned.

They stood, paired, by a garden hedge three hedges from Maggie's own, in case her parents looked out of the window. Along with other things, Maggie finally found out her man's name, Alan. Of course. She had never realised it before, but Alan was the nicest of all names, open but firm, utterly balanced.

For months she and Alan went out together. Not completely regularly. He continued his habit of appearing and disappearing. They met, if they met, at the Poco Poco, and would go off to spend the evening together. Sometimes they made love on some spare land somewhere, lying on her coat; other times he managed to borrow a car. Try as she might now, she couldn't remember their sex together, even though it was the first sex she'd ever had, and perhaps the last; except that, like his dancing, it was efficient and expressive and clean. You can't remember what is perfect. Experiences need a roughened surface, like Velcro, to enable them to stick in your mind.

Finally, of course, he disappeared for ever. She kept going to the Poco Poco in case, in case, but she knew it was ever. His disappearances had been leading up to ever all along. On one of these visits she met John. She never told him about Alan. How could she, when there was nothing to say?

So much for thinking dirty, she thought to herself. All she'd thought about was the purest sex she'd ever experienced, sex so pure that to all intents and purposes it had never even happened. If only it had been something tacky, she thought, something that I could still get my teeth into. But at least her empty memory had calmed her down, and stopped her crying in that ridiculous way. She'd even thought back to her long-ago tits without any pang from those in the here and now.

A customer whom he had never seen wanted to take out a second mortgage on his house in order to buy a property in France. It wasn't a routine request, so Mr Hawthorne, who at John's suggestion had recently started handling the branch's small amount of mortgage business, had passed it back to him. The trouble was that the customer lived far off, in Coventry in fact, so it was impossible to arrange an interview, which was the usual way these things were done. Why a Coventry dweller should choose to bank in Reddish was a mystery.

John nearly turned him down on the spot, and then asked himself why. What difference would an interview make? Should you really take into account whether a client has a fat face, or looks shifty? If you did, the wisest choice from a practical point of view would be only to lend money to people who did look shifty. They were the ones who could make investments a success. This one *sounded* shifty as a matter of fact. He wrote that the property had a substantial field attached to it, on which he proposed to grow Christmas trees as a cash crop. He could take a hundred shoots over in trays during the summer and harvest them fourteen months later as small trees. The anticipated profit was £4,000 p.a., just like that, even after expenses. You took them over in a small van, in one journey, and brought them back in a large lorry, in two journeys. The only other thing you had to do was arrange for someone to plant them and dig them up again.

Why can *I* never think of things like that? John thought. Why wouldn't a house in France make *me* think of Christmas trees? Not to mention thinking of a house in France in the first place. When you were in the thick of Stockport, France seemed like a fairy story. But if you got into a fairy-story frame of mind perhaps Christmas trees would come into the picture somewhere. He imagined row after row of them, sharpened like pencils, driving into the thick French sunshine, and casting furry shadows in their wake.

Let him have the mortgage, subject to this that and the other, in the usual way. Time for a pee. He wished he'd had one when he went to the Gents for a drink of water, less than an hour ago, but you couldn't pee in advance, more's the pity. Sometimes John went to the lavatory before bed knowing for certain that in a couple of hours he'd wake out of deep sleep with his bladder bursting.

This time it wasn't the nuisance, just the fact that the staff had seen him go so recently. I'm getting pompous, he thought, thinking I've got to ration my visits to the Gents for the benefit of the office, what do *they* care? But they did, ask them. Nothing was too trivial to fill them with glee. They loved to see your windscreen wipers or your waterworks go non-stop, the more trivial the better. He found himself walking through the main banking area towards the Gents as weightily as possible, two stone heavier than he was. He leaned back slightly as he went, like Alfred Hitchcock walking past in one of the scenes in his films, so solid that people looked right through him. Thump thump thump on thy big fat legs oh sea, he thought suddenly, remembering a poem he used to love in school.

Mrs Clarke sat with her back towards him at her loans desk, as determined not to see him as he was not to be seen. There was that complete non-rapport between them that people from the same office have when they are going to spend their lunch-hour together. Miss McCarthy and Miss Telfer, at the counter dealing with customers, also kept their backs to him, but he knew they were watching him just as intently as Mrs Clarke was, as though they could take in what was going on with every shift and ripple of their vertebrae. Miss Fielding, by contrast, turned and looked at him, in her frank slow egg way. It suddenly occurred to him that he didn't think of her as egg-like from a fertile point of view – in fact, he couldn't imagine her conceiving. She was more to do with the shell, with the spherical shape, with the beautiful featurelessness of an egg, its ability to stare at you undemandingly. Mr Hawthorne was scrunched over his desk, scribbling away as per usual. What he scribbled so avidly John was uncertain, since his productivity rate wasn't good. Perhaps he was writing a pornographic novel.

He went into the Gents. Somebody was already standing at the middle one of the three urinals. What kind of individual would walk straight down the Gents to the middle one of three, as if he thought he had to impress people instead of just taking a leak? John stood at the one on his right, angling himself away.

The man was big, in dirty overalls, and began peeing the moment John arrived, not an inhibition in sight. Thinking that very thought would make John do the opposite, he knew it at once, seize up. Even as he unzipped his flies he could sense a tiny trapdoor clanging shut. He stood at his urinal pee-impotent while the man at his shoulder pissed merrily on. Who does he think he is, John wondered, and then, with a shock so sudden he peed briefly himself, who *is* he?

This was the staff Gents, in a bank. There were half a dozen people entitled to use it, and this rough-looking man in his dungarees was not one of them. John imagined a brawny arm snaking down to hook him by the neck and drag him backwards out of the Gents, arms flailing, down the little corridor into the main banking area, a hostage, a shield, finding himself mute in front of his staff, leaning backwards with the grip, his face turning puce, his willy still hanging out of his trousers, unexpectedly exposed like a horrible maggot you come across in an apple. That was the side of things they never told you on the news, people getting shot in the crotch, dying on the lavatory, staggering down the street with no clothes on after an explosion. He remembered his mother telling him in confidence about how dad went through a nudist phase near the beginning of their marriage, having breakfast in his birthday suit, the revulsion on her face as she described it. 'Disgusting, seeing somebody *eat* things in that state.' How even more disgusting to see someone standing in the middle of a bank in that state, how much worse a *bank* was than just eating things, and worse still in the middle of an armed robbery, when onlookers wanted to concentrate exclusively on being scared out of their wits: they wouldn't know whether to laugh or to cry.

The man moved.

John stepped back, turned, hurried out at a walk that had a run humming along inside it so that he banged himself painfully on the swing door. As soon as he was outside in the small corridor he turned back, half expecting to see the enormous form crashing through behind him, the door flung to one side as an irrelevance, as in a horror film. But no, the door was swinging back to normal in smaller and smaller arcs, and then from beyond it came the sound of a faint splashing and the groan of water-pipes. Surely you didn't wash your hands when you were just about to hold up a bank? Why not? It would have a calming effect. Not that the peeing man needed to calm himself, O K then, the other way round, his calmness was so complete that he washed his hands anyway.

John strode up to Mr Hawthorne.

'Mr Hawthorne, can I ask you something?'

Mr Hawthorne looked up muzzily from his desk, as you do when you are disturbed in mid-pornography, untidy about the face.

'Yes, sir?'

'There's a man in the Gents.'

'Oh well,' Mr Hawthorne replied sneerily, 'as least he's not in the Ladies.'

'You know what I mean, a stranger.'

'Perhaps he's a customer.'

'A rough-looking man.'

'We have some rough customers.' There was something uncandid about his eyes which told John he knew the explanation, but had played hard-to-get just too much to admit it. In return, John's own anxiety faded away, but to be consistent he had to fake it, his irritation showing through.

'For heaven's sake, Mr Hawthorne, since when have customers used the staff toilets?'

'He might have got caught short. Mrs Clarke!'

A few yards away Mrs Clarke looked up from her desk. It was typical of Hawthorne to take that upon himself.

'All right, Mr Hawthorne, I'll have a word with Mrs Clarke.'

'There is one thing, sir.' Confidentially: 'Your flies are undone.'

John looked down, appalled. Yes, they were hanging open like a toothless mouth. At least – it could have been worse. With quick clumsy fingers he zippered them up, then, hardly daring, glanced over towards Mrs Clarke again. Her eyes were on his face but they'd left silvery trails in the air where she'd raised them that exact second.

119

'Can I help you, Mr Edwards?' she asked.

He walked over to her desk, enlarging his back to maximum in Hawthorne's direction. Hawthorne made a snuffling sound to show he'd noticed and to indicate contempt. But at least John didn't have to pretend to be alarmed any more.

'I've just had a peculiar experience, Mrs Clarke.'

'Oh dear, have you?'

'In the Gents.'

'In the *Gents*?' She thought for a moment. 'That's not a nice place to have a peculiar experience, I shouldn't think.' She thought again. 'Not that I'm an authority,' she concluded.

'There was a man I didn't know,' he explained, 'bit of a rough type.'

'Oh yes, I know who *he* is. He's the man who's come to mend your car. We didn't think you'd mind.'

'No,' John said, 'of course I don't mind.'

Behind him, Mr Hawthorne suddenly sneezed.

He was somewhere cold and dark. Something ahead of him ran, legs everywhere, skidding twisting stumbling, ran with the franticness that comes with running not quite fast enough but so nearly so that it is still worth going flat out just in case. Raymond sensed rather than saw the tangle of legs knotting reknotting in the dark. He couldn't smell, or rather the smells he experienced were those of his tiny awakeness, sofa dust, semen wrapped in sheep, the sequence of human bums fading away through time.

Now he was beginning to overtake. It felt as though the creature was actually beginning to approach *him*, bobbing testicles its pouchy mouth, anus a nostril, tail alert as its eyes and ears should be, while the other head, ears flattened, nostrils flared, was still careering futilely in the opposite direction. It was simply an animal. It had no smell.

Then he was up to it, his teeth grazing the creature's fur, then securing the top of its leg. Frontwards it continued to strain away, running without any geography, but back to front it suddenly voided, as though speaking turd. Raymond brought his shoulders and front legs up to add to the pressure of his mouth and finally the animal toppled to its side, its legs still running, though now without even the consolation of ground. From the back perspective it rolled cosily into the submissive position, like a bitch before fucking.

Raymond began biting first into the hard depths of its body, to give it pain and calm it. Its movements eventually became intermittent, flurries of struggle, with pauses in between as it acclimatised itself to being dead. Raymond then pressed his teeth more shallowly, and began to tear at the animal's skin, opening it up for consumption. From the backside angle it seemed to bloom red, the body unfolding itself in flesh serrations, agreeing to be meat.

But the dream meat had no taste.

It must be swimming time now. The swimming-pool was a huge box of screams. Stephen hated going inside it. The air was green. His undressed friends were bald, pink, too-near. There was something in the water which made his eyes sting and tasted warm and bad like the water in his bedside cup when he forgot to change it for a while. You were surrounded by the din of invisible screamers. The worst thing of all was having a wee with bare feet on the wet floor of the swimming-pool toilet. But now Stephen longed for all the horribleness of the pool, it was a horribleness in which he belonged, like a horrible home.

He wished he hadn't remembered weeing, it made him want to go now. As soon as he thought about it he felt a ball of wee grow inside him like an orange, round which he wanted to dance, like Indians do when you're tied to the stake. His legs twitched with the need, even though the wee would stay where it was however much it was danced. He glanced around, hoping a Gents would appear before his eyes, as kind and welcoming as a sweet-shop, but wherever he looked there was nowhere to wee, just the busy street and the big buildings on either side.

Then suddenly he remembered, and turned round. There, behind him, was the museum where they kept that worm-thing. When he went with the school to see it they were all sent to the toilets, the girls in one long line, the boys in another. The toilets were just inside, by a big open space where the museum kept all its boring things, clothes people wore in Africa, drums, and a big stone bowl that was used for crunching up corn or something in. The worm that burrowed into people was miles further in, along with the ancient Egyptians.

He felt irritated just thinking of all the things in the museum, his ball of wee made his memories of them go impatient and jumbled. He wondered for a second if he dared to go into the toilet anyway. He pictured himself going through the swing door and walking across to the Gents. Someone would catch him. There were men with uniforms and women behind the big desk who would be able to tell from the way he looked that he was just a wee-er, not somebody who'd come into the museum properly to see the worm.

Suddenly he remembered his first day at school. He'd wanted a wee then as well. He wanted to go all day long but he never went. Whatever the teacher talked about all he thought of was wee. Lots of the other children asked the teacher if they could go and she always said yes and took them to where it was, but they had to go through the door by themselves, and he didn't know if he'd do the right thing when he was inside, so he held it in all day. He told his mother when he came out of school. He felt proud because it had been hard to do, harder than any of the lessons, but she just looked sad, almost as if she was going to cry. The other time she looked like that was when he had his new spectacles. He put them on and her miserable look suddenly became clear.

Stephen turned regretfully back, pivoting on his wee-ball. The blotherin man was shutting and opening his door as usual. Stephen tried to concentrate on him in order to forget how he was feeling. Two students were coming along, right towards the blotherin man. One was a girl with a swirly skirt down to her ankles and a thin little face with big pink spectacles on, that looked as if they were made of sugar. The boy who was with her had a coat on, even though it was a sunny day. It went down to his ankles too, so that they both looked as though they'd got smaller since they'd bought their clothes, though they were still quite tall.

The blotherin man's arm was only long enough for one, so he shut it in front of the boy. To Stephen's surprise, the boy lifted up the arm as if it was a plank of wood, walked through, turned round and lowered it again. Then he patted the blotherin man on the head. The girl put her hand up to her mouth and laughed as grown-ups do when they laugh like children. The blotherin man stood with his arm still out, even though there was nobody inside it. The boy and girl held each other's hands, and began to walk on.

But as they did so the girl looked up, still laughing, straight at Stephen.

He'd known, the same as he knew in class, that she was going to look at him even before she moved her head. In the same way he knew that when she saw him she was going to notice him, not just let him slide past her eyes as ordinary things did. He tried to dead-eye her but didn't have enough time, so his eyes were only half-dead, and still had enough room to let in her look.

She said something to the boy and he turned his head towards Stephen too. Stephen couldn't deaden his eyes any more, with the girl's look jammed in them, so the man saw him as well. Then they both looked around him.

He knew exactly what they were doing, he'd seen grown-ups doing it before. They were looking to see who he was connected to. Grown-ups seemed to be able to see the invisible line that connected you to someone. Sure enough, they both looked back from Stephen to the blotherin man, who was still standing with his arm closed, as if unable to believe the student had escaped.

Then they approached Stephen.

'Shouldn't you be at school?' the girl asked. She glanced down at Stephen's school-bag, which was by his feet. 'That's your school-bag, isn't it?'

Stephen could only answer yes, so he didn't answer at all.

'I won't hurt you,' the girl said. 'I just want to know.'

Stephen looked at her and then away. Her eyes, behind the sugary spectacles, were hard and questioning. They looked like eyes that would never give up. Because he looked away Stephen saw the blotherin man who to his surprise was beginning to run towards him, his arm still held straight out so that he ran awkwardly, as if he was carrying a pole.

'What do you tazza boy?' the blotherin man asked when he'd come up to them. He didn't look at the students or even at Stephen, but kept his eyes downcast. He was walking around near the three of them as if he wanted a wee too. His arm was still poking out.

The students didn't answer him. The girl asked Stephen: 'Is he your dad?'

'No,' Stephen told her.

'*No?*'

'He's not my dad.'

'Who is he then?' asked the girl, actually pointing her finger at the blotherin man, who looked at it in astonishment. Perhaps the fact that the girl had her arm out reminded him he had his out too, and he slowly lowered it to his side.

'Who is he?' the girl asked Stephen again.

'Erma sodn wino, erma,' the blotherin man suddenly said. 'A farkin wino.'

The girl took no notice. 'Who   is   he?' she asked again. She asked each word in turn, like Mr Sherlock did when you couldn't answer, pretending that he thought it must be deafness that caused the problem, not lack of brain.

'A far kin wino,' Stephen answered, repeating the sounds as carefully as he could.

The boy student laughed. 'You're a chip off the old block, you are,' he told Stephen.

'Let's get this straight,' the girl said. 'Your dad's a wino?'

'*He*'s a wino,' Stephen said, looking at the blotherin man.

'And you're a little miniature,' the boy said, laughing. He suddenly leaned on the girl and buried his head in her shoulder, as if he might fall over any minute. The girl shoved him off, but she was laughing too. 'Honestly bosher,' she said, or something like that. Stephen began to have the feeling that everyone here was speaking Chinese.

'The thing of it is,' the girl said.

'The thing of it is,' the boy told her, 'we're going to be bloody late.'

'But what if he doesn't want – ?'

'It's only because they're not middle class. If they were middle class you wouldn't be worrying about what he wanted or didn't want. You wouldn't try to take a middle-class child away from its dad.'

They both stood and looked at Stephen again, as if the boy had been talking to *him* and not to the girl. He tried to understand what had been said. He was nearly in a middle class really, because Miss Allen's class was below his, and there were two classes above. But he didn't want to say anything in case they took him away. The blotherin man was bad enough, but behind him somewhere was the bus and Ann and home. If he was taken off by the boy student and the girl student he would be further away still – behind *them* would be the blotherin man, and then the others.

'Come on then,' the girl said suddenly, and Stephen's heart nearly jumped out of his chest. But she was talking to the boy.

'Bye-ee,' the boy said to Stephen, and gave him one of those little waves you give to babies, when you only wave the top part of your hand. The girl turned away without saying anything at all, and the two of them walked off quickly, arm in arm.

The blotherin man and Stephen looked at each other. 'I *am* in the middle class,' Stephen said, just in case the blotherin man thought that by not saying it he was fibbing.

'Fork the muddy class,' the botherin man told him. 'Er allum muddy class in this here. Allum muddle. Allum bloddy muddle here. Orlerlotonem.'

He suddenly turned round and caught a student straight away. The student and the blotherin man stood looking at each other as if they were both surprised. Stephen's wee, which had gone away somewhere after the students had begun to talk to him, came back again, even bigger than before.

8

One minute she was on time, going on her way quite placidly, or as placidly as you can go on your way when you are scared stiff that you are about to die of breast cancer, and the next, she was late. Normally it was John who did that. He would bumble about in the toilet and the bathroom for an eternity, calling out testily when anyone tried to extract him, in that same foreign language used by rag-and-bone men and people who sold newspapers; and the next thing you knew he was rushing in a fury through the house as if some conspiracy had been holding him back against his will. But Margaret was normally immune from that problem. She could travel towards her deadlines in a gentle curve.

Not that by most people's standards her deadlines were very significant, since she didn't go out to work, but they were still deadlines as far as she was concerned, and she liked to keep to them. But today, when her deadline did matter, when it might even be deadly – she suddenly thought about the word as she rushed around the hall in a sort of frenzy, getting her last-minute things together, dead line, the line between life and death, a line which might fall in front of you, in which case you would be all right, or behind you, in which case you would be dead, or across you, slicing off a breast or two as it came down, like a cheese-wire going through a cheese. Even in her rush she stopped dead, dead again, feeling the smooth pain of the deadline sliding through. Pass me the deadline, nurse, the surgeon would say, and she would hand him a little grip like those that cheesemen pulled on to keep their wire taut, and he would do that and then lower it as if he were lowering the line-drawing of a terrible blade. Her breast, firmed by exposure and terror, would give a cheesy texture to the slice, after a slight initial wobble.

That's enough stopping for nightmarish hallucinations, you have to ration being petrified out of your wits, time to rush once more. She had dressed after trying to have dirty thoughts, cleaned her teeth, and come downstairs with minutes to spare. And then, crazily, she had begun to read the newspaper. Perhaps you could read the newspaper for psychological reasons, like mental patients staring at a wall. She read about Bosnia and the signalmen's strike without taking in a single word. Then she turned the page and read about something else. She turned the page again, and this time an item came into sharp focus: *Vandals Dig Up Corpse.*

Police had found somebody's coffin in Stowmarket, Suffolk, about a hundred and fifty yards from its grave. She had been buried in March, a month ago. It was a she. They didn't say whether the vandals had opened the coffin, but surely they had, you wouldn't go to all that trouble and not. Dead a month, just time for the rot to set in. That would be a good laugh, that would, seeing how she was getting along, how far the rot had got, whether she ponged. Margaret knew, before she even read it, that the woman had died of breast cancer. *The body was that of Mrs Denise Cartwright, aged thirty-eight, who died last month of breast cancer.*

It was a shock to read it even though not in the least a surprise. You could be aware of a terrible blow heading towards you but it was still a shock when it struck. How utterly horrible of those swine to dig her up. All that digging, that hard work, just in order to be complete pigs. They were laughing at her because she was dead, because from a certain point of view being dead is like being severely subnormal. They would laugh at subnormal people too.

Margaret suddenly remembered, while she was sitting in the kitchen reading the newspaper, a subnormal girl she'd known when she was small. Called Christine. She lived down their road when they were living in Offerton. She played with Margaret and her friends even though she must have been thirteen or fourteen while they were six or seven. She didn't wear knickers, because one day Margaret accidentally looked up her skirt and saw something dark and hairy there, which she thought was a small animal, perhaps a rat. It was enough to make you hate and fear sex, not that she ever had. But perhaps those boys did. Perhaps they wanted to laugh at that poor dead woman because she had been a woman, because her breasts had gone wrong, because she was a sexual casualty. You could get blamed or lusted after for your sex even though sometimes it didn't seem to have much to do with you. It was funny to think of Christine being grown up between her legs when she was so silly and childish in her head. As she had when she was jogging, Margaret had a sudden sense of her breasts being things that had been stuck on her, but that didn't make it any easier to picture them being taken off again. She imagined being dug up from her grave, and sobbed out loud.

Raymond came over from the corner of the kitchen and licked her leg by way of comfort. Why did they have to put things like that in the newspaper in the first place? It was playing into the hands of those horrible boys. You couldn't say it was news about the woman because she was dead, no news would ever happen to her again. It was only news about the boys, and who wanted to read about them? She almost felt that the item had been put in the newspaper just to upset her. It was strange how if you had a word on your mind, like breast, wherever you looked you would see breast breast breast everywhere. It could happen with any word. She tried to think of another word it could happen with but for the moment couldn't think of any word but breast.

Now she was running about the hall she *could* think of another word: dead. Breast and dead, our words for today, children.

She'd found her coat with no trouble, and made the mistake of putting it on at once. From then on as she ran around she felt she was in a game where you have to dress up in too much and then do intricate things even though you can hardly move in all your clothes. She couldn't remember what on earth game it was, but it rang such a bell, this feeling of being a parcel on legs and running around getting so hot you begin to think your brains will explode, that she must have played it once upon a time, perhaps as a child. It would have been one of those games that make you want to shriek with rage, like bobbing for apples, and yet all the time, as a final twist of the knife, you have to pretend to be enjoying yourself.

After her coat, her shoes. She could have sworn she'd picked them out of her wardrobe first thing this morning and brought them down into the hall ready for now, and put them under the chair by the telephone table. That must have been a hallucination.

She rushed upstairs. No, not in there either.

She ran downstairs again. Her legs felt short and inadequate as if only the lower half of them, the part that poked out below her coat, really existed. The rest of her was coat and nothing but coat. She hadn't hated a coat so much since that coat her mother had got her from a catalogue all those years ago, the coat from the pit of hell.

Back in the hall she found her shoes in the understairs cupboard straight away, smirking up at her. While she was there she unhooked her brown handbag to go with her coat, unzipped her black one, took her purse out and transferred it, on second thoughts opened her brown handbag, took her purse out again, and opened it to check. Nothing in it, as she'd suddenly guessed. Why was it that when she went into a shop she took such pride in spending the exact amount of change she had on her, to within a useless penny or two, making sure she was cleaned out for the next day? Where the hell was she going to find some money for the bus?, the minutes were ticking by. Stephen! – he was the only member of the family who ever seemed to save anything, bankers or not.

Up the stairs she ran once more, to Stephen's bedroom. His moneybox was on his bedside table. John had pinched it from the bank for him. It was one of those with a combination lock on it, to be given to young investors as an incentive, and of course dear little Stephen, perhaps anticipating the eventuality that somebody in the family would try to filch his money from him, had locked it. There was just a slit at the top where you put the money in, but it would take for ever to slide it out on a knife blade.

She sat on Stephen's bed and cried out in despair. Raymond's answering howl from the kitchen reminded her that this was the second time she'd done that this morning. I'm going to pieces, she thought bitterly, how appropriate. She took a deep breath. There's a solution to everything, she told herself. She turned back to Stephen's moneybox and noticed a slip of paper lying beside it, with a number written upon it: 7P2. He still writes his nines backwards, she noticed with a pang. Dear little chap, he put his secret code right beside his moneybox so anybody could find it. Not expecting that anybody would really want to steal pocket-money from an eight-year-old.

'More fool him,' she said out loud, in sheer self-disgust, and opened the box.

★

He awoke with a cushion in his mouth and the sound of movement upstairs. He whimpered as he examined what he'd done. Quickly he leapt off the settee and through the lounge door. Margaret was coming down the stairs. He hung his head in shame at the thought of the cushion.

She didn't go into the lounge, however, but straight into the kitchen, patting him on the head as she passed. He felt a double shame, once for the cushion and once for the pat.

He remained in the hall but nothing more happened. Like other humans Margaret was unable to smell or intuit a kill, had no instinct for catastrophe. At last, still wary, he trotted into the kitchen.

She was sitting at the table, bent over as so often, fixedly sniffing paper. Raymond had watched her and John do that for many minutes at a time. Raymond went over and sniffed it himself, just to make sure. He could smell ink and beyond that had a vague sense of trees in rows somewhere far away, but nothing to explain Margaret's devout, persistent stance.

He gave up after a moment and trotted over to the corner, where a more interesting smell lay in wait, dog. He sniffed it carefully. Male, medium-sized, short golden fur: himself. It amounted to a rich deposit of homeliness, and giving a small sigh of satisfaction he stepped into it.

Once inside though, and staring out of the smell's invisible cosiness towards the room beyond, he began to wonder what to do next. Margaret was still motionless. He felt he ought to emulate her but had no paper himself to smell. He began to smell the room at large, head pointing slightly away from her. There was nothing out of the ordinary, though, nothing to waste time on. He felt his eyes sliding round to give her a surreptitious look. She didn't look back. He smiled, lolled his tongue, panted slightly. Panting reminded him of his prick, and he bent his head down and inwards to give it a rapid wash. Then he looked up again but she still hadn't noticed him. He began to feel self-conscious, and rolled his eyes around the room, hoping to see something that would take his mind off Margaret and his own unconvincing imitation of her. Nothing offered. He whimpered very softly out of frustration and embarrassment but she didn't notice, and he felt smaller than ever.

Suddenly she sobbed.

It came back to him that he'd done something, what it was he couldn't think, something bad. The stillness had perhaps been the stillness of upset, of disappointment, with the sob finally breaking through when she could hold back her emotions no longer. He got to his feet shakily, trotted over, and contritely licked her leg. She took no notice and he trotted back to where his smell was waiting for him like an undemanding friend. He sat inside it, staring dolefully at the floor.

Margaret leapt to her feet and his heart leapt too. Then sank, as she simply left the room.

He followed her cautiously, peering round the kitchen door to see if she had gone into the lounge, where something bad was waiting. But no, she was standing by the front door, pulling her coat on. She seemed busy and angry, so he went into the lounge to be out of her way. He heard her thumping up the stairs.

On the settee there was a torn cushion. He sniffed it impulsively, greedily, but it had virtually no smell of its own, though in the back of his mind there was a faint after-image of a chase, a kill, tearing at meat . . . The fur on his shoulders stood on end, and he growled. Then it became a cushion once more, and he would get the blame. For a second he had a sudden, general bitterness at how things worked, how everything large-scale, charged, doggish, turned into what was tasteless, inert, without odour, meat metamorphosing into cushions, triumph to blame, wildness to domesticity. Then he was simply aware of his guilt again, and he edged away to the far corner of the room.

From upstairs came a cry. He eyed the ceiling for a moment suspiciously, but no, the sound had remoteness in it, it had nothing to do with what had happened in this room. His heart thumping suddenly with excitement he howled in response.

They all sat in the dead van, facing forward as if they were still going along.

'Brrrm, brrrm,' Ann said, 'toot toot.'

'I'm not going to be able to do it myself this time,' Kevin said. He was still looking intently through the windscreen, as if any moment he might have to take completely stationary avoiding action, swerve to miss a sudden obstacle, weave through difficult traffic, brake to bring the motionless car to an even more stop. 'It's going to have to have a new . . . new part.'

Ann wondered whether he'd avoided naming it because the name would be wasted on the rest of them, or because he didn't know it himself.

'I said all along we should ring,' Philip said.

'You kept on saying it', Ann told him, 'when we were in the middle of nowhere, and there was no sign of a phone. At least we're in a village now.'

'There's no sign of a phone here either,' Philip said self-righteously, as if that clinched his argument.

'Perhaps when we find a garage they'll let us use theirs,' Jessica said.

'There's no sign of a garage, for that matter,' Ann pointed out.

The road they were on was lined with pairs of cottages, their small front gardens full of tulips and fruit trees in blossom, except for one, neglected and overgrown, where some misfit obviously lived. Ann wondered what it was like to be the odd one out in a village where all the women went to the Institute and made jam and all the men talked about carrots, and you had to restrict your rebellion to garden form. The straggly hedge and tussocky grass were an act of green terrorism, detonating very slowly. Add that to the feeling she had of driving along in an unmoving vehicle and Ann experienced a dizzy sense that time had come to a stop or at least slowed right down, like one of those slow-motion nature films. It was a relief to see a standard rose in one of the spick-and-span gardens tottering in some small breeze like a thin girl in high-heeled shoes.

'There's a pub, though,' Philip pointed out. 'It'll have a phone. They can probably tell us where the local garage is, too.'

Sure enough, beyond the houses on the right-hand side there was a small, white-painted pub, the Crown as its signboard announced, displaying an unconvincing painting of a crown clustered with opaque and smeary jewels.

'It won't be open, will it?' Jessica asked.

'Yes, it will,' Philip told her, 'it's half eleven.'

'I'd better go then,' said Kevin, opening his door.

'Hang on a minute,' Philip said, 'it looks a bit off, asking to use the phone when we're not getting anything. Let's order some drinks. I could do with a drink, after everything that's happened this morning.'

132

There was silence. Everyone knew exactly the sort of drinks he meant. Philip looked around the interior of the van with quick movements of his head, like a bird checking every angle.

'They might not, you know, let us in,' Jessica said in her low pure voice.

'Ye gods,' Ann said. 'We're over fourteen.'

'Only just.'

'I'm the youngest of us, and I'm fifteen. More or less. What's only just about that?'

'But they wouldn't serve us – ' she lowered her voice even more, and the word came out like poetry, as if it meant the sweetest sin you could ever imagine, sending tingles up Ann's spine ' – booze.'

I'm completely wrong about Jessica, Ann thought. She's not pure as such, she just doesn't get up to a lot. That's what it was all about, saving your skin, spiritually speaking. She wanted to be pure *Jessica*, for ever and ever amen.

It occurred to Ann that when Jessica's voice went low in order to handle sin, wickedness and above all the possibility of being found out, it sounded terribly exciting, sexy in fact. Males would forgive her pimples, her saintliness, the irritating way her head poked up when she was seated in a vehicle, her amazingly tidy eating habits, for the sake of that voice. Oh God, thought Ann, perhaps I'm a lesbian, understanding such things. But how can I be, when there's something about her that makes me want to puke?

On the other hand, there was something about Philip that made her want to puke also.

'Hang on a minute,' said Philip. 'Let me out. I want to check something.'

Kevin got out so that Philip could push the seat forward and extricate himself. Philip turned back and peered in the van. 'Wait a minute, girls, I'll just spy the place out,' he said. He was so puffed out with importance that his cardigan looked as tight as a drum. Then he turned away and set off towards the pub. He didn't run, probably realising that it wouldn't show him off to best advantage, but walked at high speed like Charlie Chaplin, his active backside contrasting peculiarly with the sluggish gardens and the empty street.

Kevin watched him go, moving his arm ineffectually as if half intending to call him back. Wet nelly, thought Ann. He's the only

133

one of us able to go into a pub and drink himself nasty without breaking the law, and he stands there while Philip does his dirty work for him.

Actually, Philip didn't do much dirty work. He took a look at the pub and came scuttling back. To her surprise, Ann felt disappointed. But then she saw he was looking pleased with himself. He pulled at his collar and waggled his head further out, as if to ensure onlookers could gauge its full beauty while he made his announcement. 'It's all right,' he said. 'They've got tables in their garden.'

They all stared at him blankly.

'We can sit in the garden,' he explained. 'Kevin can go in and get the drinks. Then nobody will know any different.'

'Well,' Ann said, 'you've got it all worked out.'

'We may as well give it a try,' said Jessica. There was that low-pitched throb in her voice again, which could make the right person go weak at the knees.

'I didn't think your crowd believed in the demon drink,' Ann pointed out.

Philip pushed his head through Kevin's doorway again for maximum effect. 'You're thinking of Methodists,' he told her. 'Don't forget the good Lord turned water into wine.'

'I bet a lot of drunks have used that argument.'

'I'm not talking about getting drunk.'

'I am,' Ann said. Keep them guessing, she thought gleefully while she watched Philip's primness evaporate as suddenly as if someone had thrown a bucket of water at him. It wasn't replaced by any expression at all, because he didn't dare have one, not knowing what she was going to say next. He was as blank as an android except for a small red boil on his forehead that looked at her like a passionate eye. 'What's the point of having a drink if you don't get a bit pissed?' she asked.

'Oh, well, yes, a *bit*,' he said. He chuckled, as if relieved that a stupid misunderstanding had been got out of the way. 'There's no reason not to get a *bit*. After the sort of morning we've had.'

By now Stephen's wee was bigger than the morning. He was standing in a huge ball of it which seemed to throb with the beating of his heart. The morning had changed places with it, and had got

134

as little as wee ought to be. Stephen had seen a programme about a car squasher once. You put a car inside it and turned it on and when it was finished all that was left was a small metal box. The morning felt as if it had gone through a morning squasher, and was now all little, with tiny people going up and down a tiny street, like Stephen had been that time when he went as small as an ant and climbed into a Polo.

He could bear it no longer.

He waited until the blotherin man had let a student out of his door and then picked up his school-bag and went over to him. It was hard to walk; each step made the throbbing worse; there was a sort of twanging all round him, right up into the sky.

'Cherwant?' the blotherin man asked.

'I've got to have a wee,' Stephen told him. 'I don't know where to go.'

The blotherin man looked at him sharply. His whole head, except his eyes, seemed to suck back in surprise. 'You go in yr willy,' he said. The further back his head went the more his eyes seemed to brighten. 'In your forkin wally. Whudya no know war ter go? In y'wully you go, if y're not a bloddy girl.' His voice had been getting louder and rougher but now he suddenly lowered it to a whisper, looking round while he spoke to make sure nobody could overhear: 'In yir bliddlin willy.'

Tears sprang into Stephen's eyes at the bigness of his wee on the one hand, and the blotherin man's inability to comprehend on the other.

'But I don't know *where* to *wee*,' he said. He said where and wee with such expression, though not too loudly, that his mouth went into a sort of grin, even while he could feel his tears begin to crawl down his cheeks.

The blotherin man's face sprang back to rejoin his eyeballs, and went bright red. He opened his mouth. A fat blue tongue poked out a little then went back in and made a little clicking noise. His teeth were yellow with black stripes. He smacked himself quite hard on the cheek. Through the pangs of wee Stephen noticed that his hand was as swollen-looking as his tongue, very red, and it had black stripes like his teeth. Then the blotherin man began to grin a huge grin, much bigger than Stephen's accidental one had been, a great big upward-curving grin like the sort of grin you might

135

draw. His teeth weren't in a row, but strung along his lips with gaps between, like dim Christmas lights. He made a funny uck-uck sound, probably by flapping his tonsils, which Stephen realised was a laugh. He grabbed Stephen's shoulder: 'Es ur secrit uva happy life, es ur,' he said, 'knowing where ter put yr willy.'

Stephen looked at the blotherin man and the blotherin man looked at Stephen. That seemed to be the end of the conversation, even though Stephen's wee was twanging now just as if he was walking though he was standing still, or as still as the twanging would let him. He felt frantic at grown-up idiocy, when you tell them something and tell them something, and even though they listen they take no notice, but cock their heads on one side like his mother did sometimes and say how sweet. The blotherin man didn't actually say how sweet, he kept talking about willies, but it was just as bad because he didn't seem to think he had to *do* anything.

I wonder if you can die of wee, Stephen thought. A boy at school called John Bassett had died once and Mr Luckett the headmaster had announced it in assembly. 'I'm very very sorry and sad to have to tell everybody that one of our children, John Bassett, died yesterday as the result of being knocked down by a car.' The teachers were all crying and all the girls, and some of the boys, though Stephen saw one or two of them grinning as if Mr Luckett had said something funny. The infants were crying so loudly that it almost hurt your ears. Some of the children said that John Bassett's head had gone flying off. There was a lot of whispering about it.

Now Stephen tried to imagine Mr Luckett saying 'I'm very very sorry to tell everybody that one of our children, Stephen Edwards, died yesterday as the result of wee.' All the boys would laugh to hear that, most of the girls too, and the infants would laugh most of all. They always laughed at words like wee. Probably even some of the teachers would laugh. Stephen felt a lump of unwanted laughter rising in his own chest, just as that sob had risen when he was sitting on the bus earlier in the morning. He tried to make his throat tight so it wouldn't come up. If he laughed now there would be such an enormous twang that it wouldn't be just his head flying off but his whole body, like Ann's had when she disappeared from the world before she came driving up in that van that was kidnapping her. He suddenly remembered about her being kidnapped. Fancy forgetting it in the first place. His wee had made Ann being kidnapped go very small like everything else.

'I'll take yi for a piss off,' the blotherin man said. He wasn't smiling any more. He cocked his face in puzzlement. 'Fra piss off?' he asked. He shook his head and sighed like teachers do when somebody has made a mistake. 'Carlya rond di black wid me,' he then said, grabbed Stephen's shoulder again, and began to push him down a pathway beside the museum.

They went round a corner and there was a little space at the back of the museum, with a wall around it and some dustbins inside. Some steps led down to a small secret door. Beyond the wall was a big yard, with cars parked in it, and people walking across, but the walled space was deserted. There was a lump of grass growing out of the paving near the bottom of the wall.

'Do yer willy in her about. War I have a drink, about, wan I have un. Wan nare abod ter kip un eye un you. Wun yer ov a little secret drink like.' He winked at Stephen, raised an invisible bottle to his lips, threw his head back, and drank invisible drink out of it noisily. 'Gar,' he then said, 'when I av a donk on, a dink in, when I av a dink on me like, an av a bit uv a dink uv it like.'

Stephen pulled the zip of his trousers down and began to wee. He aimed it at the lump of grass to stop it going everywhere. He wanted to go so much that it hurt as it came out. It fizzed up round the grass-stalks like the top of dad's beer. Some of it leaked out of the lump of grass and began to run across the ground. The ball of wee got smaller so that soon it was only the same size as him, then it was smaller than him, then it was just a ball inside his stomach like normal wee, then it had all gone, leaving an ache behind. He could feel his insides tumbling back into the space his wee had left.

He pulled up his trouser zip and turned round. He was worried the blotherin man might have been watching but the blotherin man had his back to him and was facing the wall of the museum, almost as if he was doing a wee himself, though none was coming out. He seemed to be talking quietly to the wall. He took no notice of Stephen but carried on talking in a sort of burble. Stephen tried to listen to what he was saying but it was too low and there didn't seem to be any words in it. But as he watched he noticed that the blotherin man's face was getting less red and then he understood what he was doing. The wall of the museum was a yellowish-grey colour, and he was taking some of that colour out of the wall into his face. A dot of yellow-grey had appeared on the end of his nose, which was the nearest part of him to the wall, and little fingers of the same colour began to appear on his cheeks. Stephen looked to see if any blotherin redness had appeared in the wall, in return, but there was no sign: the wall was so big it had probably swallowed it all up.

After a while, the blotherin man's eye saw Stephen, and he stepped back from the wall.

'Are you all right now?' he asked. His voice had changed again, as though its belchiness had gone into the wall along with the redness from his face, and a harder, more wallish voice had gone into the man instead.

Stephen was about to tell the man that he was all right now he'd done his wee when he suddenly remembered he wasn't all right at all. His sister was kidnapped; he should be at school; he was miles from home and didn't know how to get back.

'I want to go h–' he said. Home was one of those words that must live in your head very near to where crying is, so that if you want to cry at all when you say it, the crying would stick to the word and come out along with it. That is what happened this time. Stephen actually said home but there was so much crying along with it that the ome part got washed away, and just left the first letter.

'Ah well,' the man said, 'I got what I come here for. It's time for me to go home too.'

John wrote the wiperman a cheque.

'This is one little bugger that won't bounce on me,' the man said, stuffing it into the upper pocket of his overalls. 'Getting it straight from the horse's mouth, like. It's nice being in a bank manager's office for once without getting a bollocking. All you want now is plenty of nice dry weather so you can enjoy not having your wipers going. I guarantee when you turn them off, off they'll bloody stay.'

'It was good of you to come out.'

'No trouble. Got me out from under the gaffer's thumb for a while. I'll nip into the Griffin for a quick pint, nobody the wiser. Made me day, mate. See you.'

He turned and walked out with big loose strides, not at all like

138

the way people normally shuffled around the bank. He walked as he peed, as if he could do each of the things he did in turn, without worrying about the rest of his life while he did them. Yet bank managers bollocked him and his gaffer kept him under his thumb, unless all that was only being polite, said to please the rest of mankind who had to spend their existences worrying what other people thought of them.

Like me.

John remembered the other day, meeting Gardiner in the car-park. When worms turn, they remain worms, that was the problem.

Monday had been bleak, a different season from today. The wind was like a door slammed in your face. There were bits of hard stuff in it, pellets of frozen rain. The greyness of the day was almost blue, and the people going past the front of the car-park looked like scurrying grey animals in the blue dimness. The weather was so depressing it almost cheered you up, made you feel reckless, feel like turning.

As John was leaving for home, Gardiner was arriving back from somewhere. They met in the car-park, with the elements howling all round.

He couldn't pretend to understand what was going on in Gardiner's head. The man had only been in the branch six months, and wasn't a social animal. Margaret hadn't had a chance to meet him yet, and John was aware that to some extent he took his cue about people from her. Gardiner's hardness and cynicism were threatening from one point of view, though from another they seemed to suggest that only a mug would take the bank seriously in the first place.

'You must be in a hurry for your tea,' Gardiner said, his words bandied about by the wind.

Why bloody not, John thought, I give my mornings and afternoons to this place, isn't that enough? A piece of rain stung him in the eye. He'd actually stayed on for Gardiner's return long after everyone else had gone, except for Hawthorne, who always made sure he remained till the bitter end, presumably so he didn't miss anything.

'It's gone six, sir,' John said. 'Mr Hawthorne said he'd stay inside till you came in.'

139

'I would prefer it if my *deputy* stayed in charge, when I'm away.'

Quite without warning John became angry. What was so odd and in retrospect so sickening was that he became confiding as well. He talked about the bank not caring about you as an individual, treating its employees like children, there being more to life than trying to please people further up the ladder. He had the hostile fluency you normally only achieve when you're drunk.

Gardiner watched him with great attention, amusement and curiosity in his gaze, his face containing the sort of detached, ironic expressions you'd expect in a warm dry room, not out here on a windy car-park. Sometimes John felt Gardiner was being sympathetic; at other times he thought perhaps neutral, like a doctor inspecting a symptom: both reactions served to make John more voluble, more determined to present his case.

It became a harangue. He said that the staff mortgage privileges were like tied cottages for farm labourers: they hooked you up to the bank until you got to the stage when you would no longer be able to survive in the outside world – until it owned you body and soul. As he spoke he felt very quick-witted, with a sharpness like that of drink which enables your mind to go ahead of your words, for a while at least, until it falls behind them. Well, not your body and soul, he said, just your body, but that's a fat lot of use, since your soul's stuck in your body anyway until you die, so if they have the one they might as well have the other along with it.

Gardiner cocked his head, round which the wind whooshed and howled, twitched his lips; his eyes sparked intelligently, with the quiet promptness of the band-counter on John's compact-disc player, registering item nine, deputy manager complains his soul stuck in body . . . A hostile or even argumentative response would have reminded John that this was war and brought him to a stop, but no such luck.

They don't want initiative, they just want you to jump through hoops, he remembered saying that. And Gardiner looked and looked, perhaps amused, perhaps sympathetic, possibly amusedly sympathetic. What in the name of sanity had initiative got to do with it? The issue under discussion was John's leaving early. What sort of initiative did it show, wanting to go home for your tea? As he thought about it now, he blushed in the solitude of his office.

And he'd talked about pay. I look at the adverts in the paper, accountants get more or less what I do, to *start* with. Plus car. I've been working for the bloody bank, yes, he'd said *bloody* bank, half my life. Gardiner passed up the opportunity to say more fool you, if you'd wanted out you should have got out. Gardiner was often uncouth when he spoke, but he kept silent with complete urbanity. John had also gone on about the lack of promotion prospects. Gardiner had got *his* promotion, what did that suggest?

As he ranted on, John eventually began to get slightly uneasy. It was as though the first chill of sobriety started to creep in. But instead of slowing him down it made him rant more, just as sometimes you have to gobble when your stomach is feeling queasy. He wasn't making particular points any more, just moaning: for two pins I'd chuck it in, makes me sick, glorified salesman, place run by computers anyway, I'll do what I have to do, not a stroke more.

At last he stopped. He'd said every word there was to say; they must have been building up inside him for years.

Gardiner patted him on the arm. 'Get it off your chest, that's my lad,' he said, and went in.

John stood quite still, not daring to move, not knowing where he was. He felt as if his harangue had converted Reddish into an alien land. He was glad of the nasty conditions; if anything, he'd prefer them to be worse. He had the sort of feeling you must get if in a moment of exuberance you take off all your clothes at a party, and then discover that it's not *that* sort of party, and you wait there like a statue, hoping the frost will bite deep.

Gardiner had gone off quite cheerfully, though.

'Oh shit,' John said out loud to the wind. He had suddenly remembered that the quarterly branch review was due this week, Gardiner's opportunity to evaluate the performance of his staff for the benefit of the powers-that-be. For a moment he almost took gloomy satisfaction in the thought of such total catastrophe. He'd had the funny feeling, having said all he wanted to say, that somehow he hadn't been quite honest, even though he meant every word of it. You could tell the truth and in telling it turn it into a sort of lie. He turned that around in his mind for a second: it gave him an excuse for remaining rooted to the spot. The raindrops had softened slightly and become more frequent, so his hair was beginning to get wet. What happened was that you told the truth and that made you into a truth-teller. But he wasn't a truth-teller, he was just someone who'd lost his temper. He might just as easily have told a lie if a lie had been to hand. But the fact that his tirade would destroy his future prospects gave it some kind of retrospective integrity. He would have to pay out of all proportion, pay for each word over and over again.

Why should it make a difference? Managers wrote quarterly reviews every quarter. If it hadn't been this week it would have been next, or next month, the month after, some time in the near future. But that *would* have been a difference. He would have had time to get back to normal. The sting of the truth would die away and he'd be left with just a faint aura of the truth-teller. Gardiner would simply remember, as he watched him go about his routine duties, that somewhere inside him there was a bit of fire after all. *That*'s why the whole episode had felt like a lie. But with Gardiner putting pen to paper this very week, John's revelations would be uppermost in his mind. He wouldn't even need to make recommendations about John's future, John had done it for himself: recommended that he shouldn't have one.

It was now raining normally. Drops were coursing down John's face like tears. The lights from premature headlamps looked wobbly in the downpour, as if from a dying galaxy. John swept his fingers through his hair with sudden decisiveness, the released lumps of water landing in a distinct sequence on his upper back. What I'm going to have to do, he thought to himself, is beard Gardiner.

Even now, three days later, he still didn't know what he meant by it. Beard wasn't a word he normally used, not in that sense, whatever that sense was. But perhaps that was just as well, a new word for a new situation. He would go up to Gardiner and say something, some magic word, *beard* him, and Gardiner would look tight and suspicious for a while, and then his features would relax, he'd give a constipated nod, and the situation would be back to normal. The worm would have turned back.

As he thought about it now, panic set in, John felt it fluttering in his stomach. It was all very well to pin your faith on bearding, but today was the day it had to be done. This very day the quarterly report would be written.

There was nothing he could do about it at the moment. Gardiner had some sort of medical appointment this morning, so he wouldn't be putting pen to paper until later on. In any case, John had enough on his plate this lunch-time. What he needed to do was to push all his worry and anxiety, that horrible fiddling sense of unfinished business, ahead of him until two o'clock this afternoon, and enjoy the empty space that was left before then. Take things one at a time. He'd read somewhere, probably in some damn women's magazine, where he got most of his information about the world, that when people are terminally ill they often forget about it for hours at a time, find themselves living their lives just as if they have lives to live. That's what he must do.

There was a knock on the door. It wasn't the usual impersonal rap, but softer, more intimate, a kind of knock whisper. His voice trembled as he said come in.

9

The pub table was tip-tilted, like a small aircraft after a bad landing, though the balding lawn seemed flat enough. They had followed a little sign that pointed down the side of the pub and said Beer Garden. It was this sign that had been Philip's great discovery, and he'd ushered them round as though he owned the place, peering at the pub windows occasionally just in case anyone was taking too great an interest in them from inside.

'Nobody can see us from the road, that's the important thing,' he said.

The back of the pub was shabbier than the front, as if it couldn't be bothered to keep up appearances. A row of metal beer barrels waited by the back door like fat grey dwarfs, not unlike Philip as a matter of fact, who seemed to fill his body to bursting with glee and importance.

'What are we going to have?' he asked, for all the world as if he was going to pay for it or fetch it, neither of which he had any intention of doing. He was one of those people who couldn't bear to be a civilian. He went through life in a purple suit with gold epaulettes, carrying a torch to show you to your seat.

'I'll have a sweet Martini with lemonade,' Jessica said, in the husky voice she had acquired for evil-doing.

'A sweet Martini with lemonade, check,' Philip said. There was a pause. 'What about you, Ann?' he asked. 'The same?'

You must be joking, Ann thought. I wouldn't be seen dead drinking one of those gloppy female drinks.

'A glass of dry white wine,' she said as crushingly as possible, though it was lost on Philip who just said a glass of dry white wine, check. He couldn't care less about the details, she could have said a pint of brandy and he would have said check. The only thing that concerned him was that alcohol was about to be poured into people, particularly girls.

'I think I'll have a pint of lager,' Kevin said.

'I'll have the same,' Philip announced.

'Well, now we know,' said Ann.

'I wish you wouldn't be so cynical,' Philip said unexpectedly.

'What's there to be cynical about?' she asked. 'We're having a drink, not discussing the existence of God.'

He gave her a long look, but didn't say anything more. He hadn't been talking about God-cynicism, as she very well knew, but orgy-cynicism. You might not want somebody being a cold fish when you're about to perform an act of worship, but you'd want them being one even less when you're arranging an act of wickedness. Sin and depravity can slip through your fingers even more quickly than God. Anyway he was wrong, she wasn't really being cynical, she was just being awkward.

'Right then, Kevin,' Philip said finally. 'You know what we want?'

Kevin got to his feet slowly, one bit at a time, like a giraffe rising. He'd obviously forgotten he'd have to do all the work. Perhaps he'd been taken in by Philip's bustle. He stood quite still when he'd at last climbed up the long slope of himself.

'It's a sweet Martini –' Philip began, by way of prompt.

'Not that again,' Ann said.

'I know what it is,' Kevin agreed. He set off towards the back door of the pub. He walked without force, as if he found the air too thick. She suddenly realised that he was nervous. He was worried that people in the pub might guess he was buying booze for a gang of under-age evangelicals on the rampage. She felt some sympathy for him. She didn't mind him being nervous, it was being wet and dim she objected to, unable to knock the skin off a rice pudding, as her mother liked to say. Not that she was nervous like that herself. If she was in that position, and the landlord found her out, she would make a cutting speech, probably on the scruffiness of the pub's back garden, and leave in style. But it would do Kevin good, a trial by ordeal.

Which he survived. A few minutes later he emerged from the

back door carrying a tray. Ann watched it approach them dead level, while Kevin's body made gangly uncoordinated movements above and below it. There was something nice about him trying so hard: when the tray arrived not a drop had been spilt.

Kevin lowered the tray on to the table.

'The mother-ship has landed,' Jessica said, to Ann's amazement. It was so unlike the sort of things she normally said she might just as well have had a brain transplant.

'Well,' said Philip. He stood up and took over, doling out the drinks Kevin had paid for.

'How much was mine?' Ann asked.

'That's all right,' Kevin said.

'I still believe it's the male's job to foot the bill, where possible,' Philip said. 'Call me old-fashioned.'

'I'll call you something else,' said Ann. '*You* didn't foot the bill, Kevin did.'

'It's all *right*,' Kevin said.

'Well, Philip will pay for the next one, won't you, Philip?' Ann asked sweetly. 'Being a male and everything.'

'They've got a phone in there,' Kevin said. 'I'd better try to find a repair shop.'

'Have your drink first,' said Philip. 'We've had a terrible morning. It's time we relaxed.'

'I thought you were in such a hurry,' Ann reminded him.

'That was before I had a drink in front of me,' he replied with sudden honesty.

'That's all right then,' Ann said, raising her glass. 'Cheers.'

'Cheers,' agreed Jessica. She had starey eyes and a fixed this-is-how-I'll-look-when-I'm-pissed-as-a-fart smile, which showed just the bottoms of her upper teeth. It was like that moment in the movies when the librarian takes a clasp out of her hair, gives it a shake, removes her spectacles and, hey presto, she's become a nymphomaniac.

They drank up quickly, all aware of the need to fit in as much as they could before the real world of broken-down vans and hoe-down sandwiches caught up with them.

'I'm hungry,' said Philip. 'I don't know about anybody else.'

'You can get hot food or sandwiches inside,' Kevin said, 'but the sandwiches are two quid a throw.'

'That's a rip-off,' said Jessica. 'I'd rather spend the money on drink.' Her voice went tiny with the last word, and she laughed a tiny laugh to match. She looked at the rest of them, chin tucked into chest, out of the top of her eyes to see if they were appreciating her.

'Oh yes,' said Philip, his voice trembling, no doubt at the thought of what drink meant when Jessica said it in that way.

At that very moment Ann had an inspiration. She only ever had inspirations about what was completely obvious. She could walk along the street and the thought would strike her out of the blue that one day she was going to die, and she'd feel a terrible chill, as though it had been kept secret from her before. Or she would realise that her mother had some deep unspoken sadness. This time her inspiration was that Jessica was stuck with Philip.

Of course she was, Kevin was her brother. It had been inevitable from the start but hadn't struck Ann, for some stupid reason. She hadn't thought about the foursome from Jessica's point of view, only from her own, and with Philip grubbing about in her direction on the back seat of the van she'd taken it for granted that she would end up having to keep him at bay – or alternatively have his lips approach her just as they did the surface of his lager, like manoeuvrable thrusters on a spacecraft, or the mouths of one of those horrible fish that you see in aquariums sucking up rubbish from the bottom of the tank. She'd been kissed by lips like that before and didn't care to repeat the experience.

The perpetrator was called Jamie Davies, undersized and a know-all. While he was kissing, which seemed to last for ever, there was a fizzing sound and then a thick splash, like somebody's foot going into a bog. Her fear was that for the rest of her life she would hear that sound whenever a kiss came along. If you could imagine a revolting kiss walking round on two legs, looking like a small green and grey barrel, its name would be Philip.

But Philip wouldn't be squelching in her direction, she now realised. Not while Jessica was present. The only pairing that was possible was between Jessica and Philip on the one hand and herself and Kevin on the other. She looked at Kevin with new eyes, as you do at anything that you know could be yours. There was a lot to be said for the way he never pushed himself at the world in general, or at Ann in particular, a kind of gentlemanly modesty about it. He would only kiss when and if required, probably clonking his head en route. And if a kiss *could* be dry, his would be. Also she decided she liked his tallness. He might be gangly but at least he wasn't squashed together under pressure. There was always that feeling with barrels that they might explode at any moment, and drench you from head to foot.

'It seems silly,' Philip went on, 'paying through the nose, or going hungry, when we're chock-a-block with sannies in the van.'

There was a pause while the rest of them took this in. Even Jessica, despite her sudden conversion to wickedness, widened her eyes. The red spot on Philip's forehead caught the sun and flashed. Ann's insides seemed to glow and flow downwards, like lava. This she realised, was the moment of truth. Eating those sandwiches that belonged to the hoe-down, nicking them in fact, would be like opening a door. Once through it, and anything could happen. Knowing you have to repent sooner or later is very liberating, since you might as well be hung for a sheep as for a lamb.

There was a long silence, at the end of which, without anyone opening his or her mouth, you could tell they'd agreed. 'All right then,' Philip said. 'I'll go over to the van and get some. Perhaps Kevin could fetch some more drinks while I'm gone.'

'It's one thing boozing under-age,' Ann said. 'But if we start eating sandwiches we haven't bought here, they'll do their nuts.'

'Oh yes,' said Philip, subsiding disappointedly.

'We don't want to get into trouble,' Jessica said, sounding very unsexy for once at the prospect of being flung out of the pub garden for eating a forbidden sandwich.

But Philip wasn't deflated for long. 'What about this?' he asked. 'We get another round of drinks in, and at the same time buy a bottle or two of something. We could get cider. That comes in big bottles. Then we go and fetch the sandwiches from the van and take it all off to a field somewhere and have a picnic. How does that sound?'

'That sounds brilliant,' said Jessica, swooping down low once more.

'There's that blanket in the back of the van,' said Kevin.

'Ho,' said Philip.

'Which we could sit on,' Kevin explained. 'It's probably got a bit of oil on it,' he added.

'All right then,' Philip said. 'Same again, everybody?'

'What about phoning a repair shop?' Kevin asked.

'The repair shop will probably be closed for lunch now,' Philip said, 'so we might as well have *our* lunch first, instead of just hanging about.'

'But I thought that's what we'd come to the pub for, to use the telephone,' Kevin pointed out.

'Let's have a rest from telephones for a while. I'm fed up with the whole subject,' Philip announced.

Margaret went, taking her howl with her. Raymond had a sense of it trembling inside her locked body, waiting to be let out again. She was going to a howling place, he could smell it on her – a place lit by the moon, where heads would moan in unison, lips drawn back, teeth gleaming in the dark light. Raymond's fur bulged on his neck and front haunches; a gob of saliva dropped from his mouth and landed with a tock on the kitchen floor.

He put his paw in his empty, food-encrusted bowl and spun it away across the floor. A splatch of light made a circle in the middle of the room. He approached it, muscles fluent as if he were approaching the elemental place Margaret had found; and then used his nose to discover the light's trajectory. He sniffed. It was too thick and yellow for the moon. He looked upwards along it, through the window to sun dazzle, and a whine rattled in his throat. Margaret's dark destiny melted away in the gold. It was brightness and warm air he pined for now, the recent smells of passing cats like invisible furry walls across the lawn; the sudden flurry of birds; the flavours of pee and crap on the breeze.

He raised his front legs to scrabble at the sunbeam, and then dropped them down again, knowing it wouldn't hold his weight. He walked round and sniffed it from the other side. He put his front paws in the circle of light upon the floor, narrowed his shoulders, brought his back paws up to meet the front, pointed his muzzle up the beam, shrugged his whole body until it was solid body, as narrow as possible with no spaces in between, and tried to put himself entirely in the light; but bits and pieces of him kept falling into the coolness of the room all round. Finally he gave up and tumbled out completely.

He got to his feet and stood quite still. He smelled and listened and looked as hard as he could, in the hope that something would turn up. After a few moments something did, a shimmer of air with warmth in it, faint but definite, like the faintness of striped light beneath trees. And along with the warmth, a quality of out-sideness, of freshness, the tiniest suggestion of garden scents. Raymond turned to check the original spot of light but it held its position with shaky exactitude: this was different. He turned back and sensed again: the outsideness became sketchy, tore into ten-drils, elongated, thinned to lines in the air; then bulged towards him again, as a new waft entered from somewhere. As he pressed his nose into it, he felt it part and then flow past each side of his face. His ears trembled as it caught them on its way. Then it sub-sided.

He stepped forward and found it again, a rich new flow of air that had a leading edge so distinct his muzzle skidded upwards over it, as though it were an invisible meniscus. Suddenly he was jump-ing into it and bolting out of the kitchen, along the hall, up the stairs, the outdoor scents getting more dense and narrow as he went, until by the time he turned into John and Margaret's bed-room the cross-section was a distinct if fuzzy rectangle angling down from above and, as he curved his head to track it, the edges sharpened to coincide exactly with the frame of an open quarter-light at the top of the bedroom window.

Whimpering as he went, Raymond leapt across the room, scrab-bled up to the sill, and stretched up, front legs rotating, till his nose poked into the aperture. He shook from head to foot as the smell of the garden saturated him inside and out. As he smelled, the scene flowed up towards him; lawns, earth, tulips, garden sheds and trees liquefied in the sharp and sunny air and were sucked in by his nos-trils; craps called in dark or pale voices from many corners far and near. And something else, acrid, rank, scurrying.

Raymond rolled his eyes down without disturbing his upwardly blissful nose and immediately caught what looked like a section of autonomous grey smoke uncurling on the lawn. He watched it severely while his nose reached towards the panoply of scents.

The squirrel stopped in mid-stride, front paw raised, tail trem-bling while all the rest of it was completely still. Raymond threw himself at the opening, his nose flattening and bending back against the ungiving glass of the raised quarterlight; one front paw scratched hopelessly at the window-arm and the other clung to the window-frame by its wrist while his whole body swung. Then he fell backwards, twisting to become four-legged again, his muzzle knocking the window-sill on the way past, making his teeth clack and his eyes and nose water. He whimpered, scampering back across the room as if he'd suddenly met up with an unexpected enemy. Then, totally unconvinced by the charade but determined to persist in it out of sheer rage, he crept exaggeratedly back to the window and poked a single eye over the sill. The squirrel was still in the same place, sitting up now, its tail gracefully rising behind its back while it nibbled something in its paws with its fast little face.

Once again Raymond leapt up the window. This time his head clonked the end of the window-arm on its way up, and dislodged it; the window swung shut against his nose, and again he fell backwards.

He jumped up immediately, transferring all his squirrel hate to the quarterlight. His nose didn't hurt, it just felt numb, as though another nose was touching his own, as a strange dog's does when you kiss in the park. His paws hit the quarterlight first and pushed through; his head followed, and then part of his back. Straddled in mid-air, he stuck fast.

His rear paws felt downwards for the sill, but couldn't reach it, his front paws slid futilely across the outside surface of the main window-pane. Out of the corner of his bitter eye he saw the squirrel scurrying complacently away.

The hospital employees trotted about bearing cups of tea like those things people bear in religion, chalices or whatever they were, holding aloft their little pots of steaming liquid. Some of them were fully-fledged nurses, in uniform and with those special legs nurses seem to have along with policewomen, sensually curved, in dark stockings with a seam, culminating in functional shoes. Others were only partly nurses, with civilian suits and woollies, and a loose white coat on top, so that the effect was a bit like seeing a swan with some of its brown cygnet plumage still in evidence, though most of them were more like ducks than swans, and their eternal jolly talking among themselves seemed to Margaret like quack quack quack. Finally there were the complete civilians, size fourteen minimum, figure eights to a woman, rubbery-featured, frizzy-haired, face-powdered, lowest of the hierarchy but still with their consolatory cup of tea, badge of office.

The patients, one on every possible chair, had no cups of tea of course, and sat bereft. They were not members of this place but victims of it. Some of them pretended to read magazines but most of them stared ahead. A few of them had their husbands along too, offering consolation by dint of installing their bottoms on the adjoining seat. What was galling was that Margaret had a husband installed on the next seat too, but he wasn't hers. He was a big man who'd more or less overlapped the vacant chair beside him when she approached, but it *was* the only vacant one, and she'd asked if it was taken.

'No,' he told her, charmlessly.

She'd naturally assumed that his wife was the woman on the other side, but when that woman's name was called, very shortly afterwards, neither of them spoke, looked, touched, did anything that might suggest they were connected, prior to her departure. Possibly their relationship was on a very low heat, but if that was the case it was odd he should have bothered to come along at all. The annoying part about it was that newcomers to the room would assume she, Margaret, belonged with him. Out of the corner of her eye she glimpsed a threadbare head, fleshy cheeks, dense nostril hair, and felt that this was a bit of ownership she could do without.

Why did she think of husbands all the time? She ought to stand in the world on her own two feet, as much herself as a tree is a tree, or a daisy is a daisy, or a sheep is a sheep. Except that soon she mightn't be as much herself as those things; in a breast sense, she wouldn't be able to stand on her own two feet at all.

'Bit of a wait,' the man said suddenly.

For a moment Margaret wasn't sure whether he was speaking to her or not. His face was still set forward, but when she looked she saw that his eyes had swivelled and were giving her the greedy stare of someone hoping to have an overture replied to. It was oddly familiar, that stare, from some other situation in life apart from awkward conversations. She suddenly remembered it was the look a baby gave you, seated in its high chair, while you prepared its meal. Candid baby-hunger, coupled with a fear of some mis-understanding which could mean the heated glop being used for a different purpose altogether. She almost wanted to laugh at the in-congruity of the picture: an elephantine baby with nostril hair.

Nerves. How do people cope with nostril hair?, she asked herself, doesn't it impede breathing? And how disgusting when you have a cold. John was beginning to develop nostril hair, but not those animal tufts.

'It looks like it,' she replied.

There was a pause. His eyes still showed worried greediness but he obviously couldn't think what to say next.

'Is your wife inside?' Margaret asked.

The greed faded and the eyes looked blank.

'Being seen,' she explained.

'Oh. Yes,' he replied. Then his eyes flicked away. 'No,' he added.

'Ah,' Margaret said, and nodded stupidly, as if she quite understood.

His eyes returned. They had grown up a few years, the eyes of a child caught in a fib, and with some explaining to do. Hot eyes, hot as those of a lobster looking up at you from its bubbling pan. Not that she and John had ever run to lobsters, financially or emotionally, even on an anniversary. Lord, she must remember to buy some steak on the way home, or they'd be stuck with that chicken.

'It's me,' he whispered hoarsely.

'Is it?' she whispered back.

He nodded.

She suddenly felt out of her depth, as if she'd signed for something without knowing what on earth it was. 'What's you?' she asked.

'Being here. Seeing the quack.'

'Oh,' she replied. 'I see. It's *you*, being here.'

'Yes,' he said glumly, and switched his eyes to the front again.

She still felt not with it. 'They don't do just, um, then?' she asked. How stupid, not to be able to say the word. It had been written up on a beastly sign shaped like a pointing arm just outside: Breast Clinic.

'Yes, yes they do. They just do that, as far as I know.'

'Oh.'

'I've got a lump on my breast,' the man told her. His eyes had aged half a century, and he spoke with testy superiority. 'I've had a mammogram, the lot. Now they've got to decide what to do next.'

Suddenly his tone changed completely and for one awful moment Margaret thought he was going to sob: 'I keep imagining what it would look like if they put it in the local rag. Stockport man dies of breast cancer. What a way to go. Sometimes I think that's the worst part, the whole thing being like a not-funny joke.'

'It's like a not-funny joke for women, too,' she said, 'if that's any consolation.'

'Not as funny, and not as not bloody funny, as it is for men,' he replied, still in a rough whisper. This time he didn't sound rude or superior but oddly as if, despite what he said, he actually did see a funny side to it. You would have thought he'd aged again, if there'd been any more scope for ageing.

'I suppose not,' she said doubtfully. She tried to imagine being a man and having your breast off. It would be very embarrassing of course but it wouldn't be a mutilation like it was for a woman. You would still be able to go swimming – people would see the scar and just think you'd had an accident of some sort. Swimming? For heaven's sake, who cared about swimming?, it was sex and motherhood that mattered. And not even sex and motherhood as such but the *idea* of them. She would never be mother to a baby again anyway, but she wanted to feel that she was the same person who had been once. And if, out of a sort of absent-mindedness, she and John never got round to having sex again for the rest of their lives, that wouldn't itself be a tragedy. What mattered most was knowing at the back of your mind that you could have sex if you so wished, that you were still a sexual being, no, not being, animal, a sexual animal. If you stopped being an animal, what on earth was left? The holy aspect, the angel concealed within. Angels presumably didn't have private parts, they had wings instead. But Margaret wouldn't have anything to have wings instead of. Nance had wanted to be an angel, at least to a degree. But however hard you tried, you couldn't soar very high. Margaret remembered what John's father had said about Nance praying that the washing-machine would stop shaking about. While you were alive you were of the earth earthy, there was no getting away from it. Being dead was another matter, of course.

If a man died from breast cancer he'd be just as dead as if he'd been a woman dying from it. That much she could allow him.

'Have you told anybody?' she whispered almost inaudibly. All the other patients, even the ones with husbands here, were sitting in silence, though Margaret had a sense that deep down inside they were like a pack of animals in the wilderness, howling desolately at the moon.

'No.'

'Nor have I.'

They both looked away from each other. She felt embarrassed at their sudden secret.

At that moment in walked the nurse who called people into the consultation rooms. She was fully in white, not one of the in-between ones, with serious teeth and sharp features. Normally she stood in the middle of the room, and called out 'Mrs Whoever-it-Was' in a stern voice, as if Mrs Whoever-it-Was had been spotted doing something she oughtn't behind the lid of her desk. This time though she didn't say anything. Her upswept spectacles brought her eyes into sharp focus. They surveyed the glum out-patients and then fixed abruptly on, oh God no, on Margaret herself: and the nurse began to walk towards her. Instead of screaming Margaret found herself grinning cheerily in greeting. Then the nurse was leaning over the man next to her, and whispering in his ear.

The man nodded, and rose to his feet.

The nurse had refrained from calling out his name in order to spare him the shame of everyone knowing his breast was to be in-spected. People would think he was being asked in to comfort his wife. The nurse's thoughtfulness made Margaret want to burst into tears. All day long, and half the night, ever since those beastly re-volving thoughts in the small hours, she'd been waiting for something predatory to come along, and the nurse, with her prominent teeth and general thrustingness, seemed at last to be it, that dreaded shark, small enough and human enough to be real. But she wasn't, she was someone with enough understanding to want to spare this man's feelings. And kind enough not to be sum-moning Margaret herself for the time being: some of her near-tears were in gratitude for that.

The man didn't look round. He just strode off in the nurse's wake. Margaret felt terribly alone. At least having to talk to him had given her something to do apart from feeling scared. But now she'd better get back to fear, boring as it was. It was like doing a re-petitive, fiddly and long-drawn-out chore, the terror equivalent of ironing. A picture of Mr Mandela wielding a scalpel formed in her mind like a familiar ghost in a haunted house.

And then she was struck by a different type of misery altogether. A different league of misery. Something fleeting in the depths of her head registered a sort of pride at the sheer immensity of it.

She'd been the victim of a childish illusion. Babies cry with maximum despair in order to be comforted by their mothers – that's how she'd been working her way through fear: in her heart of hearts she'd been expecting the consultant to say there was nothing to worry about. She'd been being frightened as a way of paying her dues in advance; which was why she'd been so thorough about it. And then what? The consultant would say she was all right after all, she deserved that outcome, like a schoolchild who's swotted for an exam. And the lump would simply disappear, as if Jesus had performed a miracle.

How you could fool yourself! Miracles didn't happen just like that. It would take a *miracle* to make one happen. The lump was there, the consultant would see it, he would tell her she had a lump. Then he would tell her what kind of a lump it was, and no amount of fear would alter the fact of it.

She didn't feel frightened any more, she felt utter gloom, as if everything had turned into monochrome, what you saw, what you heard, what you smelled, what you felt. Nothing good would ever happen again. This is how the world really is, she thought, all the rest of it is like those tooters and party hats that even Stephen has grown out of. It was a lazy feeling almost; there was no reason to feel fear any more than to feel hope. She was standing on the bedrock of things. How funny that outside this clinic there were people worrying about scratching their new car or being overdrawn at the bank; there were people anticipating promotion or looking forward to their holidays. Just saying the word cancer should be enough to stop them striving for unnecessary things.

Then she realised the nurse was standing in the middle of the room, her mouth just closing after saying her name.

When John answered the knock on his office door, there was no one there. He stepped out into the corridor and caught, just disappearing round the corner into the main banking area, a glimpse of Mrs Clarke's skirt. That bit of skirt – bit of skirt! – was like a public statement they were doing something underhand. Even though, of course, they weren't; and anyway, she was actually avoiding publicity. But the bit of skirt stuck in his retina, thickish, woollen, the complete opposite of the flouncy stuff the phrase ought to conjure up.

He followed Mrs Clarke's footsteps to the main banking area. She was at the far side when he got there, just approaching the door that led to the car-park. Mr Hawthorne was hunched over the papers on his desk as if to gobble them like spaghetti.

'I'm going for my lunch now,' John told him.

Mr Hawthorne looked up, his face pink and slightly puffy. Perhaps he *is* up to something at that desk, John thought. I'll have to find some way of checking up, but not now.

'Mrs Clarke's just gone,' Hawthorne replied.

'And?'

'I was just telling you.'

'Thank you very much.'

John strode on through the area, almost shaking with a combination of fright and anger. How was it that he, John, never had the faintest idea what was going on in the world but he had only to make the most insignificant arrangement and everybody immediately knew about it? There could be parties going on in the main banking area while his back was turned and he would never be any the wiser. Mr Hawthorne for one seemed to be able to hold a party all by himself on the top of his desk. And yet John's thoughts had only to wander the slightest amount from the straight and narrow, and at once it was the talk of the town. There was Miss Fielding, more egg-like than ever seen from the back and sitting down, tapping at her console with deep pools of space between each tap, not so much typing when the thought struck her as when the individual letter or number struck her, lost in some oval universe of her own: *she* probably knew he was going off with Mrs Clarke. As he walked past the tellers one of them leaned over and whispered something to the one next door, and they both giggled in that identical way girls had, with hands flat and inefficient across their mouths.

Outside it was still sunny and he felt dazzled for a moment, like an animal coming out of hibernation. Mrs Clarke was already climbing into her car. She obviously expected him to follow her. She had said so little, had taken so much for granted, was so sophisticated in the way she handled their little arrangement. Not that she was necessarily experienced at exploits of this kind, surely not, it was just that she seemed to know how to do things in general, compared with him, anyway: like knowing Henry was called Ken. I'm an amateur at my life, John thought.

He got in his car, put his key in the ignition, and turned it. Nothing happened. I knew this would happen, he thought to himself immediately. That was true in a way. If he'd thought at all about starting his car, which he hadn't, he would have known the battery would be flat. That was typical of him, the fact that he could only anticipate problems retrospectively. He cursed, long and hard and silently. The wiperman must have switched the engine on to make sure the wipers wouldn't start up, and used the last of the charge.

Mrs Clarke drove off. She'd even remembered to put a traffic cone in her parking space. He continued to sit in his car. All I wanted was a bit on the side, he thought mournfully. Underneath the mournfulness was a sense of relief. He'd done his best, and been defeated by circumstances. What he could do now was stroll to the nearby shops and buy Margaret a box of chocolates. He was *entitled* to the straight and narrow, having done all that could be humanly expected of him to deviate.

Mrs Clarke's car backed into the car-park. For a moment he had the odd sensation that it was simply being rewound, like a video. Mrs Clarke would get out and trot backwards into the bank. But no, she came towards him head-on, and his heart sank.

'Still having trouble with it?' she asked, peering through the window. 'Why don't you hop in mine?'

'Don't you think it's a bit . . . ?' he asked, glancing back towards the bank.

'Put a bit of excitement in their lives. Anyway people are entitled to give each other lifts, for heaven's sake, in this day and age.'

He had the funny sensation of having more emotions than experiences to have them about. Bugger them, he thought, why should I do what they want? *They* were Mr Hawthorne, the egg, the tellers. At the same time he thought: this *is* what they want. But he still felt pleasantly hostile, as though he were scrunching stay-at-home colleagues underfoot. He got out of his dead car. He was scrunching his stay-at-home *self* underfoot. A Liberty scarf, he thought: freedom.

In the shop his pessimism came back. He seemed to have a peculiar ability to overlook the fact that what they were doing was buying his wife an anniversary present. Mrs Clarke was scrutinising the scarves like an expert. An expert on scarves, on walking out of the bank, on car-park attendants. Her battery would never go flat, nor her windscreen wipers become unstoppable. Her life was comfortable and woollen, like her skirt. Even her car had been comfortable and woollen, in its way: there was a little tube of mints, opened, on the tray-thing beside the gear-stick. She probably sucked one every day or so in that sensible reassuring way of hers. If they were in his car he'd gobble them in five minutes, always assuming Ann or Stephen didn't get to them first. In fact he'd felt an urgent desire to start wolfing down Mrs Clarke's tube but didn't dare. He didn't want to use up his scope for asking by asking for too little, too soon.

The scarves were indistinguishable as far as he was concerned. They all had different colours and patterns, it was true, but these seemed to add up to the same thing in the end. They were beyond him, that was for certain. He had no idea whether Margaret liked that sort of thing, either. He had the sense there would be too much detail on them for her, but he wasn't exactly sure. Was she a woman who disliked detail?

Mrs Clarke obviously loved it. She had her nose buried in the scarves as a book-lover might have his nose buried in a book. Perhaps he ought to buy *her* a scarf? That would be what somebody who had a bit of oomph in him would do. No, no, he thought, teetering back as you would at the edge of an unexpected hole, that would line her up with Margaret, that wouldn't be on at all, very poor taste. It would be far far too suggestive. He needed to be exactly suggestive enough.

'Let me buy you lunch,' he asked her.

'I beg your pardon?'

His mouth went dry. That phrase, I beg your pardon, could be a kick in the balls, it all depended how you meant it. 'Lunch?' he repeated, his voice a croak.

'Oh, well,' she said, 'I'll tell you what I've just thought of, I've got to nip home. I've got a casserole for tonight, and I want to turn the oven on low and let it do.'

'You think ahead,' John said glumly. He remembered Margaret's accidental chicken. She'd thought ahead without thinking at all. Not that he could talk: *he* just didn't think at all. 'I never can.'

'You're a man,' said Mrs Clarke, relieving the gloom slightly, though the reminder was too late.

And then, suddenly, John's moment arrived.

You did get a moment, after all. At least, he did. He'd thought all along that moments never came or at least that by the time they arrived at his door they were too late. It was like when he and Margaret used to go dancing as teenagers at the Poco Poco, and he could never keep up with the beat, no matter how fast he danced, unless he danced at tremendous speed, when he overtook it. He felt he was always at a distance from the experiences of his life, so that they took place in a sort of darkness.

But now something was happening right in front of his eyes. Mrs Clark said: 'But I can't leave you marooned at the wrong end of Reddish. Why don't you come with me, and I'll make you a sandwich.' She'd had her eyes fixed on a Liberty scarf. Now they rose and looked straight at John's. They were like the quotation marks when somebody has finished what they were saying in a book. They made sure he understood exactly what she meant.

He didn't turn away from her gaze. So often, when a woman looked him in the eyes, he flicked his own elsewhere like a frightened virgin, shying away from the possibility of sending a sexual message. Perhaps from the possibility of *receiving* a sexual message.

'That's very kind of you,' he said.

'There's this burnt orange one, or the lemon yellow. I'm a great one for lemon yellow.'

'Margaret loves burnt orange.' He had no idea whether she liked orange at all, burnt or otherwise. The only thing he knew about her colour taste was that she liked blue irises, but that was irrelevant. '*You* have the lemon yellow.'

Their looks stayed fixed. Strategy didn't matter, nor good taste, when your moment came. In fact, the bigger the risk, the worse the taste, the larger the sum of money, the better. John had a sudden mental picture of Desperate Dan bursting through a wall, and leaving his shape behind.

'That's a bit reckless,' Mrs Clarke said, in an undertone. Her cheeks had pinked slightly. 'Do you know how much Liberty scarves cost?'

'Let's be reckless for once,' John told her. 'It's only money.'

'The bank manager's epitaph.'

He wasn't a fully-fledged bank manager, of course, but it was nice of Mrs Clarke to say it.

'The thing is, where you going?' the blotherin man asked while they were standing at the bus-stop, only he still wasn't the blotherin man. His face had kept that yellowishness from the museum wall, with a special very pale dot at the end of his nose. He was the second man, who only had a drink at breakfast during the week, and saved his proper breakfast till the weekend.

Stephen knew he couldn't say home, even though his sister had been kidnapped. It wasn't home time. He should still be at school. Perhaps if he went back to doing what he should be doing, everything else would go back to doing what it should be doing as well. Ordinariness might spread. When you were sitting in class with all the other children things like your sister being kidnapped didn't happen. He hoped. The other reason he couldn't say home was that he couldn't say it.

'I'm going to school.'

'It's taken you a long time. What yr teacher will say, you did dawdle boy.' Often the man, whether he was the blotherin man or the second man, seemed to hear the things he said himself as if hadn't said them. As if a *third* man had said them. 'You did dawdle boy,' he repeated, cupping his hand round one ear to help him listen to the words. 'What he'll say,' he concluded, lowering his hand.

'But I got on the wrong bus,' Stephen explained.

'What bus should you got on?'

'I shouldn't have got on any.'

The man pushed his lips out, almost as if he was going to kiss someone. There were little curls of skin poking up from them, like when you have a cold. He shook his head and made a clicking noise with his tongue. 'You got on the wrong bus right enough,' he said. He stopped and ran his hand along the words he'd just said, now hanging invisibly in the air. 'Wrong bus, right enough,' he repeated uncertainly. He felt the words again, as if he was still not sure they should be there. Then he waved them away impatiently and concentrated on Stephen once more. 'If you shdn't of got on any. You better get a – ' again he paused, as if he wanted to look at those words too, but quickly shook his head and carried on ' – you better get a bus back to where you started from.'

Another sob came rushing up, banging against the bottom of Stephen's throat when it arrived. Luckily it was too big to go up the tube. Because it blocked most of the passage Stephen had hardly any air left to talk with so he had to speak in a tiny voice: 'I don't know,' he said.

'What?' the man said, poking his ear at him.

'Know.'

'No? No what?'

'I don't know what.'

The man's face began to redden a little. Stephen's heart thumped at the thought that the blotherin man might be coming back. He fixed his eyes on the dot on the man's nose. While it was there he'd be all right, he was sure of that. The good thing was his fright made the sob go away, and he was able to carry on in his ordinary voice: 'What bus.'

'What bus,' the man repeated. He poked his lips out again, but this time squidged them up towards his nose, so you could tell he was thinking. To Stephen's relief the blother was fading from his face. 'The bus you come on,' he said. 'The same bus as me. The one hundred and ninety five.'

'That's the date, isn't it?' Stephen asked, puzzled.

'Gar,' the man said. 'It's the bloddy bus.'

'I don't know where to get off,' Stephen said.

'Where you live?'

'Nine Glenwood Road, Heaton Chapel, Stockport.'

The man put his arms up as if someone was chucking a bucket of water over him.

'I don't want all that where you live. It's not a bloody taxi-cab. You don't tell him nine some bloody road and he rolls up at nine some bloody road like yr own personal what's-his-name, bus. Like your personal bus, like. The man in the bus doesn't want to hear where your home is.'

'What does he want to hear then?'

The man stared at him for a moment. He raised his hand to one of his eyes and pulled the top lid up and the bottom lid down with his fingers, like your mother does when you've got something stuck in your eye, and looked at him with one large eye and one ordinary-sized one. 'What he wants to hear is, *near* where you live,' he said finally. He let his eye go back to normal. 'Where you live like, near it,' he added.

'I don't know. *near* where I live. I only know *where* I live,' Stephen told him.

'That's a bogger,' the man said. He continued to stare at Stephen. Then he smiled, as he had done that other time, so his dim teeth showed. He put his hand on Stephen's shoulder. 'You get off where you got on,' he said. 'Just wait till it comes back again, then got off.'

'I don't know how much to pay,' Stephen said. You couldn't just ask the driver how much it cost to go to where you got on. In any case he didn't have *any* money to pay the driver with, however much it was. He decided not to think about that, it was too horrible.

The man jumped a little, as if somebody had hit him. Then he looked very tired, and rubbed the side of his head with his sleeve. Then his face lit up once more. 'Pay what you paid before,' he said.

'I didn't pay anything before,' Stephen told him.

The man pulled his head back and pointed at Stephen. Then he began to do a funny whispery laugh, curling his head down on to his chest, and still pointing at Stephen. 'Gar,' he said. 'Yu little bogger.'

Suddenly a bus appeared behind him, as if it had sprung out of its hidey-hole instead of coming along the road. There were some things about the man, whether blotherin or not, that made him different from other people. One was that he moved about more than other people did; another was that he often stayed in one position when you would have expected him to do something else. He stopped speaking when he felt the bus behind him, but he still pointed and stood a little bent over where he'd been laughing. Leaving the rest of his body where it was he looked over his shoulder at the bus, which was just pulling up with a squelch of its brakes because luckily there were some other people waiting.

'Siz the one!' he called out. He turned round to it, still hunched, then looked over his shoulder at Stephen. He waggled his head towards the bus and shot on to it like a monkey.

Stephen followed, his heart sinking. He kept saying inside his head, Bus driver in a rage, as if that was a line from a song. Bus driver in a rage. If you said something over and over, it became solid, like a bar, and you could hold on to it.

The man was waiting by the driver's little machine, even though he had his ticket in his hand. He looked at Stephen and shook his head sadly, as if he himself was the driver. The real bus driver looked at Stephen too, in the way somebody does when they are not the most important looker.

'I don't know,' the man said. Each piece of what he said zigged or zagged along with the shakes of his head. 'What di blather . . . yr-adder pay fa . . . di young wopper-snopper.'

The driver shook his head too, as if his head was part of the same engine that the man's head was part of. The blotherin man was still mainly the second man and not the blotherin man, even though he'd said blather, because his nose had a yellow tip and he wasn't looking all the time for whatever-it-was. His voice was still not too furry. Also he wasn't angry.

Then the bus driver stopped shaking his head and started nodding it instead. 'He pays fourteen pee,' he said.

There was a pause, and then the second man jumped. 'Ar,' he said. 'He pees fourteen pay, on he?' He whirled his hand with the ticket in it round and round, as if he was trying to stir up the words and get them sorted out.

'They all pay fourteen pee,' the driver said. He looked suddenly bored. He puffed out his cheeks, and his eyes swivelled sideways and gave the man an old-fashioned look. Stephen knew it was an old-fashioned look, because he'd given looks like that, and that was how his mother had described them. An old-fashioned look was one of those looks that feel the same on the inside as they appear on the outside. It was good to do them when you had your spectacles on because they made your eyes bigger, and your look even more old-fashioned. 'All kids do,' the driver continued. 'Under the age of fourteen.'

'Onder ther fourteen day pay der fourteen,' the man said. He pointed at Stephen. 'He's row ner bout eight,' he said.

'Then he pays bloody fourteen.'

'Don't get your goat bloddy up. He pays bloddy fourteen, he pays bloddy fourteen, includin being eight, give or take. Where air he goes,' he added. He got some money out of his pocket, and plonked it on the little tray that was fixed beside the ticket machine. 'That do yer?' he asked.

'That's too bloody much,' the driver said. 'That's more than fourteen there.'

The man peered down at the money as if he was reading a book; or as if he was looking at money put down by somebody else. 'Tha's too bloddy much,' he said. He sounded just as annoyed as the driver. He turned round to Stephen. 'Too bloddy much,' he repeated.

All three of them looked at the money which sat like a heap of brown unvaluable jewels on the tray.

'I've got to get this bus on the bloody road,' the driver said. 'Being that it's my last run. And me wife's had a bloody baby.'

The man did one of his little jumps. First of all he didn't do anything, and then he suddenly did, as if the words sank slowly down his ears the way a stone sinks down water when you drop one in. When he did his jump he pressed the backs of his hands to his chest and dangled his fingers down, exactly as if he was pretending to be a kangaroo.

'A bebby?' he asked. 'When do she had a bloddy beb? Had a blodd bebby?'

'Once upon a time,' said the driver. He shoved some of the money one way and some the other. Then he took one of the piles and dropped it somewhere under his counter. 'That's your change,' he said, poking at the remaining pile. He turned a little handle and a ticket came out of his machine. He tore it off and gave it to Stephen.

'That's your change,' the man said to Stephen.

'No, it's not, it's yours,' Stephen told him.

'Sure bloody ticket,' the man said, and turned away to go inside the proper part of the bus. Stephen took the money from the driver's tray and followed him. The man was already sitting on a seat near the back of the downstairs, by the window. His face was redder and he was looking around everywhere, as if he'd remembered the blother. Stephen almost wondered whether it would be best if he didn't sit next to him. But the man had paid his bus fare so perhaps he had to.

'Gar,' the man said, when Stephen sat down. He didn't move over, and seemed to take up a lot of space, even though he was small for a grown-up. He had the sort of arms and legs that poke

165

out. Stephen was worried to see that the yellow dot on the end of his nose had almost completely faded away. 'The rather blother,' the blotherin man said, confirming Stephen's fear, 'on di head.' He pointed forward with his finger. On the seat in front of him was a man in a hat. He seemed to be pointing at the hat.

It suddenly occurred to Stephen that the blotherin man might take the man-with-the-hat's hat off. Stephen remembered how badly he'd behaved towards the man with the coiled-up ear: he'd seemed to hate him, for no reason, unless he'd thought that the blotherin thing was buried in all the ear stuff somewhere. In which case he might now be thinking the blotherin thing was under the man's hat. As soon as Stephen thought this thought he knew that it *would* happen, just as if his thinking it had been what made it certain.

The blotherin man pulled his pointing finger back and put it to his lips. Then he lowered it, and made it and his middle finger become legs, and tiptoe down the front of himself, along his own leg, and up the back of the seat in front, all the way up to the top, towards the hat. Stephen watched in horror as the fingers stood together on the top of the seat back, bent their knees, and jumped up to the hat brim. It happened quickly but slowly at the same time, as if the fastness had slowness inside it, like those chocolates that have hard toffee in the middle. Stephen remembered when he'd dropped the teapot. It must have fallen at the speed at which things usually fell but Stephen had been able to watch it slowly. Everything else smeared when it went through the air but the teapot stayed a teapot. You could imagine putting out your hand, slowly, slowly, and feel it land on your palm like a large egg. When it reached the ground a bulge went over it, covered in cracks, like something fat in a net, and then it tinkled, went loose, scattered, and Stephen experienced a sense of relief at the thought that it was all over: the teapot didn't have to be a teapot any more.

The hat rose slowly in the air. Underneath, the man had neat flat silver hair. The top of his head had a secret look about it. The blotherin man looked at it in astonishment. Then his head sagged with disappointment at not seeing the blotherin thing there, whatever it was. He lowered the hat gently back in place. The man with the hat moved in his seat and pulled at his ear-lobe, but obviously hadn't felt his hat rise and fall back into place again. The blotherin man grinned at Stephen, his disappointment already forgotten. Stephen showed him his handful of change in order to take his mind off the hat.

'Yu keep it,' the blotherin man said.

'Thank you,' Stephen replied.

'Armour saint in holy clothing,' the blotherin man told him in his belchy voice.

The bus was going back the way they had come. To Stephen's surprise the blotherin man began to look peaceably out of the window, muttering to himself. He seemed to be in a kind of muttering doze, because he was saying nice round burbly words like the ones a baby says when it's talking to itself. Once, though, he said blothr loudly, and Stephen realised that, wherever he was, he was still on the hunt.

The bus stopped at the stop Stephen should have got off at on the way in, and he saw Ann's school quite clearly, just down one of the roads by the shops. It was so clear that he couldn't understand why he hadn't seen it last time. Perhaps it hadn't been there, like when your house isn't there during the day. And like Ann hadn't been there at the bus-stop. Perhaps she'd come back now, and made the school pop up again. Just as he had hoped: rolling back on the bus and leaving the kidnap and the museum and the university behind.

They carried on; and suddenly the blotherin man spoke.

'Whar ar,' he began, and did one of his stops again, looking at what he'd said. Stephen was used to that by now. 'Whar ar'd alight,' the blotherin man said, adding 'fum de bogger.' Then: 'De bus.' He waved his finger at the outside world. Stephen knew what he meant. This was where the blotherin man got off. Stephen's heart sank.

'I don't know where mine is,' he said.

'Wit what is?'

'My delight is.'

The blotherin man suddenly became very angry. 'Your blotherin stop has gone and gone buserk,' he said in a shouty belch. 'Is gone and flubbin gone buserk, di bus, stop.' He hit the back of the seat in front and dodged his head from side to side as if the seat was hitting him back. The man with the hat jerked forward, and the back of his head seemed to peer over at them, but was perhaps too polite to turn itself round and take a proper look.

167

The bus stopped at the blotherin man's bus-stop. The blotherin man stopped hitting the seat and put his hand above his eyes, peering at the street outside. The sun had gone in and it looked gloomy. There was some litter blowing about. It was hard to believe this was only a bus ride from near home. A lot of the people walking about on the pavement were black or brown, which made the street look more faraway than ever.

'Dar, sit di pub is open,' the blotherin man said, pointing towards a pub which sure enough had its front door open. A red-faced man in a horrible coat was shuffling into it, one arm held out to the side so he almost didn't get through the gap. He was so like the blotherin man that he might have been his brother. The blotherin man pressed his face against the window. Then he looked back towards Stephen. 'Pob,' he said again. He punched his fist on his knee as if he was angry with himself for not being able to explain it better. Then he looked back through the window. 'Di pob,' he said sadly as the bus moved off.

Stephen's heart leapt. 'Aren't you getting off here?' he asked.

'Wha's di bloddy here?' the blotherin man asked. He tapped the window with his finger, pointing back, 'Is bloddy there.'

'Where you going then?'

'Going with you, unt I? Bin wid you all di bloddy morning. One minute to the next.'

Stephen felt as if a great weight had been taken away, even though the blotherin man didn't know any more than he did himself where he should get off. With him there it would be easier to decide. It was always easier with a grown-up. It was like when you couldn't do a sum, and took it to your teacher, and before he even said anything you could see how to do it right away. If a grown-up was nearby he or she made part of you think it was grown-up too, and things became more simple. Even the blotherin man had that effect, though Stephen knew he was the sort of grown-up other grown-ups wouldn't be able to stand the sight of.

'From one bloddy min *ut*,' the blotherin man said. As he said *ut*, he suddenly yanked the rim of the man-in-the-hat's hat up, so that it leaned forward as if he was asleep. Still the man in the hat didn't look round. Stephen would never have believed that somebody could not look round with the blotherin man up to his tricks behind him. All the man did was straighten his hat again. 'Di blotherin thing,' the blotherin man said, and looked out of the window again. The sun was shining once more and the streets already looked less strange. 'To di next,' the blotherin man said, and then started mumbling again.

'What will I tell the teacher?' Stephen asked. It was one of those sudden questions that you ask before you think of them. The teacher, he then thought, with a sinking heart.

The blotherin man looked out of the window again. 'Tell him a fub,' he said. He opened his mouth and pointed at his stripy teeth. 'Went to the dentist,' he added. 'Wick,' he went on, and ran his finger over his throat, like you do to show your throat is being cut. 'Had em yanked out, orlerlotonem.' He looked angry suddenly. 'Bloddy muddy class,' he said.

Suddenly Stephen saw the biscuit factory through the window of the bus. 'That's the biscuit factory,' he told the blotherin man. 'It's near where I live.'

The blotherin man was still angry. He deliberately didn't look out of the window. 'You sod you didn't know near where you sodn live,' he said. He didn't look at Stephen either. He was looking at the hat of the man in front. He was looking at *that* so hard, to make up for not looking at the other things, that his look seemed like a strong wind, and Stephen was surprised the hat didn't fly off and go sailing down the bus.

'I forgot.'

'Yu can't fugget a fugging factory. Look at the size uv it.' He still didn't look himself but stared at the hat.

Now Stephen didn't care – he knew where he was. Road after road that he recognised, house after house, went past the window of the bus. They looked as if they were marching back from some black place where they'd been all morning. The bus passed the traffic lights, and then the other school, the one he didn't go to. Then the row of shops. He walked this far sometimes. It was wonderful to think of that, like getting back to within your depth after you've been swimming in the deep end of the pool.

Stephen got to his feet. The blotherin man began to get up too, in a complicated way as if he was pulling himself up an invisible wall. 'You don't have to come,' Stephen told him. 'I know my stop now.'

The blotherin man seemed to fall off his wall and land back on his seat again. 'Where do you think I'm going, on the bloddy bus?'

he asked. 'Heaven?' He started to climb again. He reached out as if he was going to grab the edge of the hat in front for a handhold. Stephen turned away so he wouldn't see him do it. Sometimes you could stop things happening by not looking at them, the same as when you did a dead-eye, only it was more like a dead-eye of your whole head, because you were just looking at whatever-it-was with the back part, no eyeballs at all, dead or not, just as the man with the hat had looked backwards at *them*. But it didn't work, because the man with the hat gave a sharp little cry and then said: 'Do you mind?'

Behind him in the aisle Stephen heard the blotherin man say: 'I don't bloody mind. Sure at.'

Stephen trotted up to the front. The driver pressed his brakes and they began to stop. The end of Glenwood Road went past. Stephen had a quick look down it before it was gone. There was a dog in the distance, right in the middle of the road, a medium-sized one, golden brown. It could have been Raymond's twin brother, like the man going into the pub being the blotherin man's brother. Then he was gone. Stephen felt a pang. Apart from Raymond's twin brother the street had been deserted. In the sunshine there was a sleepy, dinner-time feeling about it.

The bus brakes squawked, and it stopped – right at the bus-stop where nobody ever waited except Raymond, who used it as a toilet. The door swished open. You could almost imagine the bus-stop had been put there just for this moment.

'Are you waiting for Christmas?' the driver asked. Stephen got off. Behind him the blotherin man got off too. To Stephen's relief he wasn't carrying the hat. Perhaps he'd put it back on the man-in-the-hat's head.

'There's no school here,' the blotherin man said, looking round as if for one to appear.

'My school's along there,' said Stephen, pointing towards it. To his surprise, the swimming-bus was parked on the road beside it. Perhaps they'd only just got back, and it wasn't as late as he thought. The ordinary bus that he'd travelled here in was just driving past the swimming-bus.

'You wanna gotted out next stop,' the blotherin man told him, 'not this here here.' He rubbed the side of his head. 'Like this one here, here.'

'I walk to school. I don't go on the bus,' Stephen said.

'You jus bin on the bloddy bus,' the blotherin man told him. He waved his arm up the road, but their bus had gone now. Another one was in the distance, coming towards them. The blotherin man looked over the road and saw the bus-stop on the other side, Ann's bus-stop, the one that had caused all the trouble in the first place. 'Ar want that one there, over dare like,' he said, and began to cross the road.

'Where are you going?' Stephen called.

The blotherin man stopped in the middle of the road and turned back. 'Um going to the blotherin pob,' he said. 'It's blonkin miles frum here, blotherin thing.'

'Goodbye,' called Stephen.

The blotherin man carried on crossing the road. 'Got to get the blos frum there, to go there. Um blonkin miles frum it here. Ull have to catch the bus to fund whar the blotherin thing.'

He got to Ann's bus-stop and put out his hand. The bus came along, stopped, and the blotherin man got on. Stephen began to run towards his school.

10

The consultant was a young man with yellow teeth. He looked at Margaret's bared breasts long and carefully, as if he wanted to memorise them for later. The nurse looked too, her head cocked on one side as if to emphasise that she wasn't looking in her own right, but just following the consultant's gaze, perhaps checking that he was concentrating on the business in hand. The air felt cool against Margaret's breasts but the gaze of the two pairs of eyes created palpable warmth where it struck, as a magnifying glass does when you focus sunlight. Stephen had done that last summer, squeezing STEPHE in shaky letters on a piece of wood, which she'd come across again only the other day, in his toy-box. To her horror, as the eyes fixed on her left breast, she had a crinkly sensation around her nipple and then it popped out, like a pink snail poking its head out of its shell. Needless to say the other one remained inverted and she sat, mortified, on the examination couch, willing it to appear too, and make a pair. She felt deeply ashamed of them both, as if they were two idiot children, guaranteed to let you down on a special occasion.

'Does the other one come out as well?' the consultant asked. He had a fruity voice even though he looked young and ratty.

'Yes,' she said humbly.

'Perhaps you could . . . encourage it.'

She put her fingers each side of her nipple, her hands clumsy with nerves, and squeezed. Out it came.

'Very good,' the consultant said, with the same false encouragement in his voice that she used to use on Raymond in the days when she thought it was still possible to teach him things. Yes indeed, very good, what a wonderful trick, now perhaps you could hold up a little hoop and I'll get my nipple to jump through it. Two little hoops. But she felt more cheerful suddenly – it was a relief to be resentful.

The consultant wrote something down in a notebook. 'Now what I'm going to do', he said, while he was still writing, 'is to feel that lump of yours. I promise I won't hurt you.'

He doesn't dare look at me while he says that, Margaret realised, and felt better still, as if the only thing at stake was that she should come out on top.

He gave his notebook to the sister and stepped forward, hands in advance almost as if, funnily enough, despite what he'd said, he *was* going to maul her after all. Margaret realised it was a case of opposites amounting to the same thing, maulers and consultants would both hold their hands in front of them in that way, like the digger things on mechanical diggers, because they wanted to show you that their hands weren't really connected to the rest of them but did what they had to do in their own right.

The consultant poked one index finger out straight, placed it very carefully on the top edge of the lump, and traced out its perimeter. He nodded as if what it was telling him was exactly as expected. But what *was* it he expected? Bad or good? Fear came again and took her stomach away. She'd been sitting here worrying about being embarrassed when her life could be coming to an end. That was why, of course: you could hide *behind* being embarrassed. Bad was what he expected to find – bad was what he was being paid for.

'All right,' he said. 'Now Mrs Edwards, I'm just going to.'

He made no attempt to finish his sentence. He left it blank just as she'd said um to the man in the waiting-room. It was like one of those grunty languages that primitive tribes have on TV. Um means tit. Blank means squeeze your tit. She'd read somewhere that the Arabs have dozens of words for camel. In this clinic there were dozens of silences for 'breast'.

The consultant put a hand each side of the lump, just as she had done with her nipple, and squeezed. She drew her breath in sharply.

'Did that hurt?' he asked.

It hadn't actually hurt but it *had* taken her breath away, as if automatically.

173

'It just took my breath away.'

'Yes.'

He briskly felt around the lump again. 'Good,' he said, with obvious satisfaction. Her stomach must have reassembled, because there was enough of it for her to feel it vanishing again. If he said good it meant it was what he expected and what he expected, in his line of work, was bad.

'Thank you, Mrs Edwards. You can . . . sort yourself out now.' He waved an arm vaguely at her breasts. Put them away, he meant. The nurse tugged across the curtain that went in front of the examination couch. It was a peculiar custom, looking at people with no clothes on, but not being allowed to watch them getting dressed again. It showed that they meant well. They wanted to leave you some shreds of dignity. She found herself stifling a sob at the kindness of the curtain. Stupid doggerel words went through her mind, thank you so much for the kindness of the curtain, the very very kindness of the curtain, while her throat ached with the need to weep. She put her bra back on with shaky arms.

When she'd finished dressing she sat back on the couch. For a moment she didn't dare draw the curtain back. It was like being brought back before the judge and jury to hear the verdict. For some reason she began to sweat at the back of her neck. She heard the small click of a pen being dropped on the top of a desk. Perhaps the consultant was hinting. Pick up thy breast and walk, she told herself. She stood up, poked out her arms, worked the curtains back with stiff unnatural movements, deliberately unnatural, like when Stephen used to play at being a robot, a small soft toddler strutting around trying to look boxy and impersonal. I always think of Stephen, she thought, poor Ann. When a new child comes he blots out the path of the one before, like someone trampling over footprints in the snow. I'm such a bad mother, it's no wonder he . . . She pointed one of her robot arms slightly in the direction of the consultant, so that he wouldn't notice she meant him, that he was the one punishing her for being a bad mother. Sure enough he was sitting behind his desk, which was too big for him, so he resembled a boy in grown-up trousers. He's not too small to cut my breast off though, she thought bitterly. He in turn pointed at a chair for her to sit on. She still worked herself as if she was machinery, lowering her bottom like a crane lowering a heavy weight.

'Well, Mrs Edwards, I've had a look at the offending lump,' he said, staring fixedly at a small photograph on his desk. Margaret could only see the back of it, but it didn't take a detective to work out that it must be of his wife, with her lovely round cancer-proof lump-free breasts perched neatly in their Laura Ashley covering. 'What I need to do now is look a little more closely, by means of a small surgical procedure.'

'Oh yes,' Margaret replied, smiling and nodding, as if this was just the treat she'd been hoping for.

'It's called a biopsy, which just means taking a sample of the tissue and putting it under the microscope, subjecting it to a few tests. We do it while you wait, so to speak. Then if our analysis does suggest further treatment is required, we can undertake it on the spot. If it's advisable to remove the lump itself, for example, which I can assure you would be done very neatly. You'll never know it had been there in the first place. The good part of the prognosis is that it seems loose. I can't discover from a manual inspection that it's attached to anything, but of course that will await a further look for confirmation. Do you have any questions?' He finally managed to tear his eyes from the photograph and look at her.

She scurried through her mind trying to find one. It would seem so rude not to ask anything, like showing no interest in somebody's hobby.

'Will I be staying in overnight?' she managed to ask.

'Oh yes, whatever we do. Patients always stay in overnight with a general anaesthetic.'

'Oh. I will be having a . . .'

'Yes, yes. Goodness me, yes. When you think about it people have a general anaesthetic just to have a tooth yanked out.'

A sudden bolt of terror struck her once more. She saw her breast among clamps and pincers, being yanked out like a pink jelly molar.

'Would I have to stay in any longer? Than overnight?'

'It's possible. It all depends.'

'I see.'

'So is that all right? If my secretary gets in touch with you, some time in the next few days?'

'Yes, that will be fine.'

'Let the family fend for themselves for a day or two. That'll teach them.' He laughed, and while the laugh was still in his mouth added, 'All right then, Mrs Edwards. I look forward to seeing you again shortly,' managing to make it sound as if they'd done nothing but have a jolly time for the whole session.

'Yes,' she agreed, 'I hope so,' she added vaguely, uncertain what she was hoping.

'Good. Good morning then.'

He suddenly stood up and offered her his hand to shake. She shook it.

'Goodbye,' she said. It came out as a whisper.

His eyes somehow shrank, like a light does when you switch it off. He was already glancing down at his desk for the file on the next patient, the next offending tit. His smile stayed set to on.

The nurse came out with her to the waiting-room. All the patients still sitting there lifted mute heads towards her in unison. She could sense their admiration that she was out the other side, had got it over with. As she left the room the nurse was positioning herself in the middle to call out the name of the next patient.

Coming back into the gloomy hospital corridor along which she'd skulked with her heart in her boots an hour or so ago she felt a slight, temporary lifting of her spirits. She'd feared coming back along here with a sentence of death or mutilation on her and that hadn't happened quite yet. She had a few days' grace, a little patch of freedom to live in. But on the other hand uncertainty went both ways. She wasn't coming out here with the golden glow of the surgeon having said nothing to worry your head about, just a such-and-such kind of boil, forget all about it, you'll be as right as rain in a week or two. There were questions she hadn't asked, hadn't dared to. She hadn't asked, might you take my whole breast off? What if the lump *is* stuck to something after all? Would you do it without waking me up from the biopsy, so that when I *did* wake up I would only find out then, wake up on a perhaps Saturday and then see from the nurse's face that it was Monday morning for ever and ever amen?

She hadn't asked those questions, and he hadn't answered them. For a moment she tried to convince herself that he hadn't told her because they couldn't happen, that the possibilities had never

176

crossed his mind. But that couldn't be true. However ratty and yellow-toothed you were, however much your wife actually squeaked with breast-health in her Laura Ashley outfit, you would know that in any woman's mind whom you met in the course of your consultations those questions would be whirling like a merry-go-round.

'We meet again,' a man said in front of her. She had no idea where he'd come from. It was almost as if he'd materialised out of thin air, though he seemed very big to have done so.

'Do we?' she asked, in a small voice.

'You know, in there.' He pointed back towards the breast clinic. She suddenly realised he was the man she'd been sitting beside. It hadn't occurred to her, for some reason, that he also existed in the outside world. 'Fellow-patients.'

'Yes.'

'You got through your ordeal then?'

'I suppose so.'

He paused. She could see him, in that big battered head of his, wondering what the etiquette was of inquiring about someone's breast prognosis. 'Turn out all right?' he finally asked.

'They want to do a biopsy,' she told him. She almost cried as she said it, but felt much better when it was out. They were only words after all.

'Me as well.'

'Really?'

'You know what they're like when they've got hold of you. Same as those fellers who dig holes in the road.'

'Are they?'

'Once they start digging they never give up. Fill it in, dig it up again.'

'Thank you very much.' She suddenly shivered.

'No offence. What I meant to say, would you like a cup of tea or something? Being fellow-sufferers.'

'All right.' She could do with something to steady her nerves. Also, the house would seem empty and anti-climactic, even with Raymond in it. If the consultant had waved his magic wand and given her the all-clear, that wouldn't have mattered. She would have sung and skipped her way around the house, cooked a lovely meal for – heavens, she mustn't forget the steak, she'd *said* steak.

You can't cook steak in advance. She'd have taken Raymond for a walk, then. She'd have greeted people she knew with that extra greeting you give them when you've received a reprieve. People she *did*n't know, for that matter. The butcher when she bought the steak, she'd have been so sweet to him he'd have blushed, among all those great lumps of meat.

As it was, a cup of tea with her fellow-sufferer might settle her a bit.

'Possibly a sandwich,' he added consideringly. 'It's gone lunch.'

She wasn't quite sure she could manage a sandwich, so didn't reply. They walked down the glum green corridor side by side. The Friends' tea-room hove into view. She almost turned into it, but saw that he was continuing on. She followed. Her heart began to pound. You wouldn't think it *could* pound any more, but of course it was pounding for a different reason. She nearly said 'I thought you meant in here,' but it would seem so feeble. She always felt guilty when she misunderstood somebody.

'Have you got a car here?' he asked, turning back slightly since he was walking half a stride ahead, as if in a hurry to be wherever it was they were going.

'No.'

'Come in mine then.'

It was still not too late to say no, let's stay here. Or even to ask where it was they were going. But somehow it would seem rude. It would actually make unpleasant possibilities come nearer to the surface than they were, so that she would have no choice but to extricate herself. Oh Lord, she thought, do women let themselves get raped just out of fear of being impolite? She also wondered whether, in her heart of hearts, she was glad to have something other than cancer to worry about.

Mrs Clarke lived on a new estate just off Broadstone Road. The house was a semi-detached, plushly furnished. She took him into the lounge, inexplicably. There were only two destinations that made sense, the kitchen, so that they could go through the motions, and the bedroom. He felt a sudden film of warm sweat below the back of his neck as he thought that word.

'This is the lounge,' she said, for all the world as though he were a prospective purchaser. The lounge had a three-piece suite in a

178

plum colour, bulging and comfortable; the carpet was thick; there was one of those open gas fires, imitating coal, with an old tiled surround that must have been rescued from a demolished house. You could buy them in the junk shops of Levenshulme. This one had glazed flowers in blue, a delicate blue that seemed, in the tension of the moment, to make his heart beat faster, it had such clarity. He was not normally one to notice things like that. But still: he wasn't here to *buy*.

'Very nice,' he said shortly.

She put a hand on his arm, quickly, confidingly. 'Wait here a minute,' she said, just above a whisper. 'I won't be long. Take a seat.' And with that she was gone.

He felt suddenly large to be in the room, male. It occurred to him what they meant by a bull in a china shop. He stepped over to the settee, pulled up the knees of his trousers, something he never normally did, lowered himself. The net curtains seemed to give off a fuzzy white mist into the light that came in from the street. On the coffee table in front of him was a pink hyacinth in a bowl, and once he'd seen it he smelled it too, clean and fragrant. On a bookcase to one side were red books with gold lettering, an encyclopaedia presumably, plus some glossy-looking ones on the bottom shelf. His eyes caught something, a pipe, lying on the middle shelf in front of the neatly ranked books. A pipe. Mr Clarke's.

Everything else that was extraneous had been tidied up, cleared away. There was nothing personal around. Not that it was uncomfortable or institutional, quite the opposite, but there was no clutter. You could tell that when you went up to the bedroom you wouldn't find a pair of Mr C.'s underpants lying on the floor – it was the sort of house that wouldn't give you shocks. And yet, there the pipe was. It must simply have been overlooked.

His eyes were drawn back to it. From overhead came the dim breathy sound of water running. The pipe, rather blackened, lay slightly cocked to one side. It looked somehow as if it might be deputising for its owner, reporting back. You could imagine a bug in it; or worse, that it was a periscope. He felt more trickles of sweat run down his back as he pictured himself getting up, walking over to the bookshelf, casually raising the pipe as if he really couldn't care less, his hand being curious off its own bat, glancing at it without a care in the world . . . and there, peering up at him from the bowl, Mr Clarke's eyeball, hard as a marble. He almost cried out with horror, and that horror was instantly replaced by a more diffuse, far-reaching one, as he wondered if he was going mad with the tension of waiting.

There was nothing for it. He rose to his feet, again with heavy movements as though it was a grave matter being a man. He walked across the room. For some reason he found himself acting as if people were watching him and he had to mask what he was doing. He pulled one of the books part way out of its position on the top shelf of the bookcase and inspected its spine short-sightedly. Donk to Elf. He heard himself saying it out loud, and nodded, as if he'd thought as much. He pushed the volume back into place, bent a little and edged one out on the next shelf down, within a whisker of the pipe. He opened it, almost convincing himself that he was looking something up. Yes, there it was, he said to himself, as his finger stopped at random at an entry: passerine bird. A bird belonging to the order *Passiformes* blah blah, skim over it using the Ann method, perching birds, characterised by their feet, which are adapted for gripping branches. Feet? Do birds have feet? 'Feet,' he repeated just out loud, exactly as you might in a bookshop to show other people you were taking an intelligent interest, but below the level of comprehensibility so they wouldn't think you were actually talking to them. 'They'll be wearing shoes next,' he added.

Shaking his head sadly he slipped the volume back. Then, just as he'd imagined, his hand slipped over and gripped the stem of the pipe as if his hand were actually the foot of some passerine bird landing arbitrarily on a branch. He picked the pipe up and looked at it, as much as to say, what on earth's *this* doing on a bookshelf? but with a certain aura of who cares? at the same time. His shoulders almost shrugging. Giving it that close scrutiny you give to something you're not interested in, the fact that your mind is elsewhere allowing your eyes to become fixed and staring. But of course *his* eyes were really peering out from inside the stare, like somebody peering out into the street from inside a blank window, taking it all in.

The pipe was a straight briar, worn mouthpiece, tarnished silver ring connecting it to bowl. He was holding it side-on. Still casual: tilt it so you can see into the bowl. Easiest thing in the world. His heart was beating so hard his hand, and therefore the pipe, shook with each pulse. He looked into the tiny blackened pit. Empty, no shreds of tobacco, no eyeball, nothing. He heard himself whimper slightly with relief. And then came his mother's scratchy, strained, high-pitched voice once more: 'This isn't the time or the place.'

He stared down the bowl of the pipe in horror. It was his mother's mouth, stiff and round as mouths go when they are saying something with authority. He saw his mother's face as though it was hanging before him in the air, old, vulnerable, yet morally forceful still, mouth open in command, speaking to him from the depths of her coffin, from the depths of her cremation, her face blackening, shrinking, settling in upon itself, growing stiff and cindery, till all you could make out was the shrunken mouth, stuck in mid-word, a mouth that now exactly coincided with the charred bowl of Mr Clarke's pipe. At last she had found the exact time and place. No, that was wrong, *she* was free of time and place now. It was he, John, who had found the exact time and place, for once in his life. And his mother was telling him it wasn't, because she knew jolly well it was. Not that she was fibbing – it was the *not* she really meant, rather than the time or the place.

Anyway, this wasn't the first time, it was the second. There was a certain relief with that thought. It provided a sort of precedent: you might as well be hung for a sheep as for a lamb. He remained where he was, by the bookcase, still clutching Mr Clarke's pipe, remembering the previous time and place. He hadn't heard his mother's voice then, but of course she'd still been alive, with a time and a place of her own.

His time had been five years ago, almost; his place, a converted country house in the Cotswolds, where he'd been sent on a weekend course for assistant managers. When he'd opened the original letter in his office, he'd felt a sort of tingle going up his arm and ending at the back of his head, a tingle which he knew, through some instinct, meant that time and place were hoving into view.

It had happened after dinner, on the Sunday night. They had all drunk a lot. Sometimes you need to fill up with booze just as a car needs to be filled up with petrol, because you want to go somewhere where only booze can take you. He could tell everybody had the same idea: drink yourself to the point of new possibilities. Even the quiet woman beside him, Linda Something, was doing it.

He understood that what, all his life, had seemed the most difficult thing in the world, namely getting a woman you had no particular claim on to go to bed with you, was perfectly simple in the right situation. He remembered doing saturated solutions at a school, where you loaded a liquid up to such an extent that one more grain of whatever you were putting into it crystallised the whole lot. Here the experience felt more like liquefaction, but it had the same suddenness. Linda rose to her feet. He did the same. He staggered slightly, the first time he'd ever done so without actually walking.

'I'm going up to my room,' Linda announced. She didn't exactly hiccup but her voice went up and down as if warming up for it.

'So am I,' John said, as gallantly as possible.

'Come on then,' she replied, waving an arm limply in his direction. As he went he caught someone's eye. Even now he remembered whose: he was an assistant manager from Derby – they'd had a conversation earlier on in the day. The A.M. from Derby gave him a sudden sharp glance, through all the waver and wobble of booze, a glance that said, definitively, you lucky sod. John recognised that glance because he'd given it himself from time to time in the past.

He had a bad moment when they got to her door. She turned to him and said goodnight.

'I thought I was coming in,' he told her.

'You are,' she agreed, 'but you still want to have a good night, don't you?' The raunchiness of the reply was slightly undermined by his suspicion that it had actually slipped her mind that he *was* in fact coming in.

When she took her clothes off her body was nice but less exotic than he had hoped and even feared. It seemed normal, human. Margaret's was the same but he'd put that down to the familiarity of marriage. Women in magazines, by contrast, had a hard alien look about them, as if they came from some remote planet called Sex. As he took his own clothes off he realised that his body looked as if it had come from a different planet also, but not that one. His private parts were gloomy and pendulous; you could understand why they were normally kept private. Still, here he was; and here his private parts were; and there, already in bed, scrunched up modestly in the covers with just one ear visible, was Linda.

He hurried over to join her, very aware of the way he wagged and bounced, of his penis rising part way as if to point out half-heartedly the direction he was going. Linda's ear seemed attentive, watchful, but of course thank God it couldn't actually see. At the back of his head, beating with a double pulse like the systole and diastole of his heart, were the twin terrors of impotence and premature ejaculation, even the bitter possibility of a switch, sudden as electricity, from one pole to the other, neutral to live at a stroke.

He slid in beside her, intensely aware of the delicious warm and cool feeling of getting into a bed when somebody else is already in it. He moved round towards her and discovered she was trembling. Be gentle, he thought triumphantly. He was aware, for the first time in his existence, of a sense of the heroic. He pressed his chest to her back, tactfully keeping his lower half angled away. Then he placed a hand on her upward shoulder. The trembling was not a vibration on the surface of her body but came from far inside, was bound up with her breathing somehow. Suddenly he understood she was crying. Alcohol, he thought urbanely. No. He felt that his hand was some sort of measuring instrument, one tuned to human earthquakes, that could detect the exact level of her weeping. Boozy tears would blob up and shake loose with ease, without sharp edges to them. These tears were hard.

'Can I help?' he asked. As he spoke he felt a hot pleasurable wave pass over his chest. Strangely it seemed almost the same as the sensation you get further down when you have sex. This too was something for which he must have been waiting, just as he'd waited for a chance to commit adultery. He felt utterly mature, a man dealing with matters of concern to grown-up men and women.

'There was this man,' Linda Something replied. She could almost have begun with once upon a time. She talked for hours. The man was called Ian. There was no point in being resentful, let alone jealous – this Ian was as much a part of Linda's identity as her arms or her legs, certainly as much as her mother or her father. They'd met as teenagers. They'd become engaged. They drifted apart when he went to university. They met up again. They became engaged again. They married. They rowed. They separated. They came back together again. They'd just separated once more. They were talking of divorce. There was also another element to the problem, dating from much earlier, from her childhood. It was to do with a bicycle, and her sister, but involved her whole family set-up in a way John couldn't understand, helping to shape the sort of person she later became. When she talked about this part of her difficulties she seemed to be talking a different language almost, but John confined his responses to small noises and movements of agreement.

When she began she was, of course, facing away from him, and the effect was almost as if she were telling someone else. Then she lay on her back, talking to the ceiling but letting what she said spill over to his side of the bed. Then she turned to face him and his heart thumped at being allowed the full intimacy of her disclosures. The room was lit by the moon and he could make out her breasts looking up at him while she spoke, in the way children look attentively at a neighbour their mother is talking to, each eye unblinking. Somewhere at the far back of his mind a whining slobbering wolf-like thing was flinging itself in their direction only to crunch against the bars of the cage his mature self had erected.

When she stopped she asked him about his 'relationship'. He found himself talking with sudden intensity about Margaret, about the love and stability of their marriage. He felt the need to convince Linda that beyond her traumas and anxiety there was safety and steadiness, that these were the qualities *he* had on offer. It was the only way that he could distinguish himself from Ian, and from Linda too, come to that. When he had finished, she said 'Thank you' and kissed him on the forehead. The tone of the 'Thank you' and indeed of the kiss, their implication of gratitude, quietness, just-shared experience, corresponded exactly to his notion of parting after impromptu and successful sexual intercourse. Exactly.

He got out of bed and began to get dressed, with the word 'Exactly' stuck right in the forefront of his mind, so that he was unable to see anything else. He had been to bed with a woman. They had been intimate together. It was exactly. That's how I'll always think about it, as exactly. I will never go into it any further, but leave it at exactly. Her face had joined her breasts to look attentively up at him from the bed, in a sweet threesome. Yes, it was exactly; it was equivalent. When he later confessed to Margaret, all he said was that he'd been to bed with another woman. He told her the name, Linda, as a sort of clincher. Margaret was appalled and amused at the same time, a combination he hadn't known existed. It was like the mixing of two chemicals nobody had ever put together before: perhaps there would be an explosion. There wasn't, but the brief possibility of danger made him feel even more forcibly that what had happened between him and Linda had been *exactly*.

The thought of Margaret reminded him of how she had been this morning at breakfast, with something secretive in her manner, and that off tone of voice. Perhaps *she* was up to something too, perhaps she had a rendezvous? He felt a sudden pulse of jealousy. Then it occurred to him that he was whipping the sensation up in order to justify his presence here, and his own intentions. It amounted to a kind of do-it-yourself tit for tat. He'd stumbled upon his own hypocrisy. It was a bit like hearing yourself snore: you wondered how often it happened *without* you noticing.

The lounge door opened, and Mrs Clarke came back in. She was damp, wearing a towelling dressing-gown. It was blue, with fluffy ridges going across it. Her neck and shoulders, coming out of the top, seemed very white. It went below her knees, and her legs and feet were bare. He flicked his eyes over her toes, remembering how his children had loved 'This Little Pig'. You could see how the rhyme came about. Mrs Clarke's toes were pink and plump, cheerfully porky, like rows of piglets sucking at her feet. He wanted to suck at them in turn, so much so he heard himself making a rasping sound in his throat, and coughed briefly to cover it up.

'I'm sorry,' Mrs Clarke said. 'I thought I'd have a quick shower. Get the dust off. Oh, what's that you've got? It's – '

'Oh, just, um, Mr Clarke's, it was on the, I was just fiddling with it.'

'Mr Clarke's?' she asked, her face screwing up with incomprehension. 'That's my *fath*er's, my late father's.'

'Oh, I'm sorry.' He put it back hastily. For the fraction of a second, the tiny time in which you can propose all sorts of things before your brain moves in to separate the sheep from the goats, he wondered whether he should mention that he'd heard his mother's voice coming out of it, by way of balancing out one parent with another, and possibly making Mrs Clarke less touchy about it.

'Well,' she said, firmly changing the subject. 'What about a quick sandwich?'

He was caught on the hop. He could hardly say, don't let's bother, let's go upstairs AT ONCE, the mood wasn't right, with her sudden peevishness just fading away: a sharp push, at this moment, and it would be right back, like a wall between them.

'All right,' he agreed, and followed her into the kitchen.

'Will crab paste be all right?' she asked.

Paste? His mother used to make paste sandwiches when he was a child, but he'd never had them with Margaret. He associated them with the 1950s, along with those radio sets with valves that lit up, whooping and fizzing when you tried to tune in the Goons or *Lost in Space*. He felt a peculiar double sensation towards Mrs Clarke, half contempt and half pity.

'Yes, fine,' he answered.

'I love it,' she said, spreading vigorously. At least she seemed to have forgotten her resentment about his handling of her father's pipe. The trouble was that he felt as if he'd wandered into unknown territory, more unknown than he'd really wanted it to be. He had no idea what Mrs Clarke would love, or resent, next. Perhaps, despite the Liberty scarf, the going to her house, the shower, the dressing-gown, she had no thought at all that sex might be on the agenda. He felt a sudden chill of fear in the pit of his stomach. Sexual harassment by bank official. Crimes were always in headlines, without any 'the's or 'a's to soften the blow. Even when he did something small, and when he thought about it small things were all he *ever* did, like parking on a double yellow, he imagined the consequences in a brutal staccato, English with a mock-Gestapo accent. But *this* wouldn't necessarily be small; it might even be assault.

He could see the funny side, getting cold feet, cold everything, as the result of an ancestral briar and a crab-paste sandwich, but when all was said and done people plotted their whereabouts by means of tiny landmarks. How could he have sex with Mrs Clarke when he didn't know where she was?

She put his sandwich on a plate, and passed it over to him. Then she began scraping with her knife in the miniature jar in order to find enough paste for her own.

'If I'd had any sense I'd have put the kettle on for a cup of tea before I went up,' she said as she spread her slice of bread. She was quite relaxed. It seemed unfair that as a woman she could just be

186

there, waiting for something or nothing to happen, with no need to give herself away. 'There,' she said, completing her sandwich, 'I'll put it on now. It won't take two ticks.'

She turned away from him to fill the kettle. He stepped behind her, not quite touching. She seemed unaware of his proximity. He looked over her shoulder at the beginnings of her breasts, loose beneath her dressing-gown. Surely it would come as no surprise for his arms to snake round her waist, and his lips to press against her shoulder? Or he could simply wait until she turned round, and found herself chest to chest with him. But what then? He imagined a sudden look of horror or contempt on her face, a hand flying at him like a weapon, facing her at work the next morning and all the other mornings: an assistant bank manager with his trousers round his ankles. He remembered somebody once telling him in a pub that women always forgave you for an unwanted pass, however firmly they rejected it, because it was testimony to their sexual attractiveness. At the time he'd been much struck by the logic, but now it occurred to him that people just made up that sort of wisdom as they went along. There was no such thing as women. The person whom he was dealing with, here and now, was Mrs Clarke. He knew nothing about her, he had nothing in common with her.

Except the bank.

'Mrs Clarke,' he said, in a low voice proportionate to his nearness. He began to tell her about bearding Gardiner. He'd not even mentioned it to Margaret. It was the most intimate thing he could think of doing. In its own way it followed on from the scarf, the home for lunch, the shower. He was so close she could probably catch the sharp smell of crab paste on his breath as he recounted his woes.

'Avoir une pissoire,' Ann said to Jessica, passing her a paper plate of egg sandwiches.

'Oo, thing yew,' Jessica replied, wibbling her nose and fluttering her eyelashes as if to be equivalently posh. She was so ignorant, Ann realised, that she thought pissoire meant egg sandwich, which it did in a way.

Philip took one too.

Kevin took one, and had a tiny bite out of it, as though his mouth had been miniaturised since breakfast. 'The thing is, it was the electrics,' he said, as soon as he'd swallowed. Perhaps they were at a safe enough distance from the van for him to risk a diagnosis. 'Not much you can do about them.'

Philip took a huge swig of cider, not so much to drink as to wash down an equally huge lump of gobbled egg sandwich, on the same principle, Ann assumed, as a lavatory flush. When he'd finished he wiped the top with his hand and passed it to Jessica.

She put her sandwich down, rolled her eyes up towards the sky, and hoisted the bottle. 'Pah,' she sighed when she had finished. Philip patted her on the back with his podgy arm, as though she were a baby being burped. She laughed and placed her head on his shoulder. With her left hand she passed the bottle on to Kevin. Kevin took a nip as tiny as his bite of his sandwich had been, and gave it to Ann.

She raised the bottle to her mouth, deliberately avoiding looking at the sky as she did so. It wasn't God, it was a bottle of cider. Actually your eyes seemed to slew heavenwards automatically, and she had quite a job holding them down. She tried to grip them on to their earthly surroundings: the bumpy field punctuated by dollops of cowflop, though luckily no cows were in it at present; the hawthorn hedge by which they were sitting, with the green of its new leaves somehow separate from the branches, as if the hedge was bare but standing in a green mist; the radio telescope at Jodrell Bank, distant across the fields, on the horizon ahead of her; to one side, the footpath up which they'd come, sloping down towards the nameless village – all scrunched-up little roofs from this angle – where their van was still standing.

'At least no one will pinch it,' Ann said when she'd finished her swig. 'Unless they're an electrician, I suppose. And blind,' she added, passing the bottle to Philip once more.

'You've not eaten much,' said Philip disapprovingly as he raised the bottle again.

'I've not eaten anything,' Ann told him, watching his Adam's apple shuttle up and down like a lift. Her timing was perfect: Jessica froze in mid-bite.

'Oh Ann,' she said. 'Do you think . . .?' She lowered the remains of her sandwich to the oily blanket Kevin had provided. 'I suppose it is . . .' She moved away from Philip. 'Stealing,' she concluded.

Her voice was both hushed and squeaky at the same time: she looked mortified. And no wonder. She liked to go with the flow but the question was, which way was it flowing? If it had switched from sin to repentance she was caught high and dry, and aloneness was what Jessica feared most. She can't like herself as much as she pretends to, thought Ann savagely and then, after only the fraction of a second, relented.

'I just don't like egg sandwiches,' she said. 'They remind me of pee.' A happy and tactful word, pee: it made them all laugh, and got Jessica back on course again. This time it was her *hand* she put on Philip's shoulder. Boy, does she love that shoulder, Ann thought to herself. But of course Philip wouldn't take any more initiatives for the time being, since groping would only be priority number two while there was food around.

'Now we have chicken vol-au-vents,' Ann announced.

'Hoo, très,' said Jessica.

'What are they?' Kevin asked, equally ignorant but at least willing to admit it.

'Pastry boxes filled with a sort of sludge,' Ann told him. 'If you miscalculate your bite, it squirts out of the top, that's the important thing you have to know. Probably up your nostrils. The contents consist of liquid chicken.' She dealt out two each, to herself included. 'What I advise is, sharpen your teeth before using,' she said, and bit into one of hers. It suddenly occurred to her she was starving, and she did violence to them both, almost keeping up with Philip. Jessica did well for herself too. Only Kevin held off, taking ever more niminy-piminy mouthfuls of his egg sandwich and looking as if he had more important things on his mind. He's frightened of vol-au-vents, poor love, Ann realised.

She suddenly felt a glow of affection for him. We have our stand-offishness in common, she thought.

'What next?' asked Philip.

Ann peered into the bag they'd shoved their provisions into.

'Pork pies,' she suggested.

'Gimme,' said Philip, flicking his fingers, moving his shoulders, and shutting his eyes like cool Americans might, though probably not in response to a pork pie. Jessica giggled. Kevin worried at his crust. Ann put her hand into the bag and pulled out a pork pie, and the odour came back again, worse even than the pee of egg sand-wiches, that odour of corpses, of poor Stephen, mushed, pinked, pastry-wrapped: flattened by a vehicle.

He hadn't been flattened by a vehicle, of course. He'd been standing at the edge of the pavement, all alone.

Alone. There had been no crocodile of little children holding hands, no teachers shouting at them in extra-loud voices so the general public could appreciate how bossy they were, nobody but Stephen.

She'd only seen the scene for a second before flinging herself backwards into the darkness at the rear of the van, but could re-member it with perfect clarity. Stephen was standing forlornly at the edge of the pavement, sunlight flashing on one of the lenses of his spectacles. Nearby a down-and-out was pestering passing students. Behind, the museum looked huge and solemn. Stephen had his *back* to it.

She had known there was something wrong all along, but hadn't let herself think about it. She'd been so preoccupied with worrying about Stephen seeing *her* she'd ignored the fact that she'd seen Stephen.

'Pork pie,' she said, hoping that by saying it out loud she would make it ordinary and Stephen-free. She doled one out to Philip.

'Shouldn't it be ladies first?' Jessica asked, cornering her eyes to look cute. She said it, Ann knew, to remind all concerned that there were two sexes present.

'That's sexist,' said Philip, picking up his pie.

'Yes,' agreed Ann. 'The order is, first pigs, *then* ladies. Then Kevin.' As an afterthought: 'Then me.' Anything could have hap-pened to Stephen: he could have run away from home, or been kidnapped. Of course if he'd been kidnapped you'd expect a kid-napper to be in the vicinity. Unless he'd escaped. In which case, how on earth would he get home? He wouldn't have any money on him. He wouldn't even know where home was. He'd be stuck. He was gormless enough to get himself kidnapped again, kid-napped going, and kidnapped coming back. She almost laughed, in a despairing sort of way, at the thought of it.

'Pork pie,' she said, giving Jessica hers. 'Pork pie': Kevin. Then, almost in a whisper, 'Pork pie' for herself.

She looked at it, on the paper plate in front of her. She felt like one of those olden-day kings who served up their friends and relations in pies. She could no more eat this one than fly. She wished she'd given herself an extra vol-au-vent. Kevin hadn't touched his. He was busy chasing breadcrumbs and tiny fragments of egg around the rim of his paper plate with a large oil-stained finger. 'Can I have one of your vol-au-vents, Kevin?' she asked.

'Sure,' he said, and passed her one. He looked relieved. 'You can have both of them if you like' he added. He blushed slightly in relief. He'd been terrified of the blooming things, probably because they were called something French. He thought she was being tactful, not pushy.

'All right,' she said, and he passed her the second one. They were getting on like a house on fire. Not to be outdone, Jessica put her arm right over Philip's shoulders. Luckily for her he'd nearly finished his pork pie, and he gave her a quick interested look as she did so. With her free hand Jessica picked up the cider bottle and took a swig. We're rolling, Ann thought.

'Have my pork pie,' she said to Kevin, passing it over. 'Swapsies.' He didn't object, in fact he smiled at her. Kevin's smile made her notice how nice his eyes were, soft and brown. He seemed so kind and gentle it was hard to think of him as one of *them*, prone to singing folksy hymns, praying, believing in a God as boring and holier-than-thou as they were themselves.

Then, to her horror, a trapdoor opened in Kevin's head, and a small, peering, metallic eye rose from it.

It was Jodrell Bank, exactly above him on the horizon. But Ann stayed cold inside. She understood her dream all of a sudden. It was about how Christ wanted to pull you away from home and family, treading all over the heads of others, of the cabbages as they would seem from the evangelical point of view, the stay-at-homes, the people who were content to be what they were, and bury their dead. What had fooled her was that in the dream He had seemed so attractive. Of course He had. Attraction means pull. Magnets attract. The dream was *about* Him looking attractive, that was the whole point. It was a warning.

Kevin passed her the bottle of cider. Philip and Jessica were resting their foreheads one against the other, with their arms around each other's necks. Ann imagined having Philip's forehead-boil intimately pressing into her.

191

'I've got to go,' she suddenly announced.

'You what?' Philip asked. He didn't even bother to turn away from Jessica. He probably thought she meant pee under the hedge. 'Go.'

Jessica, quicker on the uptake, disentangled herself.

'Why?' she asked. She had paled again. Ann couldn't help feeling a kind of triumph at the power she seemed to be able to exert over her, not because she threatened Jessica's religion in any way, but because she seemed to be able to herd her further back into it when Jessica came too near the edge. That was the advantage of being on the outside, looking in.

'Oh, I've just remembered something I've got to do.'

'What?' Jessica whispered.

'Bury my dead,' Ann said, her stomach lurching immediately she'd said it. Poor, poor Stephen, she thought. 'Blah blah blah,' she added, to avoid explaining anything more.

Raymond hung in space, all four legs dangling. The window-frame bit into his chest. For a while he struggled and once he actually succeeded in hoisting the front part of himself up, finding occasional patches of grip in the skiddings of his paws against the outside surface of the window-pane. His head reared up, his shoulders crunched into the top of the quarterlight, and for a moment his whole weight levered against the back of his neck, until his back paws, as if in imitation of the front, scrabbled their way up the inside of the pane, and balanced him once more. He dangled where he was, not daring to move.

After a few moments he noticed that he could detect the spicy smell of squirrel on the breeze, and then to his horror the squirrel itself appeared, scuttling along the boughs of the trees at the bottom of the garden, and standing still at intervals with the same suddenness as that with which it ran. It came down a tree-trunk head first, and sat in a flower-bed, peering round. Then it darted forward on to the lawn and looked about itself again. Neither time did it look up towards Raymond, though Raymond knew it knew he was there. Raymond was no longer a threat that had to be taken into account, that's what it boiled down to. There was cool contempt in every inch of the tiny, quick-witted form. Even though he wasn't being looked at, Raymond rolled his eyes to one side in shame.

After some minutes the pain from his unnatural position made a howl rise in Raymond's throat. He stifled it and let his eyes roll slowly back in search of the squirrel. It was near the garden shed now, eating something again. The howl wouldn't stay down entirely so Raymond released it bit by bit, in the form of whimpers, hoping the squirrel wouldn't notice them and become aware of the agony he was suffering in addition to embarrassment.

Time passed. Raymond became bored with feeling the pain so he stopped feeling it and lapsed into a sort of doze. The sun was warm on his head and muzzle, even warmer, through the window, on his belly and back legs, where the cool breeze did not reach. His doze deepened into one of those sunlit daytime dreams where you are too lazy to discover what you are dreaming about even while you are dreaming it, except that somewhere towards the very middle of his dream there was a hot band that interfered with breathing, and to one side of it a clanging sound and the low cries of a human. Still asleep he opened his eyes to look. There was a form near the house next door, high, impossibly high, looking back at him. He woke up.

It was the man who tried to get in, on his ladder. Every so often he came to the house, climbed his ladder, and rubbed frantically at each window in turn, like a fly unable to understand why the air was hard in those places, unable for some reason to smell the glass itself, the odour a combination of water and iron. Now he was trying the house next door; at least, he had been. He was up his ladder but had twisted round so that he could see him, Raymond. He smelt of cigarettes. Suddenly he began to laugh.

It was like not being looked at by the squirrel, only worse, intolerably worse. At the bottom of the squirrel's not looking was an element of fear, a memory of the past, or even a memory of the future in which Raymond, foursquare in a dog's world, could chase after him, lips drawn back, teeth agleam. Only for the moment was he helpless, trapped in mid-air as if he was not a dog at all but an unsuccessful squirrel. But the man's laughter was a reminder that for a man a dog was never a dog but always an unsuccessful man. Even the man who didn't understand windows could laugh, however unfair his laughter might be, since stuck as he was in the quarterlight Raymond showed him that he understood windows even less.

The injustice was intolerable. Frantically Raymond began to scrabble front paws and back paws both at once, struggling to escape not so much from the window as from his embarrassment. He shot upwards, crunched into the frame again, lurched forward, and for a second looked straight down at the drop, at the strip of concrete, the picnic table and chairs, the lawn beyond. The idea flashed through his mind of jumping, no matter what the consequences, anything to leave the laughter behind; but at that exact second the laughter stopped.

The man called out something. Then clang clang he was rushing down his ladder. The ladder jerked away from the wall, clatteringly diminished to half its length, and then the man was running with it round the side of the house next door, disappearing from sight. Raymond pawed upwards at the front, struggling to put the drop at a distance, observing with a frightened eye that it grew even greater as he did so.

Then stiffly round the corner of the house came the ladder, along with the man. With a protesting rattle the ladder rose towards the window, nearer and nearer, making obtuse insensitive movements like a limb guided by a too-distant eye, as Raymond's own paw did when on the track of some elusive and skittering thing, some insect more at home in detail than he could ever be. At last it found a place to rest on the window-sill and then the man came climbing up.

Raymond wanted to slink back away from him in shame, but didn't dare rise into the quarterlight again, so he scrabbled his front paws without any pressure on the glass, to show the man he would go away if he could. He growled, because the man was an intruder; at the same time he wagged his tail and, as the man's face appeared at the top of the ladder, he licked it, in gratitude for rescue. The tangle of actions and emotions made him whimper, and that in turn reminded him of the pain in his chest, and he whimpered again. The man spoke gently, and scratched his ear. Then he raised his other hand up to Raymond's collar and began to ease him out. The quarterlight frame itself was chock-full of pain, and as successive parts of Raymond passed through it the pain leapt out and invaded each one in turn, so after a few moments Raymond barked loudly at the man, not because he was an intruder, but to tell him that it was all too much. The man spoke gently again, stopping for

194

a moment and stroking Raymond's face. Now he was near he smelt slightly of putty. Then, swaying a little on his ladder, he raised two hands to help Raymond down.

Suddenly Raymond's centre of balance shifted forward, and he had to fling his front paws outwards to land on the man's shoulders and stop himself falling further. The man lurched backwards, let go of Raymond, and grabbed the window-sill, just preventing the two of them from falling. He took one step down the ladder himself, and guided Raymond's front paws on to the top rung. His back ones were still hooked over the quarterlight frame.

Raymond slid one out and rested it on the window-pane. The man moved further down the ladder, and gave a tug at Raymond's collar. With another whimper of fright Raymond put a paw on the second rung, and brought a back paw on to the top rung. He found his body compressed like a spring, as if to go arching out in a long stride and, unable to resist his own prompt, he hurtled down the ladder, slithering past the man and careering down the rest of the ladder without regard to rungs, trying to make his running paws catch up with the velocity of the fall, and hitting the ground with a thump to the extent that they didn't quite.

He bounded round the lawn to dissipate the aftershock of the thump, and to have his revenge on the squirrel which was no longer there. As the man clanged his way down the last few steps of the ladder, Raymond rushed up to its foot and gave him a few barks as a reminder that he was trespassing. Then he ran, barking, round the side of the house, half to keep clear of any retaliation, half to show the man the way out. The gate was open. His barks changed to barks of glee as he ran out and into the road.

When Stephen got to the school gate he saw his class in a line on the playground. The trouble was, the line was pointing the wrong way. When you went to school, school was always the same, but as soon as you weren't there for a little while it all became completely different. All your friends had made friends with somebody else, the dummies had got clever, horrible children had become nice, the pictures on the wall had all changed. Now his class were standing in the playground the wrong way round, facing towards the gate. Mr Sherlock was standing in front of them, his hair flopping about as usual.

'Come along, Stephen,' Mr Sherlock said. Even the way he said it was different from how Stephen expected him to speak. He didn't sound at all worried or angry, he said 'Come along' as if Stephen had been too long in the toilets or was coming back too slowly from taking the dinner money to Mr Luckett's office.

Stephen walked across the playground to the line.

'By the way, where were you this morning, Stephen?' Mr Sherlock asked when he'd got there.

Stephen took a deep breath. He felt his face go red. He spoke very quietly, so it wouldn't be so much of a lie. 'To the dentist, sir,' he muttered.

'I beg your pardon, Stephen?'

'Dentist, sir.'

'Perhaps he extracted your voice as well.'

'Yes, sir.'

'Word by word,' said Mr Sherlock, looking happy. Stephen relaxed. You were safe when Mr Sherlock started to look happy: it meant that he'd forgotten about whatever it was you'd done or not done. 'Ooo, I don't like this word,' Mr Sherlock said, looking into an imaginary mouth. '*Slobber*: horrible word that. Yank it out.' He yanked it out and threw it on the playground. Then he trod on it, scrunching it underfoot. 'What word don't you like, Christopher?' he suddenly asked.

'Conker, sir,' Christopher replied.

'Conker?' Mr Sherlock repeated in surprise. 'Conker? You don't like conker?'

'No, sir.'

'Why ever not?'

'Don't know, sir.'

'Don't you like playing conkers?'

'Yes, sir, I like playing them. Just don't like the word, sir.'

'Oh well, nothing for it.' Mr Sherlock went over to Christopher. 'Open beak-ohs, lad.' Christopher opened his mouth. Mr Sherlock put his hand in and pulled the word conker out. He dropped it on the playground and scrunched it as he had slobber. 'Try saying conker now,' he told Christopher.

'Conker.'

'Blast it. You've got another one in there.' He put his hand in and pulled the second one out. This time he threw it far far over

196

the playground. Stephen just caught sight of it, a tiny, arcing brown dot, as it fell to earth on the small rim of lawn by the back wall. 'That should do the trick,' Mr Sherlock told him. 'Try saying it now.'

Christopher opened his mouth but no word came out.

'Got it,' Mr Sherlock said. 'Told you I would.'

'Please, sir,' Stephen said. Even though he wasn't telling a lie this time he could still only speak very quietly, as if his voice had caught a chill from the lie he had told already. 'Why are we standing the wrong way round, sir?'

'We're not standing the wrong way round, Stephen.'

'But we're not pointing at the school, sir.'

'No, we're not. You see that great big metal tube there, on four wheels? What is it?'

'It's a bus, sir.'

'Good boy! Now you know our secret. We're pointing at the bus.' He changed from his joking tone to his ordinary one. 'We're going swimming. We couldn't go this morning because we had a fire drill.'

It was true, as Stephen had thought: as soon as you didn't go to school, even for one morning, they did something completely different from usual and turned everything on its head.

'Did you think we were queuing for dinner?' Mr Sherlock asked.

'I didn't know what we were doing,' Stephen told him.

'You *have* had your dinner, haven't you, Stephen?'

'Yes, sir,' Stephen whispered. You only had to say one lie and other lies popped up all over the place. Who would have believed he would find himself lying about having had his dinner?

'You're sure?'

'Yes, sir.'

'As best you might with what teeth you have left.'

'Yes, sir.' Stephen thought of the blotherin man, with his stripy teeth, and wondered if he was having anything to eat in his pub. He was the one who needed to have gone to the dentist, not Stephen. It seemed like a cheat.

'Come on then, boys and girls, let's get on the bus,' Mr Sherlock said. Stephen felt he was doing nothing but get on buses, bus after bus, like counting sheep when you can't get to sleep at night, except that they never made you go to sleep, however many you

197

counted. The bus driver had his dark glasses on, like two holes in his face. They made Stephen remember the man with the head jumper who'd come up the stairs towards his bedroom in the middle of the night. Perhaps he had been the reason why everything had turned out so strangely. If so, seeing the bus driver's dark glasses might turn things back to normal, like when you step on a second pavement crack to stop the bad luck that would be caused by treading on the first one.

As the bus drew away Stephen realised that he still hadn't set foot inside his school, even though he'd been trying to get to it since first thing this morning.

11

When they got to the swimming-baths it was just as Stephen had remembered while he was standing outside the museum this morning: green, damp, smelly. It was horrible to see bums slide out from everybody's clothes in the boys' changing-room. What he didn't like about people's bottoms was the sort of smile they seemed to have on their faces. They would be much nicer if they were blank. The other boys didn't seem to mind about theirs, but Stephen always kept his shirt-tails dangling as much as possible, even though they were never quite long enough. If you undressed straight up and down instead of bending over you could keep a good amount of your backside covered. It made him take longer than most of the others. When he walked through into the baths themselves they were full of the screams and cries of invisible, drowning children.

A lot of the real children were in the shallow end and Stephen was just about to slip in to join them when Mr Sherlock started bellowing out his orders.

'Children, listen,' he shouted. He never changed into his swimming things; he never went near the water; for all they knew he couldn't swim at all. 'Poor swimmers, terrible swimmers, and non-swimmers, stay in the shallow end and practise your strokes. Mrs Booth will be looking after you.' Mrs Booth was the swimming-baths attendant. She always wore a white T-shirt and pumps. She was fat, and apart from the whiteness of her clothes was just like a dinner-lady, bullying people all the time. Stephen was glad he was a swimmer. 'The rest of you come up to the deep end.'

Stephen followed the others along the side of the pool. The water here seemed too flat and oblong to be wet: it looked like pale green jelly. As they waited in the cool air the children grew thinner and the legs of some of them started to shake. Most held their hands together under their chins, elbows squeezed against their ribs, almost as if they were praying.

'Which of you lot can jump in off the side?' Mr Sherlock asked.

'Me sir! Me sir!' some of the children answered, unclasping their hands so that they could poke one arm up as if they were asking a question in class.

'All right,' Mr Sherlock told them. 'Jumpers go up to the very end of the pool. Non-jumpers stay here.'

The jumpers hurried off. Suddenly Stephen went after them, even though he'd never jumped into a swimming-pool in his life. That was the whole problem: he knew Mr Sherlock was going to make the non-jumpers jump. I'm becoming a liar, he thought to himself as he went. He'd always been a fibber, but being a liar was a more grown-up kind of fibber, like going to comprehensive school. You had to fib worse or more often to be a liar. It's the blotherin man's fault, he thought grumpily to himself, I wasn't a liar until he came and sat beside me on that first bus.

No, that wasn't true, the blotherin man wasn't a liar. Whatever taking people's hats off their heads was, it wasn't a lie. It was the opposite if anything, more truthful than the things people did usually. So was asking those students for money. In fact Stephen had started being a liar even before he'd met the blotherin man. It was a lie to have got on the bus in the first place. He'd got on as if he was Ann, not Stephen, the same as he was now going to the very end of the pool as if he was a jumper, not a not-jumper. On the other hand he hadn't *told* anyone he was Ann, and they would never have believed him even if had. Nor had he *said* he was a jumper. All he was doing was going along with the others. Could you be a liar, he wondered, just by doing something, or going somewhere? Can you *do* lies, or go to them?

Sure enough, Mr Sherlock lined the not-jumpers up by the edge of the pool. Stephen and the jumpers watched them while they waited at the far end. Daniel Young was the end not-jumper. He had his arms folded. He dipped one foot in the water, or one toe to be accurate, exactly his big toe, like a ballet dancer. Then he popped it out. Then he plunged his whole foot in, much faster.

'You're not going to bath a baby, Daniel Young,' Mr Sherlock told him. 'What I want you to do is fling yourself into the swimming-pool with joyous abandon. And when I say yourself I mean all of you. Don't leave some bits and pieces on the side, just in case.'

Sometimes Mr Sherlock didn't see or understand what the children were doing, like other grown-ups. Other times his eyes were very sharp and he would suddenly pick out what was going on, like a bird picking a worm out of the back lawn. What Daniel Young was trying to do was jump in the swimming-pool one bit at a time, first his big toe, then his foot, then, probably, most of a leg. Now Mr Sherlock had spotted him he gave that up and folded his arms. Stephen, watching him, did the same. It made you feel as if you were tying your body together so no harm could come to it, folding in the loose bits as the two tortoises who lived in the house next door with Mr and Mrs Rowbotham did when their legs and tail and head vanished into their shells. But Mr Sherlock began to walk towards Daniel Young with big plonking steps, like a policeman. Daniel Young looked round at him fearfully. His arms slowly became untied.

Then a funny thing happened.

Mr Sherlock raised his hand and pushed with it, to show Daniel Young he should jump in. He was nowhere near Daniel Young but it was just as if he had an invisible arm at the end of his arm that was about six feet long because Daniel Young immediately overbalanced. His arms and legs zigzagged as he fell, trying every little corner of the air at incredible speed to find if there was a handle or foothold anywhere that he could grab. Then there was a big white splash. Stephen caught sight of one last leg before Daniel Young disappeared entirely.

The other jumpers were all laughing but Stephen, arms still folded, shivered at the thought that it might have been him. Daniel Young's head bobbed up like a ball. His hair was flattened and shiny and he looked completely different. Cyril, the cat next door on the other side from the tortoises, had once shot past Stephen soaking wet after dad had thrown a bucket of water over him, and he'd looked different in exactly the same way, as if he'd suddenly lost a lot of weight and been polished. Perhaps Daniel Young *was* different. He'd been turned from a not-jumper into a jumper in the space of a second. As soon as Daniel Young had swum to the side, the next child, Helen Rennie, jumped in.

'All right, you lot,' Mr Sherlock told the remaining line of not-jumpers, 'in you go one at a time. I'll be keeping an eye on you. When you've gone in once, line up and go in again. It's as easy as falling off a log.' And then Mr Sherlock began walking up towards the jumpers at the end of the pool. The funny thing was that Stephen could tell just from the way he was walking that something terrible was going to happen. Behind Mr Sherlock there was a little explosion as the next person hit the water.

'Now, *you* lot,' Mr Sherlock said when he'd arrived at the end of the pool. Stephen's heart began to thump so violently that it felt as if it would leap out of his folded arms like a rabbit. 'What I'd like to know is, how many of you have ever jumped off a diving board?'

Stephen forgot where his legs were, and shot downwards about six inches before he remembered them again. 'Me sir! Me sir! Me sir!' some of the children were crying, their arms pointing almost flat out with excitement, as if they wanted to grab Mr Sherlock.

'No need to burst a blood vessel,' Mr Sherlock said. 'You'll all get your chance, so don't panic. You're not panicking, are you, Stephen?'

Stephen tried to say no, but nothing would come out. There just seemed to be an empty hole where his voice used to be.

'Stephen?' Mr Sherlock repeated.

Stephen rushed about inside his head, looking for a question he *could* answer no to. Are you a girl, that would be all right. 'No, sir,' he said.

Mr Sherlock looked at him curiously for a few moments longer, as if he was trying to remember something he wanted to say. Then he loosened his head and let it look around at everybody.

'Form a line,' he said, 'and get up on the diving board one at a time. All the me-sirs can go first, to show the rest of us how to do it. What I want is arms by your side and legs together. You should slide in without a splash, just as if you've been swallowed by a shark.' Behind him at that very moment there was a squeal and then a splash as another non-jumper jumped in, probably for the second time by now. Suddenly it seemed very friendly and normal to jump in off the side. He wondered whether he should tell Mr Sherlock he was a non-jumper after all. Maybe that was why Mr

Sherlock had looked at him in that long way of his; perhaps he'd guessed.

'Any questions?' Mr Sherlock asked.

Now was the moment, if he was going to say it. The funny thing was he felt exactly the same about saying it as he had once when he'd stood on the side of the pool wondering whether to jump in. He'd felt he'd only have to go one inch further and it would all be over. But at the same time he could no more move forward that inch than fly.

'Good,' Mr Sherlock said.

They all shuffled into line. The board wasn't very high, only about up to Stephen's middle. You had to go up a little ladder, with three steps on it, to get on. The first me-sir, who was called John McGough, climbed up. He walked along the plank show-offily, waving his arms about as if greeting fans, and swinging his hips as if he was so cool he could even make fun of people *being* cool.

'Concentrate!' Mr Sherlock called out, but it did no good. John went flying off the end of the board without giving himself time to think. In the air his bottom was down and his knees were up, like a giant baby sitting on a flying potty.

Then the next me-sir went, then the next. Then it was William Watson, the first one in the line who wasn't a me-sir. He was straight in front of Stephen. He stood at the end of the plank quietly and neatly, arms by his sides, legs together. Then he made a little push with just his feet, so as not to disturb the rest of him and went straight down, just tilting slightly as he hit the water, like a statue someone was throwing in. Then it was Stephen's turn.

The only part of Stephen that could feel anything was his feet. They noticed the skim of water on the pool surround, thin and wet compared with the jelly water of the pool itself, and then the rubber-covered steps up to the board, and the grainy surface of the board itself. The feelings didn't go from his feet to his head as feelings usually did but stopped short round about his ankles, as if there was a closed door near the bottom of each leg. He felt as if he consisted merely of a pair of feet walking to their doom, with a sort of sad cloud hanging over them.

It was much higher on the board than it looked from the side. Mr Sherlock and the jumpers all had their faces turned up towards him. While Stephen felt he was just feet they looked as if they were just faces, each one like a plate which had on it, instead of meat and vegetables, a nose, two eyes, and a thin smiling mouth. As Stephen walked along the board it became horribly bendy under his lone feet. There was a distant swimming-pool below.

Whenever Stephen was going to die he always did the same things.

He did the first one when he was about two-thirds along the board. What he had to do was say, 'May Ann look after my animals.' He didn't say it exactly to Ann, or to God, but to someone in between the two, the whoever-it-was who listened when you said things like that, and could make them come true, unlike God who was too important to bother, and unlike Ann who didn't take any notice of him anyway. He thought of Rabbitty, Patrick, and Elephanty without him to look after them, sitting sadly for ever on his pillow, unable to do anything or think anything or feel anything, unless somebody did it or thought it or felt it for them. He felt a terrible aching guilt that he wouldn't be able to make them come alive any more.

He was at the end of the board. It bent horribly. It was like standing on the tip of a long, poking-out tongue. It was time for the second thing he always said to himself when he died: 'I've had a lovely life.' Tears stung the back of his eyelids as he thought gratefully of how happy he'd been.

The third thing had to be said as he was actually dying. It had to be the last thing of all, and you mustn't give your mind time to think of something else after it.

He took one last look at the pool before he jumped. Far away at the side, not-jumpers were happily jumping in. At the shallow end the little heads of the non-swimmers were bobbing about and being shouted at by Mrs Booth. None of them seemed to be looking up at him. Coming down from the ceiling was the roar of drowning children.

He jumped.

The pool froze for a moment, and then bent towards him. Not yet: there was still time for more thoughts afterwards. The pool swung further round, and grew until it filled his eyes. The water looked horribly thick. It was still smooth, he hadn't started going into it so far, now was the moment.

'Ho,' he said. He said it because once when he was little he'd said hi, and this was the answer. He said ho out loud because he knew that the splash would cover it up.

Mrs Clarke's car came to a stop. John felt he ought to tumble out of it like a paratrooper. Unknown territory: Palmerston Grove, Heaton Moor. He'd never been to Gardiner's house before.

Mrs Clarke had, though. When she told him he'd felt a twinge of jealousy. She'd bumped into Gardiner while shopping, apparently, and had gone back for a 'quick drink'. No mention was made of *Mr* Clarke, whose existence seemed minimal: even his pipe didn't belong to him. Gardiner wouldn't have hesitated, one to one with Mrs Clarke, in the privacy of his house. Going through his front door would be an irrevocable act, like entering some kind of sexual abattoir. No, surely not. Mrs Clarke with her cup of tea, her crab-paste sandwich, her *woollen* quality, wasn't designed for elemental encounters. But there was another Mrs Clarke too, no point in fooling himself, the Mrs Clarke who quietly knocked on his office door, who took a shower while they were in *her* house together, the Mrs Clarke who had piglets on the tips of her feet, and breasts loose beneath her towelling dressing-gown like presents in some exquisite bran-tub. He could howl with rage at his own cowardliness, itemising all that evidence and then ignoring it for fear, my God, some paratrooper him!, that he might be taken to court on a charge of sexual harassment, or at least be laughed at day after day as a man who'd *come on* instead of eating his paste sandwich as he was supposed to. So he'd confided in her instead, telling her about his own big moment which when all was said and done amounted to whining to Gardiner about his grievances, real or imaginary. There he, John, was, talking about confronting some ogre in the car-park, and now needing to *beard* him, and ten to one Mrs Clarke had already been to *bed* with the sod. Perhaps she was that kind, went to bed with everybody. Except John, of course. Touch me not. I'm normal, I am. All the rest of the world has sex, I have normality.

But she'd listened interestedly enough. She gave no hints that she was itching to go upstairs. If she *had* given any hints he'd have taken her upstairs.

No hints? Apart from her dressing-gown, she was naked. What more of a hint did you need? And what excuses had he got for ignoring the one she'd given? That she'd been a bit annoyed when he touched her late father's pipe. That crab-paste sandwiches seemed very 1950s. That she was making him a cup of tea.

He thought of Margaret, as she'd been when they'd first met in the Poco Poco, all those years ago. She had been standing talking to a girl-friend on the other side of the hall. Every now and again she seemed to pulse with a stray beat of whatever awful music was being played. She was wearing some sort of tufty blue nylon dress. It had all been so simple. They were as innocent as each other. He'd asked her to dance. He was a hopeless dancer but it hadn't mattered. Then he'd bought her a drink, something soft – in those days, probably orange squash. There had been no knife-edge calculations involved, no strategy. It was, what was the word for it?, normal. Even then the Poco Poco had been glum and crumbling, but what had it mattered? *They* were young. He felt sudden acidic tears behind his eyelids. Today was their wedding anniversary, and he'd dedicated it to trying to seduce Mrs Clarke. Or to getting himself seduced by Mrs Clarke. Or rather, not. And a good thing too. He knew, he'd known all along, what the time and place had been. Years ago, the Poco Poco. It even rhymed.

Anyway, his subconscious understanding of his true priorities had served him well without his realising it. He had spoken up loyally for Margaret that time he'd lain in bed with Linda; and just now in the kitchen with an almost equally naked Mrs Clarke he'd talked about bearding Gardiner, which after all affected the prospects of the whole family in addition to preventing him from committing adultery. In each case the other woman had probably been grateful for his prior loyalty also, as it may have helped to reinforce her own, Linda's to her Ian, Mrs Clarke's to the invisible Mr Clarke. Certainly Mrs Clarke had given no sign of disappointment. She had seemed fascinated by John's account of the showdown with Gardiner and had suggested dropping him off at the house before going back to work herself, telling the staff that he'd had to see Gardiner on bank business, and asking Mr Hawthorne to take over. So here they were. Palmerston Grove. Time to bale out.

They sat in the car for a few moments. Mrs Clarke had parked a few houses before Gardiner's, to be on the safe side. The houses were Victorian semis, tall and aloof-looking, with steps up to the front door. Gardiner's looked a little neglected. The small front garden had been gravelled over, and a few fleshy-looking weeds grew out of the gravel. The brickwork on the side of the house had been painted white, perhaps to protect it, but the whiteness had gone dingy and was peeling. A large flowerpot with a small dead tree in it leaned against the wall. Gardiner's car was parked in the small driveway between the house and pavement.

John got out of Mrs Clarke's car. No sooner had he shut the door behind him than Mrs Clarke leaned over to the passenger seat he had just vacated. 'Have a Polo?' she asked, offering one through the window. Stupidly, for the second time in a minute, John felt the sting of tears in his eyes. How thoughtful, he thought: she'd somehow detected the fact that he wanted one, and had chosen this moment to offer, trying to help him get the Gardiner bearding in some sort of proportion. To know him that well! His heart lurched as it struck him she must have monitored all his thoughts and feelings for the whole of the lunch-hour, but immediately he felt a sense of relief. It hadn't been up to him then, it had been up to her. She'd been in charge. A sour thought followed: other people always seemed to see further into him than he did into them. In that kitchen Mrs Clarke had been mysterious and unfathomable; he'd been an open book.

'Thank you,' he replied, taking one. His spirits rose as she smiled confidentially at him across the transaction.

'Thank *you* for my scarf,' she said in a whisper.

'Oh well,' he replied. He must have been mad not to follow up her acceptance of that ridiculously expensive scarf. But on the other hand, Mrs Clarke *knew*. To know all is to forgive all.

'I'm wearing it,' she mouthed.

'So you are,' he replied. He hadn't noticed.

'But I won't tell!' She laughed, also in a whisper.

That was the extent of it. She put the car into gear. You couldn't say it was *exactly*, as the confidences in bed with Linda had been exactly. This time it was only approximately. He'd approximately commited adultery, with the help of a Liberty scarf.

'Good luck,' Mrs Clarke mouthed, and drove off. As he watched her go, John put the Polo in his mouth. At least it would cut through the taste of that revolting crab-paste sandwich.

The sun was shining but there was a chill breeze which seemed to find its way into his clothing, making him feel naked. He walked towards Gardiner's front door. When you think about confronting somebody beforehand you only have his ghost to deal with. In point of fact John had not gone into the bearding in any detail, he'd just tiptoed around that peculiar word, but somewhere in the corner of his mind there had been a sort of spectre of Gardiner, just a brain picture which had nodded and seen reason. Of course it was totally insubstantial, and seeing Gardiner's actual house changed everything. His brain picture of Gardiner became detailed, realistic. He was able to see the man as he was: gruff, boorish, direct, unpredictable. Even worse he was able to see himself too, busily and unconvincingly retracting all he had said in the car-park the other afternoon, adding wimpishness to his whingeing.

That mental scene stopped him literally in his tracks. What if he made matters worse? Perhaps Gardiner felt a grudging respect for him, which unsaying all his complaints would undo? It wouldn't be the sort of performance that showed you were made of managerial material. On the other hand, slagging off the bank and all its works didn't demonstrate much potential either. But on the other, other hand, my God, he couldn't slink back into work not having bearded Gardiner, after telling Mrs Clarke he was going to. Bearding Gardiner was the only way he could salvage not having gone to bed with *her*.

He wondered whether he should stay here on the pavement for a few moments, and plan out what he was going to say. If he weighed his words a little perhaps they would have . . . more weight. He looked down at his feet, side by side on a cracked paving stone. He pictured his car, dead as a doornail in the bank car-park, two miles away. It made him feel itchy and impatient, the thought of his battery being flat. One of his shoe-laces had been done up neatly, the other sloppily, with a huge straggling bow. He knelt down to refasten it. Anything to postpone the moment. There was no way he would be able to prepare what he had to say in advance, his mind was a complete blank. All he could do was march up, knock on the door, and seize the moment as best he could, just as he should have seized the moment in Mrs Clarke's kitchen when her back was to him and she was only wearing a dressing-gown, with her breasts loose inside it.

He began to walk towards Gardiner's house, telling each leg in turn to make its step. It was funny how different the house seemed from its neighbours. He remembered how he'd looked at houses when he was a child: this one looked menacingly back at him from its black windows. You could almost hear it breathe.

His legs took him up a small but winding path that led through the front-garden gravel to the front doorsteps. There were three of these, quite steep. He climbed them. The door was done in green and cream paint, slightly cracked. There was a black-painted cast-iron knocker designed to look like something reptilian, or perhaps a sea-horse. He raised it, his own heart knocking in anticipation. A fraction before he released it the house screamed.

No. He realised that it wasn't a scream but a peal of laughter. What he'd heard was a woman's laughter coming from an upstairs window. Of course. How naïve to assume that just because he had to go to hospital for some sort of consultation, and after that write his quarterly report, Gardiner wouldn't be in bed with a woman! If she could have found her way in past him it would probably have been Mrs Clarke herself, making up for lost time. Since it couldn't be her it would be any woman at all, just somebody for Gardiner to be in bed with. One thing you could be sure of, it would not be a good idea for John to knock on Gardiner's door and try to explain to him about why he'd gone over the top in the bank's car-park the other day. It would, without any question, make matters far far worse. Both in terms of strategy, since Gardiner would be furious, and self-image, since he, John, would feel like a wimp on a new scale altogether, a wimp become super or mega by dint of wittering cowardice and sexual non-achievement.

He thought all this in a flash, while still holding the knocker. The conclusion was to lower it quietly back into place. Strangely, and horribly, this didn't happen. It was as if his original decision, to knock, couldn't be overruled. Even though he no longer wanted it to, John saw his hand force the knocker down hard, so that it would make a loud bang. At that moment, however, some kind of subconscious appeal procedure went into operation, and at last the order went out from his brain to his hand to stop. But it was too late: the knocker was halfway down. All that happened was that it knocked less hard than it otherwise would have, but still hard enough.

Above, the laughter stopped in its tracks.

Oh God, Gardiner would be coming.

There was absolutely no choice. John turned from the door, scrambled down the steps, and hared away from Gardiner's house like some kid who was playing thunder-and-lightning.

Even while they were kissing kissing kissing Margaret was itemising reasons. He began kissing her as soon as the front door was shut, just grabbed her and kissed. He pressed her back against the hall wall to do so. She stood there a while, scrunched by his weight, and let him get on with it while she began on her reasons. It reminded her of doing homework, trying to remember a French verb, making your mind work harder than it wanted to, though in the days when she'd done homework she'd never had the distraction of a thirteen- or fourteen-stone man pressing her mouth so hard it felt as though her teeth were bending inwards, and kneading her rib-cage with his great paws on each side of her breasts.

The first reason was: I'm letting him get away with this, for the moment at least, just for the moment, because he's desperate. In a minute I'll pull myself together, or rather, I'll pull *him* together. That was something a woman could usually do, however heavy the man was, whatever the degree to which he was squashing her almost flat, she could suddenly become his mother, be kind but firm: enough of that, don't be silly, pull yourself, immortal words, together. (What exactly *do* you pull?) But in the meantime, turn a blind eye, a blind mouth, let him have his way for a few moments, he's desperate.

At the hospital she'd thought he had less to worry about than she had, but now the sheer ferocity of his kisses told her otherwise and that, in its squashy and mauling way, was a comfort, because it put them in the same boat. She'd thought it would be nothing for a man to have a breast mutilated, compared to how it would be for a woman. As she remembered that, she thought of those lines you were supposed to say to each other after sex: how was it for you, darling? How was it for *you*? Now she felt she *could* understand how he must feel. To go through all this over a part of the body men weren't even supposed to have! Obviously, from one point of view men had breasts, but from another, they didn't. For a man to have cancer of the breast was not merely to have a part of the body you wanted (since obviously you wanted all of it) under threat of

210

being taken away, but also to have a part of the body you *didn't* want forced on you. Imagine what it would be like for her to discover she had a testicle somewhere: with cancer in it!

She felt like some lawyer, coming to grips with a complicated brief. It was funny how she could think so clearly in these circumstances. It was like pondering on something while you were standing out in the elements, except that instead of rain beating down it was kisses, driving into her face as though on a storm-wind.

Thinking of which: she was a hypocrite, letting him kiss her like this, without resisting and without kissing back. He wasn't just weather, whatever she liked to pretend, he was a man, and with a man you had to make your mind up, one way or the other.

He hadn't been kissing her all that long, perhaps a minute or so. She could let him continue a little longer, surely. And in the meantime, so as not to be a hypocrite, she would kiss him back.

When she did so he made a small noise. It was like a whimper, only triumphant. More than anything else it sounded like the faint whinny of a horse. He thinks he's in charge now, Margaret realised. What she should have foreseen, she immediately afterwards understood, would be that he'd take her kissing him back as a cue for moving his hands from her rib-cage to her breasts. Perhaps he *is* in charge now, she thought swoonily. Her breasts felt exquisite, charged and somehow golden, if gold was something you could feel.

She stopped short – it was odd how you could do that, the sensation switched off as abruptly as you might switch off a tap – as she thought of her lump, but then she remembered that he *knew* about it. The wonderful thing about adultery, she thought, in that funny state, half blurred, half sharp, that you often reach when you are falling asleep, is that you can be honest in your dishonesty. Once you are safely in the depths of a hidden assignation, you can afford to be quite open. There was no need to hide her lump. He had to take her as she was. The sensation in her breasts came back.

All your life, she thought, you defer the decision as to whether, if the opportunity should crop up in a certain way, if the exactly right man should come along, you would have a fling. You could get to old age without ever quite making up your mind. But if a lump on your breast appears, everything changes. This may be my only chance, Margaret thought. Instead of *thinking* now, and perhaps *doing* later, it has to be the other way round: do now, and perhaps think later. Make love for the time being and my mind up in due course.

'Come on,' he said. He put an arm round her shoulders and led her to the stairs.

Oh Lord, she thought, this is the big moment. She marvelled at how dry and everyday he'd managed to keep his voice. He must have been calculating the right moment, trying to work out when she'd been warmed up enough to agree to go upstairs, knowing that a tremor of doubt in his voice – doubt about whether she would agree – would have the effect of making her wonder if she *should* agree. But he'd said it firmly, not exactly as an order, more as an inevitable statement of the point they'd both got to.

It was hard, climbing the stairs. It turned a hot moment into a cold decision. Also, there was something about it that reminded you of going to execution. Even worse, she had a sense of Stephen's round and spectacled face hovering over them somewhere up towards the shadowy Victorian ceiling, like a fledgling owl, and looking reproachfully down at her. Little Stephen, Spirit of the Staircase. Why not? When you went off on a fling, you were flung from, as well as towards. Flung from husband *and* children. I'll come back soon, Stephen, she whispered inside her head. It's only for now: I have to have a little *now*, while I can. Anyway, she thought, perhaps it's good practice for you.

The thought took her by surprise, and her unaware eyes immediately brimmed. Strangely, as a result of the after-glow of her breasts, and the yearning, puckered sensation at the pit of her stomach, like the feeling you have in your nose when you want to sneeze, only to the nth degree, her smarting eyes felt sexual too, and she heard herself give that little chortle people make when they are 'snapping out of it'. It was as if her attention actually clicked as it switched back to the solid male on the stairs just behind her. He noticed it because he bent forward over her shoulder and looked at her quizzically. She found herself putting a hand back, fumbling for his groin, and giving it a squeeze. Then, squealing with laughter, she ran up the remaining stairs and turned to look down on him, hands on hips. As she did so, the words of a dreadful song came into her mind: 'I am strong, I am invincible, I am woman', and she blushed. It didn't matter, nothing mattered. He'd just think the blush was sexual desire.

'And where is this bedroom, then?' she asked, as if they'd been talking about it before.

Sexual lust was very equalising, even ordinarifying. As he got to the top of the stairs she could see that his trousers had become swollen and awkward-looking, which made him move clumsily; and his cheeks were brick-red. All the mystique in the world about sex couldn't disguise the fact that it made people totally predictable. He didn't say anything but took her elbow and led her across the landing through a tall door into his bedroom. To her relief his bed had been made: she would have felt sordid getting into an apple-pie one. He strode ahead of her and tugged the curtains across. Then he turned back towards her. 'I won't be a minute,' he said, not quite looking at her face. He went over to the door, walking from side to side like a sailor on his sea-legs, and through.

I know what he's doing, thought Margaret. He's being tactful, giving me a chance to undress in peace and get into bed. And himself, come to that. He'll be undressing in the bathroom. Yes, that was his real motive, not consideration for her feelings, but for his own. Worldly-wise, she understood there were problems, if you were a man, unzipping your flies, taking off your socks. If you took your socks off before your trousers, you looked fussily calculating: if after, daft. She shivered with pleasure at the thought that he wasn't being discreet on her behalf but out of male vanity. Ten to one he'd return just wearing underpants. What looked awkward in trousers, and over-anatomical naked, would perhaps be impressive, looming through a pair of Y-fronts. And, like any man – *any* man, she thought, with a kind of enjoyable dismissiveness – he'd adore it if a woman took the initiative with his final stage of undressing. There was nothing a man loved more than for a woman to admit, by the fumbling of her hands, that however unlikely it might be on the face of it, she was interested in, curious about, ready to admire and appreciate: *that*. Hands fumbling, she took off her own clothes; but for similar reasons, as she admitted to herself, left her bra and pants on. Then she slid into the bed.

Oh well, here I am, she thought. Then: heavens, this is the second time I've taken off my clothes since I left the house. But of course this time was to balance out the last, when she'd had to unveil her bosom to the consultant at the clinic. Balancing your actions was all-important; it meant that they'd never happened in the first place. You had a blank cheque.

The trouble was, it was so difficult getting your actions balanced with the necessary exactitude. She thought of the time when John had told her about committing adultery with that woman on the course, the assistant bank manager, Linda. Even now she found herself laughing inside at the thought of him going to bed with an assistant bank manager. It was such a workaday, John-ish, thing to have done, mixing business with pleasure.

Her first reaction when he told her the news was sheer relief. She felt as if an enormous weight had been taken off her mind, no, not her mind, her heart, the weight of Alan, whom she'd never, in all these years, told John about. And why should she? She'd asked that question of herself, with indignation built into her tone of voice – except that it wasn't voice, since of course she didn't ask it out loud – with indignation built into her very tone of *thought*, over and over again during the years of her marriage: why should she?

The affair had taken place before she'd ever met John, so in no sense had it been a betrayal, a deception, even any of his business. Yet she never quite convinced herself. There had been an unspoken assumption, when she was going out with John, that they'd not been serious with anybody before, that they were both, say the word, virgins. John certainly was; and in fact remained one for some time, to Margaret's impatience. That had been a lie in its way, letting him assume her virginity. So it had been an immense relief when he went off the rails at his assistant bank managers' training weekend. Tit for tat, though a different way round from the usual one. Once upon a time I committed, how appropriate, *tit*; then, many years later, John, even stevens, indulged in a little illicit *tat*.

But a shadow had fallen over her glee, in that very first moment. John had admitted his, his tat, and that was exactly what she had never done. Her crime was her *lack* of admission. At no point in her life had she regretted, or felt guilty about, her actual affair with Alan: he'd simply swept her off her feet (she hadn't realised before how literal that saying was). You could only feel guilty about decisions, and in the case of Alan, she'd never made one. But she had felt guilty about not confiding in John; and then, to compound it all, there was John confiding *immediately* in her. She hadn't been able to prevent the shadow appearing in her own face: disappointment, frustration, regret. And to her chagrin she saw that he saw it, and his own face darkened. He probably thought, poor sod, that she felt jealous or upset about his shenanigans with Linda. Her own feeling of guilt intensified, at the thought that his was intensifying too. But that was hardly a balance; in fact it was *another* cheat.

How going off the straight and narrow today would balance out, Lord alone knew. It was like those equations Ann got so stuck on in maths. Perhaps this fling equalled John's assistant bank manager ditto (if you put Alan to one side since that hadn't been adultery). Or, to look at it from another point of view, perhaps the minus of her ordeal at the clinic would be cancelled out by the plus of the forthcoming romp. Perhaps she'd *earned* her fling. The phrase 'forthcoming romp', made her stomach go fluttering in anticipation, and she remembered her attempts to have dirty thoughts before she left home. That had only been two or three hours ago and look at her now. Progress!

All that can go wrong at this point is not reaching an orgasm, she thought, switching from ethical to practical. That didn't seem likely on the face of it, all things considered, but perhaps being in a strange house, and a strange bed, having sex with a strange man, whose name, quite deliberately, she didn't even know, not even his first name, and vice versa, would have a last-minute inhibiting effect. More likely, just the opposite. But if it did, she'd fake it. I'll fake it, she thought exuberantly, so that he won't know what hit him. Or what hit me. I'll even scream if I think I can get away with it. And faking will probably lead to a real one. She remembered those cases when a couple adopt a child and then the woman promptly becomes pregnant with one of their own. He'll put me down as a woman who can achieve *multiple* orgasms, she thought gleefully. I am woman.

The door opened and in he came. He was *man* all right. She saw that she'd predicted correctly. His underpants cut across a large and grinning belly, looking like a small and clumsily hoisted sail. Despite her anticipation his gut struck her attention more forcibly than his obviously eager equipment. She thought of his midriff pressing wobblingly against her own, tufts of hair protruding from its soft surfaces like that spiky grass which grows out of marshland.

215

She was filled with such a panic that a sort of hysterical giggle rose up from her depths and twitched and itched in her throat. If she let it out it would bring laughter in its wake, insincere uncontrollable laughter like the laughter she had laughed with Judy outside her house this morning.

She let her gaze rise up over his body, looking for compensation – balance! – elsewhere. Yes, his chest was big and well developed, and hard-looking where his stomach was soft. Then she saw that one of his breasts was swollen and distorted – much worse than hers – with the nipple pushed to one side, making his chest look curiously boss-eyed. She sent her look hastily onwards. His face had as much expression as a dalek's. His eyes looked at her without seeing her. Unfortunately they weren't blank, as John's were on the rare occasions when drink made him uninhibited. They were filled with her private parts, even with her possibly cancerous breast. No, not hers, for the simple reason that at this stage he couldn't see hers. Only her head was visible. Anybody's. They were filled with anybody's. Already she pitied her naïve and innocent self of a few minutes ago, on the staircase with the Spirit of Stephen hovering in the dimness above, when she'd convinced herself that lust had an equalising and ordinarifying effect upon people. The expression in his face wasn't equal or ordinary, it was rock-bottom. It occurred to her that now he was virtually naked she could smell him across the room. Not that he *smelt*, as such. It was just the odour of the human body, in the same way as there might be an odour of dog, or elephant. In fact, he did make her think of elephant a little. Not too much.

For a millionth of a second, frantic to say something that would alleviate the atmosphere, she nearly said it out loud. What sex needed was a sense of humour. But how ghastly that she could even *think* of uttering such a thing. For a man to be told by a consultant that he needed a breast operation, and then to have a woman making silly jokes about his private parts, would be more than flesh and blood could stand.

Sliding back from the brink made her laughter shoot out.

She just couldn't stop it. Perhaps it was balance after all, joke in, laugh out. Or possibly you just couldn't keep more than one thing stopped up at a time. Horrors, even while she laughed her eyes were pinned to the bulge in his underpants, which visibly dwindled. It was like witchcraft or exorcism. What power! It made her laugh the more. I am woman. What a bitch! I show it by making him less of a man. What harm have men ever done me? She didn't dare look at his face for fear it might have turned into Stephen's, and sprouted a pair of poignant round-rimmed spectacles. She felt old, old. In any man she could detect the helpless little boy, even in this previously large and thrusting one, with his hairy nostrils. But not looking at his face meant she kept her gaze where it was, which made matters worse, more horrible and more funny still.

There was a knock on the front door.

They seemed a forlorn little group when she looked back at them. They'd been having a banquet. Anything might have happened. Then she had got up and gone, leaving them staring at each other, over their miserable old pork pies and thin cold cider.

Kevin had tried to come with her, of course, at least as far as the village. Philip had backed him up when he realised she was serious about going. His dreams of a teen orgy switched to a picture of a private session with Jessica, the two of them frolicking on their lonesome beneath the bald blue sky. But Ann had been firm. It was only half a mile to the village, and she was quite capable of managing that. Then she'd be on her own anyway. The rest of them had a van to repair, a hoe-down to go to, God, at some point, to beg forgiveness of. She meanwhile had business of her own.

She hadn't told them exactly what it was, apart from the remark about burying her dead, which she immediately regretted. It was tempting fate. She half suspected little Stephen had been kidnapped and/or killed, and half suspected no such thing. Her guess was that most people secretly imagined death all around them but never voiced their suspicions, just in case they were hopelessly wrong. You'd have no credibility whatsoever if you went around saying without any evidence that something terrible might have happened to your brother Stephen, particularly in view of the fact that she'd already mentioned about his bones crunching. The others would think she was obsessed and she probably was.

The village was as quiet as before, as if the whole place, not just Kevin's van, had broken down and was waiting for someone to attach it to the rest of the world again. Opposite the van, to her surprise, was a bus-stop. She stood by it.

For a long time nothing much happened. An occasional car

swished by. Faint music came from the Crown. The sun went in and out. Kevin's van on the other side of the road looked more and more deeply parked, as though nothing on earth could ever induce it to move again. A woman carrying a child went past. Where she was going to or coming from, who could say? There was something about this place that made you think that there was no point to anything, but of course if that was true it would apply all over, Stockport included. More complicated places gave you the feeling that one day there would be an outcome, that was all. A village like this one was an architectural statement of the footlingness of everything. The baby, bobbling past, glared at her in the way babies did, practising for being grown-up. I've been here for hours, if not years, Ann thought despairingly. She glanced at her watch. Nearly a quarter to two, for what that was worth. When she glanced up again a car had pulled in beside her.

The driver leaned over, and rolled down his window part way. He had severe, metal-framed spectacles and a flabby face which seemed to have outgrown its original circle and formed a second one for itself. He had a sharp little nose, though, thinner than its surroundings.

'Are you waiting for a bus?' he asked.

'No,' she replied instinctively.

'Because there won't be one till tomorrow morning.'

'That's all right then.'

'Where are you going?'

'Nowhere.'

'I'm going to Cheadle. There's a Horse and Rider there. I've ordered a saddle for my daughter.'

Cheadle. That was in Stockport, a skip and a jump from Heaton Chapel. But on the other hand she'd denied everything. Even worse, he'd taken no notice of her denials.

'I can give you a lift to Cheadle,' he concluded grumpily, for all the world as though she'd been pestering him for one.

Oh God, Ann thought, yes or no? Was it sinister that he just didn't listen? In a few minutes would he be not listening to her pleas for mercy? Or was it a good sign, proving that he was only a harmless idiot? Wouldn't a potential rapist be more careful in his approach? More slimy, even? It was promising that he had a daughter. If he *did* have a daughter. Wouldn't potential *rapists* talk about their imaginary daughters?

He took no more notice of her hesitation than he had of her negatives, but opened the car door and pushed it outwards towards her. Here goes, Ann said to herself, and stepped in. To her own amazement she realised she was squeezing her nose with her left hand as she did so, exactly as she did when she jumped in at the baths. Deep water. She sniffed loudly, to cover her tracks. The man didn't notice, he wasn't the noticing type. They set off.

'What I say,' the man said, after a few moments, 'it's one thing after another.'

Ann couldn't think what to reply. In fact it might be best not to reply anything, in case the man thought she was being too friendly. On the other hand if she didn't reply he might think she was not being friendly enough. What she did instead was stir interestedly on the seat, to show that she was following what he said (which of course she wasn't) but hadn't thought it was quite worthwhile enough to say anything back.

'To take one example,' the man went on, 'global warming. You can feel it in the air, no doubt about it, on a day like today.'

Only weather, Ann thought to herself, the great British invention. What a triumph if weather destroys the planet in the end, it will show we had our priorities right all along. Of course if you were a rapist you'd probably talk about the weather to soften your victim up.

'There again,' the man went on, 'I was reading in the paper last night about a man charged with pulling the heads off pigeons.'

He turned and glared at Ann, as if to say: you've got no choice but to react to *that*.

'Oh,' said Ann softly, in dismay, hoping even as she said it that it didn't come out sexily. Spot the connection: global warming and pulling the heads off pigeons. None, except that they were both bad. Perhaps that was all he was on about, Bad Things. Possibly he'd made a mental list.

'In front of his eight-year-old daughter,' the man continued after a pause, and Ann's heart missed a beat. He'd got round to daughters again, but this time they weren't riding horses, they were watching the heads being pulled off pigeons. Was that a sort of progression, and if so, where would it end? She thought of the picnic she'd left behind with sudden homesickness. She'd never realised before that homesickness was *portable*.

219

'There was blood on the walls and heaven knows what. This man, madman is all you can call him, had apparently given his wife the wherewithal to buy food. Then he'd gone off to the pub and tanked up, and when he got home he found there wasn't a meal waiting for him on the table. This made him depressed, apparently, so he went out to his pigeon-loft, fetched one in, and pulled its head off. Not content with that he went back out and pulled the heads off all the rest. Twenty odd there were in all.'

Jodrell Bank at that moment appeared again over fields and hedges, rising up like a great clockwork sun. Ann clutched at it as a drowning man might clutch at a straw.

'There's Jodrell Bank again,' she said.

'Oh yes,' the man replied. 'If you think of the sheer number –'

'It's like a huge eyeball, isn't it, looking up at everything?'

'It doesn't look, it listens,' he replied, sounding bored and niggled. But it was an admission that she'd changed the subject, thank God.

'Earball then,' she said impatiently, her voice fading away with the feebleness of her attempt at humour. Never mind, it might keep his mind from wandering back to unhealthy subjects. Bless Jodrell Bank, she thought. Thinking bless reminded her of how she used to go through a whole routine of God bless mum, dad, Stephen, everybody she knew, before settling down to sleep when she was young. She'd do it several times, for fear of leaving somebody out. In which case as sure as fate they'd be struck by a thunderbolt during the night. When you did God blesses you always had the feeling that people's lives hung by a thread. She didn't usually do them nowadays, partly because she didn't particularly believe in God, but she sometimes gave them a try in a crisis, on an individual basis.

God bless Stephen, she thought. Not to mention me.

Raymond darted across the road to the lamp-post that was on the other side and sniffed the rich layering of pee around its base. He couldn't concentrate though, with the eyes of the man with the ladder, now without a ladder, staring at him from beside the house. He sniffed noisily, trying to bounce the smells so sharply against the sides of his nostrils that they became real to him. He ran from point to point round the bottom of the lamp-post, whimpering with excitement as he caught the pee at new angles, but inside he had a feeling of let-down.

Deep in a sniff, he froze.

The man without a ladder had left the house and was approaching. Raymond could hear the small squeaks and grunts of his shoes, clothes, body; could smell cigarettes and the fainter odour of putty in the air; could sense the man's steady approach through his own delicately vibrating tail. He turned away from his sniff and peered.

Sure enough the man without a ladder was stepping from the pavement to the road with a slow exaggerated stride as though he expected the road to be burning hot. His arms were open as if he was carrying something invisible, though he wasn't, and his head bobbed back and forward like a bird's. Raymond watched him approach, keeping absolutely still himself. His heart lifted as he realised he was back in focus again. He knew exactly what to do. Because the man was slow-moving let him get near, near, before running off yourself. Give him some nearness now for the sake of the faraway to follow.

Raymond waited while he approached, gritting his teeth and paws to resist the pressure to do something, run at or away, holding everything back except a faint growl which vibrated gently in the back of his throat. The man without a ladder moved with ornate complicated legs, each stride wincing, delicate, slightly oblique. As the invisible thing so carefully carried in his arms grew nearer also, Raymond began to make out what it was, so that when it was only a couple of strides away he could see it quite clearly, and suddenly a sharp bark ripped through his low growling. It was himself, himself in a few moments, in two strides' time, himself carried off by the man without a ladder, and deposited back in his own garden, away from all the possibilities the street had to offer. He bucked himself into the air and ran.

Behind him he could hear a gasp and the slap of shoes as the man followed. The pavement scudded under his paws, and shortly the noises of the man without a ladder died away. At the bottom of the road Raymond dared to stop and look back. To his astonishment the man had completely disappeared. For a moment he strained forward, about to return home and find out what had become of him, so that the chase could be resumed, but he thought better of it and waited where he was. There was silence, except for the distant clatter of a magpie in a tree.

221

There was another clatter, a metallic one, coming from Raymond's own house, and the man without a ladder appeared round the side, carrying his ladder. He stopped and looked towards Raymond for a moment. Raymond stiffened. The man raised an arm and waved it. Raymond shrank down and rested his head on his front paws, watching. The man went back to the house next door. Raymond heard the clong of the ladder where it was being rested in position.

When the man had finished rubbing the windows of the house next door, he went back to Raymond's house and rubbed those. He didn't look at Raymond again, but Raymond watched him, in view and out of view, his concentration never swerving, his eyes stiff and sullen with the effort, his body as unmoving as a spider's. He watched him move to the next house, then the next. Sometimes his own stillness reminded him of sleep, and he slept, but even then he continued to watch the comings and goings of the man with a ladder.

At last the man turned the corner of the street. His ladder became long as he turned and was then eaten by the end house. As it disappeared so Raymond got to his feet. He opened his mouth, yawned, shook his head. His legs felt loaded and full, painfully so, as if they contained all the running that he hadn't done during the long interval when he'd been watching the man with a ladder. He shook one of the front ones but it didn't disperse the sensation, and at once he was off, bounding not towards his house, but round the corner at this end of the road and down the next one. In the distance there was a roaring noise, and he could smell the faraway smells of brick-dust and rat.

The air began to thicken.

For a few moments he carried on running at full speed as before, postponing the sensation of thickness and the consequent shrieking of his muscles for as long as he could, but the thickening continued, and soon he was dealing not merely with its increase but with the delayed thickness he'd already stored up, so that his legs rapidly weakened in the unsympathetic air until he was at a standstill.

Ahead of him the road sparkled in the sunshine, empty and innocent, but as soon as he pressed his muzzle forward he felt the invisible wall again, its hardness buffered by only an insignificant amount of give, so that it had the texture of the rubber ball that he

222

sometimes fetched for Stephen and didn't give back to him. Yet into his mind came the ghost of another Raymond, trotting along beside Margaret in a thin free atmosphere, passing the place that lay ahead, where the walls were broken down and men smelt of walking buildings, and going beyond it to visit the old man, top dog, who smelt of crotch. There was a hole somewhere in the air and as invisible as it, through which Margaret could go, and he too when he was accompanying her. He ran his nose over the surface of the wall to see if he could smell the gap. Sideways the air was fully open, but there was no trace of a way through frontwards. Sighing, Raymond turned back into his own road.

He found himself beside the pee-smelling lamp-post. The scents were sharp and intoxicating. His heart thumped as he realised that one of them, that of a medium-sized brown bitch, had an afterglow of blood to it, the smell of an oncoming season. As he sniffed, his fur stood on end again. *The smell was coming from behind him as well as in front.*

He twitched his ears back, not daring at first to look, much less smell, but then, unable to bear the tension, he turned his head and did both.

The old woman who carried shit was coming along the road. The shit she carried in a white slithery bag belonged to the brown bitch who trotted by her side. For a second Raymond was made dizzy by the richness of the smell, but he continued to sniff carefully to see if the promise of the pee was confirmed. Yes, there was the smell of season, faint but definite, and he bolted joyfully forward.

12

Wonderful to be out in the fresh air again, leaving that embarrassment and misunderstanding, worst of all her own cruel laughter, behind her. It felt like leaving cancer behind too, watching the door shut on Mr Lump-on-the-Breast. How lovely doors are. Clonk. All gone. There ought to be more of them. Even as she thought that, her stomach fluttered. Having your breast off was a door, too, one that you wouldn't be able to open again. Being in limbo as she was, not knowing whether it was going to be taken off or not, was like a door swaying in the wind. Best to leave it that way.

Still, it *had* been a relief to hear the door slam shut on her fling. It was all over with. Nothing had happened. She thought of her beastly unstoppable laughter, and the way her gaze had been fixed on that little tent, how it seemed to melt away through sheer eye-power. Perhaps I'm a witch, she thought; I got rid of *one* of Mr Lump's lumps, at least. Maybe he'll wake up tomorrow morning and find the other one gone too, and say to himself, Bless the day that frigid old cow climbed into my bed, and climbed out again. Bless those wonderful lump-dwindling eyeballs of hers. Then again, he might not.

Whatever, he was gone, the door was truly shut, as if it had never been opened. It was much more shut than doors in her life usually were, perhaps shutter than any door had been since the Alan-door all those years ago. Perhaps she was destined to have a certain number of locked doors in her past with men behind them, like prisoners in the Bastille. No, don't suffer from delusions of grandeur. Alan wasn't behind any locked door in her life: she was behind one in his, he the shutter, she the shuttee. Still, Mr Lump had been safely ensconced. That *was* her doing. Possibly it was the point of balance, found where she hadn't even been looking for it. Alan shut her out, she shut Mr Lump *in*.

Heaton Moor Road stretched before her like a path to freedom. Lovely clean-looking people were trotting about doing their shopping. They all looked as if they wouldn't be seen dead in their bras and panties, or their underpants come to that. A man came hurrying out of the Red Lion pub. He was wearing a respectable suit. He'd just had his lunch-break probably, a pint and a sandwich, *he* hadn't been cavorting about with hardly any clothes on. He jumped into a BMW, which seemed to clinch the matter, and drove off. Yes, there was a whole world going on here with not a bedroom in sight, no whiff of unclothed skin. She sighed. Some of her sigh seemed to go into her left breast and illuminated it a little, but she was growing tired of buckling at the knees at every twinge from that direction. I'm going to walk home so fast that I'm going to walk right through my breast and out the other side, she thought to herself. I'm sick and tired of walloping into it at every turn. She set out for home at a good clip, one which seemed to suit the bright and breezy afternoon.

She kept up such a speed in fact that she felt herself moving through the passers-by as though she were the driver of a racing car. She looked at each one in turn with half-shut gimlet eyes, quite mercilessly, calculating how many strides it would take her to catch up and overtake, not caring if the victim was some woman staggering along with heavy shopping or a poor old man shuffling with the aid of a stick. They were all grist to her mill. The slower they went, the faster she zoomed past, and the further and more penetratingly *through* her breast she felt she was going. It was a pleasure to realise how fast she could now walk, as a result of her daily jogging. I'm getting healthy, she thought, at exactly the same speed as I'm going to the dogs.

It was truly amazing what you can leave behind, she noticed, if you put a real spurt on. The whole episode with Mr Lump seemed like ages ago, as if it had happened in a different world, like the events of history. Far from being or not being an elephant he seemed to have shrunk with this sudden passage of time, and now, in her mind's eye, was more like a guinea-pig, peering wistfully out at her as he gripped the bars of his cage with tiny paws.

She walked all the way along Heaton Moor Road, and at the traffic lights crossed over, and turned right on to Wellington Road. A bus pulled up beside her and she was almost tempted to hop in out of automatic laziness, since it was only two short stops to the entrance to Glenwood Road, but she stopped herself in time, realising that if she did her breast was liable to catch up with her. The last thing she wanted to do was sit herself down and look out of a window.

Instead she hurried down Wellington Road bent slightly towards the wind that always seemed worse here than anywhere else. Since the road at this point was lined with large houses rather than shops there weren't so many passers-by to overtake, but she kept up her speed, noting with a sense of accomplishment that she was panting a little. When she turned into Glenwood Road she was travelling at such a rate that she leaned a little into the corner, for all the world as if she was indeed steering herself as you would steer a vehicle. And then she stopped in her tracks.

Raymond was in the middle of Glenwood Road, mating with the old-woman-with-the-poop-scoop's dog. The old woman with the poop scoop was standing on the pavement nearby, apparently crying.

Her distress converted Margaret's reaction from shock to annoyance. Silly old devil, weeping because her dog was doing what comes naturally. But there was something forlorn and lonely about the way she was standing on the pavement that immediately took the edge off Margaret's irritation, so that it was still hard to walk towards her, knowing there would be recriminations to come. Of course it would be all Raymond's fault. No doubt the old woman would see him as a sort of dog-rapist, cruelly taking advantage of her innocent bitch. Actually the bitch seemed entirely uninterested. She had a bored, almost sullen expression on her face. If she was human she'd be chewing gum, like a sulky teenager.

Oh Lord, why do I think that? Margaret asked herself. She had a picture in her mind of Ann grumpily chewing away while some hideous boy did *it* to her. I'm a terrible mother, she said to herself, so forcibly it was almost out loud. She wasn't sure whether she was a terrible mother because Ann was inevitably doing such things and the thought hadn't occurred to her before, or because Ann was obviously *not* doing such things, and she shouldn't have had such an awful thought about her in the first place, comparing her with a dog in the street. Anyway I can talk, she thought.

Not that Ann would ever know about it of course, but perhaps these things left their mark, a sort of decadent softness of focus about the face. Except of course that my decadence suddenly stopped in its tracks, whatever *that* looks like. Made my eyes go poppy, in all probability.

The real point of course was that she just didn't think enough about Ann. She didn't know whether Ann indulged in nasty blasé sexual intercourse, which those comments about selling her body this morning might suggest, or whether she was so innocent that she could make comments like that without thinking twice about them. Her own thoughts and worries were all centred around Stephen, that was the problem. Blast him, for occupying all her attention. Immediately, she felt another pang for blasting Stephen. Poor little chap, he was too small, his spectacles too round, to be blasted.

Meanwhile Raymond didn't exactly look in the seventh heaven, any more than the bitch below him. It was odd seeing one dog-face on top of another, like having a *list* of them. Raymond's looked more frantic than anything else. He had rolled his eyes so you could see their whites, and his mouth was stuck in an insincere grin, with his teeth clenched tight. He was letting out a series of high-pitched little sounds that seemed a cross between sobs and barks. Perhaps *he* feels guilty, Margaret thought. His tail wasn't wagging, it was pointing straight back, like a spear, so stiff it trembled.

'Oh dear,' Margaret said, when she arrived at the old woman with the poop scoop.

'They've been like that for I don't know how long,' the old woman with the poop scoop whispered back in a tear-drenched voice. She didn't look at Margaret. She sounded pathetic and despairing.

'Have they? Heavens. I wouldn't have thought Raymond would have the concentration. He can't usually settle to anything for more than a minute or two.'

'No, no,' the old woman said, suddenly impatient. 'He can't get off. They're stuck.'

Margaret looked at her for a long moment. If I allow myself the teeniest-weeniest bit of a laugh, she thought to herself, I will laugh so much I will die. It'll be like that laughter I did this morning, when 'dad' became sentimental about his teapot, and then when Judy was talking about her Naughty but Nice party, and the laughter I did this afternoon, while I was looking at Mr Lump's little tent, only even worse. For a day which is one of the most miserable and frightening days I have ever had in the whole of my life, I keep on being the victim of horrible onslaughts of laughter.

'I didn't know what to do,' the old woman said. The threat of laughter receded, and Margaret's heart sank. There was something in the old woman's tone of voice, or rather, whisper, a certain testiness about it, which suggested that what she *had* done was something silly. 'I thought perhaps I should phone the police, but then I thought better of it. You couldn't say they're doing anything wrong, could you? Then the fire brigade. You hear about how they rescue cats from up trees and people with heads stuck in the railings, and that sort of thing, so I thought for two pins I'd give them a try. There's the telephone box just round the corner, on Gower Road. But when I got there I didn't like to. I had them round to my house once, when I thought I had a gas leak. You never saw anybody look so gigantic with their helmets on. I just couldn't bring myself to explain to them over the phone. So in the end I phoned the vicar.'

'You *what?*'

'The vicar. I go to his church every week.' Her tone of voice suggested that it was about time he did something for *her*. 'He's on his way.' Obviously conscious that Margaret disapproved, her voice had become pompous and self-righteous. Another minute, and she'd launch into a diatribe against Raymond.

But for goodness' sake, Margaret wanted to say, you can't ask a vicar to do that. Whatever vicars did do, which never seemed to Margaret to be all that much, that surely wasn't part of it. It seemed too literal. But at the same time she could understand the old woman's desperation, standing here on the pavement clutching her poop scoop. How many friends would she have, to fall back on? If not the vicar, who?

'Come *on*, Raymond,' Margaret called impatiently.

Raymond pretended not to hear. The bitch took several strides forward and Raymond perforce went with her, tottering along on his back legs like one of those dogs at a circus that pretends to be human and wears a funny hat.

228

'Raymond!'

Again he tried to ignore her, this time unsuccessfully. After a moment his eyes flicked nervously in her direction, then away again. There was something so doleful and hangdog about him that Margaret felt her heart melt. What a wonderful expression that was: you do actually sense a softening in your chest.

'Oh Raymond, what have you done to yourself?' she asked him gently.

Her tone was instantly too much for him, and he started to howl, clamping his jaws together and making a little circle in his lips at the front like a dog in a cartoon. The desolate noise triggered off the bitch, and she began to howl too. Their interweaving sounds seemed to convert Glenwood Road on a sunny April afternoon into the Russian steppes. It was too much, it would attract attention, there would be eyes and ears in all those blank houses. The last thing Margaret wanted was to be somehow associated with the dogs in a public performance. 'Shut up!' she cried, not loud but savagely.

Raymond immediately shut up. The bitch, less attuned to her voice, went on regardless for a few moments, until she noticed Raymond had stopped and her howls dwindled away too, as someone's voice does when he realises he's the only one singing in church.

Trying to capitalise on a rare moment of obedience, Margaret strode up to Raymond.

'For heaven's sake,' she said, in a tone of voice that told him the joke had gone far enough. She grabbed at his haunches and tugged. To her horror, he gave a sharp, completely sincere cry of pain. It wasn't a matter of ignorance or a psychological block: he really was stuck.

'I think we ought to wait until the vicar arrives,' the old woman said. 'I'm frightened they're going to be hurt.'

'I don't see what the vicar can do that we can't,' Margaret replied. 'He could marry them, I suppose.'

The old woman seemed to bridle and shrink at the same time, so that she looked both bleak and bad-tempered. Margaret hadn't meant to be cruel, she'd only been trying to lighten the atmosphere, and she felt annoyed with her for being so hurt and worried. If Raymond's private part – not that it was ever in the least private:

229

he was addicted to washing it, with horrible splashy and gobbling sounds – if it should snap off, so much the better for the dog-race at large.

With inevitable timing the dogs staggered towards the centre of the road like a pair of drunks, just as a car approached. She caught their joint gaze at the very moment that they spotted the danger and froze, neither daring to leap out of the way for the pain it would cause if they weren't unanimous. Margaret suddenly remembered, physically remembered, with the feel of the scarf round her leg, what it was like trying to synchronise with your partner in the three-legged races at school sports days. For the dogs, of course, it was a six-legged race, four plus two, Raymond's remaining two trying to maintain purchase on the poor bitch's back.

The car crawled past the hypnotised dogs and pulled to a stop. A young man got out. He had bushy black hair, a pleased look on his face, an open-necked collar. He didn't look like a vicar but he obviously was.

'Hello, Mrs Hamilton,' he called breezily to the old woman. 'What have we got here then?'

What do you think? Margaret asked him, not out loud. To her surprise, though, the vicar proved to be decisive. Obviously realising that Mrs Hamilton was too squeamish and terrified to be any help he turned to Margaret.

'Why don't you grab the bitch and try to keep her body straight while I give a heave on the poor old chap and see if I can get him out?'

'All right,' Margaret said. She bent over and put an arm down each side of the bitch's body, to act as a sort of splint. The vicar crouched low over Raymond from behind, almost as if he was making a strange threesome, put his arms round his neck and began to pull him back. The bitch tensed and squeaked with pain. The vicar, his face only inches away, gave Margaret a politely friendly look. Raymond delivered a despairing moan and then came free. He promptly sat down in the roadway and began licking the inflamed part, as per his usual habits. The bitch hobbled off to Mrs Hamilton's welcome.

'Thank you very much,' Margaret told the vicar.

'Any time,' he replied blandly.

Unexpectedly, she felt a sudden hot surge of resentment. What

230

did he mean, any time? How often did he think she required the services of a vicar to un-, un-, whatever you might call it, un-effword her dog? It was like rubbing in all the incompetence of the situation, spreading it around, making it define her. And he of course was the vicar as hero and helper, comforting Mrs Hamilton, aiding herself, sorting out the animals. What a self-fulfilling prophecy, Margaret thought. Another idea came to her, like one of those Thoughts for the Day that were sprinkled about in women's magazines: life is *exactly* what you make of it. How can it be? she asked herself immediately, when you were at the mercy of lumps on your breast? Still, the two contradictory things seemed to be true, you are at the mercy of lumps on your breast, life is what you make of it, side by side, both at once. In which case, she thought, I'll bid a not exactly moving farewell to the vicar, and yank my dog unceremoniously home by his collar.

As she did so, it struck her to wonder what on earth the dog was doing out of the house in the first place. There were no clues inside either, though the cushion on the settee in the lounge had been badly mauled. It's not a question of Raymond being in the dog-house, she thought, suddenly tired: this *is* a dog-house.

One of Ann's mother's most annoying habits was speaking to you when you'd just come home after a hard day at school as if she'd last seen you two minutes ago. She seemed to think that all the time you spent outside the family mansion was unreal, a dream. The funny thing was that when she spoke in that way, sure enough whatever you had been doing did become dreamy and unimportant. This was home, centre of the known universe, and everywhere else was shrouded in fog.

'That damn dog, he's always destroying something,' mum said. 'I'm going to have to throw one of those cushions away, from the front room.'

'Hello, Ann,' Ann said. 'How nice to see you. Have you had a good day at school?' My God, she asked herself while she was actually still speaking, why am I saying this? What a moment for sarcasm: I didn't *go* to school.

'Has something happened?'

'Why should something have happened?'

'You're home early.'

'Oh yes, I am a bit.'

Ann spoke lightly but it was too late. She could see her mother's face come into focus. It was something that actually happened physically. All the different features, instead of just ticking over each in its own sweet way, seemed to get together like a sort of posse to pounce on whatever you were saying.

'Why are you, then?'

What should I say? Some drivel about the anniversary? No, that wouldn't make any sense, being that dad won't be home for hours yet. There was nothing for it but the old standby.

'You know. Bit of a headache. Time of the month.'

'Oh,' relieved. Then: 'But I thought you were on one the other day. A week or two back.'

'Time flies when you're enjoying yourself.'

'I suppose so,' mum said doubtfully.

'For goodness' sake, mother. You're supposed to have the hab-dabs when I *don't* have a period, not when I do.' Ann wished with a passion that they could change the subject. She'd have to remember to keep washing out her knickers and flushing the loo. Who'd be female? Especially a lying female. 'Stephen's not home yet?'

'*Ste*phen? No, of course not. *He*'s not likely to be suffering from a headache, I hope.'

'I wasn't sure what time he came home these days.'

'Same time as always. He'll be here at about half past three. Not long,' mum added, looking at her watch.

'Oh, I may as well go and meet him,' Ann said, with such careful casualness she almost found herself inspecting her fingernails.

'Why?'

'Why not?'

Why on earth were people so suspicious? Ann asked herself. *She* didn't query every little thing people said to her. She might be being lied to all the time. What was so maddening about being challenged like this was that from the point of view of the lie-victim, mum in this case, what was being said must be so unimportant that it wasn't *worth* querying. The same thing had happened at breakfast, with her father. You couldn't help wondering what would happen if you told a real whopper. If you'd murdered someone and hidden them in the garden shed for example, would people question you even more, or would the whole thing go into reverse, so that they would show no curiosity at all?

'He's old enough to come home by himself,' mum said. 'If he wasn't I'd be meeting him, wouldn't I?'

'I just feel like stretching my legs.'

Mum nearly spoke, then thought better of it, and relaxed. She had obviously been going to point out that Ann had never felt like stretching her legs in the whole of her existence up till now, which was true. Ann understood why her mother had stopped herself from speaking: a penny had dropped – the wrong penny. She'd decided that Ann and Stephen were going to go off to buy their parents an anniversary present. So now they'd *have* to go and buy them one. What a way to lie: buying people a present when you didn't intend to.

'I'll be off then. We'll probably go to the park after.'

'Stephen will like that,' mum said, nice as pie now she'd convinced herself that Ann had had a period and left school early so that she and Stephen could be sweet and thoughtful offspring. If only she could know the truth, that Ann had thumbed a lift in the middle of nowhere and had sat in a car with an individual who'd sounded bonkers in a menacing way and who'd come as near to raping her, on a moment-by-moment basis, as it was possible to get without showing any actual signs of doing it, that she had taken that chance not in order to pretend-to-be-interested-in-walking-Stephen-home-from-school-but-really-to-buy-her-parents-an-anniversary-present, but in order to pretend-to-be-buying-them-an-anniversary-present-so-she-could-*really*-walk-Stephen-home-from-school. The trouble with alibis is that sometimes you really have to *do* them.

'All right then,' Ann said.

'All right then, love,' her mother replied.

All right then, all right then, Ann repeated under her breath as she trotted towards the front door. This household was enough to drive you over the edge all by itself, with everybody parroting each other, interrogating each other, living in each other's pockets. Raymond, who'd given her an ecstatic greeting two minutes ago, now gave her an equally ecstatic farewell, wagging his tail so frantically his whole bum swung from side to side. Only as she walked out of the front door did he remember that when you said goodbye to people it meant they were going, and his head and shoulders drooped with disappointment. He sighed accusingly, sat down, and began to lick his privates as if that's what had been on his mind all along.

Ann got to the school just as the children were coming out. They scuttled along waving their arms and shouting to each other. There were hundreds of them, every possible child you could imagine, except Stephen. She began to tremble, half for real, half putting it on for good luck, though it was news to her that you could shiver on *purpose*. She'd been hoping against hope that her glimpse of Stephen outside the museum had been a dream, and that he'd been here all along.

Perhaps she ought to have told mother what the problem was before she left the house, but what good would that have done? It would only put her in the same boat, not knowing whether something had happened to Stephen, or whether he was safely at school and it was Ann who wasn't quite all there, buzzing through the centre of Manchester when she should be installed in school herself, and seeing visions as she went. But when deaths were announced in television plays, they came out in instalments. I'm afraid I've got some very bad news for you. Albert's had an accident. Yes, it's serious. Well, he's dead. The idea seemed to be that you needed to be acclimatised, one stage at a time. So perhaps it *would* have been kinder to tell mother what she thought she'd seen, and let her get used to the possibility, however faint, of Stephen being kidnapped or murdered. Too late now, anyway. The more Stephen didn't come out, the more she became aware of her heart sloshing about in increasing panic.

Just as the flow had been switched off, and there were only odd droplet children still appearing, he finally plopped out through the doorway. She could recognise him by his worried glasses. Oh Ste! she thought, you little darling. What a sweet thoughtful chappie he is, not letting himself get murdered!

He didn't seem particularly surprised to see her. He pushed his glasses up his nose with a wiggle of his face, just as you'd wiggle your middle if you were hoisting up your skirt or trousers. Then he waved towards a small boy on the other side of the road.

'Whenever I wave to Gary,' he said, 'he's always saying the same thing to his mum. His mouth is in the exact identical position.'

'Have you had a good day *at school*?' Ann asked him, trying to give sinister overtones to the *at school*.

'Yes,' he replied. 'We went swimming.'

'Oh. Where did you go?' she asked, wondering suddenly if he'd been to some gala in the middle of Manchester.

'The usual place. Reddish Baths. The same ones you used to go to when you were at my school.'

Blast, she thought. 'What else did you do?'

'Nothing.'

He didn't look up but trotted along the pavement beside her. Now was the moment. Should she ask about what he was doing at the museum, or never say anything? If she did ask she'd have to say what she was doing there herself. The important thing surely was that he hadn't been murdered. The rest could go into oblivion. Anyway, as far as she was concerned, nothing *had* happened.

'Why I'm meeting you is,' she said, 'I thought you and I ought to buy mum and dad an anniversary present.'

'All right,' Stephen said. He said it just as he'd said 'Nothing.' The neutrality of the way he said things could drive you berserk.

'Don't if you don't want to.'

'My money's at home.'

'Oh if that's all that's worrying you,' Ann said, feeling more cheerful, 'you can pay me when we get back.'

As Stephen came out of the door he knew somebody was waiting for him at the school gate before he'd even looked. When your mum and dad came in to see a teacher, school didn't seem quite so school-ish, and the same now. But it wasn't a mum- or dad-feeling, so it must be Ann. Immediately he realised that, his heart sank. Ann had never ever come to meet him from school. She couldn't, because she was at school herself. So he'd been right all along. She *hadn't* been at the bus-stop this morning, or on the bus. The blotherin man and standing outside the museum had been real. This afternoon, in school, after they'd come back from swimming, he'd wondered whether they were. They'd done a project on badgers, and doing it made him think that perhaps this morning had been some sort of dream. The only reason why it was a bit real was that he was so hungry. Could you have a dream in which you didn't have anything to eat, and then feel hungry in real life?

If Ann was here then she hadn't gone to school, which meant that she was probably dead. This Ann must be an angel. The real

Ann wouldn't meet him even if she wasn't at school, she'd be too mean, but an angel might.

He looked at her. She didn't have wings. But angels wouldn't wear their wings if they were in a place like Heaton Chapel because people would make fun of them and even pull their feathers off. A boy called Damien Birkett in the next class up from Stephen had once killed a moth in the playground for no reason at all except that he wanted to show off. She did look a bit like an angel though. You could see through her if you looked very hard indeed, a little way through anyway.

He walked slowly down the pathway to the gate. He didn't really want to be with Ann if she *was* an angel. He'd seen an angel once in a church and the very thought of it sent a chill through him. The eyes were white all over. He thought of looking up at Ann and her looking down at him, her eyes creamy and blank. Another thought struck him. If your home, and your mum and dad, stopped existing while you were at school all day, and only came back into the world again when the children returned at night, then if one of the children died perhaps mum and dad wouldn't be able to find their way back into the world at all. It might be like losing the key to somewhere.

He tried to remember if he'd actually seen their own house, number 9, when he'd got off the bus and looked down Glenwood Road and seen the dog which looked like Raymond's brother. Suddenly he had an awful thought: did dogs go to heaven? It was an awful thought that he'd had before, so he had it quickly this time, while he was still walking towards the angel. If dogs did then ants would have to. Which meant that if you killed an ant, as he had done the other day when he was trying to get himself small enough to climb inside the Polo, you would be a murderer. But if they didn't, then people wouldn't either, because dogs were halfway between ants and people. Which meant that mum and dad and Raymond would be dead for ever and ever, and so would he be when he died. And Ann.

He reached the gate. She wasn't an angel. She wasn't dead either. She was just Ann. She looked so much like herself that it already seemed silly to imagine her being anybody else. Sometimes Stephen had the thought that the people in the world nowadays, the people he knew, would live for ever, because they were so like themselves you couldn't imagine anything happening to make them stop. All the people who died in the old days weren't like themselves. They were like people in books, they weren't so good as modern-days people at being real. Nobody could be more real than Ann.

He felt so relieved he could hardly speak. She asked him about school, quite suspiciously, just like her usual horrible self, nothing dead about her at all. Then they went off to buy mummy and daddy a present. They got on a bus and went into the centre of Stockport.

It made Stephen feel quite sick, getting on another bus, and *still* not going home. He'd been going on buses all day long. He also felt sick because he was hungry but he didn't tell Ann about that because it would mean talking about all the things that had happened that day and they had decided not to talk about them. They didn't say anything to each other when they decided because that would be talking and what they had decided was *not* talking. They decided without saying a word. The emptiness he carried about in his stomach was almost as big as the wee he'd carried this morning. He felt even worse when he put his hand in his pocket and his fingers came across some money there. It was the change the blotherin man had made him keep. He didn't dare tell Ann because he'd already told her he didn't have any. He hoped it wasn't too much.

They went into lots of shops and didn't buy something. When Stephen complained, Ann said not buying things would show a lot of thought. Stephen had a picture in his mind of the present, when they finally got one, having thoughts all over it, like grey worms. He couldn't understand why they didn't just buy a box of chocolates, which was the most presenty present he could think of, and would have the advantage that he and Ann would be given their share. At the moment he was so hungry that the thought of it made his mouth fill with spittle. He could eat a whole boxful by himself, not one by one the way you were supposed to eat chocolates, enjoying each in turn, but munching through them the way you ate potatoes and meat, just to get them swallowed. He couldn't take much interest in the hard uneatable things Ann was looking at, pots to put plants in, or glasses for wine. In the end she chose a fruit-bowl from Debenhams, made of glass. It cost eight pounds, four from her, and the other four owed by Stephen. It didn't have any fruit in it of course.

Then they got on yet another bus and went home. Ann was going to put the present in her room. She hid it behind her back but not very well, and in any case everybody in their family always knew when they'd been bought a present, but you had to pretend you didn't, so it ended up that the person getting the present was the one who had a secret, not the person who'd bought it. The secret hopped from one side to the other, like a traitor in a war.

'Did you have a nice day at school?' Stephen's mother asked, in a very ordinary voice to show that she didn't know about the secret.

'Yes,' said Stephen. In his head he changed 'day' to 'afternoon', so his 'yes' wouldn't be a lie. 'I'm very hungry,' he added, to change the subject in case it still was. Being hungry wasn't a lie.

There was a crash from the staircase and Ann called out: 'Shitting fucking bloody hell!'

'Ann!' mother cried, 'stop that!'

'She could have killed herself,' yelled Stephen, suddenly in a fury at the shock of whatever-it-was that had happened.

'If she'd killed herself she wouldn't be swearing her head off,' mother told him. Sure enough they could hear Ann stomping up the rest of the stairs, muttering to herself. Stephen could tell she was still swearing but not quite loudly enough for mum to be able to prove it. It sounded like a foreign language: ger blod fuddin sittle ell. 'Go up and get changed,' mum said bad-temperedly to Stephen because she couldn't be bad-tempered to Ann. She'd forgotten he was telling her about being hungry, and he didn't dare to remind her. He went up the stairs himself. He muttered as Ann had done, but used a foreign language from the outset, just to be on the safe side.

As he went into his bedroom a stange thing happened. He remembered the men with head jumpers so vividly he felt as though one of them had opened a door in his mind and walked in. He hadn't thought about them for hours, but that made the memory all the sharper, like when a huge monster is pressing and pressing at the window and finally the glass gives way so that it shoots halfway across the room at you in one go, just with the squashed-up speed of its pressing. He spun round to make sure a man in a head jumper hadn't come through his door in real life. There was no one there. He turned back to his room. There was no one there either but he had the feeling there had been. He remembered what Ann had told him about a present showing a lot of thought, so that when you looked at it it was covered in grey worms, which were the thoughts you had in the shops where you *didn't* buy the present. He felt that the man in the head jumper had left a dark worm behind him from his presence in the room at some previous time today, something that wriggled and slid round corners in the air that kept it just concealed. He went across his bedroom to his moneybox in a complicated way, trying to keep behind invisible corners himself.

He did the numbers on the box's little dial. Just as he opened the lid he froze. He had a sudden picture of the worm-thing in the box, like a genie in a bottle. But he didn't dare shut it again because there it would be, waiting for him. He would never be able to tell anyone and he would have to open it sooner or later to pay Ann. He couldn't use the money the blotherin man had told him to keep, because that was from this morning, which they didn't talk about. Anyway, it was only change, it wouldn't be enough. Let there not be a monster in my box, he said inside his head, and lowered his eye until it was level with the opening. There was just dimness inside, but the worm was dim too. Darkness was what the men with jumpers over their heads lived in, the same as Percy and Bubbles lived in water. He remembered the way they had stayed in the television even when it was switched off.

Flip. He opened it completely. This was a special way of doing things when he was frightened that he had learned over the years. Do them just before you're ready to. You think about something and then do it before you've finished thinking about whether you're going to do it or not. The moment that you actually do it is bad: it's like doing something when you've just been shaken out of sleep – you don't even know whether you've got any clothes on or not. But then it's all over with.

It was all right, there was no worm inside. Stephen sighed out loud with relief. Then he put his hand in to get some money out, and once again his heart missed a beat. His money wasn't all there.

He stared at it, letting his eyes run over the money again and again, hoping that if he did it hard and often enough he could *look* the missing money into existence. But it wasn't there. He didn't even need to count, he could remember how much the amount was, the sort of pile all the different coins made together, even when they were shuffled up.

239

He sat on his bed appalled. It was all true. There was a dark worm in his room. The men on the TV *had* stayed on when the set was switched off. Somebody *had* made a noise in the kitchen last night. A man with darkness where his head should be *had* climbed up the stairs towards his bedroom. Stephen wished that the blotherin man was with him now, getting his words mixed up, waving his arms and legs about, getting redder and redder. The blotherin man hadn't understood a lot of things, but Stephen had a feeling he would understand this. And after all that searching for blothr he was used to looking for things that weren't there any more.

Instead, in came Ann.

'Gimme,' she said, 'you owe me four quid.'

Stephen looked at her, but couldn't speak.

'I'll tell you what,' she went on, 'you can give me three. I get more money than you.'

Still he said nothing.

'I know it's unusual,' Ann went on. 'Normally I like to be mean. I might have charged you four pounds and ten pee, for the interest, if I'd felt in the mood. But I've decided to change. I'm going to be holy from now on. If you carry on snivelling I'll probably let you off another pound, so snivel away. I've been keeping such religious company that I've become good myself. The holiness must have rubbed off. Tomorrow I'll probably give Fiona Buchan enough money to buy a Kit-Kat *and* pay for her bus ticket. *And* I won't spit in her eye. Talking of spitting, poor old Jessica will probably spit feathers, because the more of a saint I am, the less of one she'll be able to be. I'll be a saint right on her manor.'

'Somebody's stolen some of my money,' Stephen finally managed to say.

'For goodness' sake, Stephen, that's a bit feeble. I don't see why you need to fib through your teeth now I've become holy. You've only got to snivel.'

'But they have.'

'Just give me the two quid and we'll call it quits. But don't think your fib cut any ice, it's whimpering and wailing that does the trick.'

Suddenly weary, Stephen took two pounds out of his box and gave them to her.

'We'll give them their present when dad comes home,' Ann told

240

him. 'If it's not shattered into a million pieces. I haven't dared look.' She left the room. Stephen remained on his bed staring at his money-box. Then he remembered he was alone with the worm and hurried out and down the stairs.

'Hello, Stephen,' his mother said, when he arrived in the kitchen. 'I know, you said you were hungry.' Then her eyes widened and she stared at something over Stephen's shoulder. 'Oh no,' she whispered.

Stephen thought: she can see the men with head jumpers too. He turned round in horror to see what she was seeing, but there was nothing there. He looked harder, in case they were in the form of a worm. 'They're not there,' he said finally.

'I know they're not there,' mum said. 'I forgot to buy them, that's why they're not there.'

'Forgot to buy what?'

'The steaks for our anniversary dinner tonight.'

'Oh, I thought you meant – ' Stephen said, stopping himself just in time.

'I forgot all about them until I thought about getting you something to eat. Oh well. I'll have to put that bally chicken in the oven and hope for the best. Damn damn damn. I was going to remember that steak if it was the last thing I did, and then I go and forget all about it.' She looked, to Stephen's surprise, as if she was about to burst into tears. 'If it was the last thing I did,' she repeated.

'I don't mind,' said Stephen, 'I like chicken.'

As he turned from Palmerston Grove into Heaton Moor Road John had a mental picture of Gardiner in hot pursuit. He knew it was a fantasy brought on by childhood memories of knocking on front doors and running away but he had the distinct impression that heavy feet were pounding the pavement, until he realised it was the thumping of his heart. Nevertheless he looked over his shoulder a couple of times as he walked on. No Gardiner. Of course he wouldn't have come after him: in all probability he was in his birthday suit. The thought of that made John suddenly want to laugh and he felt himself relax for the first time today. He had tried to beard Gardiner, he'd done his best: and failed. The fact that he'd now have to pay the consequences for *not* bearding him seemed irrelevant for the moment. It was as though he'd been assigned a task, found it was impossible to do, and been let off. Time to worry about the rest later.

He turned into the Red Lion pub. He needed to ring a taxi to get him back to Reddish. But not straight away. His sense of relief evaporated at the thought of how appalling it would be if Mrs Clarke found out he'd failed to beard Gardiner. Doing so had somehow been put in the scales against not going to bed with her. To say he'd not done that either would be like admitting he was impotent. Whatever bearding was, one of the things it had *become* was a dry, out-in-the-big-wide-world, equivalent of sex. His heart sank further as he thought: I'm good at discovering equivalents of *that*.

The pub was dim and nearly empty. It was gone two and the lunch trade had obviously dispersed. He ordered a beer, then used the telephone to book a taxi for half an hour's time. Mrs Clarke would think he'd had quite a conversation with Gardiner. What a man I am, he thought bitterly. Beyond an archway four men were playing darts, and since there was no one else to look at he watched them. Almost immediately one of the group said he had to leave for a few minutes to drop his car in at a local garage. The others joshed him because it was a BMW apparently. That information gave John a slight lift. Even BMWs could need seeing to. The man was going to return in a courtesy car in a few minutes. In the meantime the other members of the group asked John to fill in. Beer and darts. Margaret's anniversary card had come true.

Arriving back at the bank was almost an anti-climax. Nobody seemed to have noticed or cared that he'd been gone. Except Mrs Clarke, obviously. You could tell by the way she completely ignored him that she was aware. She was hunched over her terminal at the far side of the main banking area, beyond Mr Hawthorne who was still scribbling pinkly away. Her desk seemed further off than usual, though surely she couldn't have moved it. She looked like someone viewed through the wrong end of a telescope. She was no longer in the least bit woollen. Her form had the precision of distant focus, and every angle in it seemed sharp and off-putting. She possessed the sort of muteness that could make you want to hit somebody, just to break through.

But why? They'd parted on perfectly good terms. She'd expressed gratitude for the Liberty scarf, as well she might. As he

242

thought that, he discovered new possibilities for self-dislike. He'd been trying to *buy* her with a scarf, how degraded can you get? He'd *wanted* to be a bastard. It was a miserable ambition, and how pathetic to fail in it.

No, he wasn't being quite fair to himself. He hadn't really thought in terms of *buying* Mrs Clarke, but simply of establishing an inappropriate relationship with her, spending as much on her as he was spending on his wife. Of course that led to being a bastard by a different route; but he didn't have time to follow that one through now. He'd think about it later. What was on his mind for the moment was that Mrs Clarke had accepted the scarf, and the fact that nothing indiscreet had taken place at lunch-time surely made it more of a gift than ever. As they parted she'd given *him* a Polo. The smallness, inconsequentiality, and welcomeness of the gift made it equally intimate, in its own way. Yet with nothing further happening between them, and with every reason on her part to assume he had bearded Gardiner, here she was, hunched and sullen. The only explanation was that she'd come to feel disgust or contempt for him in retrospect, when she'd had time to go over what had happened, and what hadn't happened, between them.

He felt leaden-footed as he went into his office, almost too tired to walk. How he wished her hostility was because he'd made an unwanted pass. How dismal, that it was for the opposite reason. *And* my fucking car has a flat battery, he remembered as a clincher.

He rang Reddish Windscreens and spoke to the man he'd got in touch with this morning. As he expected, the man took the line that he was being put upon, but finally agreed to send someone over, as a special favour.

The man materialised nearly two hours later, long after the bank had closed its doors to the public. For the whole of that time John had done his work at half-cock, never able to put his mind fully to anything. It wasn't so much a matter of feeling insecure, though that came into it: the worst part was being conscious of an untidiness in the background, like trying to get on with paperwork when your hands need washing. Also, he didn't know whether he would have to get angry or not.

It was a different man from this morning: small, wiry, with poking-out ears. He had thinning grey hair and was wearing an oily denim overall that seemed so snug and worn you couldn't imagine him ever taking it off. John gave him the keys and he went off to find the car. He was back twenty minutes later. John was in the banking area, so received the verdict in full view of everyone.

'I've had to put you a new battery in,' the man said, wiping his hands against his thighs, and taking a scrawled invoice out of his pocket.

'Surely the old one only needs a bit of a charge?'

'It's shot. It's a rubbish one. I'll put it in your boot if you like, so you can take it home and try it yourself.'

John wondered whether it would look better to argue or accept. How ridiculous – the only thing that seemed to matter was the figure he cut in front of the staff. If the batteryman was in fact a heart surgeon telling him he needed a transplant, it would come down to the same thing: what reply would earn most respect? Tell him to come off it, or concede with good grace? He conceded with good grace. I always bloody do, he thought to himself.

When the man had been let out there was a short silence. Mr Hawthorne broke it with a butlerish cough from his desk.

'Excuse me, sir, the day's transactions have been balanced.'

'No problems?'

'No, sir.'

'All right everyone, you can go home.'

He went back to his office. Almost immediately there was a knock on the door. It was Mrs Clarke. She didn't look quite at him.

'I've decided I can't accept this,' she said, and placed the Liberty scarf, neatly folded, on his desk.

'What?'

'It wouldn't be right. It was very generous of you, but it wouldn't be right.'

His head seemed to swell and glow, so that he felt he was looking at her out of a child's balloon. What on earth was she getting at? Was she suggesting that services hadn't been rendered; that the punter was entitled to his money back? If so, that was no let-off, since it would have been *his* failure to provoke the rendering.

No, no, that line of thought was all wrong. If the transaction had been so sordid, she wouldn't be bringing the scarf back. Suddenly he felt that an enormous weight had been lifted from his shoulders. The whole business had been much more innocent than he'd ever imagined. Or rather, since he'd hardly been innocent himself,

244

much more *mixed*. Mrs Clarke, like him, had been uncertain, confused, guilty, contradictory. How strange, that being guilty meant you were more innocent than you seemed.

'I'd like you to have it, really,' he said. Shit, his voice had come out husky, as if he wanted to compromise her, them both, again. 'I truly can't,' she said, finally looking at him to emphasise her firmness. He felt a momentary twinge of resentment. Being firm made her seem superior. It showed that her earlier uncertainty had sorted itself out. This was getting ridiculous: you can't be resentful about *every*thing.

'If you're sure,' he said.

'I am. But thank you for the thought.' She gave him another, knowing look, as much as to say, yes, *that* thought, then left the office. He felt as if he could burst into song. She *had* known. If they hadn't gone to bed together it had been at least in part because *she* hadn't dared to either. If she had been mute and hostile this afternoon it was because she was being mute and hostile about herself. There hadn't been muteness or hostility in that last look she'd given him, a look which hung in the air after her eyes had gone. It was a friendly look, a companionable look, a look of shared non-experience.

The door opened and she was back. He abruptly moved all his limbs, his head, anything to hand. Whatever position he'd been in was compromising since he'd been thinking nakedly about her. Naked was what he felt. For a fraction of a second his hands nearly scooped his groin.

'I just wanted to ask, what happened with Mr Gardiner?' she asked.

'All right,' he mouthed daftly, as if there was a bug in the room.

'Good,' she whispered, and with a wink disappeared once more.

Her second exit, a second after the first, left him at the opposite extreme, back in gloom. His impotence had been forgiven in one direction, then proved in another. He was like a child, miming the words because he couldn't trust his tone of voice to carry the lie. He'd not bearded Gardiner; he'd not even had the courage to read the letter Gardiner had left on his desk for him last night.

He found himself digging into his wastepaper basket to retrieve it. Penance! He'd make himself read it now, word by word, each one carefully, in turn.

Don't forget to contact Greenaways and by the way if you've got time give the Amos Baking Company a boot up the arse. Oh just a thought. Don't worry about our little conversation in the car-park on Monday. I've forgotten it already. In any case, I agree with most of what you said. Sod the sodding bank, I say. I fill my quarterly reports with utter crap in any case. That's what they want when all's said and done. And the last thing we need's them finding out what we really think! Yrs K.G.

John stared at the scrawl, horribly unsurprised. Perhaps his eyes had picked this up somehow this morning, without him noticing. Perhaps he'd just been leading himself a dance. Possibly it suited him to run around all day like a scared rabbit, prevented him from worrying about other things, life, Margaret, his mother, being a bastard.

What does it matter, he then thought, triumphantly. The bearding's taken place after all, one way or another. Or at least as good as. Approximately, the word for today. He had a sudden vertiginous sense of release, far more intoxicating than anything he'd felt at Mrs Clarke's house. Indeed, he hadn't felt free there at all, but imprisoned by expectations, his and hers. *This* was freedom!

He snapped his briefcase shut and almost clicked his heels, skipping out of the office like people did in adverts.

In the main banking area Mr Hawthorne was sitting at his desk, writing away. Everybody else had gone home. It was too much.

'Haven't you got a home to go to?' John asked, his good temper smoothly converting itself into a sort of savagery. What the two moods had in common was energy, exuberance almost, *attack*.

Mr Hawthorne looked up. His face was soft and bleary. It looked . . . like something, a certain sort of face, a face in certain particular circumstances. John realised what it looked like: like a face caught in mid-wank. He'd never disturbed such a face but he knew what it would look like. There were such things as mirrors.

Mr Hawthorne said something, not quite a word.

'What the hell are you scribbling away at all day long, a pornographic novel?'

'I don't think that's fair,' Mr Hawthorne replied, his features becoming petulant, as they were designed to do.

'What's not fair?'

'Leaving me to stew like this.'

246

'What the devil are you talking about?'

'I've been wanting to talk to you for days,' Mr Hawthorne announced. His features changed from petulant to something else, something they were *not* designed to express. Their smooth rubberiness almost squeaked as they sharpened into aggression. 'I can't do mortgages. It's the MIRAS scheme. I can't make sense of it. I've been working all the hours God sends, racking my brain.' He shot one hand downwards through the air, as if he were hacking someone to the ground. 'Looking things up in books,' he added, as if that were the final torment.

John stared at him in astonishment. It was just a month or two ago that he'd suggested to Gardiner that Mr Hawthorne should go on a weekend course on MIRAS, the tax allowance scheme for mortgage interest, and take over the minimal amount of property business that came into the branch. It had never crossed his mind for a second that the man wouldn't be able to cope. On the contrary, he'd seen it as a little responsibility for his super-efficiency to feed on, like giving a couple of sugar-lumps to a hungry horse.

'This place makes me sick,' Mr Hawthorne went on. 'Most of the people I knew at school are earning more than me. They haven't got a care in the world. But as soon as I come up against something I can't do, I'm left to rot at my effing desk for day after day. The bank cares as much for you as if you were a dog.'

John's own savagery had switched back to good humour as effortlessly as it had gone the other way. I'm being *bearded*, he thought gleefully. No, that wasn't it. The bearding would wait till tomorrow. This was the car-park scene. How merciful I'll be, he thought, how understanding. But that would also wait until tomorrow. This was the moment for a low profile, a touch of amused urbanity.

'I think it's time for us both to go home and relax,' he said. 'We'll have a proper chat about all this tomorrow.'

'Yes, sir,' Mr Hawthorne said, his eyes suddenly becoming cautious and watchful.

'I'm sure we can get something sorted out.' That could be taken either way, as a threat or a promise. So be it. Mercy would be the more merciful after a poor night's sleep. What did they call it in industrial relations? A cooling-off period. He'd gone to a seminar

247

on industrial relations at that course for assistant managers in the Cotswolds.

Mr Hawthorne made an odd kind of bobbing movement, almost a bow, and backed away. For a moment he looked as if he was going to say something more, but obviously thought better of it and began to pack his things away. John deliberately took his time checking security to let Mr Hawthorne leave first.

It had turned overcast and a little chilly during the course of the afternoon. He'd had a long day, with suffering and anxiety on all fronts. Not that he'd accomplished much. He'd got his car re-paired, kept on good professional terms with Mrs Clarke, found out what was the matter with Mr Hawthorne, approximately bearded Gardiner. He'd stayed level, that was the important thing. That was what survival meant, when all was said and done.

The engine caught sharply as soon as he turned on the ignition. All credit to the new battery. Then, with a sort of lazy impertinence, the wipers started up again. His hand fumbled at the lever. No, they were switched off. For a moment he bowed his head to the steering wheel. Shit. That fool this morning claimed that he'd cured them. All that had happened was that the battery charge had got too low to keep them going. He remembered bitterly how he'd admired the man's loose-limbed confidence, and the way he'd peed so uninhibitedly in the Gents. If you're good at something basic like peeing it probably means there's a low ceiling to your ability. I'm good at more complicated things, John thought sadly, like not going to bed with women. He should have realised what that wiperman looked like as he swaggered about the bank this morning. Like what he was, a cowboy.

At least there was no Ken, or Henry, to observe and sneer.

He set off, through the early evening jam in the centre of Reddish. By the time he was travelling down Bollington Road the sky had darkened further and it had begun to spit with rain. That cheered him up a little: the weather was catching up with his windscreen wipers.

As he turned off Manchester Road on to Denby Lane the sight of the Poco Poco struck him so forcibly that he pulled to a stop. How ridiculous that something that wasn't there any more could catch your attention like that. It was almost completely flat now, a field of crumpled brickwork. A crane and two bulldozers looked like enormous yellow animals grazing on it. Pink dust still hung over the surface from where the demolition had been going full blast, though all the workmen had gone home by now. He got out of his car and leaned against it, hands in pockets, looking at the wreck of the Poco Poco. At nothing, in other words. This is the time and the place, he thought, remembering what his mother had said to him. No, that was an illusion. Time and place only existed within people, that must be the answer, time and place joined together in a person, or in a relationship like that between him and Margaret. How cheap, he thought, to use the demolition of the dance hall where you met your wife as an excuse to cheat on her; to pretend that your own history and geography no longer existed.

He turned back to his car, got out his briefcase, opened it, took out the bag containing the two Liberty scarves and, without giving himself time for second thoughts, flung it on the debris. With love, he said to himself sarcastically. It was a peculiar present but as expensive a one as anybody could hope for: *not* giving your wife two Liberty scarves.

He got back in his car and did a three-point turn to head back to the Elf garage on Manchester Road. It still wasn't raining quite hard enough to fully lubricate his wipers, which wiped with a trembly action. It was almost as though patches of dryness were falling among the wet.

The flowers and chocolates at the Elf garage had a measly quality. Buying them seemed as functional as buying petrol. The garage man winked as he wrapped them up. 'Nearly forgot something, did we?' he asked.

'Not really,' said John irritably, and then tried to smooth things over: 'Just took a bit of time to get round to it.'

John came in with presents, sweetly unimaginative ones, chocolates and flowers. Stephen and Ann looked pleased: that was what was supposed to happen. Margaret kissed him. She felt she was being a cheat, letting things become romantic when there was all the breast business she should be confiding to him. Even with her chest scrunched against his she was monitoring it: was the delinquent one beginning to glow again? But how could she bring the subject up at a moment like this? It would be like throwing his gifts

249

back at him. She would keep her secret until tomorrow. That would be her own present to him, coping with the whole burden by herself.

There are tin anniversaries, paper anniversaries, silver anniversaries, she thought: this is my not-telling-my-husband-about-the-possibility-of-breast-cancer anniversary.

'There's something I have to tell you,' she said softly, still in his arms.

His heart sank. He wanted to push her away. He'd remembered his suspicions of this morning as soon as he'd come through the door. Her eyes seemed over-bright. He remembered how he'd decided that those earlier suspicions were provoked purely by self-interest: he'd wanted to give himself the excuse to have a fling. But perhaps, by pure coincidence, they were well grounded too. After all the complications he'd been through he felt enraged at the thought that he might have to cope with *her* complications as well. He suddenly wanted to push her away and had to hold his arms rigid to stop himself doing so.

'Oh yes?' he asked, through gritted teeth.

'I forgot the steaks,' she said, bowing her head in mock-shame.

He held her tight and kissed her again, feeling true shame himself. 'I'll tell you what,' he said. 'I'll take you out for an anniversary dinner. Ann won't mind doing the honours with Stephen, will you, Ann?'

Surprise, surprise, thought Ann. But why not? There were no hoe-downs to go to, and she still had the peculiar sensation that somehow or other she'd rescued Stephen, even though her logical brain, what there was of it, knew that couldn't be true. She might as well continue down the same track. 'All right,' she said, with only enough bad grace to maintain her self-respect.

'No! no!' Stephen cried, and burst into tears.

'Whatever's the matter, darling?' Margaret asked, rushing over to him. The sight of him taking off his spectacles to cry more freely made her feel her heart was going to burst. The swirl of sensations in her chest flooded into her breasts as well, washing away any unevenness between them.

Raymond picked up the emotions sweeping through the room. He began a howl in sympathy, but cut it off immediately. It would have meant sitting rigid, head raised, concentrating fully on making the sound and therefore being unable to keep up with what was going on all around. Instead, he rushed to each member of the family in turn. The scents they carried were so strong they made his head spin: distant fields, rotting material, chlorine, strange houses, intimate skin, antiseptic, alien body dirt that was stronger and more enticing even than the old man's groin. It was as if place after place crashed together in the one room, and Raymond whimpered with the stress of negotiating the tangle. No one responded to him in any case: all they gave him was their smell.

'There are burglars,' Stephen said. He nearly said worm, but stopped himself in time, knowing they wouldn't understand.

'What burglars, darling?' mummy asked, putting her arms round him.

'They stole my money.'

His heart missed a beat as he felt her go stiff. Usually when he told her something bad she just said don't be silly.

'Oh Stephen,' she said. She looked as if she was half going to cry and half going to laugh. '*I* took it. I needed some change and I didn't have any left. I forgot to put it back.'

'That's all right,' said Stephen, relieved. But he still didn't want to be left with just Ann. He put his spectacles back on. There was a tear on one of the little windows. The fear of burglars must have fired it out of his eye so hard it reached the glass. It looked soft and blobby. Even though what his mother said switched the robbers off, they were still there, just as they had been still there when she switched off the television. 'I don't want you and dad to go out tonight,' he told her.

Margaret glanced over at John. 'I've got that chicken in the oven,' she said. 'I had to cook it up anyway.'   ˙

'That'll be fine,' John said.

'I'm sorry.'

'What are you sorry about? We're a family. We'll have a family anniversary.' Listen to me, he thought. Nice as pie. Good job Mrs Clarke can't hear it.

'Thank you for your trust, Stephen,' said Ann. Though, come to think about it, he hadn't got any particular reason to trust her, seeing her career about in foreign parts in that clapped-out van. She hadn't got any reason to trust *him*, come to that, being that he was

251

in foreign parts himself. But some things were best not inquired about.

'I'm hungry,' Stephen said.

'Oh darling, I forgot, you were hungry *hours* ago,' Margaret told him, beginning to feel irritated at feeling guilty about him all the time. 'Here, have a biscuit, to tide you over until the chicken's done.'

She gave him a biscuit. Raymond came snuffling over to see if there was anything in it for him. He glanced swiftly around to check if the others were likely to be inattentive enough to let him persuade Stephen to part with some, but everybody was looking fixedly at the biscuit so he gave up and went back to his blanket.

'Try not to crunch so loudly, Stephen,' mother said. 'It does something to my nerves.'

'I can't help it,' Stephen told her. 'The loudness is in the biscuit, it's not my fault.'

Ann explained: 'He always crunches like that. Even when he has *soup* he crunches like that. He's got crunchy teeth.'

Raymond licked his genitals. They glowed, almost painfully. They'd obviously been used in the recent past. He licked them once more. Yes, there was still the taste of bitch. For a moment he felt uneasy, and the image of a spider came into his mind, unmoving, maddening, mocking. He sniffed. No, the scent was definitely of bitch. He placed his head on his front paws and sighed contentedly. He must have had a good day.